PRETTY LITTLE LION

SULEIKHA SNYDER

Published by Sourcebooks Casablanca, an imprint of Sourcebooks
P.O. Box 4410, Naperville, Illinois 60567-4410
(630) 961-3900
sourcebooks.com

Printed and bound in Canada.
MBP 10 9 8 7 6 5 4 3 2 1

To those we lost and to those who are still here. All my love.

Weary of struggles, I, the great rebel,
Shall rest in quiet only when I find
The sky and the air free of the piteous groans of the oppressed.
Only when the battlefields are cleared of jingling bloody sabres
Shall I, weary of struggles, rest in quiet,
I the great rebel.
I am the rebel eternal,
I raise my head beyond this world,
High, ever erect and alone!

—from "Bidrohi" by Kazi Nazrul Islam,
translated by Kabir Chowdhury

1

THE VIP LOUNGE AT THE Manhattan Grand sat just below the hotel's trendy rooftop restaurant. Floor-to-ceiling tinted windows offered up near-perfect views of the city skyline awash in the neon lights of Times Square. Near-perfect because you had to ignore the periodic drone sweeps and the occasional ominous black helicopters…ignore them or lean fully into them, posting dramatic snaps with a drone in the background. Fortunately, Meghna Saxena-Saunders wasn't interested in anything outside. Unfortunately, what *did* hold her interest wasn't suitable for Instagram pics or Twitter updates.

> Check out this view! #toomanykillersinthisroom #criminal-activity #relationshipgoals

Guaranteed to go viral? Sure. Also guaranteed to ruin everything. Just like the man across the room. A room with an ice sculpture of a naked woman—top-shelf vodka flowing down her breasts and painstakingly carved nipples. And scantily clad real women circulating with shots of the vile stuff. They'd signed iron-clad NDAs to work the gig, knowing they'd walk away with hefty paychecks and tips besides. The hefty dose of fear was an unfortunate side effect. Not that you would know it from the way the three redheads strutted through the room in tiny bikini tops and leather miniskirts. She wanted to salute them, to applaud. They were bold, breathtaking, brave, under the slobbering scrutiny of the drunken guests.

But *he* was still watching *her*. He'd been watching her all night, tracking her movements around the party with the focus of an apex predator stalking prey...but with the care and caution of someone who existed in a hostile world that needed no excuse to punish him. All of the guards in the room operated under the latter assumption. *Step one foot out of line and you die.* He knew the consequences of being caught paying her too much attention, of drawing too much attention to himself. And yet he tempted fate.

Meghna wasn't concerned by his interest so much as intrigued. She was used to the attention of men—counted on it, really. She wore bright-red lipstick to draw their eyes to her mouth, picked curve-hugging dresses to pull their gazes to her tits or her ass... and she smiled *just so* while sliding stilettos between their ribs. The pin in her coiled updo seemed to vibrate at that thought, like a sentient extension of her murderous impulses. Meghna shook off the tingle of anticipation, the burst of adrenaline, reminding herself that she was here to seduce, not to slaughter. It would *not* do to leave bloodstains on Mirko Aston's carpet. Not tonight at any rate.

So she returned the man's gaze, infusing it with an equal amount of focus and just a dash of sexual interest. It wasn't a difficult task. Not the challenge it had been when she inserted herself into Mirko's life, using all her training to tolerate his hands on her body and his cruel kisses. *This* man was as beautiful as he was dangerous. A black T-shirt and jeans, meant to help him blend into the background like the rest of the hired security, clung to his rock-solid body like a lover. His skin, several shades darker than her own light brown, glowed with health and vitality. She doubted it came from any kind of product—none of the high-end brand names she'd shilled as an influencer. The smooth curve of his shaved head begged for hands to cradle it…to guide it down between her thighs. *Focus, Meghna. Observe. Find his weaknesses, not your own.* She took the mental reprimand like a slap, all the while tilting her head and laughing breathlessly at something that had made Aston's cronies chortle.

It was easy—pretending to be interested in what they were saying. They didn't expect real engagement, didn't expect her to actually *listen*. So most of the time, she eventually feigned disinterest and wandered away. Just a few feet. So she could eavesdrop in earnest with a drink in her hand. And the few times that she stayed in the circle…? Well, that was infinitely valuable as well. That was why she was here, with her arm looped through Mirko's, periodically blinking her heavily made-up eyes at him in vapid adoration while his right-hand man seethed. Sasha Nichols had never liked her, regarded her with barely veiled suspicion. Born of a Russian mother and an American father, with loyalties one hundred percent for sale. Dual nationalities and an utter lack of conscience were something he and Mirko had in common. He required careful monitoring, even in situations like this—where she was nothing but a pretty prop for his boss.

Her watcher was getting in the way, though. Splitting her attention. Sending prickles across every inch of skin bared by her bias-cut slip dress. He was as different from Mirko and Sasha as night from day, and not just because her fair-haired and pale-skinned "protector" and his equally Nordic-appearing henchman were the whitest of white men. And Mirko a white *human* at that. The stranger, who was very likely not a security guard at all, was a supernatural like her. Her instincts identified him as a shifter of some kind, the specifics of which she couldn't guess from this distance. Unlike Sasha, who had shifter blood but couldn't actually shift and resented the whole of the universe for it, this man didn't have any obvious insecurities. And unlike Mirko, who'd bought and paid for every companion in this room in one way or another, Mr. Shifter didn't have to demand the room. He already owned it. Simply by standing in an alcove and spanning it with his gaze. Did that include her?

No. Never. Her kind belonged to no one. *Don't forget that, Meghna. Don't forget why you're here.*

As if that were a possibility. She scoffed at the warning voice. She didn't have the luxury of forgetting. Not in this world. Not in this life. Not after the Darkest Day, and the light that had been shined upon supernaturals afterward. Eventually, many humans had gone back to their idea of "normal." Work and school and leisure activities. The grocery stores had been restocked after the calamities that had plagued the past few years. The grief for those lost to sickness and violence had dulled to a throb instead of the sharp, persistent spike. The economy was slowly rebounding. The TV shows and streaming channels and podcasts were much the same as they had been…though perhaps a bit more patriotic and pro-government than before. Those who had never experienced oppression or an -ism lived as they always had: oblivious, privileged.

Her own upbringing should have marked her for that callous delusion that the only color that mattered was the green of money. A rich man's pampered daughter, born among the Washington elite, into a higher caste and generational wealth, raised in her uncle's Bollywood and Hollywood circles. *Should have. Could have. Would have.* But she'd never had the chance to be simply that vapid socialite who voted conservatively because of her tax bracket, who thought she was better than everybody else because of an accident of birth. Because there was her upbringing…and then there was her *other* heritage. Her other inheritance. Her duty. Her destiny.

Meghna gently slid her arm out from Mirko's. He barely

noticed, caught up as he was in some outrageous—but no doubt still true—story about doing vodka shots in a Moscow brothel with the American president and the Russian prime minister. It was nothing she hadn't heard before. Nothing she could use. But the handsome supernatural watcher in the corner...? He was an unknown quantity. He could make or break what she'd come here to do, what she'd worked so hard for. All because he couldn't take his eyes from her.

Meghna saw only one solution. Well, one solution that didn't involve the stiletto in her hair. She had to fuck him. Tonight.

━━━━━━━━━━

She was a billion bloody times more gorgeous in person. The photos hadn't done her one bit of justice. Flat, lifeless, caricatures of the flesh-and-blood woman crossing the room. She glowed— golden-brown skin, golden-yellow dress clinging to every curve. It was like watching the sun move across the sky. And Elijah Richter should've known better than to stare straight at the sun, but he did it anyway. Like he'd been doing all night. It was the job, right? The gig. The op. What the whole team agreed he'd do. *Who* the whole team agreed he'd do, rather than targeting Aston and the like.

Meghna Saxena-Saunders. Influencer, celebutante, ex-wife to a handsome Hollywood hotshot. Both of their faces graced entirely too many magazine covers while their names popped up all over digital gossip blogs. Everyone with a deciding vote at Third Shift had come to a consensus months ago that another pretty boy wouldn't move her now. That had eliminated several members of the team outright. One would think they ran a modeling agency. JP, once Joe Peluso and now their newest recruit, whose face had literally been on Wanted posters, was a move to the other extreme. So that had left members like Elijah who were too rough and tumble to be considered pretty. He was tall, muscular, honed by the military and special ops. As different as possible from Meghna's movie-star ex-husband and her string of smarmy Eurotrash lovers. More importantly, unlike JP or Danny, he was single.

"You're the honey trap this time, mate! Our Pretty Little Lion!" Finn, who volunteered as their beautiful bait for most missions that required it, had crowed while they mapped out the initial op. When there had still been time for jokes. *"I hope you're up to it... so to speak."*

"Damn right I am," he'd assured him before forbidding Finn from ever using that wretched nickname again. Naturally, that had made his entire team all the more determined to make it stick. They drove him mad, the whole lot of 'em.

But the hell of it was, he *was* very much "up to it." His cock was swelling in his jeans just looking at Meghna come toward him. His skin was tingling with the awareness of her. The subtle scent of her perfume. The faint hint of her sweat. He wanted to lick it off her. Touch his tongue to the inside of her wrist and then the back side of her knee and see if it tasted the same everywhere. That was the cat talking. Wanting to mark her, so he'd know her anywhere. He'd lived with his dual nature for more than four decades, and most of the time, he could keep the lion leashed... but not right now. He didn't *have to* right now. Not in this instant, where he needed to sell to his target that he was absolutely off his head for her.

So when Meghna stopped just a few feet away from him, chatting with one of the waitresses and taking a glass of champagne from her tray, Elijah amped up his own glow...or what passed for a glow at any rate. The brooding stare he'd been told "melts panties." *"Not mine,"* Finn had interjected during that particularly awkward digression. *"But only because I go commando."* Luckily there was no such thing as sensitivity training in a black ops outfit. Elijah reckoned half his team would fail the course. Mostly Finn Conlan. *All* Finn Conlan. God save him from pansexual vampires who couldn't keep their gobs shut. And God send him straight to this woman sipping slowly from a crystal flute as she glanced at him from the corner of her eye.

Smart. She couldn't flirt with him right out in the open. Not with Aston holding court so close by. So she drank. And studied some hideous piece of art on the wall. Then another. Until she found herself directly in front of him. "Who are you?" she wondered in a throaty murmur that was a sharp jolt to his groin. "You're not one of Mirko's usual guards."

"Mack." An alias. For one of his men whose sacrifice would never be forgotten, whose loss still stung. It was a good reminder, too, of what he was actually here for. The mission. *Always* the mission. "A friend got me this gig," he added gruffly. "Said it would be easy money as long as I could be discreet."

She tilted her head, studying him like *he* was a piece of art. Her thick black hair, coiled up high like she was from a fifties girl group, didn't move at all. Pinned in place. Just like she had *him* pinned in place. "Is it?"

He made a show of swallowing hard. Of scuffing the carpet with one boot. All while keeping his gaze steady—professional now that he had company and parties interested in that company keeping an eye on her whereabouts. "Is it what?"

Her red lips curved into a sultry smile. She had to know the power of it. Like a siren. Maybe she *was* a siren. Or Jessica sodding Rabbit in human form. "Easy?"

Fuck. Elijah barely restrained a laugh, maybe a groan, and then he took his first big risk of the op since getting assigned to the party's detail. "Don't know about *it*, love, but *I* am."

Twin flames lit up in her toffee-brown eyes, melting the irises. Melting him. And *he* wasn't wearing panties either—*thank you very fucking much, Finn.* So he knew his risk was paying off even before she murmured, "Hall closet, five minutes," and sashayed away. *Damn.* That fast. That simple. Probably a trap. But he couldn't not go. It was too important. So he counted off in sixty-second increments. Watched Meghna touch Aston's arm, whisper some excuse, and then leave the VIP Lounge. He kept his eye on Aston after that. Jealousy, possessiveness, too much give-a-shit about where his girlfriend had gone wouldn't serve Elijah's purposes at all.

His luck held out. The oily blond arms dealer barely blinked when Meghna walked out of the room. He went right back to braying to his mates. *They* were most certainly racist. Assuming their largely Black and brown security guards were basically furniture, treating the female waitstaff like playthings. A who's who of rich, entitled criminals who thought themselves above the law. He recognized a Chicago crime boss, an LA movie producer, and a few of New York's most notorious Eastern European mobsters. All being recorded, thanks to the Spider hidden in the sole of Elijah's shoe. The specialized bug, invented by Third Shift's hacker extraordinaire, spun into every bit of available tech and fried the original unit, leaving no trace. Handy for keeping tabs on this unsavory lot. Crawling into their smartphones, the hotel's security cameras, and whatever other devices might be in the room. And it meant Elijah didn't have to surveil them personally. Good, because he'd already had enough of their boasts and their toasts. Of their casual disregard for human and supernatural life. He'd spent years watching bastards like this strut 'round like they owned the world. Before and after 2016. Marching in Charlottesville. In Washington. Dancing to the tune of their dictator. Doing things in clear view of law enforcement that no one with darker skin would ever get away with. All while Elijah had to keep his own temper in check, his voice soft and his shoulders hunched to minimize his size lest he get three slugs to the back for jaywalking.

Elijah tried to keep his expression impassive as he scanned the group one more time. You wouldn't think from looking at these arseholes that they'd lost one of their own just a handful of weeks ago. Aleksei Vasiliev. Dead on a Brooklyn warehouse floor. He'd already been replaced in the cabal by another ambitious mob boss. One villain was as good as another. No wonder Meghna's departure hadn't made much of a dent. Because women didn't mean anything either, right? They were just accessories or sex toys and nothing else. Elijah would've dinged himself on the same account, but misogyny wasn't what was driving him tonight. Or any other night. His mum had raised him better than that. If he'd had the luxury of fighting his way into this shit show with Meghna as his equal, he would've taken it. But he didn't have that luxury. He didn't have that time. Whatever Aston and his crew were up to, he needed a way in *now*, and she was the most expedient way to get that foothold.

He left his post with a curt nod to the rest of the hired muscle. Names and faces he didn't need to remember. Hopefully they wouldn't remember him either. The top floor of the posh Midtown hotel had a basic layout. Everything in clean lines and variations of beige. A few suites, one event space, the swanky VIP Lounge, two closets, and some washrooms. Half of why it required little effort to get him on the party's security detail. Just a few hacks, a few words whispered in a few dirty ears. He exited the lounge and easily found the hall closet. Before five minutes were even up. And hesitated with his hand on the doorknob.

You can just tag her with a tracker and be done with it. Or he could test out the new subdermal bug that Joaquin had been working on for months. *"And exactly how am I supposed to get under her skin, 'Quin?" "I'm sure you'll think of something, Teacha."* He didn't *have* to be Meghna Saunders's honey trap to reel her in this way. He and Jack would never demand such a thing of their operatives, and he tried to hold himself to the same standard.

He didn't have to...but he *wanted* to. *Hell.* It was that, not anything else, that made him pause for a half minute before he yanked open the door and went in to her.

"Second thoughts?" The closet was cramped, dark, but her

voice was like a beacon even as his eyes adjusted. Her scent too. Rich and spicy. Guiding him toward her. Around a box on the floor and something like a mop or a broom.

"No thoughts," he told the shadowy shape of her, "just action. That's what you want, right? Why we're here?"

"What if I told you I just really like closets?" she asked in the driest of tones, reaching out to grip his shirt, curling her fingertips into his chest. He'd noticed earlier that her nails were painted the same alluring red as her mouth, but now he could feel that they were clipped short. A practicality at odds with her bombshell image.

"We can do a whole world tour of closets," he offered. "All the posh hotels. Even Buckingham Palace if you like. Only the best for a beautiful woman like yourself."

"Sandringham's are better," she said in the offhand way of the very rich—the way that told him she'd been in the queen's country home more than once.

And him growing up on a council estate. *Fuck*. Meghna Saxena-Saunders wasn't just out of his league, she was out of his tax bracket, out of his entire bloody universe. A concern if he were embarking on some sort of relationship instead of a targeted seduction. But one night, a handful of nights if this went well, and then it was over. Elijah couldn't afford to forget that. And he couldn't afford to waste time with banter either. So he covered her hand with his, pressing it flat above his heart. And then he peered down at her, lion eyes adjusted to the darkness, taking in her whole gorgeous face and the "well, get on with it" tilt of her chin. If she was disconcerted by the shine of his pupils, she didn't let on in any way but the soft catch of her breath…right before she arched up and kissed him.

Because she had no time for banter either. Just this. Slipping her free hand around the back of his neck. Pressing her open mouth to his with no teasing preambles. It was focused and fierce and went straight to his veins. Like a drug. A drug that tasted of sweet honey and pepper and skin. The heat of her tongue finding his. It was the most passionately planned of assaults. More professional than any siege he'd ever laid. Lije knew the exact minute he lost the upper hand…if he'd even had it to begin with. It was when she smiled against his lips, the victorious curve rocking him to the core.

"I don't just like closets," she whispered. "I like the look of you, too."

Christ. It went right to his cock, that whisper. He was at full mast, his own plans be damned. He had to turn the tide. So he hauled her against him, palming her arse over the clingy silk of her dress, slanting his mouth over hers. He didn't touch her hair. Knew better. It was too perfect. If it went one strand out of place, it would rouse suspicion neither one of them could afford. But he touched everything else, by god. The long column of her throat. Her satin-smooth arms. Her thighs, bared once he hiked up her skirt. The heat between them. He wasn't shocked to find she, too, had gone commando. And the reminder of his teammate's TMI should've deflated his erection, but all it really did was crystallize his resolve. Remind him what the real goal was here. Not the sex he was initiating as he slipped two fingers inside her but the connection he was making because of it.

Meghna was a means to an end. Nothing more, nothing less.

2

IT WAS NO LONGER A good world for vampires. It had never
been particularly a good world for anyone. Some would say that
everything had changed for America in 2016, but Tavi Estrada
had lived long enough to know that history was doomed to repeat
itself, and humans were doomed to self-destruct. It was just that
the speed with which they descended to hell had quadrupled in
the twentieth and twenty-first centuries. Nuclear weapons, man-
made diseases, global fascism. Countries that had once seemed like
bastions of reason, cradles of democracy, had fallen one after the
other like dominoes. All because of human greed, human ambi-
tion. Humans' belief in their own superiority. Even the revelation
that they weren't superior, that more powerful beings existed on
earth, had not tempered that arrogance.

A prime example was posturing right before him. Mirko
Aston. Despite rumors on the Dark Web that he was some sort
of powerful supernatural, he was just a man. With blood and air
and ego keeping him alive. Oh, he'd certainly amassed powerful
friends—Tavi among them—but any one of them could snuff him
out should they choose. He was mortal, breakable, disposable. But
useful. For now. A conduit to so many criminal syndicates around

the world. If you wanted drugs, Mirko Aston could find you the newest designer narcotics on the market. If you wanted sex, he could send you an entire shipping container full of unwilling options. If you wanted weapons, he could supply those as well. He was like the big-box store of darkness and debauchery.

What did that make Tavi? The FedEx? The UPS? He facilitated so many of Mirko's transactions. Made sure they went exactly as planned. *What can brown do for you?* Wasn't that, after all, his MO? Making himself indispensable to those who would otherwise see him deported, detained, or dead? It helped that he'd taken on a vampire's pallor after so many decades in the shadows, losing the warm skin tone he'd inherited from his Taino mother and favoring his white Cuban father. It made it easier for his unsavory associates to ignore that he was one of the few nonwhite guests left in the room. Mirko's latest girlfriend had swished away in a cloud of silk and secrets. Most of the hired security guards were Black and Latinx—not because Mirko was open-minded but because he felt that was their appropriate place. And the brooding supe with the impressive arms who'd held up the far wall all evening had gone on break. Perhaps an extended break. He couldn't really blame the man or Meghna for finding other places to be. Mirko's private party would go on into the wee hours of the morning, maybe even the next day. The drinks would flow, the clothing would be shed. Lines of cocaine were already appearing on tabletops, being sniffed from wrists. Tavi would watch. As he'd always done. Watch, wait, act accordingly.

"Thirsty yet, Estrada?" The snide voice was like the persistent whine of a gnat. Instantly annoying. Wholly unwelcome.

Sasha Nichols. A human from a shifter line who seldom left his master Mirko's side. He thought himself a big player in this game. Didn't know he was just a pawn. Easily sacrificed. Tavi settled back into the leather banquette, tipping his half-full tumbler of whiskey in a mock salute. One of his many tiny rebellions—sipping the amber liquid while Mirko poured vodka down his cronies' throats. "As you can see, I'm far from parched."

He would never be so stupid as to drink blood in front of these men. He'd killed in front of them, of course. He'd done what he had to. But slaking his actual thirst was a vulnerability he could not afford to show them. In the early days of his involvement with Aston and his friends, a few had asked to be turned. That, too, was something he'd opted not to share. The likes of Sasha Nichols being given the gift of a longer life and enhanced abilities…? *Ha. No, thank you.* Tavi had never been that careless. To turn someone without thinking it through. *"Not true,"* a voice piped up in the back of his mind, in the cruel part of his memory. *"You were that careless once. Dare you be that careless with me as well, Octavio? Try. See what will happen."* He silenced the trilling mockery with another sip of whiskey. With words. "What do you want, Sasha? I'm already bored of looking at you."

"Watch your tone, vampire," the henchman sneered, no doubt wishing he could run back to Mirko to play tattletale. To add this latest insult to the ledger they kept of Tavi's slights against them. Or wishing he could turn into a bear like his ancestors and swipe at Tavi's face. "You think you're indispensable? You could get a stake through the heart at any given moment if Mirko wishes it."

Tavi laughed, adjusted the scarf at his throat, and threw one arm along the back of the banquette. As unbothered as could be. And then he let a little bit of the monster through. In the tips of his teeth. In the flash of his eyes. In the dangerous silk of his voice, softer than that of his scarf. "Just as, at any moment, I could tear your head from your neck. Pity you'll never know what it feels like to have that power."

Sasha paled, which was a feat considering the man was already the color of uncooked rice. He stumbled back a few steps, bravado draining like the blood Tavi would never take from him. "Fuck you!" he snarled.

Miracle of miracles, Tavi was actually enjoying this ridiculous party now. He grinned. "Is that what this is about? You're jealous of Mirko's beautiful companion, so you want one of your own? Lo siento, Sasha, but my dance card is full."

"You're delusional." Nichols's homophobia made him scramble three more steps away. Made him utter slurs in both Russian and English that Tavi had heard before and would, no doubt, hear again. How utterly predictable—Sasha was more horrified by the prospect of fucking a man than being killed by one.

This was not a problem Tavi could relate to. He'd fucked many, many men. And killed many too. An equal-opportunity predator. All were welcome to succumb to his sharp kisses. "*You* came to *me*," he said with a shrug. "I was just minding my own business. Maybe, in the future, you should mind yours."

At a safer distance now—or so he thought—Mirko's aging errand boy was free to posture once more. "Just wait," he warned, lower lip curling like a petulant child's. "When our plans are put into motion, we won't have to depend on *your* kind anymore. We'll have our own resources. That day, you'll be out on your ass."

Tavi wasn't exactly devastated at the prospect. But still… "It's not *my* ass being put on the curb that you should be concerned with," he pointed out. "I haven't let Mirko down yet. It wasn't *my* pet Bratva vor who ended up a literal dead end just last month."

Sasha had been so sure that Aleksei Vasiliev would prove a valuable connection. Crowing about the greater access to test subjects and key pharmaceuticals. Mirko was none too happy with Sasha's poor choice of allies and had been not-so-subtly freezing him out in the weeks since Vasiliev's permanent hibernation.

Tavi's barb hit its target with unerring aim, and the nonshifting bear growled at him ineffectually. "You'll pay for your arrogance, Estrada," he promised.

"Send me a 'Save the Date' so I'll know when to cry." Tavi

dismissively waved his whiskey glass. "Until then…? Do us both a favor and stay the hell out of my sight."

Nichols listed forward, as if he were preparing to say something else. To continue needlessly bothering a supernatural more than twice his age and one-tenth as patient. And then self-preservation finally, *finally*, kicked in. He shot Tavi one last glare and stormed away. Likely to find another target for his ire or another way to get back into his boss's good graces.

It was a perfect snapshot of humanity's problem as a whole. What would be their undoing when all was said and done. They never knew when to stop pushing, when to stop taking and stealing and killing. Not until it was much too late.

"*When will* you *stop, Octavio?*" The voice from his mental vault taunted him once more. "*Or is it already too late for you?*"

Tavi downed the rest of his whiskey in one gulp, drowning out reminders he couldn't afford to let surface. If it all tasted like ashes in his mouth, so be it.

───────

Meghna Saxena-Saunders was going to be his undoing if he wasn't more fucking careful. For all his attempts at taking his mind elsewhere, at focusing on anything but the intimacy of the act, Elijah was keenly aware that he'd just gotten the best sodding blow job of his entire life. The back of his head hit the wall, echoing like an empty thing because she'd gone and sucked out all his brains through his cock. His control was somewhere on the floor with her, stayed there as she rose from her knees and smoothed out her dress. Her hair was still perfect. Her lipstick barely smudged, even with his come glossing her mouth.

Who seduced who? He couldn't say. But it wasn't finished. Not nearly. *Pull yourself together, mate.* It took him a second or two, but he managed it. Shaking his head to clear the fucked-out cobwebs. Tucking his cock back in and zipping up his jeans.

"Fuck," he said with completely sincere admiration. "That was brilliant."

"I know." She gave a shrug that, even in the darkness, illuminated her confidence. "I should probably get back to the party... but there are a few people inside who might pick up your scent from my skin."

Because it wasn't just any party, was it? There were bear shifters inside. Vampires too. Elijah had no love for either, and he admired her forethought...while simultaneously cursing himself for his lack of it. They'd missed something obvious when they hadn't taken that into consideration. "Makes it risky, doesn't it?" He played off his unforgivable error as a bit of added spice to an already ill-advised assignation. "Will they notice if you don't go back?"

"No." The roll of Meghna's eyes was echoed by her scoff of disgust. "I doubt Mirko even cares where I am. He'll remember me two days from now, when he's come down from the high and painfully hungover."

There was no love lost between the pair, clearly. So why were they together? For appearances? For social clout? Because her father owned an armaments factory? Elijah would have time to answer those questions later. His most pressing one had to do with the pair of *them*. "Sounds to me like you have two days to fill, love. What could you possibly do with all that time?" he wondered with a charming smile that would rival Finn's.

Meghna brushed a nonexistent speck from her shoulder. And then did the same for his...but let her hand linger. "Are you asking what I think you're asking?"

He glanced down at her fingers before meeting her gaze. There was a test here. Or a trap. She could bring down an entire room of pissed-off wankers on his head if she felt like it. He let the awareness of each of her fingers seep into him. Her pulse through her skin. Trying to gauge the lies versus the truth. The loss versus the potential win. "Depends," he said slowly. "Do you think I'm asking to fuck your brains out for the next thirty-six hours? Then yes."

Her palm made a slow slide from his shoulder to his chest. No calling this off. No shouting. No one would be coming for his head except her. As she'd already done. With mouth and tongue and just a hint of teeth. "All thirty-six? With no breaks?" She tsked, her lips making a teasing moue. "That's going to chafe."

It was like the crack about the closets. Unexpected. And just like then, he laughed. He didn't want to find her so charming. Didn't want to enjoy this all quite so much. But it was already too late for that, wasn't it? When he was talking about nonstop fucking and looking forward to the prospect. "I'm keen to try if you are," he offered, mimicking her earlier shrug.

She kept up the seductress routine, trailing fingertips along his belt buckle as if reminding him how easily she'd undone it not too long ago. "How do I know you're not after something?"

"How do I know *you're* not after something?" he countered. "You're the one who came up to me."

Meghna's eyebrows rose. "Makes it risky, doesn't it?" she echoed him.

She was fascinating. So much more than the profiles he'd read and the intel he'd gathered over the last few months. Sexy as hell and sharp as a knife. "You a risk-taker by nature?"

"I'm here with you, aren't I?" she replied almost immediately.

She was good at the dance. Evading questions. Asking them. Pushing and then pulling back. He was impressed. More than a bit turned on. But he reined in the beast this time—both the lion and his dick. "Give me an hour and an address," he said. That would give him time to scrub off her scent in the WC, do one more tour of the party room, and check in with HQ. "I'll wrap up here and then wrap up for you." He glanced meaningfully at where her questing hand had ended its journey. Atop his already raring-to-go-again erection.

"Daring but conscientious," Meghna murmured with some combination of admiration and approval. "How did you know that's just what I like in a casual hookup with someone I just met?"

Because it was what he liked, too. What he prided himself on. "Just lucky, I guess."

She leaned in, capturing his mouth with hers even as she released his cock. "Oh, you'll get lucky," she whispered as she brushed the lightest of kisses across his lips. A tease tasting of lipstick and his own come. "I promise."

Elijah could only hope that was true.

3

____

MEGHNA HAILED A YELLOW CAB on the corner just south of the Manhattan Grand, pulling the faux fur jacket she'd liberated from coat check around her shoulders to ward off the night's chill wind. The mistress suite Mirko had rented for her in an entirely different hotel was downtown. She could walk a few blocks to the subway entrance at Fiftieth, take the 1 train for a few stops, and make one easy transfer to her closest line. That was asking a lot of a woman in three-inch spike heels. She could take a punch. Suck up cracked ribs. But there was no sense in tormenting her feet when god and man had invented taxis.

Besides, this way, the drones circling overhead would only capture her leaving, not her entire path. As long as she paid with cash, she was anonymous once the cab pulled away from the curb and merged with the rest of Eighth Avenue's traffic. A sea of cars, a few pedicabs that had returned after the theaters reopened last year, a few reckless assholes on bicycles going against the flow. It was camouflage. Cover. Another layer of the lie she lived.

She'd washed up and reapplied her lipstick before making her excuses at Mirko's party. She could still taste the man from the closet on her tongue. Beneath the sharpness of mints and the bite of mouthwash—which had been stocked in the bathroom not for her benefit but for those coke-fueled and booze-addled men who had to go home and pretend they didn't reek of vice. Meghna had no use for that kind of pretense. Everyone already saw her as a party girl. If she stumbled home smelling of high-end liquor and smoke, it only added to the story. If she tasted a man's come, inhaled the musky scent of his thick dick, and remembered the weight of it as she headed to her paid-for pied-à-terre…wasn't that just expected?

No. Not that last part. She was supposed to forget. She was supposed to fling the memory away like a condom wrapper or a burned-out match. She'd done so more times than she could count over the past decade.

"You don't have *to sleep with them, Meghna. You can simply dispatch them,"* her first handler had said to her during one of their increasingly rare in-person meetings. As if it was a genuine concern for her mental and physical well-being. *"Sex is not our only weapon."*

"That's funny coming from you," she'd replied, setting aside the file with her next assignment. They hadn't gone digital yet, not then. And she hadn't bothered to expand or clarify or even defend her methods. The woman they'd nicknamed "the General" didn't get to judge her. Not after the choices *she'd* made.

Sex wasn't Meghna's only weapon, but it was a damn good one. Efficient. Literally catching targets with their pants down. She could poison them. Stab them. Shoot them. Almost anything was easier when someone let down their guard for her. As long as she never let her guard down for them. And thus far, she never had. Not even for her husband. She'd wooed him for her work and then let herself enjoy being Chase's red-carpet arm candy, falling into the role and into his bed. They'd played out a whirlwind romance and elopement for the weekly tabloids, and those glossy photos had captured most of the substance of their relationship. The rest of it had been *actual* substances. Ecstasy, ketamine, high-quality weed. Meghna hadn't been high since the quickie divorce. She'd almost forgotten how it felt to fly like that, without a care in the world. Because the thing about flying was that you always came down. The woman she was now couldn't afford the hard landing. Yes, she'd hit the floor for that man in the closet—but she'd only gone to her knees because she knew he'd fall, too.

Those powerful hands clenched, hovering just above her head, as if he understood he couldn't muss her hair. His breath coming in harsh gasps as she licked him. A rumble like a purr emanating from his chest. *Did* shifters purr? That might warrant further hands-on investigation. Along with everything else about him.

"*We can do a whole world tour of closets,*" he'd murmured. "*All the posh hotels. Even Buckingham Palace if you like. Only the best for a beautiful woman like yourself.*"

Dammit. The car squealed to a halt in front of her destination just as her brain hit the brakes, too. She pressed a fifty-dollar bill through the slot in the Plexiglas divider and hurried out of the cab. Like she could outrun the disturbing reminder of just how much *fun* she'd had flirting and fellating and being fingered by a fine specimen of man. He'd made her want to *laugh*. That was almost more of an affront than making her come. She could fake both, sure, but she'd faked neither for him. Mostly because it hadn't even occurred to her. She couldn't make that mistake again. In her line of work, *everything* had to be a calculation.

Doctor. Lawyer. Engineer. Astronaut. Princess. General. These were career goals for most little girls. For the child Meghna had been once. So how was she now courting not one but *two* suspect men out of misguided duty to a country that didn't even want her? Fifty percent patriarchy. Fifty percent twisted celestial feminism. Because now she was a firefighter, an assassin, a soldier…a million little-girl dreams twisted into one often-nightmarish charge.

Girls from other cultures, *human* girls, had a quinceañera or a

Sweet Sixteen. Meghna's fifteenth birthday had been celebrated in a manner befitting her father's wealth and status, with the promise of a commensurate blowout and a fancy sports car for the following year when she was old enough to drive. She'd received a diamond solitaire necklace, a pair of Jimmy Choos she'd been eyeing all summer, and hugs from three of her favorite Bollywood actors. But the biggest and most shocking gifts she'd received that day were ones she couldn't wear, couldn't brag about, and probably should have found a way to return: a mother she'd never met, bearing news of a calling she'd never asked for.

"You are an apsara," the beautiful woman she'd only recognized from painfully awkward family photos on the mantel had said, swishing toward those very picture frames in a cloud of silk. *"Daughter to an apsara. And there is a war coming that will require your particular weapons."*

Spy. Operative. Secret agent. Those were the official words, the kind words, the English words. She'd been called far worse for the work she did. In multiple languages. The only name that mattered was Vidrohi. The network she'd been born into, the duty she couldn't forsake. In simple Hindi, it meant rebellion. It meant defiance. To her and her sisters in the network, it meant everything. That was what she had to remember. That was why she was here. Kicking off her heels just inside of the high-rise hotel suite that didn't have her name on the bill. Stalking to the bedroom as she pulled off her earrings and undid her hair. Preparing to cheat on a man she routinely pretended to adore…with a stranger she was about to identify.

Meghna undressed quickly, unearthing equipment from the bottom of her everyday bag while still naked. She ran the black light and the scanner over her skin, over the folds of her dress, looking for prints. Even a partial would do. It was amazing what the Vidrohi's network could turn up. With their tech, with their magic. Their resources were limitless. Their patience was not. She'd been working on Mirko for months now. Almost too long. They didn't have the luxury of devoting endless personal attention to all of the scum that walked the earth. *Or to handsome mystery men.* But she ignored the latter warning as she sent scans to one of her contacts. As she then wiped her devices and tucked them back beneath makeup palettes and tampons. Not that she needed the latter anymore, but they proved a simple and effective anti-snoop solution. Like hygiene products were radioactive. God forbid. You could probably fell entire dictatorships by flinging some Stayfree maxi pads like that man who'd flung a shoe at George W. Bush in 2008.

Meghna still preferred knives. They hadn't failed her once. They weren't like people. *"Poor little rich girl,"* the General had mocked her a year or so into her training. *"So angry that your father ignored you and your mother abandoned you. You should feel honored that I rescued you from such a pedestrian life. That I showed you what you were meant to be and gave you a higher purpose."* Such a high purpose. Slaying monsters. Bedding monsters. Becoming one herself. But the General hadn't been wrong. It *was* a better life than the one she'd almost led. She saw the truth of the world and she could rage against it. She could *do* something beyond throwing money at a problem and considering it solved.

Is that so? You really didn't miss having a childhood? Having a choice? If a tiny voice deep inside her disagreed once in a while, that was just something else to overcome and ignore. She buried the whisper as she took a quick shower and readied herself for her not-so-gentleman caller. Just like she'd long ago buried her conscience, her standards, and her innocence. Some things were more hindrances than they were help. Some things…you couldn't get back.

———————

The party was ratcheting into high gear with the host's girlfriend gone. Elijah couldn't *wait* to leave. So he didn't. He stayed a whopping forty minutes more after Meghna's departure, watching the drunken debauchery until his gut roiled. And the coke. So much cocaine. An amount that only white men could do without fear of legal consequence. It was early November outside, so snow in the city was still rare, but the blizzard in the VIP suite showed no signs of abating. That was his cue to go. To leave the other guards to their well-paid duty while he saw to his own. If it didn't sit quite right with Aston and his ilk…well, Lije wasn't looking for references, was he?

The minutes ticked by like hours as he watched a room full of criminals snort and shoot and bray about their various deals. And then he just…left. He'd memorized the location she gave him. Not that of the place she owned in Tribeca. It was downtown. He took the train, so it gave him time to decompress. To think. To check in with HQ.

Elijah was more than a decade removed from the desert. Sometimes he swore he was still there. When a car backfired. When someone shouted just a little too loud. The first few years they had Third Shift up and running, it was as much a PTSD support group as it was a covert black ops outfit. Him and Jackson and Mack working through all of their shit from the wars. Then they started bringing in the civilians. The people who weren't satisfied with their day jobs, with fighting for justice only to end up with sand trickling between their fingers. The supes like Finn who had nowhere else to go. That was when it had all really gotten serious. Both internally and externally. A real organization fighting real battles against oppression and fascism. For all the good it had done them. Because the fascists kept winning no matter what happened.

Elijah still remembered life without surveillance drones. Without having to show his papers whenever he set foot outside New York City limits. There were kids in primary school now who would never know anything different. Who would always understand their country to be a dictatorship dressed in the tattered remnants of democracy. Who were being taught to fear and distrust anyone different, all while upholding American exceptionalism. It was bullshit. The whole of it. He'd wondered time and again why 3S even tried. Why *he* even tried. Hence his brief foray into teaching at a private military academy. The place he'd met Joaquin, who'd also joined the Third Shift fold.

He can feel Jack's gimlet eye on him the minute he hangs up the call from the school. And sure enough, the man doesn't even wait to offer his unsolicited opinion. "Just because your friends back home call you 'Teacher' doesn't mean you actually need to teach, Lije. Don't spread yourself too thin," he warns like Elijah is a jar of peanut butter or, god forbid, Marmite.

"Teacha," he corrects, not that he wants Jackson to attempt it. The man's a whiz with most languages, but not Patwah. Not by any stretch. He'd rather listen to nails on a chalkboard. "And I have to do something. If we can't stop the next generation from turning into good little Nazis, does what we do at 3S even matter?"

"Don't say I didn't warn you." Jack flings a slew of pencils across the room with the shake of one hand, embedding them in the office corkboard like darts. "I was one of those brats you'll be trying to enlighten. I still went off to fight wars I didn't believe in for administrations who didn't give a shit."

"Ah, but you're not a Nazi, are you?" he points out.

"I'm a rich white asshole," Jack says, ever so self-aware. "Look at who's in power. These days, there's not much difference."

There still wasn't much of a difference. And yet they kept trying to make one. With Jackson's wealth. With Third Shift's skills and resources. Elijah was supposed to be in charge now. Doing things differently than he had in Iraq and Afghanistan. Not using people like the scientists and military brass who'd cooked up Phase One of the Apex Initiative and then gone on making their own monsters with Phase Two and Phase Three. But here he was. Using Meghna Saxena-Saunders just the same.

It was new to him. Playing the honey trap. Being the bait. All of the things that Finn had teased him for in the weeks leading up to tonight. Not everyone could be a walking sex tape, yeah? Conlan was the sort of bloke you could call a "sod" or a "wanker," and he'd say a cheerful "thank you" in return. Whether he ripped your throat out after depended on what side you were on. Lije had never been on his bad one. Being his boss rather helped in that department. But the department of job-related seduction...? He should've asked the vampire for pointers. A brief. A TED Talk. Stick-figure drawings. Because this wasn't dating. It wasn't taking a nice woman out for dinner and a show. *That* he could handle. *Fucking* he could handle. But not feeling anything? Keeping his head and his heart separate from his prick? He didn't have the knack for that.

"We can bring Hawk over from Prague. It doesn't have to be you." Just days ago, Jack had given him one last out. It had only strengthened Elijah's resolve. Because he was damned if he was going to have one of his people do something he wasn't willing to do himself. And because...because Meghna Saunders was *his* project, dammit. He'd done all the research. All the legwork. Stacks and stacks of magazine articles. Casual surveillance around her Tribeca loft. He knew how she liked her coffee—with soy milk and cinnamon—and her fancy gin martinis. He could rattle off her favorite club in Ibiza and what exact shade of lipstick she shilled on billboards and bus shelters all over the city. And now he knew what she tasted like. And he wanted to taste her again. He'd started this. He was going to see it through.

He transferred at Fourteenth Street and took the next subway train a few stops to a fairly new boutique hotel. One of the ones that had cropped up *after* the hellscape of the Darkest Day. This was where Mirko Aston had booked a love nest for his flashy quasi-famous girlfriend. Not a bad choice, really. Not that Elijah knew that much about love nests. His relationships had always been straightforward. Brief, but honest. He'd never been the other man. Or gotten into a love triangle or a love quad or any of that geometry. Who had time for that? And yet here he was now, about to bed a woman theoretically attached to another man.

He was thankful for Wi-Fi in the subway tunnels as he texted out a terse message to Third Shift's resident flirt. Despite not being a product of the digital age, Finn responded before Elijah got off the train and took the stairs aboveground.

Breathe, mate.

A rich bit of advice from someone who didn't have to. But the two texts that came in after, in quick succession, were more useful.

Stay in the moment.

Stay with her.

That wouldn't be a hardship. Because Meghna Saunders was the kind of woman Elijah wanted to know more of. That gorgeous, responsive woman who'd come for him in a dark, dusty room. Sure, she could have been faking it. But the slickness he'd rinsed from his fingertips before leaving the Manhattan Grand didn't feel like a lie. Going to her now didn't feel like a lie.

He was more than a decade removed from the desert. But she was an oasis. What did that mean? That he'd already fucked this up?

You're still you, Lije.

A last text. Unprompted. He scowled down at his mobile before he shoved it into his pocket before he walked through the doors of the hotel. Elijah knew exactly who he was. Exactly who he'd always been. Maybe that was the problem. Elijah Richter, son of Simon and Nakia Richter, was not the sort of man who fucked women he barely knew. Not the sort of lion shifter who went toe-to-toe with potential prey before he sprang. He was responsible. Methodical. Always in control.

But you couldn't control sex, could you? Even if you knew it was just a job, just a ploy to get close to someone. There was still the smell of her, the feel of her, the taste of her. All things he'd carried with him on the ride downtown. He wasn't cut out for this part of undercover work. He'd likely never do it again. But he'd do her. Oh yeah. He'd definitely do her.

4

GRACE MARIA LEUNG WAS THE smartest person in any given room. She'd never had cause to doubt that. This wasn't arrogance on her part, just a statement of fact. Smart. Responsible. Controlled. Always on the ball. Third Shift's in-house medic and all-around science wonk. She had a list of academic and professional achievements a mile wide. And a list of frustrations just as long. At the top of it, in perpetuity, was Finian Conlan. Clever. Impetuous. Never serious if he could help it. He was the only vampire on the American team, and that was plenty as far as everyone was concerned.

She watched him stalk across the office like it was a runway at Fashion Week, his black leather duster unfurling behind him like a cape. One would think he did it for effect, but no, that was just Finn on the average Friday. On any day that ended in *y*, really. They were both on the clock. Third Shift required that at least three operatives be at HQ at any given time, and with Elijah out on a mission, Jackson off doing whatever it was that rich white men did on the weekends, and their booed-up members enjoying some well-deserved time with their partners, that left Joaquin, Grace, and Finn to mind the store. Which really meant Joaquin and Grace were minding the store while Finn provided atmosphere and entertainment.

Looking at him, it was hard to believe he'd nearly bled out all over her hands less than a month ago. Vampire physiology was a marvel unto itself, and intellectually Grace knew that he'd healed easily after feeding, but there was no residual emotional trauma whatsoever. Like he'd recovered from a paper cut or a hangnail. It was remarkable. It was infuriating. Because *she* had yet to recover from that night. From everything that had happened.

She's rarely seen Finn so listless, so pale. For an undead man, he's the most vibrant, alive person she's ever met. She and Nate help him over the threshold of his apartment at HQ. "Like I'm your bride?" he quips, his voice more thin and reedy than it is flirtatious.

It takes a lot to eclipse flirtation in Finian Conlan's world. The wounds from the avian shifter's claws dug deep. Nate's new to all of this. He hasn't experienced this side of Finn. Never watched him fight. Never watched him falter. Never known anything but the rogue. So the human lawyer is just as pale, shaken even, as they wrangle Finn into his room and strip off his clothes. Grace is used to being the adult in the room, the one who keeps a cool head and a steady hand. But this is something else. This is something bigger. No...she's wrong. It's smaller. Compressed and tight. Wrapped around the three of them. A rope. A net. A spell.

"Stay," Finn murmurs, his eyes bluer and brighter than normal. As if dancing close to death gave him an electric charge, turned up his wattage. "Don't leave," he pleads as they press him down onto the mattress, tuck him beneath his garishly obvious silk sheets. "Don't leave me," he says again. And his hands echo the order. Skating up her arms, gently circling.

She shouldn't listen. She should go. They've worked together for years without taking this step, and there's no reason to change that up now. Right? Making it a question is the mistake. Because then there's a counterargument. Isn't this step inevitable? Finian Conlan has fucked half the Eastern Seaboard—why should she be exempt?

Nate moves before she does. The civilian. The outsider. He checks the healing wounds under the bandages she applied in the med bay. Far better than the field dressing on the floor in Brooklyn. Nate's touch is professional, impersonal, chaste. All up until he leans in and kisses Finn full on the mouth. Maybe it's leftover adrenaline from their adventures at the warehouse. Maybe it's an impulse he's been repressing for days. It doesn't matter, because he gives in wholly and unashamedly. And Grace…what kind of person is she if she doesn't do the same?

So she kisses. And she strokes. And she succumbs. Climbing into bed on the other side of her infuriating partner, her closest friend.

The friend who sauntered up now like he'd never been inside her, never made her come. "What's on tap for tonight, Gracie? Anything exciting?"

She was used to neutrality, to not giving a single one of her inner thoughts away. Her default mode was "inscrutable." So her reply was just as casual as his question. "No emergencies as of yet. Joaquin's running through everything the Spider's picking up at the Manhattan Grand." She nodded toward Joaquin's desk, where they were parked in front of multiple huge monitors and surrounded by bags of Oreos and licorice. The hacker *thrived* on this sort of thing. On amassing knowledge, on sifting through data like a forty-niner panning for gold.

Finian hooked his coat on the divider of his cubicle—despite the fact that there were coatracks aplenty at various locations on the office floor—and pushed up the sleeves of his brick-red pull-over. "Let me guess: a lot of sexts, entirely too many dick pics, and some marginally useful intel."

"That's *your* phone," Grace said dryly as she minimized her email window and her folder full of expense reports—the truly *thrilling* side of black ops. Much like in medicine, the paperwork almost always outweighed the heroics.

"Nonsense," Finn scoffed at her, wickedly overactive eyebrows doing their level best. "There's no such thing as too many dick pics on my phone."

She didn't want to laugh. Laughing only encouraged him. But a snort slipped out along with her eye roll. He flopped down in a rolling chair, grinning widely as he wheeled from side to side just inches from her personal bubble. He was like a house cat sometimes. A bratty tom. She half expected him to walk across her keyboard. And she half expected him to ignore her entirely. As mercurial with his attentions as the weather. *She* was the steady one. The person who everyone at Third Shift counted on. The doctor whose patients looked to her for miracles. Smart, responsible, and controlled...but who the hell was looking out for *her*?

"*You know better than to ask that, baby,*" she could just imagine her mother saying. "*Nobody looks out for Black women but other Black women.*" And yet the rest of the American population *still* insisted Black women were going to save them all. When they hadn't bothered to elect the one who ran for president in 2020 to do that very thing. Funny how that worked. Funny how, even on a small scale, Grace was expected to be strong and superhuman... more so than even the actual supernaturals around her. She could do it. Sure. It was a survival mechanism. Especially in this day and age. But that didn't mean she always wanted to.

"Gracie?" She heard the frown in Finn's voice before she glanced up and saw it. "You all right, love?"

Now that was a loaded question. Did he really want the answer? She'd caught him looking at his phone more than once over the past several weeks. Hoping for texts or missed calls from Nate. For some sign that the city's most eligible legal eagle would fly back to this particular roost. *Nate* he worried about. The unknown quantity. But Grace...? She was a fixed point. A sure thing. His partner in all things...now including sex. He knew he could stroll into HQ and flirt and tease and she'd *be here*.

"Have you *ever* not gotten your way?" she wondered before she could think better of it, before she could rephrase. *Fuck.* In for a penny, in for a pound. "Have you ever been rejected? Or do you just annoy everyone into submission?"

Her cocky asshole vampire shocked her then. Without even meaning to. Because he stilled. His gaze dimmed. And then he looked down. Away. His pale throat worked as he swallowed. All of it added up to an answer even before he finally spoke. "You planning to reject me? Is that what this is?"

God, no. Because if she was Finian's fixed point, he was hers. Her constant and her constant pain in the ass. She adored him. Couldn't imagine her life without him. Even when he was a total shit. "*Could* I reject you?" she countered rather than confess that right now with their teammate just a few feet away. "Is that a thing that even happens? You charm every single person you meet."

"Not true," he huffed automatically. "I kill some of them." She didn't even need to quell him with a sharp word or a withering look. He immediately barreled on with a more sincere response, his voice dropping to a velvet-soft burr. "I *have* lost, Gracie. Again and again. My family. My friends. My lovers." He shook his head, eyes far away, probably seeing decades she hadn't even been born for. "When you've lived as long as I have, you don't get to keep them all. Everyone leaves while you stay on."

Her heart twisted. Her stomach turned. And guilt for her petty resentments flooded her chest. What felt permanent and sure to her... It was just a blink in the life of a man who could potentially live for centuries. He'd almost died last month, but odds were that he would outlive her. Finn only took her for granted because he'd learned to take *everyone* for granted. "I'm sorry," she murmured. "I've never considered how rough that must be."

"I didn't tell you for pity, love." Finn bumped her knee with his. "I told you so you know that my past doesn't matter. It *can't*. So everything important to me is here. It's now. It's you and Nathaniel and this place. Third Shift. I hold tight to what I have, because I know it'll eventually slip through my fingers."

"And then we'll be your past, too, won't we?" Grace was seeing him with new eyes. Naked in a different way than he'd been when they'd had sex with Nate. There were sides to Finian Conlan she was still uncovering. Even after four years working and laughing and fighting together. "We'll cease to matter, too."

"No," he said swiftly. He took her hands from the desk, where they'd been poised over the keyboard in a pretense of typing, and closed them both between his. "This is where it stops, Grace of my heart. You're my present. You're my future. I'm not looking further than that."

Oh. Tingles traveled from where their fingers met to her arms and her shoulders. Down and up the line of her spine. The intensity of Finn's words, his stare, his gentle touch, was hot enough to sear off her clothes.

"I was giving you space," he murmured. "Because Nate wants space. But you don't, do you? You're not pushing me away."

"I couldn't if I tried," she admitted with a laugh, maneuvering her chair so they were knee to knee and forehead to forehead. Leaning in to each other. "And I wouldn't try."

He didn't do anything so unprofessional as kiss her in the middle of the office—though she wouldn't have put it past him. Instead, he just stayed with her there for a moment, letting her breathe in the wintergreen and smoke scent of him as he stroked her palms, her wrists, and the backs of her hands. "I don't have dick pics on my mobile," he confessed after a while, pressing his mouth to her knuckles. "But I do have pictures of you. Hundreds. Like a proper stalker."

Only from Finn would and could that be a compliment. As well as a comfort. He *cared*. He wasn't immune to people, to time, to *her*. Grace Maria Leung was the smartest person in any given room…and she still had so much to learn.

Manhattan after midnight was a perfect hunting ground. Eerily silent, hauntingly still in some places…and yet still somehow in motion everywhere else. The neon in the signs. The taxis and livery cabs on Eighth Avenue. The drones in the air. The rats scurrying amid the trash bags piled on the curb. Tavi felt more comfortable with the rodents than with the humans he'd left upstairs at the Grand. He reveled in the cold November air on his face, welcome after the overstuffed air of that VIP suite, which had reeked of liquor and marijuana and sweat. He'd have to go back. His presence would be missed eventually. But for now, he was free. Free to hunt, free to feed, free to *be*.

His phone buzzed in his jacket pocket. More messages from Sasha Nichols, no doubt. The pendejo had decided it was safer to taunt him via text than in person, claiming bragging rights about the all-too-coveted product being manufactured in Connecticut and its safe delivery to Mirko. *Congratulations. Give the man a prize.* Those were accolades Tavi didn't need. His place in the organization was secure by virtue of what he was. Vampire, night-stalker, predator. A creature following a lone human west down a dark street. Across Ninth and then Tenth, with the West Side Highway beckoning just beyond.

Tavi wouldn't kill this one. That was wasteful. That was wrong. He preferred to end the lives that deserved it. All this white man in his midfifties had done was be convenient. Warm and full of blood. Lean and clad in an MTA worker's uniform, he fought when Tavi swooped in on him…but only until the bite. Then he relaxed in the thrall of it. In the circle of Tavi's arms and against the wall of one of the fancy car dealerships that lined this stretch of Eleventh Avenue.

There were blood bags. Animals. Alternatives. But nothing came close to the true feeding. To the hot, gushing fluid filling his mouth and flooding his veins. The heartbeat echoing in his chest, in his ears. *Life.* That thing that had been so far out of his reach for almost two centuries now. It was close, beautifully close, in these moments. Tavi didn't hunt for cruelty's sake. To feel powerful or vicious. He did it to remember what he'd once been and would never be again.

Minutes later, the man continued on his path toward the Hudson, no worse for wear. Perhaps a little dizzy, a little bruised. He would wonder how he hurt his neck. But he'd survive. And so would Tavi Estrada, thanks to the loan of a little blood. Had a drone recorded the encounter? Probably. Did he care? No. There were dozens of known vampires in New York City now. And he hadn't left his quarry dead. A Sanctuary City had bigger problems than a postmidnight snack. The usual crop of rapists and murderers. ICE agents and Supernatural Regulation Bureau stooges still trying to do their dirty work. The rich thugs like Mirko and his ilk who always seemed to escape prosecution. The task force that monitored the surveillance feeds was overworked and underpaid and wouldn't look twice at what looked like a quick fuck.

Tavi whistled as he turned back east. La Lupe's "Con El Diablo en el Cuerpo." *With the devil in the body.* The spring in his step and the swing in his hips was no affectation, and he was almost amused when he finally looked at his phone and spotted three new texts from the pathetic wannabe bear shifter.

Couldn't take the heat Estrada?

Coward.

Mirko's whore is gone 2. Have u seen her? R u with her?

Beyond absurd. He and Meghna were civil when they spoke, which was rarely. They took care to avoid one another, as if innately understanding that the only two people of color in Mirko

Aston's inner circle couldn't be seen as allies, as potential coconspirators. He suspected she'd gone off with that strapping hired security guard she'd been flirting with right under Mirko's nose. But he wasn't about to share that speculation with the likes of Nichols. What or who Ms. Saunders did was her own affair—pun fully intended. As long as it didn't interfere with *his* agenda.

Tavi took his time heading back toward the hotel, walking around and around Times Square, skirting the police checkpoint at Forty-Second Street. The NYPD seemed to interpret "Sanctuary City" as keeping people *in* as much as keeping ICE and other government agencies out. In line. In fear. Who was the real thing that went bump in the night? Supernaturals like him? Or humans like them?

He was no stranger to political oppression. He'd fought for Cuban independence from Spain. He'd lived through World Wars I and II and been there in Havana when Castro overthrew Batista. To say nothing of the last seventy-five years. So many wars. So many dictators—and unlike many of his Cuban brethren, he hadn't fled the rule of one just to roll over for another. Tavi wasn't a member of the Resistance, he wasn't an idealist or anyone's savior, but he continued to fight in his own way. As time marched on. As the death toll rose. Not all at his hands or teeth either. Tavi was merciless, pitiless, but he didn't prey on the innocent. On anyone who wasn't capable of fighting back. The sip from the man earlier...? Just that. A sip. A snack. Something to keep him going. Something to remind him of what he was—not that he ever forgot.

"You could be more," she says with scorn. "But you refuse. Why is that?"

"Shut up," he tells her. "You know nothing of me. While you flit about playing judge, jury, and executioner. Who gave you that right?"

"This world," she spits back, brown eyes blazing. "And it gave you that right, too. If only you'd see it."

It's the last thing either of them say for a while as they dance across

the rooftop trading punches and kicks. Neither of them holding back.
He will feel her boot to his kidneys into the next day. She licks the blood
from her split lip and laughs. He uses his enhanced speed. She conjures
flame and flings a ball at him that he barely manages to duck.

Only two people in his overlong existence had ever shaken his
foundation, challenged his choices. He'd left them both behind.
Conscience was a hindrance in his business, not a help. The few
lines he'd drawn for himself were just that. *Few.* Tavi Estrada, vampire for hire. That was who he had to be. Anything else was idealism. And this wasn't the world for that.

Tavi almost let that line of thought guide him north a few
blocks to Hector's. The beloved café was another one of his lines,
another one of his small concessions. The music and the memories and sometimes even the mambo. But no, that was for his
Saturday nights. So instead, he stopped his contemplative circuit
in front of the Manhattan Grand Hotel and stared up along the
edifice. So many floors. So many windows. All hiding the evil that
worked within. The evil that he was a part of.

This was the choice he'd made. This was where he belonged
now. There was no going back. There was only going forward.
Even if that led him straight to hell.

5

———

THE ROOM WAS DIPPED IN midday light like an artisanal ice cream cone, hot with the sultriness of too much sex and not enough windows open. Her perfectly manicured short nails dug into the broad shoulders above her—just the one set, as she dug five additional crescents into her own thigh. *Focus. Stay focused*, Meghna reminded herself for what felt like the thousandth time in the past thirty-six hours. It was a struggle to listen to that stern inner voice, drowned out as it was by her ragged breaths and the husky voice murmuring beautiful filth in her ear.

"That's it, baby," the man who'd called himself Mack urged as he rocked into her. "Let me make it good. Let me make you come."

She was making all the appropriate noises, rising up to meet his vigorous thrusts, telling him he was "so big" and "so hard" and "the best I've ever had." And really, really trying not to think about how much of that might actually be true. The blow job she'd given him in the Manhattan Grand's hall closet had been engineered to put him in *her* power, not the other way around. She'd learned that at twenty-one…while other young women were doing internships and on European vacations. With the help of an enterprising jinn and a willing test subject in a virile gandharva named Atul. *"Once you have their balls in your hand, you have everything,"* her teacher had purred, demonstrating her own technique. Meghna and Atul had spent the rest of the summer practicing. Two enthusiastic Vidrohi agents learning spy craft and sex craft in one go.

But now…? Here? Almost a decade and a half later? Meghna was *so* screwed. In more ways than one. Six months into her operation, she was no closer to the intel she sought—to the information the man above her was literally pumping her for. How ironic that she was frustrated in every way but sexually.

"Am I *boring* you?" Her new mark's words were a glorious rumble, hitting her as deep as his cock, sending vibrations rippling down her spine.

"I'm multitasking," she said with a gasp of pleasure that wasn't entirely fake.

To his credit, the man who'd introduced himself to her less than forty-eight hours ago as Mack Wilson knew what he was doing—even if he didn't know *who* he was doing. He'd compelled her immediately. Impressed her. Aroused her. So much so that it hadn't surprised her when the network had verified his fingerprints. Elijah Richter, former British Army, current cofounder of a security firm known as Third Shift. As she'd noted from the first moment she saw him, he was a beautiful man. A powerful one too. The average human would not feel what he hid under human skin, the growl of the creature just below the surface, begging to run wild. But she'd understood it. She'd heard the beast and known its name. *Lion. Singha. Sher.* That secret, she told herself now, was why she'd entertained his pursuit. Why she'd allowed his mission to potentially endanger hers. *Utilize every asset, take every avenue and every advantage.* And so, she'd taken and taken and taken…

"Hurts a man's ego, don't you know? We like to be the sole focus when we've a lady in our arms." His deep-brown eyes twinkled with mirth. She pushed aside the warmth that twinkle sparked in her belly. She had no room for a real connection. No time. Neither did he...though he didn't want her to know that.

"I think your ego will survive," she assured dryly.

Like most men, he had confidence to spare. That confidence had given him the inroads his organization wanted—her, her bed, a possible path to the other man in her life—and also kept him ignorant to the truth of her. What he saw, what everyone saw, was precisely what she allowed them to see. A beautiful woman who set fashion trends and made headlines. Rich, useless, ornamental. Arm candy to the who's who of Hollywood and DC political elites alike. Meghna Saxena-Saunders was only as important as the men she was tied to after all. Her ex-husband, Chase, her father, RK, and his defense company, and of course Mirko—arms dealer to the terrorist stars.

"Mack" wouldn't be trying to make her come, would never have met her at all, were it not for Mirko Aston. It was almost funny, considering the Vidrohi was comprised of women and of nonbinary and gender-nonconforming supernaturals, and they had little use for cis heterosexual men. Except the one use she was currently engaged in. The gloriously distracting exercise that was sex. A means to an end. Sometimes a happy one...sometimes a permanent one.

But she didn't want to kill this man. Was that a weakness on her part? Everything she'd been so determined to avoid? Meghna couldn't stop to war with that question. Not when Elijah Richter's fingers found her clit and teased it exquisitely. Not when he angled his cock just so. God, he was *good*. The kind of lover she hadn't had in years. One who actually cared about her pleasure. He wouldn't be satisfied with breathy moans and tremors. With the theater of sex. He wanted the reality. He wanted her to come apart. Meghna had done it for him countless times already, and she was poised to do it again.

Of course, she couldn't surrender. Not completely. Because

that was too big of a risk. *It's just sex,* she reminded herself as she opened for him, as she rose to meet him. *Sex is your weapon.* And she couldn't let it be her undoing. If nothing else, because the General would say "I told you so." The woman had loved to lord her savvy and her skills over each crop of new recruits. She'd been hardest on Meghna, for obvious reasons. But she wasn't going to think about any of those reasons right now.

Elijah Richter deserved her complete attention. The arch of her body under his broad, long-fingered hands. The genuine cries of pleasure he could wring from her throat. The fruit of his lusty labors. He wasn't boring her. Far from it. And it was time for her to pay him back in kind.

For all the mental preparation, for all the advice from those far more experienced in such matters, Elijah was still completely and utterly lost. Being with this woman was like nothing he'd ever felt before. Her nails dug into his back like tiny bits of shrapnel. The sounds she made were needy and hungry and demanding. Calling to him on every level. Her thighs hugged his hips. She panted the false name he'd given her and it went directly to his groin, making him piston harder and drive her back and back and back until she teetered on the edge. Sweat beaded his skin while his fur prickled beneath it. The fight to keep the change back was rougher than it had been in decades. But *she* was his hardest fight. Because she, and this, was an actual challenge. Anchoring her in the present instead of letting her wander away mentally to wherever she'd just been. Pleasing her. Satisfying her. Making sure she remembered *this* more than anything else.

Meghna was supposed to be his way in. His gorgeous longish con. The team had pulled from what was left of Aleksei Vasiliev's connections in South Brooklyn...learning that Aston had something dangerous and classified that he was planning to sell to the highest bidder. All they needed was someone on the inside…and Lije inside her. A few days into their beautifully filthy affair, he could "confess" he was really after Aston's stash, planning to steal the loot before the auction and sell it back to American military contractors. A partial truth. And given how little affection she held for her boyfriend, she'd probably pretend to feel betrayed for all of five seconds before she kissed him like she was kissing him now.

Like it meant everything.

Like they'd both die if she stopped.

He didn't stop. He took it down a notch, making it perversely slow, keeping her at the brink of her orgasm and staving off his own. Because she was beautiful like this. Tangled with him, her throat bared and her hair spilling all over them both. More careful than they'd been at the party, this time she'd stayed away from the suite's door. Met him at the bedroom after he let himself in. All that hair loose and welcoming. Her soft purple robe hanging open to reveal a sinful scrap of matching lace that could barely be called a nightgown.

"This round two or goodbye?" he'd growled, hooking an arm around her waist and maneuvering her up against the wall.

"It's whatever you want it to be," she'd said.

Goodbye. Au revoir. Until I fucking see you again. *Until you give me everything I'm looking for.* Elijah hadn't come yet. He could draw it out further still, hold out for when she'd come three or four times over, but she started to spasm around his cock, pulling on him with each little quake of her quim, so he gave in. Thrusting in with one last grunt. Filling the latex sheath he'd barely remembered to put on before she dragged him to the sheets. She went to pieces around him, against him, like they'd run a marathon together and collapsed at the finish line. "Meghna." Her name was a groan he muffled along the sharp line of her collarbone. "Ah, Meg. This is fucking brilliant."

"Brilliant fucking, you mean." Her eyes shone like black

diamonds. Her skin smelled like expensive perfume and sweat and him. She kneaded his shoulders with her fists and then pushed at him, which he took as a hint to lever himself up and off her body. "Is this what you wanted from me? Why you were watching me the other night? Are you satisfied?"

"Not nearly," he told her as he pinched off the condom and dropped it into the bin next to the bed. "Not bloody nearly."

And he had to prove that, had to punctuate it, with one more openmouthed kiss. His senses were still so full of her—her smell, her taste, her filthy-gorgeous sounds of pleasure—that he didn't hear the intruder until it was too late. Until he'd already come down the hall to the bedroom. Until the litany of Russian and English curses and the whisper-slide noise beneath them, of a gun being drawn from a holster. *One of Aston's men. Here.* He and Meghna sprang apart, kiss broken, spell broken, twisting to look at the weasel-faced blond man who'd caught them completely unaware.

"You traitorous bitch!" the man snarled. "I knew you couldn't be trusted."

Shorter than him. Solid build. He smelled like a shifter, but he was human. No less dangerous for being so. Elijah processed it all in wasted seconds as he rolled forward, shoving Meghna behind him with one hand as the other popped and shifted to a claw. He didn't waste any more time feeling or thinking. He just launched from the bed with a roar. Swiped at the man who stank of gun oil and cologne and murder. Knocked the weapon away before he could fire it. Sliced his throat before he could spit another threat.

Blood spattered the wall like a macabre bit of modern art. The hot spray hit Elijah's face. His arms. Dripped from his paw. So much blood...and so much death. Because the gunman instantly crumpled to the floor, an empty sack of bones and flesh. It was only then, when time slowed back to normal speed, when the lion was quiet and the fur at his ruff receded, that Elijah remembered

Meghna. She hadn't screamed. She hadn't made a sound after he shoved her out of the way, off the far side of the bed.

Did he...? Is she...?

He whipped around, only to find her standing by the night table. Unharmed. Still naked. Entirely unconcerned about seeing him shift, seeing him kill someone. Staring at the henchman's body with the dispassion of a person who'd seen more than one corpse in her time. "Well, that was excessive," she said crisply before looking at back at him. "Are you satisfied *now*?"

For the second time in less than five minutes, Elijah was totally off his game.

6

SASHA NICHOLS WAS DEAD. VERY dead. Still warm, but not for long. The man made as ugly a picture in death as he had in life. Meghna could muster only two dovetailing emotions: anger and annoyance. *This* was not the plan. This, in fact, *ruined* her plans. "What exactly am I supposed to do with this?" She gestured as she came around the bed. There was no point in checking for a pulse. Elijah's slash had been swift and true. No doubt he had a great amount of experience dispatching problems in that manner. It wasn't neat. It wasn't precise. But it was certainly permanent. "This is going to require some explaining to Mirko, don't you think? I doubt he'll buy that Sasha tripped on a garden rake."

The gold sheen of the lion shifter's eyes melted back into deep brown. His grim determination changed to bewilderment. "Pardon?" he sputtered, bloodstained hand dropping to his side.

There was no point in keeping up her charade. Playing the hysterical bystander. Meghna knew better than that. It was a waste of time. Unnecessary theatrics. Besides, everyone knew that the best defense was a good offense. She needed to keep Richter off-balance in order to maintain her ground. "You killed my target's closest henchman," she pointed out coolly. "He's going to notice. That is more than six months of work down the drain."

Just as she'd hoped he would be, Elijah was still scrambling to process what she'd revealed. "*Your* target?" He looked at Nichols's body and then back at her, brows drawing together with confusion.

Meghna didn't bother with an answer. She just set about recovering her bra and underwear from the corners of the room, quickly buttoning up the cashmere sweater dress that Elijah had stripped from her without preamble at the beginning of their latest encounter. She probably shouldn't have bothered getting dressed when he went out for a bodega egg and cheese, but now having a dress within close reach proved useful. She would leave everything else behind, of course. The few personal items she'd kept in the suite weren't of value—clothes and accessories easily discarded—and packing them up would just waste the time she'd already run out of.

Aston would not take kindly to this development. He'd come after her for the murder, not so much the cheating. But it boiled down to the same conclusion: all her work, all her effort had been for nothing. Her mission was blown. So she needed to go before suspicion fell on her. Somewhere public. Somewhere where she couldn't be touched without causing a media shitstorm.

Elijah was making his own preparations. Scrubbing his hands in the en suite bathroom. Returning to tug on his clothes. A comm emerged from a hidden pocket, and he slid the device behind his ear. But he hadn't let go of what she'd said. Of course not. He would be a terrible operative if he let such things slide. "What do you mean *your* target? Who do you work for?" he demanded once they were both as presentable as they could be under the circumstances.

"No one you've ever heard of," she assured, crossing out of the bedroom and into the short hallway that connected to the suite's sitting room. "No one you need to concern yourself with." He stalked after her. Foolish lion. Thinking she was prey. "You don't seem worried about shifting in front of me," she said over her shoulder. "Why is that?"

"You don't seem worried about me killing in front of you, now do you?" he countered easily. "Besides which, you're a supe. I can smell it on you. But I can't make heads or tails of it."

"Because I don't *have* a tail," she quipped. "I doubt you could even guess what I am, Elijah. Have you even heard of my kind?"

He shook his head, brows knitting together. "Siren?" he guessed.

"I've lured a few men to their deaths in my day, but no. I am an apsara. They say we were court dancers for Indra, the king of the heavens. Celestial beauties, nymphs, often sent down among humans to tempt sages away from attaining power through prayer. That's just the Hindu origin story, though." It was the story she'd heard from the woman who'd given birth to her. One she'd listened to with a healthy dose of skepticism. She'd done her own research afterward. "You'll find tales of us all over South and Southeast Asia. Cambodia…Bali. Always beautiful. Always accomplished in the arts. Somewhere in the past two thousand years, we became accomplished at *more*." They'd formed the Vidrohi with other supernatural women from around the region. Left behind the heavens to help those on earth. They'd weaponized for themselves what cisgender men had used for millennia.

"Not so much tempting the sages as taking them out?" This wasn't a guess but a cool statement of fact as Elijah glanced from her to Sasha Nichols's body and back again. As if he were piecing her nonreaction to the man's gruesome demise together with the story she now told.

"We have many skills," she evaded deftly. "I speak eight languages. Play the guitar and the piano. I know Bharatnatyam, flamenco, and the Argentine tango. I have an MBA. And this isn't the first time I've seen someone die. It probably won't be the last."

"Well, it's the last bloody time today," he growled. "I'll call a crew. Get the body cleaned up and the scene sanitized, and then you're coming with me. We'll get this all sorted."

"I think the fuck not." She drew herself up, cold fury cloaking her more thoroughly than the cowl-neck sweaterdress she'd donned. Funny how *his* abrupt turn—from lusty supernatural security guard to efficient killer with tech—wasn't to be questioned. She was supposed to just fall in line, like a good little girl, and do whatever he demanded. "You're not taking me anywhere, Elijah Richter. In fact, I'd like to see you *try*."

He stopped short. Statue-still, like she was Medusa turning him to stone. "You know my real name." His already-granite jaw hardened even further. He was still impossibly handsome for it. The facial hair that shadowed his cheeks and chin had a bit more salt and pepper now than in the ID photos Vidrohi's contacts had included in his file. He'd bulked up some from the weight on his New York State driver's license, too. She had no complaints whatsoever, at least not when it came to using the resource that was his well-hewn body.

"I know your real name," she affirmed. "I know what you do. I know what you are. And I have no need for any of it."

"*Any* of it?" One of his brows went up. Along with his back. "You sure needed a piece of me not twenty minutes ago, love," he reminded. "Or was I a target, too?"

That was rich coming from the man who'd infiltrated Mirko's VIP party and immediately set his sights on her. Meghna stared at him without flinching. "You don't get to ask me that. Unless you have an active fetish for fucking women in closets, and any connection I had to Mirko was purely coincidental. Go ahead and call your team," she added. "Explain to them how you've messed up this operation because of that 'piece of you' that you had no problem offering up. I'm sure they'll be thrilled."

Elijah made a low, rumbling sound. A reminder that no matter what he seemed to be, he was no mere mortal man. It rippled across her skin like a warning. But it didn't faze her. Meghna, after all, was no mere mortal woman.

"Don't move," he bit out before turning away to activate his comm and contact whoever he needed to.

She didn't have to listen. It would be the perfect time to make her exit. To burn this mission and never look back. She could return to the bosom of social media and red carpets and dressing up on theme for the Met Gala. Back to Chase's beach house in Malibu or her father's compound in Great Falls. The Vidrohi wouldn't begrudge her failure. They'd value that she got out alive. Because there would always be other operations. Their work was never done.

Meghna stayed right where she was. Later, she would blame curiosity. Wanting to know what Richter was planning. And efficiency too. Because anything his people had learned about Mirko's upcoming deals could be passed along to the Vidrohi. Those were better excuses than the broad expanse of Elijah's back under his T-shirt. Or the all-too-fresh memory of how those taut muscles felt under her hands.

The SUV crawled uptown from the swanky hotel where Meghna had her paid-for crash pad. They hit every possible red light. If Elijah hadn't known better, he'd say Wyatt was doing it on purpose. Making this painful ride even more excruciating. But no, generally the drivers on the Third Shift motor pool weren't sadists. There was only one person to blame for this. Maybe two. Definitely himself at any rate.

Meghna wasn't speaking to him. Not anything but strictly necessary words since they'd evacked from the hotel and climbed into the transport vehicle. Her back was straight, her shapely legs neatly crossed, her profile smooth… There wasn't a single sign that she was displeased with him, but she smelled like anger, like a fellow predator braced for an attack. It was a mess of gorgeous contradictions, just like her. She was laser-focused on her mobile, thumbs flying across the screen as she Instagrammed and tweeted about her skin-care routine and the club she hit last night. "Plausible deniability," she'd said when she caught him looking. That had been six blocks and fifteen minutes ago.

He knew all about plausible deniability. It was why he and Jackson had masked Third Shift as a private security and investigation firm. Why they'd recruited supes and humans who had other "first shift" gigs. Lawyers, cops fed up with the system, doctors like Gracie Leung. They'd been hiding in plain sight for more than a decade. Just like supernaturals had been doing since the beginning of time. Long before the world plummeted straight into the fascist shitter and they'd had to step up to balance a few of the scales. Congress. Parliament. The United Nations. NATO. There were admitted supes everywhere now—some trying in vain to yank their countries back to where they ought to be, while still others aligned with the rich and the corrupt to make them even richer and even more corrupt.

The United States was barely that anymore. The Sanctuary Cities like New York and Los Angeles and Chicago were basically city-states, forming a Sanctuary Alliance with other territories and rebelling against the new Patriot Acts. By early 2018, they'd declared total control within their jurisdictions, pushing back against ICE and the Supernatural Regulation Bureau. But that defiance hadn't really changed shite nationally. Detainment camps for asylum seekers and migrants were still active along the northern and southern borders. Only now they were outfitted for supes, too. The cages migrant children had finally been freed from... They were full of shifters and other things that went bump in the night. DC was still a cesspool of left versus right—supposedly progressive versus entirely too conservative—with none of it doing much in the long run. There were committees and subcommittees, of course. Proposed bills about supernatural personhood and citizenship. It'd all been tied up in political red tape for years.

Third Shift wasn't tied up at all. They did what needed to be done. Locally, globally. Wherever they could be of service. Off the books. Under no one's orders...but maybe a few suggestions from a committee at the Department of Defense. It was almost a laugh, because when Elijah and Jack had dreamed it up, buried in dirt and sand and a war neither of them had a personal stake in, they hadn't reckoned what was coming. How the dominoes would fall one after the other. Just how *badly* they'd be needed. The world had always been on fire, after all. You didn't notice how deep the burns were after a while. But 2016 had made the flames taller, brighter, hotter. And then 2017 and 2018, too. And so on.

Jack had an inside line to the firefighting efforts, courtesy of a spotless military service record and friends in the DoD. Former Lieutenant Tate had been introduced to a very exclusive, very secret group embedded within the U.S. government and dedicated to combating fascism. Missions frequently came to 3S through that pipeline. Aston was one such mission. Elijah couldn't afford to fuck it up now. Not when they were so close to figuring out what the man was up to. Who *his* secret group included and what their ultimate aims were.

The cleaning crew was supposed to be done with the first phase of suite sanitization by now—disposing of Sasha Nichols's corpse via a laundry cart and a service elevator, cleaning the carpet, tossing the trash, wiping the hotel security cameras of any damning footage. Then the second phase of work would begin. Making sure no DNA was left behind. Painting over the bloodstains on the wall. Removing any fingerprints and footprints. All in all, it wouldn't take *that* long. At the rate traffic was moving, they'd probably be done before Elijah got to the Third Shift HQ in Hell's Kitchen.

Jack had been running the show solo for the past few days.

Tying up the last loose ends of everything that had happened with Aleksei Vasiliev and Joe Peluso, making arrangements for Peluso to go toes up in prison and resurface with a new identity. Jack Tate was the sort of white man who'd never known suffering—at least not until he saw it firsthand in Afghanistan and Iraq, experienced it in blood and bullets and broken bones. He was born with a silver spoon in his mouth and a silver stick up his arse besides. His family could trace itself back to the *Mayflower* and the Salem witch trials, had memberships in all the high-society social clubs and a box at every major opera house in the country. That he owned property all over Manhattan and Brooklyn was a given—and a bonus for Third Shift. His wealth and status and skin color allowed him entry to rooms Elijah could never, even in the twenty-first century, gain access to. He could rub elbows with the Senate majority leader and the president without them ever knowing he opposed everything they stood for. Again, hiding in plain sight.

Jack was Elijah's polar opposite as far as most people were concerned. Polished. Lean. Fashionable. White. Sometimes, when high-profile clients came in for meetings, Elijah was mistaken for his bodyguard instead of rightfully assumed to be the cofounder of 3S. But it was more than just the obvious differences. Jack was a sorcerer. Elijah was a shifter. Jack was American. Elijah had dual citizenship with Britain and loads of uncles and cousins and aunties who still lived in Jamaica. Jack was U.S. Army. Elijah was British SRR—Special Reconnaissance. But they were of like minds where it mattered: Third Shift. Getting things done. Keeping collateral damage to a minimum.

Was Meghna Saunders collateral damage? That remained to be seen. Elijah shook his head of all the thoughts swirling 'round in it, glancing out the window to gauge their progress north. Miracle of miracles, they were actually up to numbered streets and avenues. He touched the comm at his ear, switching to B Channel. "Report?"

"Just finishing up now, sir!" the tech in charge of the cleanup assured. "ETA to incineration is eight minutes." They'd burn the body. Burn the cart. Burn the van they used for transport. Not particularly great for the environment, but that was the least of Third Shift's worries. "The suite is clean. The occupant can return at their leisure."

Good. Very good. Lije repeated the words aloud for positive reinforcement. But he had no intention of letting Meghna return at her leisure or anybody else's. Whoever she worked for, whatever she was after, she was about to become Third Shift's latest asset. Whether she liked it or not.

7

THE DARK-GLASSED MIDRISE BUILDING WAS just steps from the Hudson River. It had that slick sheen of a new construction, incongruent with the surrounding older brick buildings, mostly warehouses, at the very west end of Manhattan's West Fifties. Like slapping a shiny filtration faucet on the old sink that was Hell's Kitchen. Meghna was both repulsed and impressed. Third Shift was bold…making their headquarters so visible when discretion was the better part of valor. But then again, wasn't she doing more or less the same thing? Operating in the spotlight, drawing people to her, trading on her looks and her connections and her charms— both natural and supernatural?

The driver pulled the nondescript black SUV around the back of the building and down into an underground parking garage. Meghna tucked her public smartphone away into the shoulder bag she'd brought with her. Wallet, keys, other devices, other incidentals. She'd left everything else in the suite. There was a fifty-fifty chance that she wouldn't ever be going back there, and she wasn't sorry for it. It was a pied-à-terre, a love nest, a set piece for a play. Mirko had a mansion in Westchester and a penthouse in Midtown. She spent most nights in a loft in Tribeca, and that was where a few of her personal belongings lived full-time. That hotel suite had just been a place she stayed once in a while. A place that had brought her no joy...not until last night and this morning. When Elijah Richter had tried over and over again to get through the barriers she'd long ago erected between her body and her mind...and nearly succeeded.

She'd enjoyed going to bed with him. She'd almost forgotten that they were using each other, lying to each other, all while pleasuring each other. There was no forgetting it now as they slipped out of the parked SUV and walked across the well-lit garage. There were three other black SUVs of a similar make and model, along with various cars she presumed belonged to the operatives themselves. The driver walked ahead of them, like he didn't want to be around for whatever she and Elijah were heading into. And indeed, when they entered a corridor with two elevators, he offered Richter a jaunty salute before pressing his finger to a biometric scanner and hopping into a car by himself.

Elijah scanned his own index finger and then made an after-you gesture when the doors to the second car opened. "We're the only ones with access to these lifts and the garage," he said, pronouncing the word the British way, like her Indian-born father did *GAH-rahje*. "There's visitor parking 'round front."

Meghna could drum up any number of trivial things to say in response. She was used to that. Insipid cocktail-party conversation was the same whether you were in DC or Aspen, hanging with ambassadors or rock stars. She chose to stay silent, settling against the back wall of the elevator. There were no number buttons to press. Just another biometric scanner and a touch screen. Elijah swiped this way and that until the car shot upward smoothly and soundlessly.

And then they were stepping out into the heart of Third Shift. An entity she'd only vaguely heard of. Still, she probably knew more about Richter's agency than he did about the Vidrohi. There were secret organizations and then there were *secret* organizations. Hers had existed, in some form or another, for thousands of years. It would probably exist well beyond their lifetimes, into the future, if humankind didn't manage to destroy the universe first. They had the training camp, sure, but they didn't have a centralized hub, a headquarters. No home base. *No home.*

The office had a largely open floor plan. With a long, glass-walled conference room along the back that looked to be their command center. Everything was decorated in black and white and steel. The glass panels shielding the back room were lightly frosted, showing the shapes of the people inside and nothing more. The floors were carpeted with tightly woven gray fibers. Overall, it appeared to be a normal place of business, with cubicles and dividers in the center and a few offices along the sides—if you discounted the alarming amount of high-end tech. And the low hum of activity and energy that seemed to vibrate through the space. Expensive monitors were everywhere, showing everything from news feeds to stocks to CCTV from god only knew where. Visible surveillance cameras were mounted at the top of some of the floor-to-ceiling columns that marched toward the back— probably cover for the invisible ones. There were digital world clocks set high up into the same wall as the elevator, ticking away the hours in cities like New Delhi and Tokyo and Prague.

And here. Time was ticking here in New York, too. They likely had a matter of hours—if that—before Mirko realized Sasha was missing. That he hadn't detoured to some den of iniquity en route to catching her in flagrante. Precious hours. Meghna knew better than to waste them. She'd already wasted too many. Her window for convincing Mirko that Sasha was paranoid and her loyalties were above reproach was a slim one.

That window was growing narrower even as Elijah walked her to the back of the floor, to the conference room that was already buzzing with movement and chatter. Five people were scattered around the space, bent over laptops and tablets and files or studying 3D modules they'd brought up from projectors positioned above the long, black table that dominated the center of the room.

"Jack and I've got offices. An actual conference room for client meetings. But we spend most of our time back here in Command. Easier. More efficient," Elijah said before adding, "Would you like to inspect our closet space?" in his best snooty *Downton Abbey* accent. It was strange hearing the crisp higher pitch from his lips after the rough comfort of his real one. It almost distracted her from what he'd actually said.

When it registered, Meghna narrowed her eyes. "Are you sure *you* don't want to inspect something? Didn't get your fill earlier?"

"All in good time, love. All in good time." Elijah broke away from her side to go confer with a tall white man. Brown-haired. Generically handsome and radiating privilege in a way that spoke of frat parties and hedge funds and an Ivy League education. His shirt, collar undone and with the sleeves pushed up, was tailored. So were his gray suit pants. The matching jacket was draped over a nearby leather captain's chair. His hands were devoid of any rings. He was clean-shaven, and he and Elijah had a matching mulish set to their jaws.

"I have to go back to Mirko," she said, interrupting whatever Richter was telling the bespoke bachelor. "Before he realizes I was in any way involved."

"The hell you do." Elijah whirled back to her, his eyes blazing. "Going back now *guarantees* he'll catch on."

She bristled. She couldn't help rolling her eyes as well, even though her media training had mostly broken her of the habit. "As opposed to the subtlety of vanishing from my suite and coming here with you? Not suspicious at all," she spat. "He'll just think I booked an extra-long spa vacay. No big deal!"

"Joaquin could arrange that if you'd like. They've done similar things for cover in the past." Elijah gestured toward a brown-skinned operative swiping through the 3D blueprints of some sort of facility. "Joaquin Serrano. Hacker extraordinaire, all-around tech guru, and Starbucks flat-white addict."

"That sounds like an actual compliment, Lije, and I'll take it! I'll take the assignment, too!" they assured, light-brown eyes dancing with obvious delight at the prospect. "I can populate your social media with photos and status updates. Make it look like you jetted off to the hot springs. Easy. Just give me a few base images to work with." They held out their hand for her phone, wiggling their fingers impatiently.

Meghna felt compelled to unlock her device, call up her photos, and comply—even though Joaquin didn't have any supernatural powers that she could detect. Maybe it was their dimples. Or the charmingly awkward way they scrubbed at their curly black hair. Or the T-shirt they wore that declared "Fuck the patriarchy! Read romance!" She had no intention of giving in to Elijah Richter as easily.

"As far as I can see, I have two options," she told him. "Getting away from all of this and surrounding myself with as many paparazzi and clout-chasers as possible. Or going back into the fold. Pretending nothing happened. Playing out the charade for as long as I can. If I can get what I went in for, great. If I can get out alive, even better."

His brows rose, and he crossed his powerful arms over his chest. "What *did* you go in for?"

Meghna was entranced by the flex of his forearms, but she wasn't about to share any answers as a result. *No.* "Closet space," she said tartly.

———————

It was like watching a sexually charged tennis match—this give-and-take between Elijah and Meghna Saxena-Saunders. But Third Shift had no time for spectator sports. Grace cleared her throat and tapped her fingers on the smooth surface of the conference table to get her boss's attention. "What's *our* play? What do you need the team to do, Lije?"

She had just a handful of days off before her next shift at the Queensboro Community Hospital. They'd started noticing the wide gaps in her surgery schedule over the past year. And despite her flawless work in the OR, the board was considering not renewing her contract. She supposed that should worry her. Maybe it would when it came to that. In this moment, she was only concerned with what she needed to do for 3S. She'd long ago learned how to compartmentalize her life. Her brain. Her heart. It was what made her an excellent surgeon and a valuable operative.

Elijah would have snapped at anyone else for interrupting his verbal and ocular standoff with the woman who'd been his mark up until a few hours ago. He'd decided Grace was a cut above "the ragtag bunch of gits" that made up Third Shift. Treated her like she was Wendy among the Lost Boys. So all he did was register her questions with a sharp nod. He stalked over to the table and swiped across one of the projection consoles, bringing up a string of text and two file photos.

"Joaquin's already harvested quite a bit from the Spider and from Nichols's mobile phone," he said. "The most recent, and most relevant, number belongs to a vampire going by the name of Octavio 'Tavi' Estrada." Elijah gestured to one of the photos. It was a grainy surveillance picture from the VIP party of a man in profile. Dark-haired. Well dressed. "He's on a number of watch lists. FBI, MI6, INTERPOL. He has his fingers in a lot of pies and his fangs in a lot of necks."

Grace felt rather than saw Finn react in the seat next to her... and it sent an answering shudder through her. A shudder and a frisson of alarm. Finn Conlan was not a subtle person. He flirted wildly, spoke too frequently, and allowed his eyebrows entirely too much expressive freedom. So when he went deathly still and equally silent at the mention of Tavi Estrada, she knew it could only mean trouble.

"Estrada is an intermediary," Elijah was saying, reading Joaquin's report off a tablet. "He helped arrange the transport of the bioweapon Aston is so hot to sell. He knows what it is and where it's going. He knows when the auction will take place."

"*I* would have known all of that." Meghna slapped the conference table with her palm as she exhaled in frustration. "Damn you, Richter. I was *so close*. Mirko took me everywhere, and the auction was next on my appearance list. And you had to go off half-cocked. Literally."

Elijah slapped his own palm down, like they'd moved from tennis to some sort of high-stakes card game. "I don't recall you complainin' at the time, love."

Grace tuned them out, canting her body toward Finn. "You know him," she said in low tones beneath the command-center chatter. It was not a question.

He seemed to go even paler than his usual sun-loathing pallor, paper-white and waxen. His lashes fluttered like dark butterfly wings, and his chest rose and fell in the mimicry of human breaths. "Intimately," he admitted quietly after three interminably long beats.

Finian had known a great number of people intimately. It was a source of pride. *Defiant* pride. His queer polyamorous fuck-you to a world that demanded conformity and spit on anyone who stepped out of line. Grace had maintained a defiant sort of pride of her own in keeping her notch off his bedpost. Keeping him wanting. Keeping him her colleague and friend. For all the good that had done. Finn had gotten her into his bed anyway...no matter that she'd put him there first. She'd fallen between the sheets so hard and so fast that she was still spinning weeks later. She suspected that Nate was keeping him at a distance for similar reasons. They'd grown too close during the showdown with Vasiliev and Joe Peluso several weeks before. So they'd redrawn the boundary lines. There was no pride *or* pleasure, however, in learning that this Tavi Estrada had gorged on something they'd only just tasted themselves.

Because Finn—her exasperating, infuriating, beautiful beloved—looked absolutely gutted. And Jackson and Elijah finally noticed.

"Why are *you* so quiet, Conlan? Out with it," Elijah snapped, pulling his gaze from Meghna, who'd been his primary focus since they arrived.

Finn reached for Grace's hand beneath the table. She squeezed his fingertips as he pasted on a devil-may-care smile and punctuated it with a brow quirk. "Estrada and I go way back," he said. "All the way back to 1960. Before any of you lot were even a twinkle in your mum's eye. He's ruthless, efficient, almost as charming as I am. But unlike your friendly neighborhood vampire, he can't be trusted. Because he has one interest and one interest only: whatever benefits himself. No matter who gets hurt in the process."

Finn's light tone ended on a dark note, and his gaze flitted to the smooth obsidian surface of the conference table before meeting Elijah's once again. It was probably clear to everyone in the room who'd gotten hurt in the process. And a perfect opportunity for ribbing, for jabs at the comrade who was always taking potshots at the rest of them. Grace leveled each and every person with a death glare that telegraphed "Don't you dare." Joaquin, Jack, even Meghna, who was a veritable stranger despite being a minor celebrity…none of them escaped her warning.

Lije nodded back tightly. *Message received.* "He can't be trusted…but can he be turned? Can we use him?"

"Yes," Finn assured. But his grip on her hand betrayed his private doubts. And so much more. "As long as you know he's as likely to shiv you in the back as he is to help you. Estrada's an opportunist. And he'll fuck off to parts unknown the first chance he gets. Leave you holding the bag."

Elijah didn't look at Grace this time. He just leaned on the table, palms braced, and kept his attention locked on the only vampire in the room. "No, he'll leave *you* holding the bag—so you'd better suss out where you're going to put it. I want you on this, Finn. You've history with the man. You know how he operates. I'd love to bring someone else up to speed, but we just haven't got the time."

Apparently "don't you dare" only went so far. Grace wanted to say something. To intercede on Finn's behalf. But before she could, he spoke up for himself. "Of course," he said, flashing a wide, false smile. "I wouldn't expect anything less. Can't wait to stage a reunion with my old pal Tavi."

"Then I'm running point." Grace followed up immediately. Without even having to think about it. She just held Finn's hand tighter, like she could will him some of her warmth. "Because I know how *Finn* operates, and I'd like to keep the mission running smoothly." And whatever past he had with Tavi Estrada, they would face it together.

"For what it's worth, Tavi's always treated me kindly. He keeps to himself for the most part. Doesn't join in all the 'reindeer games' with Mirko and his men," Meghna added. "Out of everyone in that crew, he's the most approachable. Because he has his own agenda. I have no idea what it is, but his loyalty isn't to them."

"Good," Jackson Tate, their other boss, chimed in from the other side of the room. "File a mission plan. Gear up. You know the drill. Now to the second photo and the second most relevant phone number. That's a genetic researcher named Gary Schoenlein. Last known whereabouts: a private research lab just outside Hartford. His phone has also pinged in some odd locations in the Atlantic Ocean that we're still narrowing down. The communications on Nichols's phone are brief. Cryptic. But they indicate that Aston's bioweapon has an unpredictable element that involves mutation."

Elijah swore audibly, repeating the word *mutation* with obvious frustration. "Where have we heard that before? Haven't we got enough mad scientists mucking about with DNA? Sending their experiments out into the world?"

He was referring to Joseph Peluso, who'd been newly rechristened JP Castelli and newly recruited into Third Shift. The military had created an entire elite unit of genetically modified shifters—infusing human soldiers with supernatural DNA—and was purportedly keeping an eye on the operatives who left active duty. They hadn't done a very good job with Peluso. Which was in part why Third Shift was knee-deep in dead Russian gangsters now. Elijah was still infuriated by the whole thing—especially their new werewolf recruit, who got under his skin even more than Finn did.

"Lije, if I were you, Dr. Schoenlein is where I would go next," Jack told him. "We need to know exactly what this weapon does. And how to stop it. Bonus: It would get you the hell out of town while Aston's still wondering where his guy went. Stay out of sight an extra day or two if you need to."

Grace watched the tennis match go back into play. Elijah and Meghna Saunders volleying glares back and forth before they came to some sort of not-silent-for-long accord.

"I'll go along," Meghna said after a minute of this communication. "But my operation remains my own."

It was a sentiment Grace could appreciate. Her operations were always her own, too. And so were her people.

8

COMMAND EMPTIED OUT QUICKLY AFTER the impromptu briefing, but it felt sodding interminable to Elijah. Seconds stretching into minutes into hours until it was just him and Meghna and Jack left alone in the conference room. He watched them make uneasy introductions to each other, shake hands like they were meeting at some high-class Washington, DC, cocktail party. Maybe they *had* met at just such an occasion and cagily weren't saying so. It wouldn't be the first lie either of them had told.

"I've met your father several times," Jackson said, like he could read Lije's mind. Sense the suspicion and the prickling anger. And after all these years side by side and knee-deep in black ops, that wasn't too far from the truth. In a lot of ways, his best friend knew him almost better than he knew himself. "Gandiva Corp., right? Defense? He's always spoken very highly of you. Top of your class at Yale. Wharton MBA? First million before you were twenty-five?"

These were all things in the dossier they'd collected on her, but Elijah also knew Jack was telling the truth. He'd heard her accomplishments right from the source. Rajkumar "RK" Saxena, CEO of Gandiva Corp. Fallen out of favor with the current administration, overlooked in favor of more right-leaning contractors, but still a powerful force in political circles.

"What can I say? I'm a daddy's girl." Meghna smiled, but it didn't quite reach her beautiful brown eyes. "I wish I was as proud of his accomplishments, but I can't complain too much when his weapons paid for my first car, my education, my shopping habit. I've benefited from his blood money. Made my own."

Elijah didn't interrupt the awkward small talk so much as bull-doze his way in. "That's quite a turnaround from getting arrested for protesting in front of the Gandiva warehouses in 2007," he pointed out, recalling the shaky YouTube video of the rowdy gath-ering. It featured a striking eighteen-year-old Meghna with bright-pink dye in her hair and a "Here are your WMDs!" sign...enjoying her freedom of expression while American soldiers like Jack were in Iraq with him, fighting in the name of it. He was still sussing out what they were fighting for these days. All he knew was that they had to win. And they'd need her cooperation to do it. "Quite the little rebel, weren't you?"

Meghna turned from Jack to him, the curve of her mouth now matching the coolness in her eyes. "I was still a teenager. I grew up. I learned to be a pragmatist instead of an idealist."

Jackson responded before Elijah could, ever so helpful. "I hope you'll be pragmatic now. If we pool our resources, we will all get what we need."

"I don't need your resources." The diplomacy didn't change her tight posture, her impassive face. She crossed her arms, another barrier between them.

Just hours ago, Elijah had her pliant beneath him, felt her orgasm, watched her whole facade melt away as she gave in to plea-sure. He'd caught a glimpse of something true, something honest. But perhaps *this* was the real her and not the other way around. Cold, efficient, focused. He thought he was the honey trap...but she'd closed the trap around him.

He pushed down a growl at the discomfiting thought. Resisted the urge to rub the itch at the back of his neck. "Maybe *we* need *your* resources. Ever think of that?"

Meghna looked around the tech-heavy room, out to the floor beyond. Distinctly unimpressed. "If this is all you have…I can see why," she huffed with a wrinkle of her nose that she probably wouldn't want to know was damn adorable. "You need all the help you can get."

Jackson, the right arsehole, proceeded to laugh like it was the funniest thing he'd ever heard. With good reason. "Lije…why don't you give her the full tour while you two clean up?" he suggested with the smugness of somebody who had spare millions to spend on secret bunkers and horse ranches and the like. "Joaquin and I will get the rest of the mission specs in order in the meantime."

Elijah wasted no time in taking the suggestion, guiding Meghna out with a firm hand on her elbow. She, shockingly, allowed herself to be guided. Her pulse was calm. Her heartbeat even. But he could smell her disquiet. Taste it. She was still furious with him. With all of this. She wouldn't give up a single bit of why. He could almost respect that…but he couldn't let it stand. They had to know who she was working for and to what end. Sooner rather than later.

He took her back to the lifts. Scanned in for a trip to the Locker. It was below the garage. Under the river. But there was no likelihood of it ever being flooded. Not unless the mighty Hudson could get through multiple layers of concrete and reinforced steel.

"Ready for a road trip?" he asked once the doors closed in front of them.

Meghna moved perpendicular to him, leaning against the lift's far wall, giving her a clear view of both him and the entire car. Her voice was as remote and reserved as her posture. "Do I have a choice?"

Was she having him on or what? "Yeah. You made it already,"

Elijah said. "We're not *forcing* you to stay here. You opted to throw your lot in with us for your own reasons."

She didn't appreciate the reminder. "And I'm already regretting it. I've made too many questionable decisions lately. Like fucking you to neutralize you. That really worked out well."

Elijah tried not to take it too personally—after all, his mission profile hadn't been all that different. Fuck her to get a line on Aston. But the idea that she had other ways to "neutralize" marks sent a chill down his spine and prickles across his skin. "So you could've killed me instead?"

"I could've. I didn't. Because that would've been even *more* questionable. Too many witnesses," she said with the ease of someone all too familiar with the process. "No easy way to dispose of your body—you're the only one who has a cleanup crew on speed dial. We don't work that way. So you got to live. You got to come. I'd say that's a win-win."

We don't work that way. Elijah heard it. The "we." But he reacted to all the other words, so she didn't realize she'd let something about her own people slip. "I'm not sure I like hearing about my potential disposal. How do I know you're not going to knife me in the back at the first opportunity?"

"Because the first opportunity passed me by. So did the second, the third, the fourth…" Something flickered in Meghna's eyes then. Not so cool. Not so remote after all. "We kill because we *have* to, not because we *want* to. Isn't that how we justify it? How we separate ourselves from humans like Mirko and his friends? How the military frames it? 'Us or them'? You're not a threat to me, Elijah. Unless you make yourself one."

He had no desire to threaten this woman. No, it wasn't even in the Top Ten of things he'd like to do to her. And that brought up a question he really didn't want to ask. Even thinking about it made his stomach lurch. *Meghna on her knees. His come slicking her lips.* "What about sex?" he wondered. "Is that something you're forced to do as well? A 'have to' and not a 'want to'? All for the sake of your mission?"

"No." She looked oddly discomfited by his concern. And a little angry too. Her fists clenched as the lift stopped on the proper level. "Sex work is part of my work," she said. "I accepted that when I took it on. I do what's necessary…but only what, and *who*, I'm willing to do. That's what you're really asking, aren't you? Whether I *had* to with you? Whether I faked it?"

Christ. He hadn't considered *that* at all. Not until this moment. Because her coming on his cock had felt pretty fucking real to him. But how much did he really know about her? How much could he trust? Maybe he needed to be less worried about whoever she was working for forcing her into people's beds and more worried about the people who landed beneath her? "Meghna…"

"I enjoyed every minute of it. But don't worry; it won't happen again." She stepped out before him into the Locker. Like she owned the place. Elijah had the distinct feeling that, before this was all over, she would. She'd conquer the world. And him along with it.

———————

"I enjoyed every minute of it. But don't worry; it won't happen again." The words echoed in her mind, bounced off the tile walls of the shower stall, taunting her with the sound of her own false confidence. She'd stopped Elijah Richter's tour before it began with one simple request: "Where can I get cleaned up? Does this Locker have a locker room?"

Now, water sluiced over her, urging her to linger under the hot spray. But she had no time to indulge. She just efficiently and ruthlessly scrubbed every trace of him from her skin. Every little bit of the past day and a half. The role she'd played. The hours she'd wasted neutralizing someone who didn't need to be neutralized. And the ridiculous assertion that she wouldn't fuck him again…

which basically ensured that she would. That, too, was something she let the drain take away from her.

The clothes she'd left outside the bathroom door were probably already being whisked away for disposal. No, knowing these black-ops types, they would probably go over her things with a black light hoping to find traces of Mirko's DNA. And then they'd code some sort of tracker to it and send a SWAT team to his next known location. Blowing it—and everything she'd been working toward—sky-high.

Get ahold of yourself, Meghna. And she did. Literally. Washing the last of the generic but serviceable shampoo out of her hair, scraping her scalp with her fingertips. She still had a job to do. It was just a different job. She would make the necessary adjustments. Go along and find this doctor. Ultimately, she would still end up where she needed to be—at the cross-section of whatever all these disparate and degenerate people were up to. Something so dangerous that it could shake what was left of the known world. A place where agents before her had gone…and had yet to return from.

Ayesha, a Bangladeshi jinn from Sylhet, had been incommunicado for more than a year. She'd been a Vidrohi operative for centuries—no amateur. And if she wasn't dead, then it was likely her talisman had been taken from her and she'd been forced to do someone's bidding. Meghna barely knew the woman, had a mental snapshot of a stunning beauty with dark-brown skin and curly hair who'd been at the training grounds in the mountains once or twice. Her last known whereabouts? A party plane with Mirko and his associates. Meghna had managed to meet some, not *all*, of those associates. Like Sasha. And Tavi Estrada, who seldom spoke to her but always did so with courtesy the human men lacked. But she hadn't uncovered who else was on that fateful flight…or where it had gone. Now, thanks to Third Shift's interference, that information might be lost to her forever. Or closer to her fingertips than before. It all depended on what she did with this so-called partnership. On what she did with Elijah Richter now.

Meghna finished up in the shower, toweling herself dry quickly and dressing in the dark jeans and shirt she'd picked out from Third Shift's collection. These operatives were the opposite of apsaras, who always dressed to impress and to seduce. No sequins and stilettos or saris to be found. Most of their "costumes" were practical. Their facility was minimalistic, all dark fixtures, darker walls, black tile, and reinforced doors. Built for function, to hide bloodstains and secrets. It wasn't teeming with people. She'd passed no one in her journey from the main gear room, where weapons of all kinds were secured in glass cabinets with bio scanner locks, to the showers. She would likely pass no one on the return trip.

And the top bosses of Third Shift didn't seem to care about her being left to her own devices. Presumably because they had surveillance on every inch of the space. If she so much as left an ass print on the bathroom counter, they would know. Luckily, Meghna hadn't been that indecorous, that carefree, in a very long time. Turning sixteen had changed everything for her. No more fun. No more friends—at least no real ones outside the network. Everyone was a tool to be used. Everything around her a weapon. Even her marital "foible" in her midtwenties had been mostly a ruse, engineered to get her close to one of Chase's producers in order to take the slimy serial rapist out of circulation. She'd lived in lies for so long, sometimes she forgot what the truth was.

That wasn't so different, really, from growing up wealthy in a white-adjacent upper-class Indian household. Daddy and their circle had raised her to believe she was better than 99 percent of the world. Then she'd been trained by apsaras, by her *mother*, to embody it. Because lives depended on her excellence, on her perfection, on her privilege.

Lives still did. She couldn't forget that. So she couldn't play cat-and-mouse games with Elijah. Whatever they'd started in that closet had to stay there. And even if she did give him access to her body again, she could never, *ever* give him access to her heart. The tiny, shriveled thing that sat in her chest. Meghna wasn't even certain it still existed, save for the fact that she was walking around, alive. She'd cared for her husband as much as she was able—still cared for him. Chase was a sweet, uncomplicated, accommodating man. As down-to-earth as his popularity was sky-high. His top priorities were good roles, good drugs, and good times. He'd never suspected her of wearing two faces, of having ulterior motives, and they'd remained in contact after the divorce. But love? No, she'd never loved him.

"You have mommy issues." Her assistant makes this announcement with clinical detachment. As if her years of experience in PR has given her the ability to diagnose such things on the spot.

"How would you know? You've never even met my mommy." She glares at Em over the rim of her martini glass.

"I send flowers to your father every Father's Day and pick out his Christmas presents. In all the years I've worked for you, you've never asked me to send anything to your mother."

Because she doesn't need anything from me. Meghna almost says it aloud. She just barely bites it back, drowning the words in crisp top-shelf gin. "Maybe she's dead. Ever considered that? Thank you for opening that deep and devastating wound, Em. You're fired."

Em doesn't even blink. It's the fourth time this week she's been fired in conversation. "She's not dead. As you well know. So yes, mommy issues."

"Why is this relevant?" The tablet Meghna set aside on the kitchen island has pitches from a fashion magazine. She graced their cover three years ago, and now she's been bumped down to single-page features that have questions like "Favorite travel must-have?"

"The Himalayan campaign for Vogue India. *You've turned it down twice. They're going to stop calling."*

Technically not the Himalayas. Too risky, even for a Vogue *location shoot. It's a multipage travel romp through parts of northern Bengal. Siliguri. Kurseong. Darjeeling. Still too close to home—so to speak. "I told you: I spent enough time up there when I was younger. I don't have any desire to go back."*

Em's shrewd gaze is penetrating even through the thick lenses of her black-rimmed glasses. "She still lives in some fancy resort there, doesn't she? Some yoga retreat?"

"Shut up, Em." Meghna scowls, sloshing the last of the gin out of the cocktail shaker. "Did I mention you're fired?"

Because her assistant is a shark who knows not to take no for an answer, she keeps pushing. "They're going to ask Priyanka Chopra."

"Let them." Meghna shrugs. No matter the feelings, both professional and personal, she has about Priyanka Chopra, she's not going to begrudge a gal a job. "I'm sure she'll be happy to do it."

Em's sigh is the kind of sound that speaks volumes. "Do you care about your career at all?"

If Meghna were the kind of nightmare boss that people write exposés about, this is where she would yell. But she saves the nightmares for those who deserve it. For the men who die in her bed. "I pay you to care about my career. But let this one go, Em," she asks quietly. "Please."

Finally, finally, the older woman relents. She shakes her head, jabbing sharply at her own tablet. "It won't kill you to let your walls down a little, you know," she murmurs as she likely sends Vogue India *an email they're going to hate.*

The rest of Meghna's martini almost goes down the wrong tube. She chokes. Sputters. "That's where you're wrong," she wheezes out. "It absolutely will."

Feelings were a weakness, a vulnerability too easily exploited. Meghna had learned early that there was little value in sentiment. Fathers ignored you. Mothers abandoned you. Then, when you were old enough to be useful, they miraculously remembered you existed. The General. *Ha.* Otherwise known as Purva Saxena, thousand-year-old apsara, ex-wife of a defense contractor, and absentee mother of a daughter who'd only become useful fifteen years after conception. She'd married RK to procreate, to propagate her species, and left for the "yoga retreat" when Meghna was all of three months old. Meghna had grown a hard shell even before her training…and during those grueling years, she'd reinforced it with steel and platinum. *The General. Not Mom. Never Mom.* She checked the integrity of that shell in the mirror as she applied eyeliner and lip gloss. As she dug into the bottom of her purse for one of her burner phones.

She had this week's Vidrohi check-in number memorized. Next week's too. Just a fraction of the information filed away in the brain few people realized she had. What *was* it with her ability to survive without vital organs? Perhaps her next check-in needed to be with a supernatural doctor.

Unlike the smartphone Joaquin had given back to her in the conference room, the simple pay-as-you-go burner didn't have foreign languages programmed into its keyboard. It pained her to use English letters instead of Urdu or Devanagari script—it was hardly discreet—but beggars couldn't be choosers. She couldn't trust that Joaquin hadn't bugged her primary device or cloned the secure messaging apps. Part of her job was to adapt, to do whatever needed to be done with whatever resources she had at her disposal. Or *for* disposal. So she thumbed out a quick, vague message in "Hinglish" indicating her plan had changed but she was still on course.

And then she repeated a variation of that message to herself. *You're still on course, Meghna. Don't get distracted. Don't let anyone get in your way.*

9

ELIJAH WAS ONLY AFRAID OF a handful of things in the world. Top of the list? Disappointing his mum. She'd cried when he cut his locs before enlisting. Full-on sobs, like he'd severed a limb. *"Aw, Mum, don't be daft,"* he'd told her, wrapping her in his arms, towering over her by more than a full head. *"It'll grow back, yeah? It always grows back."*

"Damn fool," she'd called him in return. *"You're caging your lion. And for who? For the army?"* She'd shoved at his chest, not lacking in strength just because she lacked in size, slipping into Patwah and her fur as she scolded him for turning his back on his heritage, on his self-preservation to fight in the white man's war.

"You moved here," he'd reminded her. She was part of the Windrush generation, which British MPs and the PM were still pretending to care about even now, years after the fucking Windrush scandal and sodding Brexit had proved the contrary. Raised in Clarendon on the southern coast of Jamaica, Mum had settled in Tottenham with his grandparents as a teenager. Then she'd ended up with his father in Hackney. Had four kids—four cubs at that. "You married Dad. I'm as English as I am Jamaican. As human as I am lion."

"You don't have to tell me, Teacha." Mum had sucked her elongated teeth, wielding his nickname with the gentle mocking he deserved, stroking his face with her half-shifted paw. "But you'll always be Black to them."

Elijah had never forgotten that lesson. Not at training. Not in the desert. Not even when he was having a pint with Jack at the Scottish pub on Forty-Sixth and Ninth. He remembered it now as he pulled the lion to the surface. Not the shift, the change, but the power behind it. Coursing through his veins, his pores. His beard growth thickened. The stubble on his scalp spiraled out into hair and then locs. That was a neat trick he'd developed—the locs. And taught his sisters, who were still finessing how to incorporate braids so they didn't have to spend seven hours in a salon chair while their stylist stopped to eat fish fry or watch West African soaps.

It was a rush, like the best possible high, as his locs expanded down to his shoulders. His human mane. His beast uncaged. Elijah reeled in the spirit before he could sprout back hair and fur between his toes—a lesson learned decades ago when he'd first experimented with shifting only parts of his appearance—and gave himself a good once-over in the mirror. He didn't look much like the hired muscle who'd worked Aston's VIP room. But his mum was right: he would always be a Black man.

That was still dangerous in America. In the world in general. *More* dangerous now that there were checkpoints at state lines and the country's northern and southern borders. He and Meghna would get stopped on the way to the lab, asked for their papers, asked why they were crossing out of New York. That was just a fact of life in the six years after the 2016 election—what the leftist blogs and resistance podcasts called the Darkest Day. Nine out of ten people stopped at borders were people of color. If those people were lucky, they got through because their papers were up to snuff. Or they were let off with a hefty fine. Unlucky…? Well, that was what the detainment camps were for. Housing more and more of the unseen and the unheard all the time. Refugees, asylum seekers, citizens, humans and supernaturals alike.

Elijah riffled through his personal lockbox for IDs that matched his new look. He was sliding them into his wallet when Meghna walked back into the room, smelling of the standard soap and shea butter lotion they stocked in the Locker's shower facilities, braiding her still-damp hair. If she was surprised by the length of his hair, she gave no indication. The woman was entirely too good at keeping her thoughts contained. *Her* personal lockbox was internal. "Getting your papers in order? We should be fine at the checkpoints," she said as she wrapped an elastic around the end of her thick plait. "My father's security clearance extends to me."

She'd picked out skinny jeans and a black sweater from the wardrobe closet. She had practical trainers on her feet instead of stiletto heels. Her makeup was subtle—he wasn't stupid enough to think it was nonexistent. Still, she looked more fresh-faced and innocent than the glam goddess who'd been on her knees in that closet or the stunning sexpot who'd taken him in bed. The naiveté—or maybe arrogance—of her assumption only underscored the image. "That might be enough if you had your moviestar ex or your criminal on your arm, love. But we can't take any chances traveling together," he reminded her. "Everything's got to hold up to scrutiny."

"Point taken." She grimaced, surprising him with her immediate acknowledgment. And then with the return of the flighty flirt from the party. The one who batted her eyelashes and played the men around her. "I should know better than to be so careless," she said lightly. "Two days into our acquaintance, and I'm already slipping."

"*Acquaintance*? Is that what we're calling it?" He snorted, slipping his wallet into the inner pocket of his jacket and then moving to the weapons cabinets. He didn't like how easily she shifted gears, going seamlessly from badass to bimbo and back again. It was uncomfortable…and purposefully so. She meant to keep him off-balance. So he'd best keep his feet planted firmly on the ground. "D'you need anything? We don't like loaning out firearms, but we've loads of blades and other little toys."

She was already moving to the wall with the KA-BARs. There were switchblades, Swiss Army knives, and daggers, too. Throwing stars. Hatpins. Even a few forks and spoons. Everything and anything a stabby girl's heart could desire. "Pretty," she murmured appreciatively. "And deadly. I can relate."

"Thought you might." Elijah unlocked the cabinet for her so she could do a proper bit of shopping. She scooped up a nice little dagger and two hatpins, as well as a pouch of stars. He didn't bother sifting through the merchandise himself. He had his weapons on him at all times, and they'd always served him well.

So why did he feel like he wasn't nearly armed enough against her? This gorgeous, dangerous supernatural who hadn't even revealed the full extent of her powers yet. *We*, she'd said in the lift, claiming kinship. Separating humans as *them*. And her explanation of apsaras… That had told him next to nothing. A cursory internet search had offered up the same information. Maybe she could destroy him with a single thought. Maybe she was a magic caster like Jack. Maybe she didn't need powers at all to wreck him. Maybe all she had to do was smile and crook her finger.

Elijah hated feeling vulnerable. He hated feeling vulnerable to *her* even more. But he was just going to have to get used to it…and find a way to turn it into an advantage.

Finn was uncharacteristically silent as they gathered up anything they'd need from their cubes and headed for the elevators. Once the doors were closed behind them and he'd scanned in for his living quarters, he finally spoke. "He turned me, you know. Octavio Estrada. Made me what I am."

She hadn't known that, actually, but it didn't surprise her. Finn's reaction in Command had been so raw, so unlike his usual light-hearted and annoying antics. "Do you know where to find him?"

"I always know where to find him. It's a bloody nuisance." Finn's hand hovered over his chest. The left side. "It's like a pulse. Like that old movie *Highlander*. I just *feel* him."

"The Whoosh," Grace supplied. When he paused his brooding to look at her with his trademark brow lift, she shrugged. "I watched the TV show in syndication. We didn't get fancy cable until I was a sophomore in high school. Ba wanted us to focus on our studies, not rot our brains."

Mama had wanted that, too. Had *demanded* it. Between both of their parents' views on hard work and good grades, Grace and her siblings had no option but to excel. But they'd been allowed to watch TV as long as they finished their homework right after dinner each night. And while *Highlander* with her brother Ernie had been fun…it was *ER* and *Chicago Hope* that had changed the course of her life. Those hours were when Dr. Grace Maria Leung, Dr. Freeze, was conceived.

It was nothing compared to how a vampire was made, though. Through bites and blood loss and blood gain. Death and rebirth. She'd studied all the ways the human body could break down so she could—as a surgeon—circumvent them. Or so she'd thought until she'd met supernaturals like Finn and Elijah. She was a master in the OR, nearly unparalleled, but no amount of skill and study could explain a man shifting into a lion. Or why ingesting blood could keep someone alive and youthful for more than a century.

"Do you hate him for it?" she wondered. "Is there…and I hate *myself* for this pun…bad blood between you?"

Finn's delighted cackle made the terrible joke completely worth it. He lost some of the brooding and the pallor and gained a twinkle in his bright-blue eyes. "Didn't know you had it in you, love," he said. And his smile remained even as they stepped out into the subbasement that comprised his home. It sat just above the Locker…and well below the dangers of the sun, which wouldn't kill him but didn't make him feel particularly perky either.

She'd been over a dozen times in the past few years. One memorable time in the past month. *Cool hands skating across her skin… hot mouth against the back of her neck…a warm whisper directed at someone else, urging them to "Come and join the fun."* She was grateful that he was occupied with her questions and didn't notice said memories heating her cheeks. They hadn't talked about that night in the weeks since. They hadn't really *needed* to. Because they fell into step beside each other in the hallways. Reached for each other's hands in times of crisis. Still argued and pretended it wasn't flirting. Though where Finn was concerned, nearly everything counted as flirting.

They'd gone on much like they always had. Just…*more* somehow. And that strange new intimacy was apparent in how Finn finally addressed her concerns about him and Estrada. "I'm… conflicted, I reckon," he admitted, tossing his duster over the back of the red leather sectional and then turning back to her. "I don't hate what my life has become. Only the circumstances that led to it." There was none of the lightness he employed amid the others. None of the truths wrapped in equal parts leering and lies. His brilliant-blue eyes were subdued, full of contemplative depth only she and a select few others knew him capable of. "I would've liked to have had more of a choice. An 'informed decision,' you might say. I trusted Tavi Estrada, and he used that. He used it to mold me into what he wanted me to be. A vampire. An agent. He could've just used the truth."

Grace echoed his weary laughter with a gentle one of her own as she playfully shoved at his shoulder. "Finn Conlan advocating for the truth. Who would've guessed?"

He drew her in for a hug, still so somber and serious. "You know I've never once lied to you, Grace of my heart," he murmured against her temple. He smelled like nighttime and whiskey and the smoke he swore he couldn't shift into. "I might tailor things for others. But never for *you*. You see all of me as I am. You have from the start. So did he. The difference is, you would never hurt me."

Why did her chest ache all of a sudden? With something deep and profound that defied diagnosis? "Not on purpose," she assured fiercely, glad he couldn't see the emotion she blinked away as she ducked her head.

"Precisely. And that's why you're here with me, and Tav is… probably at Hector's." Finn's brows furrowed in contemplation as he broke their embrace and stepped back.

"Hector's on 54th? So close?" It was a popular family-owned Cuban restaurant and music venue within walking distance. Twenty minutes, ten or fifteen at a good clip. How utterly bizarre to realize that one of their potential assets was so easily found. Practically under their noses this entire time.

He nodded. "The café used to be on Columbus Avenue. Upper West Side. It had just opened the year we met. Run by the one-and-only Hector himself. Tavi swore that Hector's rice and beans tasted just like his bisabuela's. He could only eat just a little bit, so it was my prevampiric job to finish the plates. A delicioso task, if I do say so myself."

Grace winced at his atrocious Spanish accent, but she gave him an A for effort. It was still better than most of his attempts at Cantonese. What was more worrisome, though, was Estrada's adherence to habit after all this time. "And you think he still goes there? Isn't that a risk, given his line of work?"

"I daresay he doesn't give a damn." Finn snorted. "We all have the things we can't give up. The things that we make excuses for. For Tavi, it's Hector's. If he's in the city on a Saturday night, that's where he'll be. Sitting in with the band. Playing guitar and singing

PRETTY LITTLE LION   83

old Cuban songs. Drinking too much rum. We saw Celia Cruz there, you know. Tito Puente too. It was grand. A different time. Can't say I blame him for wanting to revisit it."

But it didn't fit the image they'd constructed of the cold and cunning vampire who had no allegiances, no loyalty to anyone except himself. Grace didn't like that. An anomaly meant a complication. It often made the life-or-death difference during surgery. "What about you? You've never wanted to revisit that time? Never had the urge to drop by and see if he's there?"

"No. I've never had the need. Why dwell on the past?" Finn pressed a smacking kiss to the bump of her high ponytail, as if to signal a change of topic, a change of tone. Maybe he didn't even realize he'd just told a flagrant lie. More to himself than to her. "What do we think? Dress to impress? Show up with my new love on my arm, shove it in his face that I've traded up?"

Grace almost opened her mouth to ask if he was really that petty. Except she already knew the answer. Yes. Finn was definitely that petty. "If you think I'm going to hang off your arm and bat my eyelashes at you, you've got another thing coming," she warned instead, following him down the apartment's marble-tiled hallway and toward his bedroom suite.

"If I wanted that, I'd ask Nathaniel," Finn pitched over his shoulder.

It was her turn to cackle with delight. Mostly at the mental picture of one of New York City's most eligible bachelors batting his eyelashes. Not that Nate had been picking up their calls. The official excuse was that he and his law partner, Dustin Taylor, were too busy setting up their own firm after being forced out of Dickenson, Gould, and Smythe. Unofficially, she knew Nate was running scared. He'd experienced the full gamut of Third Shift adventures in a very short time. The adrenaline rush. The crash. The affirmation of life after it was all over. He'd slipped out of Finn's bed without so much as a note.

"Why does everyone leave me?" That vulnerable murmur, imbued with so much hurt, when Finian turned and found the empty space where their lover should have been… It clicked into place for Grace now. Why Finn nurtured his promiscuous reputation. Why he let people walk away without chasing them. Because it was easier than trusting them to stay. And Tavi Estrada had left him, too.

She had no plans to do the same. As infuriating as he was, Finian Conlan was her partner, her closest friend. One of the few people outside her family who she trusted completely. They were ride or die. Maybe ride *and* die, because there were no guarantees in black ops. Grace would always have his back. And as she only admitted to herself in her most private of moments, he would always have her heart.

10

THE TWO-HOUR DRIVE TO HARTFORD County, Connecticut, was surprisingly painless—once they got past the checkpoint at the state line. Elijah had magnanimously held on to his "I told you so" when the border guard pored over their identification, scanning and rescanning and making a few calls before letting them through the barriers. Perhaps he'd remembered that she was carrying several sharp objects on her person. As they left the New York city limits behind, heading toward fields and farmland, trees on either side of them, Meghna could almost pretend that they were weekenders heading out on holiday. Except for the weight of the blades against her skin and how warm the steering wheel felt under her icy palms.

The car was one of Third Shift's. A nondescript mid-luxury sedan with plates registered to an innocuous person who didn't really exist. The heat was on low, accounting for the November chill outside but also factoring in that lion shifters like Elijah ran naturally hot. But Meghna was cold for different reasons. Cold deep inside, below the surface, and she couldn't quite figure out why. Elijah was a perfectly acceptable travel companion. Unlike many men, he had no problem with her driving, had let her pick the music, and didn't argue with the Third Shift-issue GPS as it offered periodic directions in Joaquin's smooth voice. He seemed perfectly content to just sprawl in the pushed-back and reclined passenger seat, one massive arm propped against the window, and catch up on the rest neither of them had gotten the night before. All while Meghna's body and mind were at war.

She'd veered off course before. The feeling of imbalance wasn't new. She'd felt similar vertigo during her protest phase as a teenager—largely brought on by meeting her absent mother for the very first time and developing a strong urge to tell both parents to fuck off. And there were the weeks of partying with Chase that proved a cover could sometimes be *too* deep. But she'd always returned to her duty in the end. Learning how to use her powers of influence, how to incapacitate a man with the right notes of music or the right dose of poison. Traveling to Milan and Paris and Tokyo to shill makeup and underwear while taking down corporate slime. Funny how no one ever noticed the major companies losing CEOs or key board members in every country stamped on her passport. That wasn't something she did much of anymore. The Divisive States of America had made it much harder to travel in the past five years, and she couldn't risk being barred from reentering. Still, she'd always stayed focused. She'd known what the goal was. A million tiny rebellions that would add up to one overall victory for the Vidrohi and for people who deserved a better world.

This was different. Unsettling. Elijah Richter had only deceived her for a handful of hours, thanks to the fingerprint scanning apps on her encoded devices, but those were three hours too many. And she'd let Nichols catch them in flagrante. *Reckless.* Allowed Elijah to kill him. *Dangerous.* Thrown in with Third Shift without more than a cursory protest. *Lazy.* A woman who worked efficiently and alone, now making rookie mistakes left and right and turning to a cis male-helmed agency for help. Yes, her palms were icy. Her innards were frozen. And her head was clearly filled with bricks.

"We dug up everything we could find on you." Elijah's voice didn't interrupt or intrude on her interior monologue so much as slip across it like a sheet of silk. "Didn't get even a whisper of what you really are. And I employ one of the best hackers on the sodding planet." He was looking at her, not out the window, and his expression was equal parts contemplation and admiration. "Joaquin found *nothing* suspicious."

There were reasons for that. "Because almost everything hackable is legitimate—all apologies to Joaquin's skills. I'm sure they're thorough, but so am I." She shrugged. "I've worked hard to maintain my image. As far as anyone is concerned, I'm a party girl with too much time on her hands and too much money in the bank."

Elijah tilted his head, studying her with the same heated, speculative gaze that had intrigued her in the VIP suite. Here, it wasn't intriguing so much as discomfiting. He saw too much. More than she should let him see. "Never let anyone in, eh? Not even your fancy friends?"

Meghna couldn't hold back a snort of laughter. "My fancy friends aren't that fancy or that friendly." She kept everyone in her social circle at arm's length, and with good reason. "The less they know about the real me, the better."

He made a *hmm* noise that told her he wasn't done with his light interrogation. "What about your parents? Do they know what you do?"

Fuck, that wasn't a question she wanted to answer. She tried not to clench her jaw, knowing that he was studying her every move, down to her subtlest micro expression. She kept her hands light on the steering wheel despite the urge to grip tightly. "Your extensive research didn't give you any insights?"

He shifted in the seat, honestly too brawny to sit in it comfortably. But probably also wary of telling her exactly what he knew about her background. "RK and Purva Saxena. Married for all of a year in 1986. Divorced by the time you were six months old," he rattled off after a moment. "No custody arrangement. Your mother went back to India before you even took your first steps."

"Sikkim," she elaborated, though she wasn't quite sure why. Probably because adding to his dry recitation of facts was something to do besides curse the General's name. "So far north, it barely resembles what you'd think of as India. She runs a yoga retreat and wellness center for rich people who'd rather align their chakras than climb Kangchenjunga." That was the official line anyway. It kept tourists and other hapless humans away from the private compound and training camp, from the one place in the world that had any centralization of Vidrohi resources.

"Highly unlikely that you'd trust her with the particulars, then. Makes your father an even less likely candidate, as he'd be overprotective." Elijah tapped a rhythm on his kneecap with two fingers. Two powerful, talented fingers that she knew could draw music from her throat. "So you play the poor little rich girl whose mum left and whose dad overindulged her. But that's not the real you. It's all an elaborate ruse. A cover."

Oh, he *wished*. "That's where you're wrong, Elijah. That *is* the real me. My mother abandoning me, my father filling my life with *things*…all of that helped make me into what I am." Meghna had no illusions. She wasn't some comic-book superhero with a public life and a secret crime-fighting identity. Batman making the dregs of Gotham City society pay after losing his parents. "I used money and privilege and my supernatural heritage to get what I want. You can give it pretty explanations, nicer names, but at the end of the day, there's nothing deep or profound here. I kill people. And I'm good at it."

Elijah laughed, not one bit disturbed by the pronouncement. As if she'd admitted to being good at knitting or part of a bowling league. "How has no one noticed that men around you keep dying?" he wondered.

"I'm very discreet," she said dryly. But then she sat up a little straighter, acknowledging the seriousness at the root of the question. The logistics. "There are actually a few Reddit forums devoted to conspiracy theories about my career. My background. How I just 'came out of nowhere' and got famous. And I've been targeted in hate campaigns more than once for being seen with someone questionable—like Mirko. Luckily, I have a *very* good publicist."

That made Elijah laugh again. "No publicist is *that* good."

Em comes close, she almost said. "That's why this is the last high-profile asshole I plan to be linked with," she murmured instead. "I need to course-correct before it does irreparable damage to my reputation as everybody's favorite South Asian celebutante."

"Or irreparable damage to your life?" Elijah suggested.

"Oh, that ship has sailed," she snorted. Sailed, wrecked, and sunk to the bottom of the Mariana Trench.

"And this is what you call getting what you want?" he scoffed. "I don't think so. I haven't known you long, but I know enough. You wouldn't risk everything on a lark. You're not the kind of person who kills indiscriminately. Aston would already be dead were that the case. Half his mates too. I think what you want is bigger than that." Damn the man for his insight. Just like she'd feared, he saw more in her than she wanted to show. "I think you want a better world, a safer world."

And you. I want you. But she wasn't going to admit to that aloud. Not when she was still warring with it herself. He could have her past, her mommy issues, her body, and her partnership on this op, but he couldn't have that admission. Not yet. "I think you should spend less time analyzing me and more time studying mission specs," she said tartly.

"All right, Meg. Q and A's over. For now." He made a show of retrieving his tablet, paging through docs.

She finished the drive staring out the windshield at the road ahead, letting Rage Against the Machine drown out everything but what she needed to keep. Her priorities. Aston. Ayesha. The big picture. Not the memory of Elijah's mouth on hers or how welcome she'd felt in his arms. *Sex is a tool*, she reminded herself yet again. It held no significance to her. *He* held no significance to her. Only success did.

Meghna was frightened, or agitated. The subtle hint of fear rolled off her skin like a perfume she'd sampled at the shops. Elijah could relate. Because he was pretty fucking terrified himself—of just how quickly a simple operation had gone to shit. *Again.* He was supposed to be a *leader*, and he'd cocked things up. *Literally*, as Meghna had wasted no time in pointing out. The clinic was their chance to right the course. But there were no guarantees. Blueprints of the facility didn't mean they knew what they'd discover there. There were too many unknown variables. For instance, going in after dark didn't ensure the place would be empty. And he had no idea what Meghna was like in the field. Hell, he still wasn't entirely sure he should trust her…but the proof of that pudding would become clear soon enough. He just had to stay alert. Stay in it. Stay the course.

Elijah made a show of stretching lazily, "waking up" from the nap he hadn't really been taking after putting away his tablet. His fingertips brushed the car's ceiling as he observed, "We're almost there, eh?"

"Just a few more miles," Meghna affirmed, automatically reaching to turn down her music. "We have everything we need?"

"Even a pair of pants for when I inevitably shift." He tapped the small utility pouch he'd be handing off to her once inside the clinic. "And some tech from Joaquin."

Her gaze flicked from the road to him and back again. "American pants or British pants?" she asked abruptly. Almost as if she couldn't help herself. That surprising wit that had made him laugh from the first was another fascinating aspect of the multifaceted mystery that was Meghna Saxena-Saunders.

"I think you know where I stand on British pants." He regretted it as soon as he said it, because he was immediately back in the tight confines of that closet as her nimble fingers undid his fly, found his bare prick, and stroked. He had to choke down the memory—*again*—and shift about in the already-uncomfortable passenger seat. Now was not the time for a hard-on. He was a grown man, for fuck's sake. He had better control than this. *Usually.*

Thankfully, Meghna let the sexually charged moment slide, despite being the one who'd initiated it. She just nodded as if his answer was completely aboveboard. "My primary concern is the surveillance. I can't afford to be caught on film. I'm too high-profile. No amount of fake Instagram posts will explain away my face on security footage."

Funny how that hadn't been a concern when she hooked up with him right outside Aston's party. Maybe because all the night's footage from that floor of the hotel had been erased before anyone could review it. Standard operating procedure for the criminal elite. He was just glad the Spider had pulled what it could from the cameras and the active devices. It was likely still active now, during whatever revels were still happening. He had no idea when it stopped crawling or spinning or what have you. "That's where Joaquin's toys come in," he noted aloud. "You got a taste of what the Spider can do back at HQ. This time we'll test out the Honeybee."

Meghna sputtered with laughter, her eyebrows rising into her hairline. "You realize that sounds like a high-end vibrator?"

He snorted. *Welcome to Third Shift, home of perpetual perverts.* "'Quin names all of their creations after bugs. Bit of an amateur entomologist along with a professional hacker. This one's meant to sticky up the security feed and put it on a loop. It should give us about an hour of free movement."

She was still chuckling as she flipped her turn signal and guided the car to an exit ramp. "How did you even meet Joaquin? Your team seems to be quite an eclectic bunch."

Understatement. Elijah grinned. He was proud of the people he and Jack had recruited over the years. All with a wide variety of strengths and skills and backgrounds. "I used to teach a few courses at a military school just north of the city. They were one of my students." Which was why Joaquin got away with calling him "Teacha" like only his mates and his family did. Because in their case, it was literal.

"What?" Meghna looked like she was trying to put together two ill-fitting pieces of a puzzle. The casually dressed charmer who'd demanded her phone plus military training. There was a reason it didn't quite add up.

"'Quin's parents sent them to the academy," he explained, hoping his tone conveyed the proper amount of disgust. *"They sent a queer enby kid to a school full of attractive boys to straighten out,"* Joaquin had marveled on more than one occasion. *"Buena suerte, Mami y Papi."*

"Proper Dominican Catholics. Father was career army. 'Our child can't be queer. Can't be nonbinary.' You know the homophobic song and dance. And one day I'm faffing about in the grading software, and a D for Joaquin Serrano goes right to an A. While I'm logged in." He'd spent a few minutes wondering if he'd hit the wrong key or the software was glitching before he'd realized what had happened. "So I look up their room number. Track them down in the dormitories. I find this kid with a hardware setup worthy of the CIA, wearing a T-shirt that says 'Binary is for code, not gender' and a shit-eating grin."

Meghna laughed again. The sound was like bells or a cascade of water. Something he wanted to use as a mobile ringtone for the rest of his life. "What did you do? Turn them in to the administration?"

"Fuck no." He'd hated the academy's headmaster. Colossal

bastard who thrived on control and didn't give one shit about providing actual education. "I told Joaquin that if they finished out the term with an honest B average, I'd give 'em a job when they graduated. They did. And I did. They've been with Third Shift ever since," he said with no small amount of pride.

He didn't want to play favorites, but he played favorites. Joaquin and Grace were his most cherished operatives. One the kid he might've had if he'd married young, the other the adopted sister who reminded him of the three blood sisters who constantly took the piss out of him in their WhatsApp chat. Amani, Ciara, and Naomi would *love* Gracie. A pea in their pod, that one. She and 'Quin, along with Jack, made him miss all the family he'd left behind in England just a little bit less.

"You really love them, don't you?" There was wonder in Meghna's voice. As if she couldn't quite wrap her mind around the concept. "Not just Joaquin but your whole team."

Elijah responded with a noncommittal grunt. Not because he was afraid to admit how much he cared but because he wasn't sure he should admit that to *her*, this woman he still didn't entirely know. Except for how she tasted and how she sounded when she came.

She yet again accepted the moment for what it was and moved on, changing the topic. "We're just about there." Was this how she navigated all the parties on Aston's arm? Dancing lightly from thing to thing before anyone could get too suspicious or too uncomfortable? "Two miles till we reach the turnoff where we stash the car. It should be dark soon."

The sky was already graying, providing them cover. Not just for their mission but for whatever this messy thing was between them. Elijah pulled out his tablet and swiped through the blueprints and headshots, memorizing every detail anew. He'd let Meghna do the same before he wiped it clean. Pity they couldn't do the same with their slate.

11

THEY'D WAITED UNTIL FULL DARK, leaving the car miles away, camouflaged in the brush, and infiltrating the clinic through the HVAC ducts. An easy fit for Meghna, but not so much for Elijah, who was broad-shouldered and thick of thigh, built like a football player. Somehow, though, he'd squeezed through. Shifting various body parts with that eerie ease he'd displayed when dispatching Sasha Nichols. As expected, they'd emerged in the basement. Now they were working their way up the four-story facility. So far, so good. Which meant something was bound to go wrong.

From the blueprints she'd looked over on Elijah's mission tablet, it looked like the research laboratories were on the ground floor. No doubt it was easier to contain and dispose of any shady experiments if you didn't have to haul them down four flights or wait for an elevator. The hallway was quiet, cold, sterile, with a handful of reinforced doors set at about ten feet apart. Elijah stayed behind her, moving cautiously—"guarding your six," he'd said—mindful of cameras even though they'd activated Joaquin's Honeybee. They had approximately fifty-four minutes before the surveillance would go back online. A lot could happen in fifty-four minutes.

Like the rattle of a lab door just ahead. And a far more menacing noise than that. The growl lifted the fine hairs along the back of Meghna's neck. An inhuman rumble that sounded like no animal call she'd ever heard. Even before the door flew open, practically banging against the wall, she knew danger was imminent. But she couldn't have guessed what that danger would be. A terror. What some might call an abomination. Neither wolf nor bear nor cloven-hoofed beast but some sort of chimera. The patchwork monster looked like something out of a David Cronenberg or Guillermo del Toro movie. Misshapen. Nightmarish. Horned and fanged and hairy. That was as much observation as she could make before the quasi Minotaur sprang. And before an enormous golden-furred, dark-maned lion leapt to meet it.

Elijah knocked the creature back, his fully formed paw bigger than Meghna's entire head. She'd seen all sorts of supernatural beings in her time. Not just bear shifters or werewolves. A chupacabra. A Jersey Devil. The yeti who lived up the mountain from her training camp. The mammalian science experiment Elijah was fighting was not naturally born but *made*. A killing machine in truth. One that knocked Elijah into the wall while letting loose a bloodcurdling howl. But the lion shifter only roared in return and shoved right back. Like a bumper knocking forcefully at a pinball.

As they locked in battle, she rolled to the side, pulling blades from her belt. She was no physical match for shape-shifters, but neither was she helpless. So when a human male emerged from the open lab behind Elijah and his opponent, she flipped and slid to meet him—and pinned him to the wall with ease. One arm across his throat. A blade at his belly, encouraging him to stay still.

Dr. Gary Schoenlein himself. The ID photos in his dossier had been accurate. He was a pink-faced man with sparse blond hair combed over his balding pate. He didn't look like an evil genius. In her experience, evil geniuses seldom did.

"Schoenlein," she murmured in greeting, her register one he

could hear amid the shifters' snarls. "What the fuck have you done?"

The scientist didn't seem inclined to answer. His watery green eyes darted back and forth behind the fogged frames of his glasses. He huffed out a sour breath that hit her nose like a slap. So she repeated the question with a bit of power behind it. The apsara's seductive thrall.

Schoenlein fell under the spell quickly. His eyes glazed over dreamily and his thin lips curved into an eager smile before opening to do her bidding. "Everything," he told her, pride infusing the word. "I've created a miracle." She dragged him, unresisting, inside the laboratory—away from the fight, which Elijah seemed to have well in hand. Or paw, as it were. It was immediately clear where the "miracle" had come from. A huge cage that spanned the back half of the space. A quick assessment revealed a bed but also a pile of hay and other foliage on the floor. And some sort of toilet set up in one corner. It was a terrible existence for any living being. A jail cell in the name of science and progress and war.

"Tell me," she urged Schoenlein as she held him immobile and enchanted. "Tell me all about your miracle. Was that berserker out there just a human once? I want to know how brilliant you are."

"The American military thought *they*'d perfected shape-shifter engineering. Petty fools. They're just one country out of many. Russia. China. So many superpowers are cashing in," crowed the researcher. Their very own Dr. Frankenstein. "Not only have I copied their formula, but I've enhanced it. Our soldiers will be unstoppable."

"Our?" she repeated.

"Aston would like to take sole credit." Schoenlein sniffed derisively. "He's nothing more than a thug in a shiny suit. *I* did the work. *I* produced results."

You *are an officious asshole*, Meghna thought but didn't say aloud. "Like the shifter in the hallway?" she prompted instead. "Is that one of your soldiers?"

He struggled a little in her grip, craning his neck to peer over her shoulder at the yawning doorway, where signs of obvious struggle could still be heard...and then went suddenly silent. A few seconds later, a blood-streaked and stark-naked Elijah appeared on the threshold. He was dragging his dead opponent by the scruff. "*Was* that one of your soldiers?" he corrected gruffly as he tossed the body into the room. Dr. Schoenlein yelped, his face reddening and limbs flailing.

"Answer him." Meghna concentrated, expanding her power, calming him, reeling him back in. She kept one arm across his neck as she freed the pouch on her utility belt and tossed it to Elijah so he could get dressed. "Answer us both."

"No," Schoenlein said, gaze focusing on her face once more. "An early prototype. A failure. Our success rate with the previous iterations of the serum was dismal. But you can't make an omelet without breaking a few eggs."

These were living, breathing beings—not eggs, for fuck's sake. Meghna swallowed her disgust and continued pressing the man. Fairly crooning her next question. "So you've finally perfected this serum?"

Schoenlein beamed. "Indeed. It meets Mr. Aston's specifications and is ready for mass production. I've spoken with his liaison, and they should be receiving a case of the first successful batch any day now."

Meghna's blood chilled at the implication. And she made the logic leaps easily. The upcoming auction. It wasn't for a weapon. It was for *this*. Mirko was going to sell a serum that could transform humans into shape-shifters to the highest bidder. "Are you sure you sent him all of it?" she asked. "Do you have any more here or at another facility?"

"No!" The scrawny human shook his head, a hint of fear

overlaying the glaze of his eyes. "No further batches will be produced here. It's not secure enough. I've even forwarded the formula to Mr. Aston's people."

She couldn't waste time savoring the irony of Schoenlein acknowledging his clinic wasn't secure. "You won't remember this conversation," she said softly. "You won't know we were ever here."

The man sank back, dazzled and dizzied, and slid down along the wall until he hit the floor with a thump. Elijah's reaction fell more on the side of alarmed and appalled. And a thin pair of track pants did nothing to mitigate his bare brawn. He looked glorious and dangerous, skin glistening with sweat and blood. "Did you do that to me? 'Charm' me?" he spat the word like a curse. "Give me a little of the ol' Jedi mind trick?"

Meghna's skin burned with the implication. "The trick was *you*," she reminded. "Sent to my bed for *your* mission."

He flinched. They were already experts at causing each other pain. Just as they'd expertly given each other pleasure. "Meg…"

"Look at me." She cut him off with a slash of her hand, gesturing across her body. "Do you think I have to *force* anyone to want this?" It wasn't an egotistical assertion. Just a fact. He hid his teeth and claws. Her weapon was always on display. Her shining hair, her flawless skin, the breasts and hips she'd inherited from that woman she could barely call a mother. Her face. Her annoyingly beautiful face. It had given her powers long before she was told she had supernatural ones.

"No. You're sodding gorgeous." A growl tore from Elijah's throat. His eyes flashed gold…like they had two nights ago in the hotel's hall closet. When he'd stolen her breath and her sense. No one had forced her to want him either. But he'd never believe that. Not now that he knew her currency was lies. He exhaled loudly, grabbing the back of his head and a handful of locs in frustration. "I still want you now. What sort of fool does that make me?"

The same kind of fool she was. Forgetting she had a job to do.

Wasting time on personal dramas instead of immediately pursuing the lead they'd been given. Standing here craving his hands on her, remembering the soft rasp of his beard stubble between her thighs. Many men in her life had told her she was gorgeous. Elijah had made her *feel* it.

Meghna choked down vulnerability she couldn't afford. She let the charm Elijah had insulted spread across her skin like armor. Not enough to affect him. Just enough to protect her. "I won't apologize for what I am," she said. "Apsaras were the original influencers. We changed the course of history. Started and stopped wars. Put kings on the throne. Created dynasties."

His brows quirked with amusement. "Is that what you're about then? Creating dynasties?"

"No," she assured. "I'm more into ending them. But right now, we need to go after Aston. Stop the auction and whatever else he has planned. Your evaluation of my supernatural abilities and interrogation of my career goals can wait. Nothing else matters except the job."

"The job. Right. Can't let anything get in the way of the bottom line." He huffed, his frustration obvious. At her? At himself? The circumstances? She couldn't let herself wonder. Couldn't care. Not right now.

"What would you tell your operatives?" she asked coolly. "To pursue a potential asset or to address their personal shit on company time? What *should* the priority be?"

To her surprise, Elijah found the questions hilarious instead of needling. "You've *met* my operatives, love. They multitask." He roared with laughter, every bit the lion, as he called back to their bedsport of that morning. When she'd been equal parts distracted and disarmed as he moved inside her.

And the gorgeous sound of his amusement reverberated through her body, echoed to her bones, setting every nerve alight. Reminding her why *she'd* multitasked, nearly compromising everything for this man. Why she wanted to do it again and again.

He'd spent months studying her—stalking her, really—and two glorious days in her bed. And he had no idea who she really was. That much was crystal clear as they left Dr. Schoenlein napping in his locked laboratory and quickly checked the rest of the doors. All locked with keypad access. All easily unlocked, thanks to a digital unscrambler. Only the last was occupied, by a man who didn't even have the chance to reach for the gun he wore at his hip.

Elijah watched Meghna clean the blood from her stiletto blade in quick, efficient movements before tossing the scrap of cloth away. As easily as she'd discarded the men in her path. Charming one. Stabbing the other. The slender blade went back into the knot of her hair, and it was only then that she acknowledged he'd been staring.

"Draupadi, the cursed queen of the *Mahabharata*, swore she wouldn't tie up her hair again until she could wash it in the blood of her enemies," she said, dusting her palms off on her black pants. "I think about that every time I use my pins. Not particularly sanitary as vows go, don't you think?"

"Does being sanitary really matter in times of war? When all you want is revenge?" He shrugged. "She made her promise and spoke it into being, didn't she? There's power in blood. And there's power in hair. My mum taught me that—that cutting it lets the weakness in. Like Samson in the Bible."

Meghna cocked her head, a hint of a smile playing at her lips. Lips that had shilled high-end makeup on billboards all around New York City for those lucky sods who could still afford it. "Are you afraid I'm your Delilah, Elijah?"

Oh, and wasn't *that* a loaded question. Her eyes were liquid and dark with knowing. He could imagine her tying him to a chair like in the song. Cutting his locs and drawing "hallelujah" from his lips. "Hallelujah" and "fuck you" and "damn me to hell." He could imagine it…but that didn't mean he believed it or feared it would come true. "I'm afraid of a lot of things, love, but not that," he assured before pivoting and peering down the corridor.

Elijah's eyes sharpened with his natural night vision. The clinic was still dark. Eerily silent. It wouldn't remain so for long. He had no doubt they'd tripped an alarm somewhere or landed on some security footage despite Joaquin's looper. Or maybe Schoenlein had woken up from his impromptu nap and set loose more hounds. They couldn't afford to linger. Elijah didn't *want* to linger, knowing what they did now. That it wasn't a bioweapon Aston's cabal was shopping but a bio *serum*. One of the fruits of which lay rapidly cooling at Meghna's feet. Distracted, Elijah hadn't caught his scent. But now that he was dead, the man's supernatural status was obvious. Feathers had begun to sprout from the back of his head. Now they were tinged with red from the fatal wound in his eardrum. Meg had drawn far less blood than Lije's average kill. But she'd still drawn blood. Which meant they had to go. *Now.*

They wordlessly moved the dead shifter's body back inside the lab from which he'd come and conducted a quick sweep, turning up another huge cage but little else. Elijah swallowed bile and repressed a shudder. Americans liked to pretend they were only recently in the business of putting people in cages, but a look at history proved differently. Like the circuses and traveling shows that had hawked looks at kidnapped Africans and people with disabilities. Like chattel slavery, the effects of which still impacted America and the Caribbean today. People who were in any way different had always, always been deprived of dignity and freedom.

Elijah liked to think that Third Shift was changing the world little by little...but moments like this made him wonder if they'd made any difference at all. He exited the room without looking closely at the lab benches or searching any of the file cabinets—suddenly needing nothing more than to put distance between himself and the metal bars and the narrow cot within them. He moved forward, up the hallway, trusting that Meghna would follow. And she did, her footsteps light and sure. Almost as if she were a cat shifter, too. Maybe a cat burglar. His chest rumbled with a much-needed laugh that he didn't dare let escape. Not until *they'd* escaped at least. They still had three floors of the clinic to clear—and less than forty minutes in which to accomplish that—and then a hike to where they'd stashed the car.

Their mental countdown clocks ticked away as they took to the stairwells. He'd recovered his shoes, so the flights weren't as belabored as they could've been, but the aches and pains that had come from fighting the Minotaur-like hybrid didn't make it easy. By his estimation, he'd cracked at least two ribs, sprained his shoulder, and pulled a leg muscle that corresponded to his leonine form's hindquarters. Nothing that wouldn't heal swiftly, nothing to really complain about, but Lije wasn't getting any younger and pain was a reminder.

Most people didn't retire from black ops. They left it toes up. Elijah had no desire to cark it for his country, especially after surviving multiple deployments with coalition forces in the Gulf, but he knew it was a likelihood. Each and every mission could be his last. So he took care as he and Meghna worked their way from the fourth floor down to the third and then the second. Senses on high alert. Listening, watching, *feeling* for anything that might be wrong. They encountered no more engineered shifters. No other researchers working late on the weekend. It was quiet. Almost *too* quiet.

The reason for that became obvious when they retraced their steps to their entry point in the basement and came face-to-face with another of Schoenlein's prototypes. The shifter had scales like a snake or a lizard, the slitted pupils of a reptile as well, but bat-like wings sprouted from his shoulder blades. He didn't run toward them so much as flutter and slither. "Intruders!" he hissed like a cartoon villain. "How dare you hurt the doctor?"

"He's not hurt," Meghna murmured, and Elijah recognized

the lulling quality of her voice from the magic she'd worked on Schoenlein. "He's just asleep. As you should be. It's so late. Aren't you tired?"

The power wasn't just her voice, though. She wasn't simply singing a siren's song. As he repositioned himself to better cover her, Elijah noticed a subtle glow emanating from her skin. Likely invisible to human eyes or shifters with other things to worry about. There was something suddenly otherworldly about her. She looked more beautiful, ethereal, like one of the elves from Lord of the Rings. He could very well believe she'd come from the heavens. And if their new friend wasn't amenable to enchantment, she would swiftly consign him to hell.

Fortunately for all of them, the reptilian shifter was nodding along to Meghna's observations. As if, yes, it was indeed incredibly late and he'd far rather be tucked away in bed instead of confronting them in front of the air ducts. She began humming. A haunting melody Lije couldn't identify. All he knew was that it sent uncomfortable shivers down his spine. And either it or Meghna's powers further transfixed their opponent. He swayed on his feet for a few seconds before passing out.

Meghna waited a few seconds and then cautiously prodded him with one boot. When he didn't move, she turned to Elijah. "It was a snake-charming song from a Bollywood movie." Her preternatural apsara glow dimmed as she shrugged ruefully. "I've always wanted to know if it would work."

Elijah didn't know whether to laugh or shake her for taking the risk. "And did it?" he asked instead of either of those options.

She hopped over the prone supe and scrambled up the wall to the ventilation duct, as nimble as a teenage gymnast. And then she glanced back and gave Elijah a wink. "You'll just have to live with the mystery, Mr. Richter."

12

THE MISCHIEF, THE MIRTH THAT had fueled her as she climbed out the ventilation duct and dropped onto the frost-edged ground below didn't last long. Meghna was a mess of contradictory emotions by the time she and Elijah got to the car and buckled in. Magic still sang in her bones from charming the hybrid shifter. Energy coursed through her veins. What could she do with that? How could she channel it?

They were barely a few miles from the clinic when she told Elijah to pull over. Not remotely out of the woods. Still in danger of pursuit, because the doctor and the bat-snake had surely woken up by now. But the need she vocalized was guttural, thick, and demanding. The need in her soul was even worse. Something all-consuming. Hungry. Something that demanded to be sated. And it wasn't more than two seconds after Elijah steered the car onto the shoulder that she was unbuckling her seat belt and diving across the console that divided the bucket seats. Climbing into his lap. Burying her hands in the thick locs he'd grown for this trip. She could still smell the lion on him. She would always smell the lion on him. Maybe he could taste the temptress in her. The apsara who was a tool of passion.

Meghna seldom gave in to her own lusts. Her entire existence was built around manipulating the lusts of others. But here, on this dark stretch of road, with this dark stretch of man, she let herself plunge straight into selfish debauchery. Claiming his mouth, burying the fear and tension and impulse that had guided her every move inside the research facility. Erasing everything but the here and the now. The scent of him. The feel of him. The adrenaline racing through her veins.

"Meg," he gasped under her siege. "Meg, love…" But he didn't stop her. Didn't remove her from her awkward perch on his knees, pressed between his chest and the steering wheel. No, he just toggled the lever that pushed the seat back, giving them some room. Then he slid his hand up along her spine until he was cradling her neck in one large palm—and he kissed her back. Hard and furious and just as desperate for distraction, for completion, as she was.

Somehow they got their pants and her underthings sorted. With the expert contortions of two people who'd managed tight spaces before. A condom materialized like a conjurer's trick, and then there was nothing stopping them but misgivings they were too far gone to voice. It wasn't like the hotel room. The choreographed seduction where her mind was on a thousand other things as her body did the work. She was *here*. Present. All in. Just as he was all inside her. Surging up into her, meeting her when she slammed down and took him, grinding her clit against the outer ridge of his cock.

It was quick. Frantic. Chasing orgasm like they'd been chased in the hallway. Two predators. No prey. Equally matched. Elijah nipped at her throat. She sank her nails into his shoulders. They panted nonsense words and sounds against each other's ears, and Meghna told herself that the sex was just as meaningless. They were blowing off steam. Two people who'd already done this before, so what was the shame in doing it again? In enjoying it for what it was? Bodies grinding. Lips exploring. Fingers diving down between them as Elijah worked her clit with his thumb and she stroked his sac. Sweat and salt and skin and precious seconds until she was falling apart on top of him. Meghna took the pleasure and the escape. Grabbed it with both hands. Not because she needed information. Not because she needed to know Elijah's game. But because she needed to come, and he was the one bringing her there.

When it was done, she moved back to the passenger seat. Tugged on what was left of her clothes. The air between them was hot and musky, smelling strongly of what they'd just done. She rolled down the window to let the cool air take it away. To let common sense return. And it did with two words. "The Naga," she said. The snake hybrid back at the clinic. It hadn't sat right with her. Seeing him there. A tool of a mad scientist and her so-called boyfriend's schemes. "They're incredibly rare supernaturals. Schoenlein shouldn't have had access to that DNA. How did he get it? How did he create that shifter I put to sleep?"

If Elijah was disturbed by her change of subject, change of attitude, he didn't let on. He simply continued cleaning himself up, disposed of the condom out his own window, and fumbled around for the hand sanitizer that almost everyone kept in their vicinity these days. "Good question," he said as he rubbed alcohol solution on his palms and then offered her the bottle. "Lucky for you, we have someone at 3S who can provide answers."

"You have a Naga on staff?" She couldn't hide her skepticism. She could hide how her skin still burned from his touch and her body was still wet and wanting, but she couldn't hide that. The sharp sting of alcohol filled her nostrils as she ruthlessly scrubbed her hands with the sanitizer. Like that could clean away some impulsive car sex.

"No, I have a Naga's cousin on staff," Elijah said as he put the car in drive, getting them back on the road. "Is there anything else you'd like to know about my personnel? Fancy a look at the HR files?"

"You have a *human resources department*?" she sputtered before she could think better of it. What was it about Elijah Richter that made her forget all of her poise, all of her media training? Meghna just replied, reacted, without taking a moment to consider her goals. Just like she'd pounced, kissed, fucked, without giving a damn.

"Well, *supe* and human," he corrected, amusement brightening his eyes. "Off-site. Everything's done digitally and securely. Safer that way."

Third Shift's HR office could've been on the moon for all she cared. But unlike with Mirko and his goons, she didn't feel the need to tune out. To play the bubbleheaded arm candy while she mentally ran mission scenarios and went through her social calendar. Meghna liked listening to Elijah. She liked the timbre of his voice, the notes of his accent—at times so very rough-and-tumble London and at times the lilt of the Caribbean. And she liked what he had to say about Third Shift.

The Vidrohi...they were a collective, not an organization. Camaraderie—any kind of attachment—was incredibly difficult just by virtue of how they operated. It was hard to bond with people through encrypted messages, masked voice calls, and anonymous intel drops. And that was the point. Because if you bonded, then you felt things. And if you felt things, it made it that much harder to fuck a stranger or kill one for the cause. Meghna knew that not all sex workers viewed the job as such. Many had spouses, children, perfectly healthy emotional lives. But being an apsara was something different. Something that went beyond a business transaction between two or more consenting adults. It was seduction in the name of deceit and espionage. With or without her powers engaged, it was a *lie*. And thanks to how her kind had evolved with their allegiance to the Vidrohi, sometimes that lie was fatal.

Evolved. Wait. The chill that grabbed hold of her then had nothing to do with the late fall air rushing through the open window. What if *that* was why Ayesha had really gone missing? Had these mad scientists figured out a way to extract DNA from *all* types of supernatural beings? "What else do they have, Elijah? What if they have material from ifrits and other jinn? What if they've made an apsara? If they start moving beyond shifters, imagine the damage they could do."

"No worries, Meghna. We're going to stop them before they get that far." Her non sequitur didn't faze him. Maybe nothing about her fazed him. "Besides which, they had a starting point with the military when it came to shifters. They don't have a biological template for anyone else. Unless they've got some other sorts of supes in their mix."

"Just Tavi Estrada," she said immediately. But one didn't need to *engineer* more vampires. It was much simpler. All done with a bite and a transfer of blood. "I think he's been holding out on them, though. He's not the type to create more vampires willy-nilly."

Elijah nodded, digesting that bit of insight. "One point in his favor then, but I'd reckon Finn doesn't want to give him any at all."

That brought them to the parallel op taking place tonight. Just a simple meeting between Estrada and Third Shift's representatives. In Meghna's experience, the things you expected to be easy seldom were. "He keeps to himself," she said of the quiet vampire. Dark-haired, dark-eyed, the sort of handsome frequently described as "rugged." The few times she'd seen him unguarded, he'd smiled like a saint and danced like a sinner. "I don't really know what he's doing with Mirko, why he chose *him* of all people to align with. It's never made all that much sense. But I suppose the same could be said of me. We all have our reasons."

"And you're still not going to tell me yours, are you?" Elijah huffed and shook his head, glancing at the rearview. There were no headlights reflected. If anyone had caught on to them breaking into Schoenlein's facility, they weren't on their tail yet.

"No. I'm not." Meghna felt no shame in admitting it. As far as she was concerned, Elijah knew everything about her that he needed to know. Where to kiss her. How to touch her. And when to turn his attention back to the road and steer them toward New York. He put dancehall on the radio…and turned the volume up loud enough to drown out the tiny internal voice itching to tell him "pull over" again.

Hector's was a two-story establishment in a converted brownstone just across the street from one of the many Broadway theaters. A blue awning and a bright vertical marquee emblazoned with a palm tree advertised the restaurant's name with just enough panache to draw in tourists for a prix-fixe meal and some drinks. Grace felt simultaneously overdressed and underdressed once she and Finian went inside.

"I miss the old place," he murmured in her ear, giving her arm a reassuring squeeze. "But this is just about what it looked like there."

The front dining room was elegant, with white tablecloths and dark wooden furniture. Ceiling fans spun slowly and wooden window shades were set into the wall, bringing to mind a grand old house in Havana. Half the tables were populated by people in jeans and T-shirts with their *Playbills* sticking out of their shopping bags. Heads swiveled to take note of her in her slinky dress and heels and Finian in his tight-fitting black leather and eyeliner. They probably looked like minor celebrities or like trouble—which would be more accurate. *Welcome to your authentic New York experience*, she wanted to tell the gawkers ruefully. Instead, she focused on the bright side. The city's economy was slowly bouncing back after the past few years. Tourists had returned in droves, and the theaters were all open again. Border checks and increased drone surveillance be damned, the Big Apple was still the best city in the world. Grace didn't want to live anywhere else.

"So where do we start?" she asked Finn as he swept her past the maître d' stand with nothing more than a dazzling smile at the confused young woman standing there with menus.

He nodded toward a set of stairs at the back of the dining room. "The Santiago Lounge."

When they reached the top of the steps, it was the moment Grace felt like she hadn't dressed up *enough*. An intimate club-like venue with rum cocktails, small plates, and live music, the lounge was filled with men in sharp linen suits and women in bright dresses. There was a quintet of musicians on the stage to their right, a bar buzzing with thirsty patrons to their left. Grace didn't need Finn's tight posture and clenched jaw to tell her that Tavi Estrada was indeed in the house.

He was the incongruous fifth in the band. The only man not wearing a guayabera or a jaunty fedora and, at least visibly, decades younger than the silver-haired horn players and the men on the drums. He sat on the edge of the stage, a guitar in his lap, finishing up a haunting Spanish ballad. His smooth, low voice entwined with the trumpet like a lover, and if half the audience didn't care...it didn't matter to him. He was the music and the music was him. Nothing else existed. She recognized that feeling. It was her in the OR.

"I'll get us a drink," Finn bit off sharply, not as spellbound by Estrada's performance. "Don't break any hearts—or any legs—while I'm gone."

By the time he returned with a blackberry mojito for her and a rum punch for himself, she'd found them a shiny black high-top near the stage. Not that it was necessary to stay in the band's sight line. She had no doubt in her mind that Tavi had seen them enter, recognized Finian, and knew exactly where in the lounge they were. They didn't have to wait long. Sure enough, once he finished his heart-rending tribute to lost love and said his thank-yous to the band, the vampire immediately made his way to their table against the wall.

Finn clapped softly as he approached. A golf clap. There was nothing sincere about it. Petty was definitely the theme of the evening. "You still have them eating out of the palm of your hand, Tav," he said by way of greeting. "Makes it that much easier to take a bite of their necks, doesn't it?"

The other vampire didn't even blink at the dig. "Never thought I'd see you in the audience again, Finian," he said, like they were old friends instead of something far deeper and stranger, before turning to Grace. "And who is your beautiful companion?"

"It depends what you're going to do with that information," she murmured, taking a slow sip of her mojito, prolonging the moment...and slipping her free hand into her purse. She activated the Cricket that Joaquin had furnished her with before they left HQ. It was a privacy shield, emitting a high-frequency noise that would mask their conversation for eavesdroppers. "You have a reputation, Mr. Estrada. Not just for singing but for selling."

His polite demeanor slipped a notch, the agreeable smile of a musician greeting his fans wavering. With his enhanced vampiric senses, he likely heard the Cricket and knew what that meant. "So I take it this is business, not pleasure?" When their only answer was shared silence, he reached for Finn's rum punch and drank half in one gulp. That, more than the pettiness, more than the niceties, spoke of the history between the two.

"I take no pleasure in discussing your business," Finn assured him as Estrada thunked the glass back down on the table, sloshing rum and juice over the rim. "But it's come to our attention that you've been running with the wrong sort of a crowd."

Estrada gave a theatrical shudder. "God forbid!" he exclaimed. His polished voice was devoid of regional accent. Unlike Finn, who'd clung to his Irish brogue. "If you don't like my new friends, I don't know what I'll do with myself. I might cry."

The sarcasm dripped from his tongue like the distilled molasses he'd just downed, so Grace took the perfect opening to ask him, "Are they really your friends?"

"No." He snorted and helped himself to the rest of the punch.

It wasn't an answer that pleased Finn, who growled his frustration. "So *why*, Tav? Why are you working with these people?"

"Maybe I've changed." The shrug was elegant even if the man himself seemed more like a pirate than a gentleman. His dark hair curled around his face, a few streaks of silver the only markers of age. The scarf thrown carelessly across his neck was a brick red, almost brown, like dried blood. "Maybe I've sold my soul to the highest bidder. You were always worried about the state of my soul, weren't you? Here we are."

"That's bullshit, and you know it," Finn snapped. He leaned forward across the small table, his eyes blazing and his normally easy tone filled with fury. "I understand you being out for yourself...but traffickers? Racists? People who'd gladly see you dead for who you are and who you love? There's no way you've changed *that* much."

The smile Tavi Estrada flashed them didn't reach his eyes. They were flat, lifeless, like dirty copper coins. "*You* haven't changed at all. Still giving impassioned sermons." Maybe something in how she moved or breathed betrayed her, because his gaze flicked to Grace. "Did you know?" he asked. "Has he told you that he was a priest once?"

Oh. So many things fell into place with that one revelation. Like the tumblers on a safe, now unlocked. It didn't hurt...but she ached. Not for herself but for her friend, for her partner. A man of so many contradictions, so many vulnerabilities, all hidden behind the devil's own tongue and the most beautiful blue eyes she'd ever seen. Grace channeled Dr. Freeze, the Ice Queen, and marshaled her physical responses once more. There was no need to give Tavi more weapons against Finn. Not when he had decades of them in his arsenal already.

"Seminarian," Finn said softly, drawing his former lover's attention back to him. "Acolyte. But never a priest. I never finished. I never took holy orders. And why might that be? Care to hazard a guess, Grace of my heart?"

Oh, *here* was the pain for herself. Hearing his nickname for her like this. Not as an intimate joke between the two of them but as a gauntlet thrown for someone else. But she knew better than to flinch. This was not her fight. She was just collateral damage in a conflict that had begun decades before she was born. And more importantly, they had an asset to finesse. "Because that was when he turned you—both into a vampire and into the spy game," she said aloud.

"Aye," Finn confirmed. "And he fucked me too. But who are you fucking now, Tav? And for what purpose? What could be worth consorting with the likes of Mirko Aston?"

For a moment, Estrada's cool veneer slipped away, a sharp surge of emotion darkening his eyes and flushing his cheeks. Only a moment. Then it was gone and the mask returned. With the dead eyes of a shark circling its prey. "Do you really expect me to answer, Finian? To tell you everything? It's not so easy as that."

Grace had been caught between Finn and another man before. In a far more pleasurable clinch. That night suddenly felt like years ago now. Where she and Nate had fussed over Finn's still-healing wounds and put him to bed…and then joined him there. This was different. This wasn't about healing or affirming life. It was dark and painful and dredging up a past she had no part of. *That's why he needs you,* she reminded herself. *That's why you came. To remind him to stay in the light and in the now.* She stepped forward, angling her body so Finn was behind her. It was time to take control of this little reunion.

"Then what's the incentive you need?" she demanded. "Money? Information? For us to say 'please'? What's your price, Estrada? You say you sold your soul… What will it cost us?"

"Ay, *querida*." The vampire sighed with air he didn't need to breathe. And here was the Latinx accent he'd code-switched away before. Along with the honesty. "You can't afford me."

13

HE'D BEEN IN THE SAME city as Finian Conlan hundreds, thousands of times since they'd last been in each other's company. He'd felt the city blocks stretching between them. The years too. None of that compared to being mere inches apart. The boy, who'd never really been a boy and had long since become a man, was still one of the most beautiful creatures Tavi had ever laid eyes upon.

"We can't *afford* you? That's despicable, Tav. You were ambitious, sure. Selfish, certainly. But not *evil*." The righteous indignation in his voice was almost funny. The disappointed look in his eyes was anything but. It was the same devastation that he'd displayed as a young seminarian when Tavi flashed his teeth outside St. Patrick's Cathedral after weeks of flirting across the pews and chaste coffees after mass. A show of hope dashed, of a candle pinched out. *"So you're a monster, then. And you've come for my immortal soul?" "I have no interest in your soul. Just everything else."* It had probably been their last honest moment before he'd overridden the young man's suspicions and taken him, turned him...ultimately abandoned him.

"Why Mirko Aston?" Finn demanded in a fierce whisper. And the second part of the question, the silent part, was like a scream. *Why Mirko Aston and not me?*

The memories, the bite of conscience, itched like a mosquito's conquest of his skin. Tiny raised dots of what could've been. Maybe that was why Tavi actually told him a tiny sliver of truth this time. "Because Aston knows where all the bodies are buried. And I need access to that cemetery."

"Because he has something on you?" The woman who'd wisely kept her name to herself—though Finn had ruined that by calling her the "Grace" of his heart—didn't hesitate to ask further questions. She was focused. Unyielding. Clearly protective of Finian. "Or because you have your own designs on the information he hoards?" She was striking too. Tall, brown-skinned, with the high cheekbones of a supermodel and eyes even darker than his own. And her voice was the kind of smooth, commanding tone that both inspired one to fall in line and to fall at her feet.

"If you were me, would you answer those questions?" he countered. "No matter what my alliances are, my reasons are my own."

"If I were you, I wouldn't be in this position to begin with," she shot back. "I don't truck with fascists, Estrada. Never have. Never will."

If Finian wasn't already besotted with her, he would be soon enough. He couldn't possibly resist. They were men of lies. Grace was a woman who radiated truth. The rarest gem in today's world. A lure to thieves like them. Tavi was almost envious. It had been entirely too long since he'd loved anyone. Longer still since he'd wanted to. He'd had other priorities. And yes, his own designs... yet to be carried out. It wouldn't do for Finian and his warrior woman to get in the way.

He had one mission and one mission only: getting to the island. Everything else was either in service of that or a roadblock.

"If you're here to appeal to my better nature, I'm sure you've realized that's a fool's errand. Nothing and no one can shake me from the path I'm on. Not even you, Finian. Or your friend here, with her passionate convictions." Tavi pushed away from the table, out of the sphere of whatever dampening bug they'd activated. "This was a waste of your time."

Finian glowered. All that tumultuous emotion radiating from every line of his body. He might pretend to be the suave, continental vampire, but he'd never quite learned to shield himself. As to Grace? She was cool, collected, a child of the night in spirit if not in body. "Was it?" she murmured, tilting her head. "I think we've learned quite a bit, even with your reluctance to share."

They'd thought to neutralize him with nostalgia, putting Finian before him. But it was *she* who posed the real threat. She saw right through him. Worse, her forthrightness made him want to expose who and what he really was—the person even *he* didn't recognize anymore. He'd known someone like her once. Someone who brought up these impulses in him. That couldn't stand. It was too much of a risk. He had to separate them. Divide and conquer. Sooner rather than later. Only then would he have a chance to control the situation...to control Finian Conlan.

Finian's asleep beside him. The light sleep of a human lover, not the death-like rest of the vampire. He wore himself out last night, despite the vigor of youth. Rum on his tongue and rum driving his hips. Tavi should feel regret. He doesn't. He simply climbs out of bed to the fire escape of the nondescript apartment he's rented. Lights up a cigarette and watches the moon hang over the Upper West Side. It only takes minutes for the steps above his head to tremble with a slight weight. Her. Of course. Always watching. Because this is their game. Going back decades now. Nearly half a century.

"Enjoying your honeymoon?" she wonders caustically.

"Fuck you," he says, inhaling nicotine that won't get him any higher than alcohol gets him drunk. He shouldn't look up. Shouldn't honor her with that acknowledgment. He still does.

"This is a departure for you, Octavio. Caring. Staying." It's not jealousy that sharpens the needles in her voice. In all the time he's known her, she's had many lovers—husbands and wives too—and never given

him any indication she'd like him to join the ranks. No, this is spite, pure and simple. And he's missed it. What does that say of him? "Does the poor man in that bed know what you really are?"

"Why are you so obsessed with what I am?" he counters. "Don't you have dragons to slay? Wrongs to right? Bottles to inhabit?"

"Fuck you," she echoes him, dark-brown eyes glittering just as brightly as the bejeweled brass ring she wears on her middle finger.

He should get back to Finian. To, yes, what feels like a honeymoon. A vacation. A break from the reality of his existence. Tavi stays outside. With the moon and the stars and her judgment. Until he's done with one smoke and then another. He doesn't ask her why she's in Manhattan. She doesn't wonder the same of him. They sit in mutual silence, in mutual contempt.

In mutual understanding.

Until the rising sun drives him back inside.

Tavi worried his lower lip with his front teeth. Dragged a hand through his hair. All affectations. Bits of theater he'd learned over the years to seem vulnerable or conflicted when he was neither of those things. He stepped back into the dampening field and dropped his voice to a weary whisper. "Okay," he said, as his shoulders slumped. "Okay, I'll play along. But not here. And not now."

He could *feel* the relief coursing through Finian's veins as if it were his own. Even now, after all these years, everything he'd done, the altar boy still believed in his inherent goodness. It would be sweet if it weren't so damn naive. How had he ever survived this long as a vampire? Grace, however, still had her guard up. *Smart.* And proving he'd assessed her correctly.

"If not now, then when?" she challenged, one hand on her partner's arm. Calming him. Grounding him. Reclaiming him.

"Monday," he said, flicking his gaze between them. Lingering deliberately—not that it was any sort of hardship—on Finian's brilliant-blue eyes. "We can meet Monday morning."

That would give him plenty of time to find something, any-thing, to break the Grace of Finn's heart.

———————

Elijah took a long, circuitous route back to the city. He turned a two-hour trip into a four-hour one, and it was close to 3:00 a.m. when they stopped just a few klicks outside one of the checkpoints between Connecticut and New York. He'd dragged it out as long as possible, but it still wouldn't do to have them logged as return-ing at such an odd hour. Just for the sake of plausible deniability. If they'd been made by the blokes back at the clinic, they'd been made. Nothing to do about it. But better safe than sorry, yeah? No one from HQ had checked in with red alerts. Sasha Nichols's disappearance and Meghna's coincidental flounce hadn't raised alarms yet. He wasn't naive enough to think that meant they were in the clear. So they caught a couple hours of shut-eye right there in the car.

He'd expected an argument from the glam girl in the passenger seat, but Meghna hadn't so much as blinked. She'd just asked for him to turn the heat on as a concession to her physiology and then turned toward the window and closed her eyes. Until promptly at 6:00 a.m. when she jolted awake just moments after him. "Any word?" she said instead of "good morning."

"Not yet." He turned, reaching into the back seat for his dopp kit. There was a mini bottle of mouthwash within it, and he took a hefty swig, swishing and spitting out the window, before passing it along to her. "Don't reckon that'll be the case for long, though. We made too much noise."

"*You* made noise. I was perfectly subtle," she said before she rolled down the window to do her own swish and spit.

A dozen filthy thoughts popped into Elijah's head. As if he were Finn or JP, who had no filter and no home training. He reined them all in and covered them with light sarcasm. "Well, pardon me, love.

Guess I should've just let that genetically engineered monstrosity tear you to shreds, eh?"

"It was *not* going to tear me to shreds," she said automatically. "I could've handled myself."

He had to admire her confidence, because he couldn't say he'd had the same thought when he went barreling at the beast full tilt. He was a lion. He went into every fight assuming it was kill or be killed. Anything less than that meant he was leaving himself, or somebody more vulnerable, unprotected. Only since starting Third Shift had he begun to let his guard drop a bit...because he knew he had a team watching his back.

"You're used to doing it all alone, aren't you? Handling yourself?" he observed, glancing at Meghna. "Well, that's not how we do things at 3S. We look out for one another. We *trust* one another."

"So you trust me?" Her brows rose with skepticism.

"Do you *want* me to trust you?" he countered. "I don't think that fits your agenda."

Maybe that was why it had all gone sideways at the clinic. Why they'd learned a little but still made a big mess. Because he and Meghna were on shaky ground with each other. They'd started with lies and they were still lying, still keeping parts of themselves on lockdown. Their narrow escape was the price.

As if he'd summoned it, the portable comm on the dash came to life. "ETA?" Joaquin's voice. Light and soft, but no less insistent for it.

"Forty-five minutes, I reckon? We're on I-95 in Greenwich. Just closing in on the Port Chester checkpoint. Why?"

"You might want to reroute, Teacha. Don't come to HQ."

Dread uncurled like a dragon in the pit of his stomach. Fuck. Fucking *shite*. "Explain," he bit off, gripping the steering wheel hard enough to break it.

His tech geek didn't mince words. "You've been made," Joaquin said apologetically. "I just pulled it off the party-suite feed. From

Aston's phone. They know about Connecticut. They caught a glimpse of Ms. Saunders on the surveillance video."

"So *I've* been made," Meghna corrected, her posture straight as a pin. "Guess covering my digital footprints was pointless, wasn't it?"

"Tweeting from Ibiza is never pointless," Joaquin assured her, even pronouncing the city's name with the traditional lisp. "Don't go home. Don't call anyone you love. Sit tight. Elijah will take care of you."

The vote of confidence should have been comforting. All it did was put Elijah further on edge. Because he'd done a bang-up job of taking care of her so far, yeah? "Thanks, kid," he said nonetheless. "I hope that's not you angling for a raise."

"Jefe, please." Joaquin scoffed. "I could hack into payroll and *give* myself a raise," they pointed out before signing off.

Ending on a light note did nothing to ease the ensuing tension in the car. It felt thicker and thicker with every mile. Getting through the New York State checkpoint had become the least of their worries. So it was ironic that they breezed through in mere minutes. With the guards scanning their IDs and waving them through with no questions whatsoever.

"That was too easy," Meghna said as they continued south on I-95 toward the Belt Parkway and Brooklyn. "I don't like it when things are too easy."

Like breaching Schoenlein's clinic had been. "Easy" was a warning that things were about to get difficult. So it came as no surprise whatsoever when the comm rattled again and Joaquin's voice piped up as clearly as if they were in the car, too. "Was Ms. Saunders attached to her places in Tribeca and WeHo?"

"Joaquin…" Meghna had a condo in West Hollywood and a loft in Tribeca. Expertly designed setups that had been showcased in a number of fancy magazine spreads. The dread dragon in Elijah's gut flapped its wings. "What's happened to her properties?"

"They're on fire," Joaquin said, tone all businesslike this time.

"Engines en route in both cities. No preliminary reports yet, but I think we can infer arson given our intel."

Yes. Yes, that *would* make sense, wouldn't it? Aston's people had acted quickly, recklessly, but emphatically. Their message was clear. They'd sent Meghna a *literal* burn notice. *Helluva way to break up with someone*, Elijah thought grimly.

"Goddammit!" Meghna followed up with curses in Hindi that he vaguely understood, thanks to his Punjabi mates back in Hackney. She thumped her head against her seat, fists clenching in her lap. "This wasn't supposed to happen. *None* of this was supposed to happen."

Because he'd come in and mucked up her solo operation. She didn't say it aloud, but the implication was clear. "I'm sorry," he said as soon as Joaquin went off-line. "We didn't mean for you to lose your homes—"

"Fuck my homes!" Meghna cut off his apology before it was even half out of his mouth. "In our business, we live every day prepared to lose our lives. I don't care if those assholes make a bonfire out of my CD collection and my throw pillows. What I care about is that we've completely lost control of this mission. That *I've* lost control of this mission."

It was uncomfortably close to what he'd been thinking before Joaquin's communications. "We'll get it back, Meghna. No matter what, I promise you we'll get it back. You've just got to trust me. You need to let us help."

Her beautiful dark eyes blazed at him, turning him to ash like her loft. "What if I can't? What then?"

Elijah didn't have an answer for her. He wasn't sure he ever would.

14

AT HALF PAST SIX ON Sunday morning, the VIP suite had long since emptied of everyone but Aston's closest associates. Sprawled on couches and chaises, clothing in disarray—if they wore anything at all. The man himself had commandeered the same banquette that Tavi had availed himself of a few nights ago, apparently seeing its tactical advantage and relative privacy compared to other parts of the circular suite.

Mirko raised bleary, red-rimmed eyes as Tavi approached. His silk shirt was unbuttoned halfway, his sports coat a sacrifice to the hedonistic gods. But he looked in better shape than Rossi from Chicago and the Hollywood hotshot, Keegan, both of whom had misplaced their pants. "Where is Sasha?" he demanded, pouring himself a restorative shot of high-end vodka.

"'Am I my brother's keeper?'" Tavi quoted, voice heavy with irony. He imagined his old seminarian friend chuckling…even more clearly after seeing Finian again last night. He could also picture quite vividly Nichols's reaction to him claiming brotherly ties. The purpling of the man's face. His ineffectual threats. It was beautiful, really. And fucking hilarious.

Mirko wasn't nearly so amused by his Old Testament reference.

He cursed in Slovak, kicking the nearest table and scattering white powder across it. Thousands of dollars' worth of cocaine had been circulating during the party. There was as much of it ground into the carpet as there was up men's noses. But this was of no consequence. No, Aston had bigger things to occupy his mind, higher costs. "He was in contact with the clinic. I'm awaiting news on the latest results. He knows time is of the essence."

If time were truly of the essence, Mirko Aston could just contact the clinic himself, couldn't he? He wanted to have total control and yet delegate to flunkies at the same time. But this wasn't something you pointed out to self-proclaimed supervillains. To ambitious arrogant men who wanted to take over the world—and the universe after it. Tavi shrugged again, making a show of retrieving his smartphone from the inside pocket of his jacket. "Sasha's last message to me was just before 10:00 a.m. yesterday." *Fuck u. i will catch the whore and then come 4 u.* Not anything worth repeating aloud. Nothing that inspired any sympathy for what fate might have befallen Mirko's number one bootlicker. Tavi hoped he'd tripped and fallen through a subway grate and been eaten alive by giant rats. "I can confer with Dr. Schoenlein at the clinic, if you like. Unlike Sasha, people tend to find me charming and easy to work with."

Aston grunted his assent, his gray eyes narrowing shrewdly. "Or else they'll find your teeth in their throat."

A quip about the mark of Cain rose and then died on the tip of Tavi's tongue. Such jokes were wasted on Mirko, who had very little interest in anything that didn't involve money, drugs, or murder. Or power. Oh, he so loved power. Because he'd been born without it. "Carajo, Aston," he swore lightly. "You know I don't kill them unless I *have* to. Body disposal isn't as easy as it used to be when I was young."

"Acid baths," Mirko said, trailing one fingertip through the coke or heroin on the table and then licking it. "We use acid baths. Or lye. It is good when there are too many to bury."

Being on earth for the turn of two centuries meant Tavi had spent all of that time mastering his emotions, his reactions. He didn't even flinch. Drug cartels had been using lye for corpse dissolution for decades. It was the *we* that disturbed him. And the *too many to bury*. There could be only one thing Aston was referencing, since he had no ongoing hits on his enemies in play. *Carajo.* Not so lightly this time. "The island?" he asked casually. "I can't imagine there is much free real estate for graves."

Just hours ago, tucked away at Hector's, he'd said something flowery and metaphorical about needing access to the cemetery. About Mirko knowing where the bodies were buried. Not letting himself think about how it might be literal. Of course, they would need to dispose of the failed trial subjects. They could not afford to leave witnesses, evidence alive. *Not even the innocents.* The implications brought bile and rum and blood to the back of Tavi's throat. But again, he had years of practice swallowing horror, choking it down.

Aston made another grunting noise of assent, momentarily distracted by his wake-up cocktail of drugs and alcohol. It would be his last indulgence until the next such party. He insisted on remaining clearheaded most of the time. Needed no anesthetizing to order so many deaths. "Our facilities take up most of the real estate," he boasted after downing another drink. "We have only made a little bit of space with our lye. The ones who were not viable. Those of our own who turned against us. You know how it is. Examples must be made. The bulk disposal will occur after the trials are complete and the product is ready to be administered."

If Tavi could have breathed a sigh of relief, he would have. The prisoners—the *women*—were all still alive. And he now knew more about the island than ever before. All because of Aston's cocaine-laced loose lips. He'd been waiting years. Biding his time. Gathering intel. Gaining access. He was closer than he'd ever been to his goal. Mirko, the consummate braggart, was careful in one thing and one thing only: the identity of the man who pulled his strings. He'd never once uttered a name. It had never appeared in a communication or a document. As if the island and the facility it housed were owned by a ghost. There were rumors. Suspicions. But never anything of substance. Nothing to connect one of the world's most famous billionaires to Aston's circle.

Roman Hollister. That was how he was known now. He'd changed his name countless times. Changed his face. But Tavi had always seen him for what he was. A true monster. Even among monsters. A killer of women, of children, of the old and the infirm. He followed no code. Kept to no laws. He just amassed money and power. He'd courted a century's worth of presidents from both parties. He'd swung the Senate to his whims. He *was* the Illuminati. And he was the darkness, too.

Tavi had been inching toward him for decades. Infecting his network at the roots, tracing it to the source. Now here was Aston slowly allowing him access to the entire poisonous garden. *Finally.* The small victory should have tasted sweet. But it was stale on his tongue. Like blood from a corpse. Because he couldn't shake Finian's questions from the night before. *"Why would you throw your lot in with people like this, Tav? You were ambitious, sure. Selfish, certainly. But not evil."* Or his lovely companion's fierceness on his behalf. *"Then what's the incentive you need? Money? Information? For us to say 'please'?"*

They were young. They still thought you could keep your honor while playing the game. They were wrong, weren't they? They *had* to be wrong. Or he'd spent two hundred years without a soul for no reason at all.

"Tell me more," he murmured as he dropped down to the banquette next to Mirko. "Tell me all about the trials."

But before Aston could begin, his phone vibrated. Rattling across the table like a snake. Mirko grabbed it, answering it with a sharp bark of "What?"

Tavi didn't have to strain to hear the voice on the other end of the line. His supernatural senses meant he could hear a whisper across the room if he chose to listen for it. "The lab!" cried the hapless lackey who probably wouldn't have a job for much longer. "It's been compromised! The doctor and one prototype are still out cold. The other two prototypes are meat. Headed for the incinerator."

"Who did this?" Mirko demanded. "Who *dared*?"

"The cameras captured only one person," the lackey sputtered. "The woman, sir. *Your* woman."

Meghna. Tavi's mental curses echoed the ones Aston spat aloud as he threw the cell phone across the room. This was an unwelcome development. And after last night's strange little reunion...? Not remotely a coincidence.

———————

Finn and Grace had fallen into bed the night before out of necessity more than desire. They'd climbed onto opposite sides of his king-size mattress in mutual silence after filing reports with HQ. Just before dawn. Going back to her one-bedroom in Astoria had made little sense, and using the guest room seemed silly given what they'd already done in this one. Besides, there was a gulf between them on the massive bed. Both emotional and physical. One that Grace wasn't sure she wanted to cross, even after she woke up around half past seven. What felt like five minutes after she'd shut her eyes.

She lay there, in the darkness, next to a man who didn't breathe. Whose chest didn't rise and fall. He literally slept like the dead. She knew from experience that he woke up with no significant change in movement or sound. It was eerie when you weren't used to it. When you weren't used to *him*. Grace was glad Finn hadn't initiated sex the moment they'd stumbled—half-exhausted—over the threshold. It would've felt too much like erasure...a desperation to replace the memories of Tavi Estrada with the reality of her. Enough had been erased at Hector's already.

Grace still felt invisible now, as the sun rose outside this underground haven. Maybe her hand was visible on the pillow next to her cheek? Maybe her legs had materialized beneath the covers? She was returning in pieces. And the vampire four feet away might as well have been thousands of miles across the desert.

"Gracie?" He turned to her then. Waking as soundlessly as she'd expected him to. A pale sylph against the black silk sheets. He swore he wasn't psychic, but it felt oddly like he'd picked up on her thoughts. "Thank you."

"For what?" She shifted to face him.

His eyes glowed just faintly. Like the blue flames of a gas burner on low. "For being you," he said hoarsely. "For being with me last night. It was…harder than I reckoned it would be."

Nearly everything came easy to Finn. He'd led a charmed life these past few years with Third Shift, work-related injuries notwithstanding. For him to admit difficulty was significant. Grace felt the punch of it to her solar plexus. Tavi Estrada had genuinely gotten under his skin. First at the briefing and then in person. More so than she'd even suspected. And now he was seeking reassurances. A tether. A port in the storm. Grace had always been that for him. This time, though…this time, she hesitated to let him drop anchor. "I'm not a replacement for him, Finn," she warned. "I will not be *used* because you miss him."

"I wouldn't want you to be." His words came out in a rush, almost cutting off her own. "Not you *or* Nathaniel. I'm not using you. You're nothing like him. You could never be, love. You have to believe that. What you give me…it's nothing Tavi Estrada was ever capable of."

Was that deliberate? The cynic that took up most of the space in her brain couldn't help but wonder. Had Finn connected with her, and then with Nate, because they were so different from Tavi? Because they'd never betray him in the same ways? Because there was no way either one of them could remind him of the one he'd lost? She didn't ask the questions aloud. They weren't productive, not when there was still intel to gather. She'd said all she really needed to say by stressing that she was no substitute for his first love. "Do you think he'll tell us anything useful tomorrow?" she asked instead.

Finn sat up, a mound of pillows pressed between his shoulders and the headboard. "I don't know," he admitted quietly. "I wish I could say 'aye.' But it's worth a shot, isn't it?"

Everything was worth a shot at Third Shift. It was how they rationalized so many of their missions. How she'd rationalized so many of her choices. And any further rationalizations were cut short by the sharp trill of her phone on the nearest nightstand. As well as Finn's on the far side. *Fuck.* That couldn't be good news. She scrambled for the device with one hand even as she shoved the bedcovers away with the other. Sure enough, the ten little words on her screen had her rolling out of bed and into action.

Arson. Saunders's residences. No casualties reported.
    Present at HQ ASAP.

Finn's dismount was slightly less graceful, for all that he was a creature of the night. He hit the marble floor with an audible thump. "Jesus, Mary, and Joseph!" The curse was so very Irish, so very Catholic, that it brought a smile to Grace's face despite the emotions warring inside her. Maybe the memories that Tavi Estrada was stirring weren't all problematic. Maybe, just maybe, they were reminding Finn what it had been like to be human. What it was like to be her and Nate.

Grace excused herself to the guest bathroom, cleaning up quickly and throwing on a set of the clothes she kept at Finn's for just these sorts of emergencies. Less than ten minutes tops. By which time there were already follow-up texts on the encrypted app 3S used for all communications.

Simba and Nala en route to safe house.

Simba? From *The Lion King*? And calling Meghna *Nala*? If that had gone out to everybody on the 3S roster, Elijah was going to *kill* Joaquin. Or, at the least, lock their Nintendo Switch in the vault. Grace snorted as she met Finn by the front door. He was chuckling, eyes bright. "Simba. Can't believe I didn't think of it first."

The next messages wiped away any more merriment, dried the laughter in her throat, and replaced it with sand.

Two fatalities reported in a Los Angeles nightclub
    shooting.

Chase Saunders spotted at the scene just prior. Status
    TBA.

It was barely 5:00 a.m. in California. Aston's people had already managed to target Meghna's ex-husband as well as burn down her homes. Their operation was in trouble. *Big* trouble.

15

MEGHNA WAS NUMB. EXCEPT FOR the persistent buzzing in her chest. Like a hive of bees had taken refuge inside her rib cage. Not because she had no place to go—she would always have some place to go, whether that was her father's house, or her family's haveli in India, or a motel room in the middle of nowhere—but because, for the first time in a long time, she wasn't the predator but the prey. Aston had moved first. Quickly. While most of the country still slept. While *she'd* slept, nestled against the window of Elijah Richter's getaway car. Coke-addled and meth-brained on a two-day bender, her cruel and cunning so-called boyfriend had still managed to best her.

And Chase. *Oh, god, Chase.* Joaquin had buzzed them with the update just minutes ago. He'd been shot outside a Malibu nightclub just before dawn. Rushed to UCLA Medical Center with GSWs to the shoulder and thigh. *"They missed his kill spot on purpose,"* she'd told Elijah, voice devoid of emotion. *"It was a message. Telling me no one's beyond their reach."*

"No one's beyond ours either, Meg." He was so intense, so very *solid*, that she'd almost believed him.

It wasn't even 9:00 a.m. and TMZ had already blasted the

news all over social media. So many venerable news institutions had died over the past few years, but the tabloid had survived like a cockroach in the nuclear apocalypse. They still had sources in every ER and morgue and county clerk's office known to man. Maybe known to supes, too. Perhaps they were staffed by literal ghouls. That would explain so much.

But Meghna couldn't waste thoughts on trash journalism. Or even on her endearingly earnest ex-husband, fighting for his life in the ICU. *Poor, sweet, perpetually stoned Chase.* She had to stay here, now, in the present. Looking toward the future. A future where Mirko Aston died at her hands. Where his entire organization fell apart. Where the women he'd victimized were either freed or avenged, depending on what had been done to them.

"You all right, Meg?" Elijah had been good about giving her space after Joaquin's update, but he spoke now. Gruff but gentle. Wary but worried.

She turned to look at him, pulling the seat belt tight across her chest with the motion. Almost relishing the harsh slide of it against her bare throat. Because it reminded her where and when she was. "Why do you call me 'Meg'?" she wondered. It wasn't *terrible*, as far as nicknames went. Just...*odd*. It reminded her of the little girl from *A Wrinkle in Time*. The one who'd gone to the ends of the universe to save her father. Meghna had never felt that particular pull for her own paternal figure. She'd never felt a particular pull toward anything except the Vidrohi.

And the man beside her. The one who took a careful hand off the wheel to brush a wild strand of hair back from her forehead. "Because you haven't told me to stop," Elijah said, his fingertips trailing sparks across the delicate whorls of her ear and the soft flesh of her lobe. "I'll stop if you hate it. If you'd prefer your full name. But I gotta tell you, love, 'Meghna' is too unreal and untouchable for the likes of me. Posh. Gorgeous."

The bees inside her fell painfully silent. As if the only thing left of them was the cavernous space for his words to echo and the slow drip of honey along her bones. *Oh. Oh, Elijah. I do not deserve a man like you.* "She's not. She's really not. I think *you* might be too unreal for *me*." The words tripped from her lips before she could second-guess them. And she twisted back into place, directing her eyes out her window, as if that could erase what she'd confessed.

He let her. Bless the man and the lion under his skin. They didn't push, didn't press, didn't ask for more. Elijah just kept driving along the Belt until he took an exit and directed the car to a small private turnoff. "Welcome to Safe House 13," he said then.

Meghna's gaze flickered over the old-fashioned—but clearly expensive—wooden sign. Bergen Beach Equestrian Academy. As they crested the sloping road toward the grounds, the gray stone main house and matching outbuildings came into view. As well as the first of what were no doubt several paddocks. It was the kind of place her father would've sent her had she been interested in riding when she was a child. Complete with her own horse. "The existence of a Safe House 13 implies there are at least twelve other safe houses," she murmured.

"We just like the number thirteen," Elijah said, which was neither a confirmation nor a denial. "Like you and your closets."

"Not that again. I think we've done that joke to death, don't you?" But Meghna could hardly complain. If pressed, she would never give up the locations of Vidrohi bases. As it was, she only knew a few—and they might not even exist anymore. It was a security measure employed across the network. Constantly moving. Constantly changing cities and countries. There was no known leader. No one central hub. Nothing to tie anyone together except their common purpose and, among the apsara and the jinn, their supernatural roots. If you were caught, you were on your own—in theory.

Ayesha's disappearance had been too important to ignore. Too disturbing for the network to disavow. If the wrong person learned her secrets, learned the *Vidrohi*'s secrets, hundreds of years of resistance work would be for naught and their enemies would have an invaluable weapon at their disposal. Maybe they already *did* have that weapon at their disposal, if they'd taken possession of Ayesha's ring. No lamps—they weren't practical in the twenty-first century and really hadn't been in the eleventh century either, from what Meghna had heard. All someone would need was the simple bespelled talisman that gave Ayesha her autonomy…and she was in their service until it could be cut from the finger of the thief and returned to its rightful owner. So Meghna, who loved nothing more than a good excuse to cut things, had volunteered to go in after her. She already moved in similar circles to Mirko Aston—better circles, aspirational circles. Her family connections and public persona were a shield many other agents didn't have the luxury of. She could operate in plain sight. A date with her had cachet, social capital. And she presented as just enough of an airhead that her marks didn't take her seriously. But she had no safe houses to hide in if things went bad. All she had was her face and her name.

Was she a little envious of Elijah for having Jack Tate and their team on his side? Maybe. Envy was just one of the many uncomfortable emotions she was sitting with now. One of her many deadly sins. Along with pride. And lust. So much lust.

Even now, it was coursing through her. Not like the bee-laden anxiety of losing ground to Mirko. No, this was a low-level awareness of the shape-shifter beside her and all the things they'd done together in less than a week. The places he'd touched. The stretches of skin she'd tasted. He was the only mark who'd marked *her*, tattooing want into her flesh. And she couldn't let him know that. Not after the things she'd already let slip. So she straightened in her seat, sliding her fingers along the tight band of the shoulder belt. "Is using an active riding school for a safe house really wise?" she asked, proud of how her tone betrayed none of her lecherous musings.

"It's not as though we have operatives on premises regularly. We occasionally use the tack house to regroup, hide assets, et cetera." Elijah said. "Was just there for some business last month." Then, as if he were confiding some great secret, he dropped his voice to a conspiratorial whisper. "But that's not the *real* secret bunker. Jack's got his own setup. And, lucky you and me, we've the privilege of using it."

There was a crackle from the comm resting on the dash next to Elijah's smartphone. She braced for Joaquin again, for more awful news, but it was a gravel-rough voice she didn't recognize. "I heard that, asshole. You mean Doc and I didn't have to sleep on that sofa bed?"

"Sod off, JP," Elijah returned in kind. "You get the upgrade to the master suite when you're at my level. Not when you're faffing about in 3S business as a civvie and making a bloody nuisance of yourself." He reached over and shut off the device. "Forgot that thing was activated," he grumbled.

Meghna chuckled. It was…*cute* to see this powerful man turn so cranky so quickly. This JP was like a thorn in the lion's paw. "He certainly activated your temper."

"New operative," he admitted ruefully. "We don't quite see eye to eye, but he's a helluva fighter and an invaluable field medic."

There was more than grudging respect in the words. It raised Elijah another notch in her esteem. Though she certainly didn't need to admire him any more than she already did. He'd saved her life more than once. And it was clear how much he cared for his people, even when they annoyed him. He was a good person. A *genuine* person.

Meghna had gone through the motions of being a "good Indian girl." She'd attended temple with her dad well into her early twenties, danced to Bollywood songs at annual Diwali and Republic Day functions, and said her respectful namastes to every uncle and auntie she encountered. It had served her well to play the role.

Especially as she trained with the Vidrohi and learned to use her apsara powers. No one could mistake the sari-clad sweetheart for a supernatural siren, right? Her teenage protests at the Gandiva headquarters had been waved away as a phase. Even when she got her MBA and made her name as a brand influencer, it had still been *acceptable*. She was successful, no? Shilling makeup and clothing and trading on her "exotic" South Asian good looks was fine as long as she made money and acted as a representative of the model minority. Her father's fortune and influence had excused quite a bit.

Eloping with Chase and landing in the tabloids had ended the pretense of normalcy once and for all. It was then that she'd been shifted from "good Indian girl" to "celebrity embarrassment" in the eyes of the northern Virginia Hindu community. She hadn't cared at the time. The drug-fueled months with Chase had been a welcome respite from her calling. And slicing a predatory producer's throat in an upscale suite at the Beverly Wilshire had been the ultimate victory. An affirmation that the Vidrohi could trust her to do her job. But, now, she missed the mundane sometimes. In her secret heart. Being valued for her piety or her Hindi proficiency or her Ivy League education instead of her skill at seduction and her penchant for murder. It had been…*simpler* to be *that* Meghna Saxena.

Why was being near Elijah Richter bringing up these private, long-stifled feelings? *Ugh.* She resisted the urge to squirm in her seat, hating the vulnerability that she'd long since learned to put aside. What was it about this man, this shape-shifter, that made her acknowledge just how *human* she was? That was the last thing she needed when her objectivity was already in question.

———

The screens in Command were filled with fire and smoke. LA County firefighters trying to contain the blaze that had spread to two surrounding buildings. The FDNY tackling a no-less-daunting task in securing the four-story brick building that had imploded and was now a pile of cinders and rubble. And there was a third feed running. Maybe the most haunting. Yellow "Caution" tape stretched around the coppery sidewalk stains just outside Malibu's Blue Elephant club.

Grace had seen her share of gunshot wounds. Patched them up with dispassionate precision on the table and in the field. Sutures. Duct tape. Whatever tools were at her disposal. She still didn't have the tools to heal emotional wounds. For Ernie's all-caps texts and crying-face emoji about Chase Saunders being in critical condition. He loved so much louder than she did. Even a celebrity crush was one of his own. All Chase was to her was data points. Intel. A warning. It was all he *could* be. Because if she lost objectivity…she would lose everything.

Finn. You mean Finn. No. That was a ridiculous thought. Finn was forever. There was no losing him. The very idea was like losing the stars in the sky. Even if he *felt* just as far away as those stars right now, a million miles removed as he sat beside her. Grace reached for her phone, swiping through her apps as she swiped away the doubts. It was almost 10:00 a.m. Jack had only just crawled off the ceiling—metaphorically, though his sorcery skills made it likely he could do it for real. Elijah and Meghna Saxena had arrived without incident at Safe House 13. No further attacks on Meghna's known residences or loved ones had taken place. It was the calm before the next storm. And Third Shift needed to use that time to batten down the hatches.

Jackson already knew of her and Finn's impending meeting with Estrada at a diner near the Empire State Building. They'd filed that before catching a few hours of sleep. But he was making Finn repeat the details out of sheer anal-retentiveness. Grace, for her part, was trying not to analyze the words her partner used. His tone of voice. His posture. How it all spelled "distance." He wasn't still in love with Octavio Estrada. She knew that as surely this morning as she'd known last night. But there was unfinished business there. And the lure of his past. A person couldn't serve two masters—the past and the present. All that did was impede the future.

Grace half listened to the briefing as she thumbed through her day-job email. And as if punctuating her ominous thoughts about serving two masters, a new message appeared in the inbox. *URGENT: MEETING WITH CHIEF.* All-cap subject lines were never good. It usually meant a Nigerian prince needed her bank account number. Or Ba wanted help with his Alexa device, his laptop, his iPod, and oh did she know he'd met a nice Chinese boy last week at the grocer's? Grace grimaced and scanned the body of the message. It was no better than the histrionic header. The hospital chief of staff and board required her presence at an emergency conduct hearing tomorrow.

Shit. What conduct? She hadn't been on the schedule in a week. Not since the aneurysm grab and go that she could do in her sleep—but had done with a flourish while wide awake. There hadn't been any complications. She'd checked in with the attending on the case twice just to be sure. Jack wasn't the only anal-retentive one in this conference room. She was Grace Maria Leung, and she'd never made a professional mistake in her life.

There was only one logical explanation. *Estrada.* He'd done something, arranged a complication for her in the handful of hours between their midnight meet at Hector's and now. Not as loud a message as Aston's, but one sent emphatically nonetheless. He'd perceived her as a threat and acted accordingly. She could almost admire it. *Almost.* "Damn it," she muttered, just exasperated and energetic enough for all eyes in Command to turn to her.

"I can't be at the diner tomorrow," she explained when Jackson raised his eyebrows. She'd been trained by a Black mother. She knew what the tiniest expressions meant—because god forbid she ask for translations when her ass was on the line. "Something's come up at the clinic. Likely a distraction created by Estrada, but I can't ignore it. To do so would raise suspicions."

Jack didn't even blink. Like Elijah, he'd decided she was always to be trusted. He pivoted, both physically and verbally. "Can you handle the meeting alone, Finn?"

Finian tilted his chair back on two legs, showing off, before he let it hit the ground again with an audible thump. As if to assure everyone, quite literally, that he wasn't off-balance. "Of course I can," he scoffed, waving one hand. "Even if Tav thinks I can't. He doesn't know Gracie's with me no matter what."

Any other woman would probably find such a declaration romantic. But Grace was her Ba and Mama's child. She'd been raised to be smart, shrewd, cynical, and two steps ahead of everybody else. Honors and AP classes. Double majors. Internships every summer. Med school. Residency. Third Shift. Finn had bled all over her palms barely a month ago. This was nothing. This was his deflection and his charm. "Separating us physically still isn't optimal. And *that* is what Estrada is counting on," she pointed out. "I have no personal connection to him. I'd kill him without a thought if I considered him a real threat. Can you say the same, Finn?"

"I'm not a child, Grace." His blue eyes turned stormy. Nearly gray in Command's harsh fluorescent lighting. "I've lived more decades on this earth than anyone else in this room will ever see. Just because I haven't killed Tavi thus far doesn't mean I won't."

It was the most harshly he'd spoken to her in years, but that wasn't what struck her. No, it was the *intensity* of his last sentence…as if he was trying to convince himself he was still capable of taking lives. Of taking a *lover's* life. And what could she possibly say in response? Nothing came to mind, and the moment stretched between them to the point of discomfort. A rubber band pulled to the limits of its elasticity.

"Let's hope it doesn't come to that," Jackson cut in, snipping the tension.

But Grace was still very much aware of how a gulf had widened even farther between her and Finn. He was a vampire. She was a human. He was emotion. She was reason. And tomorrow they'd head to two very different meetings...the course of which could change both of their lives.

When her gaze flicked back to the surveillance feeds on the monitors, the fires were out. All that was left was ruin.

16

"STAY PUT" AND "SIT TIGHT" were bits of advice that Elijah was brilliant at handing out and absolute shite at taking himself. The itch of having to wait things out spread from the back of his neck and along his shoulders as he parked the company car in the riding school's employee lot and hopped out to swap the license plates. Or maybe that was just the weight of Meghna's gaze on him, coolly assessing his every move. The plate switch took mere minutes, as did the walk to the members' clubhouse and cabanas where Jackson kept his secret suite, but Elijah was aware of every excruciating and arousing second of her study.

He'd mostly left her alone with her thoughts after word of her places going up in smoke came in. He was learning that giving her space, not pushing her to open up, actually brought her closer. Funny how he'd figured that out, picked up her cues, the changes in her scent that signaled her comfort or her lack of it. They'd only really known each other a few days, but it already felt longer. Maybe him studying *her* all that time had led to this strange shorthand between them. Maybe it was the fucking. Maybe it was something else—the bond between two people working toward a common goal. *No. Who are you kidding, mate?* It was probably the fucking.

Meghna might've turned sex into a transaction, into a job, but he wasn't nearly so mercenary about it. He could count the number of women he'd slept with in the past decade on one hand—the last someone he'd met at his cousin's wedding in East Ham. He and Janice had kept up emails and texts for a short while, but Third Shift came first for him. He'd ghosted her without meaning to… earning a blistering lecture from his mum about "breaking a nice Jamaican girl's heart." *"Maybe I'm not cut out for 'nice girl,' Mum. Ever think of that?"*

Meghna was not a nice girl, by her own definition. By his…she was a fascinating, infuriating, beautiful woman. One who slipped off her shoes just inside the door of Jack's suite, subtly pushing him to do the same. She wandered ahead of him into the space, taking in the floor-to-ceiling murals that distracted from the lack of windows and the track lighting along the ceiling that illuminated the art and the sunken living room. The king-size bed was off to the left, raised up a few steps, decorated in shades of bronze and silver. The furniture was in similarly muted metallic hues. Because the walls…the walls were Jackson's soul. Vivid splashes of red and blue and purple telling a story that only his best friend could interpret.

"What do you think?" he asked as Meghna walked the perimeter of the room, a mimicry of what she'd done that night at Aston's party, except barefoot and in a far more conservative outfit.

And just like that night, she came to stand before him. "I think it fits him," she said simply. "The leather couches, the boring knickknacks, the bronze and silver and gold…that's who he shows the world. The paint? That's who he is inside."

She'd taken Jack's measure effortlessly. Like some people took a breath. Bloody brilliant. It made Elijah wonder… What did she make of him? What had she learned from their time together? How many layers of his skin had she peeled back so far? Did she know his weaknesses? Would she exploit them? He wasn't sure he cared.

Somewhere, Danny Yeo was laughing at him. Last month, in the middle of the tangle with JP and Aleksei Vasiliev, the junior operative had warned him of—or maybe cursed him with—the devil of this thing growing inside him. *"You're always doing things for the greater good. But have you ever, ever done something for just one person? Risked it all for them? Have you ever loved someone that much?"* He was risking a whole hell of a lot right now for this woman. He wasn't about to call it love—not yet—but it was obsession and passion and hunger and *need*. "Who am I inside?" he wondered hoarsely. "You know yet, Meg?"

She brought her hand up to his cheek. Her touch was cool, but her eyes…oh, her glorious eyes were on fire. "Give me time, Elijah," she purred, like the cat he could've sworn she was. "I'll know every inch of you."

He couldn't say who kissed who first. Him. Her. They came together as equals. Closing the inches, the centimeters, the kilometers, and the miles. Her palm skated up behind his head to cradle his skull. He enfolded her in his arms. It was every bit a dance, choreographed by forces he couldn't have named on pain of death. Her mouth led, his followed. *Fuck*, she tasted so sweet. Not like a quick fuck in a closet or a hot shag in the car, but something almost *honest*. Elijah groaned and leaned into it, deepened it, chased it, and held it.

She gasped his name into his tongue. *"Elijah."* Music to their steps. To how they stumbled together toward the bed. Meghna pulled at his locs. He tugged at her jeans. They got naked and tangled and tripped. Not a smooth number, but something chaotic and clumsy. Modern dance, not a sodding waltz. He kissed behind her thigh. She licked under his sac. He damn near put his fist inside her. She damn near swallowed him to the root. She was a fucking goddess when it came to sucking a bloke off. And he understood it, even as he was helpless against it. There was power in how she licked his cock. In how she played with his balls. He would give up the security code to Fort Knox, the key to the Crown Jewels, the location of the Holy Grail, just to keep her mouth on him.

But he wanted more from her. And he wanted to give her more, too. So he wrapped his fingers in her hair and urged her up, face-to-face. Where she was just as vulnerable as he was. No games. No lies. No power plays. Just the two of them with everything laid bare. Everything except one thing. He broke away just long enough to rummage in the silver, steel, and glass nightstand, sheath himself in a condom, and slick up his cock and his fingers with lube. She was wet already, but their fuck in the car had been none too gentle. He wanted this to be easier in every way possible. She sighed and gasped under his preparation, bucking up to take his fingers, to help spread the lubricant he drizzled from the small bottle. "You don't have to be careful with me," she murmured, even as she accepted and opened to the contrary.

"Yes, I do, Meg," he whispered, sinking into her inch by precious inch. "And I *want* to take care with you. I want to take my time."

They had nowhere else to be. Nothing else to do but wait. Everything to lose. Everything except, at least in this moment, each other.

———

It could've been hours that she spent in Elijah Richter's arms being kissed and caressed and brought to repeated orgasm. It could've been minutes. It was so consuming, so dizzying, yet so strangely fleeting. Meghna only confirmed that they'd managed to while away most of the day when he left the bed to wash and she went looking for her purse and her various devices. There were three missed calls from her assistant on her business phone. A slew of frantic text messages and emails from sponsors and industry friends. She ignored the latter and listened to the former. The first two were professional but slightly passive-aggressive inquiries on her well-being and whereabouts. The third was to inform her that Em had taken the liberty of sending out a press release about Chase's shooting and how "Ms. Saxena-Saunders appreciates your thoughts and prayers in this difficult time." Unspoken but heavily implied was that Em would appreciate actual correspondence from her employer at some point in the next twenty-four hours. Meghna made a mental note to give the PR wunderkind a substantial raise while she thumbed out a quick "thank you" and a vague implication that she was in hiding from the paparazzi.

Em had been with her since before Chase. The formidable fortysomething from Montreal was a former publicist for one of the CBS soaps. She'd begun representing individual celebrities and athletes after her show got canceled, like so many of the grand old daytime dramas over the past two decades. Meghna had wooed her away to exclusive personal assistant work with a hefty paycheck and a promise of more autonomy than most famous clients gave their people. It more than served her purposes to have Em in charge of all her non-Vidrohi affairs, freeing her up for her *real* commitments. *Not like the commitment you made to Chase, right? Who needs that?* Her conscience, usually muted for her own sanity, managed to land a vicious blow before slinking back to its cave in the back of her mind.

Meghna shuddered, tossing her phone onto the nightstand and trying not to consider that it was symbolic of how she'd tossed her husband aside. She reminded herself again that their split had been entirely mutual and entirely amicable. He didn't expect her to rush to his side in the ICU. For one thing, as per Joaquin's reports, his newest girlfriend was already there. For another, she couldn't make him, or herself, more vulnerable than they already were. Mirko had targeted Chase because of their past relationship. What damage would he do if he thought there was a *present* bond? Who else would he go after? Em? Her father? Her social circle?

Meghna was on a text chain with several other media

personalities and celebrities of color. It had been running for years. Back when the most controversial topic was how many towels somebody owned. Before 2016. Before 2017 and 2018 and 2019. So many years where the messages became how to get out the vote, how to stay positive, and "How political is too political in your Instagram stories?" Among this chain were journalists, two TV actresses, and an Oscar-winning movie producer. People she knew had her back if scandal broke. People whose careers she would always support. People who had no idea that she was an apsara and even less of a clue that she was actively involved in rebellion and sedition. Not just voter mobilization campaigns and fruitless fundraising to flip the Senate seats they hadn't gained in 2020. They'd cried together after the presidential election went red in 2016, making the Darkest Day the Drunkest Day, too. And then, two days later, Meghna went out and made sure a Republican lieutenant governor with a taste for beating up sex workers had a heart attack in his bed. If it also appeared that he'd fallen out of bed and hit his face a couple of times before finally croaking…so be it.

Denesha kickboxed to blow off steam. Waheed did yoga and meditation, though he insisted on calling it "mindfulness" so as not to culturally appropriate. Hallie and Honey, who were sisters, loved their Wino Wednesdays. Meghna killed in the name of Vidrohi. She was always going to be two steps removed from the Text Chain of Doom, from the friendships it should have strengthened for her. No one in her life saw her real face. Not even her father.

They talked once a week. A perfunctory call with occasional prodding for her to find a nice man and settle down. As if such normalcy was even achievable in this hellscape of a world. As if he and her mother had given her a rosy view of the institution of marriage. Daddy had no idea that her rebellious phase had lasted far longer than the protests outside his munitions factory. That she no longer had to dye streaks in her hair to feel like an edgy outsider, because she'd found something so much edgier. Her knives.

But none of the distance between her and her celebrity text buddies or the awkwardness between her and her father would matter to Mirko Aston. He would use those connections, destroy them if he could. She couldn't allow that. But she couldn't stop it either. Not right now. Not without putting her own safety in jeopardy. So that meant compartmentalizing. That meant locking the memory of Chase's sunny smile and dirty jokes in the vault next to her conscience. It meant focusing on what was immediate and present and closer than everything she regularly pushed away. *Like Elijah.*

She watched him emerge from the bathroom and pull on his boxers, tugging the soft cotton plaid over the frankly glorious globes of his ass. It was a shame to cover up a butt like that. It deserved a billboard next to hers in Times Square. "Why did you choose *me* as your entry point to Mirko's organization?" she wondered, tucking her arm behind her head, hoping he hadn't noticed the tension of her clenched fist, of her clenched jaw. "Because women are easy?"

"Because *sex* is easy," he was quick to reply, as if expecting her to level him with a well-deserved feminist diatribe. "Or at least it's supposed to be. You've said it yourself. It's the job. And it's a way in that doesn't involve bloodshed. Low risk, high reward, innit?"

"Normally," she agreed. "But I'd say we're risking quite a bit now, aren't we? We've compromised ourselves and our missions."

That was when sex became the most complicated thing in the world. Not a slap of bodies for transactional purposes, two people using each other to get off and get ahead. There was nothing remotely *easy* about her and Elijah Richter choosing to go to bed together again and again after that initial bout of dalliance and deception. About getting used to it. Finding it…comfortable. It had only been a handful of days, but she already knew how the lines of his body felt under her palms. And how biting the meeting place of his neck and shoulder made him moan. She knew blow jobs wrecked him entirely and that he was never satisfied by fucking until she was wrecked, too. And she craved that gentle intimacy of waking up with him. Those early hours in the car where they weren't operatives, they weren't running a play, they were just Elijah and Meghna. Two lovers striped and warmed by rays of the rising sun.

Yes. She was most definitely compromised.

"Do you regret it?" He climbed back under the covers with her, turning on his side and propping his head on his hand. "You're the one who pulled us over on the road, love. I wouldn't've laid a hand on you again without your say-so. No matter how much I wanted it."

That was novel. Most men she dealt with were not predisposed to keeping their hands to themselves. Especially if they'd already been given the go-ahead once. "Ongoing enthusiastic consent" was a foreign concept to the bulk of her marks. She'd buried three of them after they'd failed to grasp the nuances to her satisfaction. Unmarked graves in Mumbai, Lisbon, and Nashville.

"No. I don't regret any of it." Not the killings, and not the pleasure she'd found here with this man who was the antithesis of those dead ones. "I probably should. This can't go anywhere or *be* anything. But I'm not sorry."

"Me neither." Elijah's eyes shone gold before melting back to their natural dark brown. She'd yet to figure out if that signified something specific. A change of mood. A change of light. His inner lion coming to the surface and then subsiding. But even with that question unanswered, he wasn't a mystery to her. She'd grown to understand him in this short span of time. They were as alike as they were different. Goal-driven, determined. But like most shifters, he had a pack. She hunted alone.

He reached out, tracing the furrows between her brows. "Some deep thoughts in here, Meg. Reckon you'll tell me what they are?"

"No." She smiled her apsara smile. The one he already knew

was fake. And then she shoved him down flat on the mattress and climbed atop him. He was already hard again, the boxers serving more as a wishful end to their sex play than an effective one.

But Meghna didn't move to take them off, to take him in. Instead, she sat there, knees digging into his hips, cradled against the taut lines of his pelvis. Aphrodite's saddle. The Adonis belt. The iliac furrow. There were so many names for the sharp cuts. All she wanted to call them was *hers*. He was beautiful. A dark-skinned god like the Hindu deities of old, before all the whitewashed art. There were scars marring the smooth planes of his skin. Knife slashes. Bullet wounds. Evidence of the battles he'd fought. Evidence she didn't wear on her own flesh because it healed—on the surface at least. An apsara's best weapon was her beauty after all. But compared to him…compared to Elijah, Meghna's looks were shallow. A tool. Not something carved by years and experience and violence but still so fucking stunning.

She leaned over, hair spilling across his chest as she kissed his firm belly. No defined six-pack or eight-pack like some Hollywood hero but hard just the same. She pressed her mouth to one of his pecs, licking his flat nipple and appreciating the rumbled growl it elicited.

"Meghna…?" There was a question along with the arousal in his voice.

"I never get to linger," she said softly. "*That's* not the job." Even when she'd been married to Chase—especially those first six glorious months after a PR-stunt Vegas elopement—the sex had been frantic and often drug-fueled. She had fond but hazy memories of being on Ecstasy and Red Bull, waking up hungover before he headed out for a call time and she rolled in to a photo shoot. This…this was different. This, she could soberly savor. For as long as the mission lasted.

"Have at it, love. As long as you like. I'm not going anywhere just yet." Elijah stretched out beneath her, arms out to his sides, urging her to look her fill. To *take* her fill.

So she did. Learning the geography of his beautiful body, committing each point of the map to memory, traveling far and wide before landing at his lips. And she stayed there until they had to break for breath. Until he pulled back and whispered, "*My* turn."

Meghna pulled back, too, muscles locking, lungs seizing in as close to a panic response as she got. *No*, said every protective instinct she had. If she didn't linger, then it was a given that her lovers weren't allowed the privilege either. To view her body as the art it was…that was fine. But to find her vulnerabilities? To kiss them and stroke them and touch them? When was the last time that had happened? *With Elijah. Each previous time with Elijah*, needled the same instincts that had frozen her in place. He'd already gotten further under her skin than anyone else ever had. And now he wanted to go deeper. To explore to the core of who she was.

"Meg?" he prompted, so maddeningly perceptive. So patient and kind. "Everything all right, love?" He brushed wild strands of her hair from her face—from his face, too—his touch tender and tentative. "Where've you gone off to?"

So many places. Nowhere at all. Both answers teetered on the tip of her tongue. In the end, she gave him neither. She simply rolled to the side and spread herself out like he had just a short time ago. Hands at her sides. Knees bent. She felt vaguely like a frog pinned out on a tray in high school biology…which was not the sexiest thing to be thinking. That he could cut her open like this.

"You look like a virgin sacrifice." He laughed softly…which was an even more unsettling image than that of a dissected frog, mostly because she hadn't been a virgin for more than fifteen years. "You really don't let your guard down, do you? Not for anyone."

"I want to. For you." The confession was difficult. It tasted like broken glass. She remembered their last go-round, how he'd been generous with lube and with his time, wanting to take care of her, to make it sweet and hot and good. Could she be even half as generous with herself? Meghna didn't know.

Elijah aligned himself along her side. He reached down for one of her open palms and entangled their fingers. He did the same with their legs. "Everything I find…all the things that I uncover… it'll still be yours. I promise."

Meghna did two foolish things in a row then. She kissed him. And she believed him.

17

WHEN FINIAN ARRIVED AT THE Tick Tock Diner alone, Tavi felt
the closest thing to satisfaction he'd experienced in a long time.
At last, success in one small endeavor. His old lover standing in
the aisle of the Thirty-Fourth Street tourist trap, surveying the
tables and booths—looking both beautiful and mistrustful. One
of those things could, and would, be changed. Finn would trust
him again. Or die. Those were the options. He couldn't allow for
anything else. Hence the unfortunate professional distraction that
had lured the lovely Grace away from this meeting.

Alone, without his formidable female companion, Finian
Conlan was every inch the vulnerable prey he'd been sixty years
ago...but also something else. Something new. And not just
because of the twenty-first-century clothing. Distressed blue
denim and long-sleeved black T-shirt. A puffy down vest—
also black. No pretense of a winter coat to ward off the crisp
November air. He looked...comfortable. Like he'd lived, *truly
lived*, in the youthful skin that Tavi had both cursed and blessed
him to inhabit. Their gazes locked and Finian swiftly moved
toward Tavi's booth by the Eighth Avenue windows, Starbucks
holiday cup in one hand and mobile phone in the other. The

consummate millennial New Yorker—save for the flash of his razor-sharp canines.

"Tav. Still early, I see. Casing the joint or what?"

"Finn." The new nickname was more natural on his tongue than it should have been. "Still suspicious, I see." He sat back, one arm across the back of the banquette, his favorite pose of indolent disinterest.

It didn't fool his protégé one bit. "The fires," Finian said, dangerously soft. Too soft for anyone but a fellow vampire to hear. "The movie star. Did you do it? Was that your call?" There was fury in the questions. And disapproval. "Because I've nothing to say to someone who would see an innocent man shot to further his own goals."

Always that core of Catholic morality with this one. It had never taken root with Tavi. He was too cynical to be spiritual, too practical to be moral. And revolution had been his first and only religion. "You really are determined to believe the worst of me, aren't you? No. I had nothing to do with yesterday's unfortunate events. I was just a bystander to the orders for the woman's properties. And the target practice was handled entirely outside of my hearing range."

Finian snorted. "Likely story."

"*True* story," Tavi corrected gently. "I can be trusted in this, amigo."

"Leopard shifters don't change their spots. Neither do vampires like us." Finian set down his coffee—likely something full of sugar and caramel, achingly sweet—and slid into the bench seat across from him. "I'm not your bloody 'amigo.' We were never friends," he growled, apparently remembering those years far differently than Tavi did. "Talk," he added tersely.

"No pancakes?" Tavi raised his brows, mock-wounded. Young human Finian had quite the sweet tooth. Pancakes drenched in maple syrup, loaded Belgian waffles, pastelitos de guayaba or piña.

Watching him tear into treats had given Tavi such joy. No wonder he'd taught him to tear into throats.

"I've lost the taste for them. Wonder who I have to blame for that?" Finn's eyes flickered to the expansive menus the waitress had left after seating Tavi fifteen minutes ago. There was something like longing there in his expression. And it was gone when he focused on Tavi once more. "Get to it," he snapped.

"What? No pleasantries either, mi amor?" The deliberate needling was immature. Poorly done of him. Tavi didn't much care. This was the most genuine fun he'd had in a long time. As innocent and diverting as he was allowed to be.

It was the same feeling he'd had in 1961, alight and alive because of this man. This man who was now scowling at him. "Pleasantries were last night. And don't think I don't know that whatever called Gracie away was your doing," Finn accused, annoyingly on target. "You wanted me here by myself. Well, you've got me. Now let's see your cards, mate."

"Not here." Tavi had more than just cards to show. His hand was bigger, more dangerous than that, and the pot far more valuable than money. He slid out of his seat, tossing a few bills on the table for the waitress's trouble. "Let's go," he said. "If you want to turn me, then you have to come with me."

Finian snorted, shaking his head. "Nearly every mistake I've made in my miserable life is because I followed you somewhere I oughtn't've."

Tavi laughed. "Is that a no?"

"It's not a no. It *is* a 'fuck you, you fucking fucker.'" His opinion of the matter eloquently delivered, Finian joined Tavi in a brisk, eye-contactless departure from the diner. Their seats would be filled quickly, but it was still best not to acknowledge that they'd wasted the establishment's time.

New York City was only just struggling back to normalcy after several years in chaos. Working out its Sanctuary City laws.

Recovering from one crisis after another in the wake of 2016. Police corruption. Natural disasters and epidemics. Jails closing. And, of course, the emergence of supernaturals in every walk of life. In offices, hospitals, the theaters, and City Hall. Tavi loved this place. How it throbbed and sang and seethed. Every few months, some hack would write an op-ed about how NYC was "over" or "dying." They couldn't be more wrong. New York City was here, breathing him and Finian in as they descended into the nearest subway station. Welcoming them into the belly of the beast. Or maybe into its veins.

They swiped through the turnstiles with their respective Metrocards, and Tavi had to laugh at the sheer humanity of it. Vampires at diners while the sun was still in the sky. Vampires taking the subway. Such mundanities. Somewhere, a goth teenager was experiencing a keen yet inexplicable sense of disappointment over two creatures of the night hopping on an A train to Fulton Street. But this was what supernaturals *did*. For thousands of years. Existing alongside humans, navigating human society, with none the wiser. Were it within his power, Tavi would curse the day humans had discovered the truth and decided that they could exploit it for their own gain. Men like Mirko Aston, already a blight upon the world, had moved in quickly.

"What new scheme have you got knocking 'round in that head of yours?" Finn leaned one shoulder against the wall of the train car, a scowl etching his face.

"The same scheme as before," Tavi said with a shrug.

They both stayed stationary, balanced, as the ancient train bumped over the subterranean tracks, a few hard jerks startling the handful of other passengers spread across the car. "So you're leading me into a trap then?" It sounded like a question, but it was more like a certainty. Finian's brooding expression turned into a feral smile. "Taking me away from all that I know and hold dear all in the name of power and glory?"

Was *that* what he'd promised when he gave Finn the gift of an extended life? Tavi winced. Basura. Just complete trash. His recall of the past clearly had a few holes in it. As for the present… "There's no power and glory in this." Not for him at any rate. That wasn't why he'd signed on with Mirko. Why he'd seemingly thrown out the few ideals that had fed him during his youth in Havana.

The rest of the trip downtown was made in silence—discounting the busker who got on at Fourteenth Street and warbled an off-key rendition of "Hallelujah" while he strummed a ukulele. As if that song hadn't been abused enough since the death of Leonard Cohen. Tavi moved to stand by the door after a crowd got off at West Fourth. And then Finian followed him off the train at Fulton Street.

Mirko had many meeting spots all over the city. He loved conducting business in Midtown because thousands did, affording his international cronies effortless anonymity. But his home base was the Financial District. It held all the hallmarks of the legitimacy he ultimately craved. He had a suite at the Cipriani, like several Wall Street bigwigs and media personalities, in the hopes that rubbing elbows would let him come away with some of their cachet. If it didn't work…well, that was of no matter. Because Aston would surpass them, or destroy them, in the end. He wanted to stamp out the rich, the poor, the liberal, the intellectual elite, the brown, the devout, and the atheists alike. When all was said and done, he wanted a world that looked like him… and that followed his rules.

That meant Tavi's days with Mirko were numbered. They had been from the start. Could he trust Finian Conlan with that knowledge, with more, when the man couldn't even trust *him*? Tavi was just coming to an answer when he felt a sharp prick at the back of his neck and his limbs atrophied. "Sorry, mate," he heard Finian whisper as everything went dark. "I've learned my lessons. Maybe you will, too."

Maybe.
Maybe not.

––––––––––––––

A slew of lawyers worked for Third Shift. Grace could have called any one of them to walk into the emergency meeting with her. Neha Ahluwalia, for one, was raring to prove herself as an official member of the team. But Grace knew better than to cross-contaminate her two careers, to allow even the most tenuous connection. So it was Nathaniel Feinberg who went with her into the den full of white lions, who helped her deflect the bullshit Octavio Estrada had strewn in her path. Not because Tavi cared in particular about her medical career or the consequences but because it got her out of the way. Away from Finn. While they'd been trying to turn Aston's pet vampire, he'd been plotting to steal away her partner. She could almost admire it.

In less than twenty-four hours, he'd fabricated several documents indicating that she'd practiced medicine at another independent hospital—performed two emergency surgeries on days she hadn't been scheduled at Queensboro. If she'd actually done so, it would be a blatant breach of her contract and grounds for immediate dismissal. Grace took in the charges without blinking. Sitting ramrod straight in the uncomfortable conference room chair—the ones in 3S Command were way more ergonomic—and looking from pale face to pale face. The chief of staff and three out of five hospital board members. "Have I ever given you *any* indication that I would be so incompetent and so careless?" she asked them icily. "If I didn't know any better, I'd say someone falsified these papers in order to discredit me and force my resignation before my contract renegotiation."

No one sitting at the far end of the long table was the person in question, but it didn't stop them from fidgeting like they were guilty. Chief Davidson cleared his throat, cheeks going pink above his white beard. The cardiologist played Santa every year for the children's ward, but that was the sum total of the man's resemblance to a cheery and beloved saint. "You know we value your work, Dr. Leung. Queensboro Community Hospital has been very lucky to have you with us for the past several years. Surely you can't think we'd attempt such a thing."

Nate, who'd been letting her run the show thus far, leaned forward just slightly in his seat on her left. He grinned like a shark. "Let's hope that's not the case, *Mr.* Davidson," he said with deliberate arrogance. "Because if my client is wrongfully ousted from her position here, you *will* be hearing from me."

The meeting went on for a grand total of fifteen minutes after that nicely leveled threat. Grace didn't even bother offering explanations for where she'd actually been on the two dates in question. All she gave them was her terse assurance that she was Not Pleased at being summoned and would be happy to warn other Queensboro surgeons of this sort of behavior. With that, she and Nate said their goodbyes and made a beeline for the elevators.

"Finn was right," Nate murmured as soon as the doors closed behind them, awe in his voice and mirth twinkling in his eyes. The brief hesitation—the awkwardness—that had laced their interaction before they walked into the conference room together was gone. "You *are* a badass."

"Because I've had to be. Because I didn't have any other choice." The words bubbled up from some hidden spring six layers beneath her skin. From the river of fire that ran through her center. From the vault she'd kept locked as she sat in front of the board. "Not Chinese enough for some people. Not Black enough for others. 'What are you?' and 'Where are you from?' from assholes who don't know what to make of my face and think they have a right to a definition. The only thing I could ever control was being strong. Being smart. Being the best in my field. The best in *the* field. Ice Maiden Grace. Dr. Freeze. The one Elijah can count on in the middle of his Lost Boys. I've never had the luxury of weakness. Of being shielded or protected from everything awful in the world."

If Nate was shocked by her outburst, all it manifested as was warmth radiating from his entire besuited body. The warmth he'd shared with them in Finn's bed before he fled it. "You deserve to be taken care of." He came off the side of the elevator car and joined her in one long stride. "You deserve a soft place to land."

She did. She really did. "You and Finn were my soft place not too long ago. My safe place, too." Grace held his gaze. Did he see his departure and distance in question form on her face?

Maybe so. Because he wasted no time before drawing her into his arms. "We'll take care of you," he murmured as his lips feathered her temple. "*I'll* take care of you," he said against her skin. An absolute breach of attorney-client ethics. Grace hoped whoever was watching the elevator's CCTV got their jollies. She just let herself be held. Let herself believe, for a few seconds, that she *was* safe.

Was this how Finn felt around Nate? Secure? Grounded? Human? Was that what scared him so much that he'd let Nate keep his distance for weeks? Had it driven him to Tavi Estrada? She wasn't the only one with pertinent questions, it turned out. "So, uh…what exactly *is* the deal with you and Conlan? Open relationship?" Nate asked when they were safely ensconced on the N train and making their way west, back toward Third Shift HQ.

"No." She hadn't whiled away years pining for Finn. There was no secret flame she'd been tending since their first meeting six years before. No throbbing core of unrequited lust between coworkers to deal with. She'd, frankly, spent more time wanting to stab him with the nearest sharp object than wanting to kiss him. A reaction he inspired in many, not just her. And she had the proud distinction of being someone who'd actually *done* it. March 2018. She'd jabbed a ballpoint pen right through his hand after he wolf-whistled at the surveillance photo of an attractive South

American couple who were running weapons while pretending to be art dealers. *"Oi! What was that for?" "Midmeeting inappropriate behavior. And terrible taste."* She'd bandaged him up in short order, and he'd stopped being salacious during briefings for almost two weeks. There was nothing about their relationship to open, because they were never closed.

Grace knew what Nate wanted to hear. A simple explanation. One that fit society's heteronormative definitions. "He's my best friend. My partner in every meaningful way." Finn listened to her. He deferred to her. He *craved* the boundaries she set for him, albeit not necessarily in the form of periodic stabbing. It was nothing as defined as a formal BDSM relationship. She didn't spank him on alternate Wednesdays, though she'd definitely had the urge. It was like a tether between them. A flexible band of give and take, of mutual respect and frequent teasing. One look or one touch conveyed a thousand things. *I trust you. I've got you. I love you. I'm not amused by your eyebrow gymnastics, so please knock it off this instant.*

"I've been with other people. Finn's been with…everyone." She laughed ruefully. "But none of that changes us."

Nate frowned speculatively. "Because he feeds from you?"

She'd asked herself that same question early on. And dismissed it. "Because we draw from each other. Not blood, Nate. Strength."

He digested that and sat with it for a while. She could see him turning it over in his mind, this handsome white-haired man with a thoughtful, faraway expression. "That's how I feel about me and Dustin," he said finally, reminding her of his law partner, his own best friend. "But it's more than that with you and Finn. You have to admit."

"What's 'more' in this instance?" Grace countered. "If you mean sex…the first time I kissed him was that night at his place. You and I found out together how he tastes. And what he's like in bed."

The faraway look in Nate's eyes this time was decidedly more heated. As if he, like her, was recalling all of the ways they'd touched each other, learned each other. Tongues, lips, fingers, sighs, and whispers. "It doesn't bother you at all that he might be sharing all of those things with Estrada right now?"

"Of course it does." She was practical and realistic, not entirely impervious. "But not because I'm jealous. I know my place in Finn's life. I'm confident in it. I'm worried for *him*. For what Estrada will drag him into. What feelings he'll stir up in him. Finian has a good life now. Friends. A purpose. A future. Tavi is his past. And the past is like quicksand." It felt strange to articulate aloud the fears she'd been mulling internally. Strange but…*right*. "I don't want him to get caught up in it with no way out."

Nate's cross-examination of her was cut short by the N train arriving at Times Square–Forty-Second Street. They hurried off the car and into the humid bowels of the station. It was still that nebulous period between fall and winter, but the heat was already cranked up. Grace was relieved to emerge aboveground a few minutes later, with the crisp breeze cooling the sweat on her face and easing her choice of lightly lined trench coats. She'd thrown the knee-length tan trench on over a severe black pantsuit. And she noticed now that Nate was dressed nearly identically. His own suit had pinstripes and his trench was longer, but they'd coordinated nonetheless. Right down to the blue ties that matched the shade of Finn's eyes.

"He's really something, isn't he?" Nate marveled, the tenor of his thoughts clearly on the same scale as hers. "To inspire such loyalty from you. To turn me inside out in a matter of days. How does he do it? Why do we fall for it?"

Grace had to laugh. More questions. Of course he had more questions. "Why do I feel like I'm on the stand, Councillor? It's been nothing but interrogation since we left the hospital."

"Because I want to understand." Nate shrugged helplessly. He was so adorably bewildered. So adorable in general. No wonder

Finn had been infatuated by him before they'd even met. "Not just him. All of it. Why you are the way you are. Why you both do the things you do."

"We've already shown you that." In Aleksei Vasiliev's ware-house when they'd fought for their lives and the lives of innocents. And yes, in one another's arms. "You know exactly who we are. The next step is on *you*. You can accept it, accept us. Or you can choose not to…" She mimicked his shrug.

He flinched. As if the very idea of the latter was unthinkable. It was a good sign, all things considered. It was an even better sign when he followed her through HQ's front entrance, hands in pockets, handsome face a mask of quiet contemplation, and let her swipe him in.

"Well?" she prompted gently when they stood in front of the elevator bank. "Has the jury returned a verdict, Councillor? It's all right if they're not ready."

"They're ready. *I'm* ready." One of his perfectly manicured hands emerged from his trouser pocket. He used it to reach for hers. To squeeze her fingers. It was a small gesture that felt as big as the hug he'd given her back at Queensboro. "I wouldn't have answered your call if I wasn't."

18

WHEN ELIJAH AWOKE, IT WAS to the insistent alert of text messages and an empty bed. Both raised his alarm. *Meghna's done a bunk. She's gone. You sodding idiot,* he cursed himself even as he thumbed through Jackson's messages about how Finian had brought Octavio Estrada in for questioning and thus far the man had been uncooperative. And by the way, why aren't you picking up your messages, you asshole? He shot off a rude reply to that line of inquiry as he rolled out of bed, bare feet hitting the hardwood floor. There was a Post-it note there, next to the logical place where his feet would fall. *Looking for food. Not AWOL.—M.* The relief that coursed through him in that minute was ridiculous. Like he was sixteen, not forty-fucking-six, and a pretty girl across the way had smiled back at him.

Except the pretty girl was an accomplished assassin and she had his number. She'd had it from the get-go. *Fuck.* Elijah grabbed his clothes from where they were strewn and headed back to the WC for a quick cleanup. Jack's kitchen was fully stocked. The man had a pathological obsession with Cheez-Its, at the very least, so there was no real need for Meghna to leave the suite. Unless something was wrong. Unless the last few hours between them had been a lie.

Fur prickled up his spine and back down again. The extra teeth throbbed in his mouth, begging for release. *No*, the lion inside him insisted. *She's true. She's mine.* He wanted to believe what the cat knew. He had to confirm it. So he went out onto the grounds, following her scent. That rich, seductive essence that could only belong to her. And him. He was all over her. She hadn't washed him from her after this last time—not thoroughly enough. But that wasn't the only thing he picked up as he tracked. There was a hint of copper, too. Of *blood*.

His mobile vibrated in his trousers. A message from 'Quin awaited him. Perimeter breach at Thirteen. Six or more hostiles on the cams. Team en route. Sit tight.

Sit tight? That wasn't an option. Neither was staying put. Not this time. Even before the choice was yanked out of his hands.

Elijah broke into a run as the first spray of bullets hit the spot where he'd just been. He kept moving until he spied the next set of buildings just over the hill. The stables. They'd provide temporary cover if nothing else. Better than staying out in the open. That was certain death. He tapped out a quick 911 to HQ on his mobile as he moved, then shoved it back in his pocket and switched to wrist comm as he scanned the landscape for shooters. This wasn't the deliberately sloppy message of the club shooting in Malibu. They were smart, whoever they were. Pros. They knew to conceal, to hunt.

Unlike vampires, shape-shifters didn't have an expanded life span. The average lion shifter in the wild, without any immediate family or pride, had a life expectancy of fifty. Factor in the life expectancy of the average Black man in America, especially when he constantly ran afoul of law enforcement and the criminal element alike, and Elijah had never counted on living to a great old age. He was forty-six years old, he hadn't seen his mum and dad in ages, and the clock was ticking. He'd already willed his belongings to Jack and all of that legal rubbish. *"What makes you think*

I'm going to live longer than you?" his partner had sputtered. *"Bruv, have you seen yourself? When you finally croak at 102, they're going to name an entire chain of CrossFit gyms after you."* Lije would just be happy to have his ashes scattered in Jamaica. In Rocky Point where his gran and granddad had lived before moving to London, or the caves at Jackson's Bay.

At least, that had been the plan. Until now. Plastered against a stable wall, listening for hostiles, hoping for Meghna, Elijah really fucking wanted to *survive.* Sod dying young. Sod giving Jackson bloody Tate his vinyls and his vintage Clash T-shirts—what was Mr. Dave Matthews Band and Savile Row going to do with his stuff anyway? He'd drink the good whiskey, of which Elijah had plenty, and chuck everything else in the bin.

He propelled off the wall, pulling a partial shift. Maw and claws. The ripple of pleasure-pain went through him in delicious shivers, and he had to swallow the urge to roar. Wouldn't do to give up his location, now would it? The horses were none too happy with the change, stamping and whinnying in their stalls. They'd smelled the cat on him before, but it was stronger now, more threatening. That couldn't be helped. They weren't his prey. They'd have to get over it.

Especially when a single shooter appeared at the open entrance to the horse barn. All black. Night-vision goggles even though it was barely dark. Tactical vest. It was overkill. Doing it up like an extra in an action movie. But the gun in their hand? That was no prop. Elijah didn't waste any more seconds on observation. He struck before the hostile could radio their mates and give up his hiding spot. Crossing the barn with a leap. Delivering a slash across the throat like he'd done to Aston's man. And then a snap of the neck to be sure. The shooter fell to the ground in a heap, and Lije immediately knelt to pat down the body. No ID. Two clips and a KA-BAR. When he pulled off the goggles and the mask, it revealed a nondescript white male. Brown hair, flat and lifeless brown eyes. In no way memorable. Just the kind of person you'd want on a professional hit squad.

"Fuckin' hell." Elijah added a few more colorful words as he tugged the corpse out of sight behind some hay bales. Lucky for him, there was no one to hear but the horses. At least for now.

Team on premises. Hold your position. The readout on his wrist comm would've been hard for human eyes to make out in the dimness, but he had no problem. Message received. Loud and fucking clear. He hated waiting, but he did it. Counting the minutes. The seconds. Until the pop of gunfire reverberated through his skull like a succession of tire blowouts. Elijah could guess what it was about without having to raise his head or pause for breath—JP drawing the shooters away from the stables. The gargantuan wolf leading them in a merry chase…hopefully to where the rest of the team was waiting. That meant the window for a safe egress was rapidly closing. Precious minutes before the shit hit the fan entirely. They needed to go. Close this up. Shut this down. Burn this safe house location. But not yet. Meghna was still out there somewhere, between the tack house and the stables. He couldn't leave without her. *Wouldn't.*

She was true and she was his. That was all that mattered now.

———————————

Meghna hated getting shot. It was so inconvenient. Especially when she'd done nothing to warrant it except go looking for something more substantial than cheese-flavored crackers. An apsara could not live on Cheez-Its alone. She couldn't live with two bullets in her either. Not for long. Luckily, she'd taken one in the thigh and the other in the upper left arm. Not immediately fatal. No major arteries hit. But the wounds hurt like a bitch and made it hard to hide from the multiple shooters she'd counted. At least four. Professionals who knew how to get a job done. They'd only missed a kill shot because she'd tucked and rolled behind a ridiculous piece of topiary that was still putting up the fight against fall and winter. A figure atop a rearing horse. It had a wide enough base of branches and leaves that she couldn't be seen. Unfortunately, that meant she couldn't see her pursuers either.

So she listened for them. The crunch of dry grass and branches under their feet. The changes in the wind. All while scanning around her for her next shelter. Another topiary sculpture a few yards away? The stables? There was a secure room in the tack house, Elijah had told her, but there was no way of knowing she'd be able to access it. It could just as well be a death trap.

Third Shift's safe house was *not* getting a good Yelp review. *One and a half stars. Pleasant company, but no actual safety. Would not recommend extended stay. Fuck and flee.* Meghna tried not to laugh. Any sound might give away her position. But laughing was better than whimpering in pain, right? She sucked in a great big gulp of air, pushing the agony down beneath the breath. These had to be Mirko's men. They'd found her, followed her, Elijah's unmarked car be damned. *How?* One would think *they* were the supernaturals in this equation. Had the good doctor lied about his experiments? Was there already a wave of genetic hybrids stalking the streets on Mirko Aston's say-so?

No, said her gut instinct. Because things would be even worse were that the case. Because Mirko would be first in line to power up with a proven serum, and he was still very much human. *They're just people, Meghna. They're all just people.* She needed the reminder. She scrambled up from her crouch, flinching as fire raced along her shoulder and up her hip. Her skin was trying to knit around the bullets but couldn't. Her supe cells couldn't charm their way around lead. And so the healing hurt as much as what had necessitated it. Until she got the bullets out, she was living and dying at the same time, a vicious cycle of pain.

Meghna took another steadying breath. And then another. And then she ran. Zigzagging across the manicured lawn—still pristine

even with the grass dry and browning. Each crunch felt as loud
as a boom of thunder. The massive stables were just ahead of her.
There was no guarantee she'd be safe inside them, but the possibility of shelter was better than the certainty of being an open target.

It all went a little blurry for a bit. How she got to the stables.
How Elijah was suddenly there, too. His hands on her as he
checked her over. Had he come after her after finding his bed
empty? Had he dodged bullets or caught them?

"You with me, love?" It sounded like he was willing his voice
not to shake. "I need you to stay with me, breathe through the
pain." She tried to stay focused—that was her thing, right? *Focus,
Meghna.* On his face. On his eyes. Not on the blood welling from
beneath the makeshift bandage despite the tourniquet he'd tied
with his belt. "We have to get you to the egress point," he murmured. "And we need those bullets out, yeah? Sooner rather than
later. Just breathe."

Her pupils were no doubt dilated, her inhalations shallow. Both
signs that were worrying Elijah. But Meghna knew her body was
fighting with the bullets as best it could. She clutched at his hand,
squeezed it with all her strength. "I do not need a Lamaze coach,
Elijah Richter. I need to get the hell out of here."

He didn't even wince at her crushing grip. He brought their
joined hands to his lips, choking back a laugh or a sob, or both.
"I'm working on it, Meg. The team's on the grounds. We've got
backup. We've just got to get to them."

"Sure. I'm up for a sprint." She struggled to sit up, and he swiftly
moved to help her, propping her against the stable wall. *Oh. Fuck.*
Her wounded thigh was decidedly *not* up for a sprint. Or even a
brisk walk. "I hate getting shot. Have I mentioned that?"

The sound Elijah made was definitely a laugh this time. "I don't
much like it either," he said. "Makes you reconsider the job when
these are the perks, eh? I had no idea how lucky I was when this
assignment landed in my lap."

"You mean when *I* landed in your lap." She smiled faintly, even while glancing over his shoulder to make sure they were still concealed from the hit squad.

Elijah was doing the same. "And look where we are now." He masked his sweep with a theatrical gesture. "Luxurious accommodations. Killers on our trail. Remind me to take it up with HR when we're back at HQ."

The HR callback made her snort. Which moved her chest. Which in turn moved her arm. Which then hurt like a motherfucking bitch. Meghna was growing increasingly tired of the pain. Especially if she was resorting to multiple swear words in an internal narrative she tried to keep in check. She tried to keep *everything* in check. Because that was her calling, her mission. *Everything in service to the cause.*

"Meg? You okay?" Elijah's distress was clear on his handsome face. It was nice to be worried about. To have someone's concern. How long had it been since anyone cared enough to ask how she was?

You're slipping again, Meghna. "I'm fine," she assured him, gritting her teeth against the intense discomfort. The dizziness. "I'm not dying anytime soon." Brave words. But her voice was dropping, low underneath the whickering of the horses, who were nervous about the predator among them. They could smell the lion and they expected attack. They could smell her, too, and didn't know what to make of her.

"You should go," she told Elijah. "See if the coast is clear. I can handle myself."

"I know you can handle yourself." He didn't want to leave her, but he'd have to do a circuit of the stables to make sure their egress was clear. That Mirko's people weren't waiting outside to ambush them. "You're a bloody superhero."

"I'm bloody, that's for sure. But I'm not a superhero. Not like you. You want to save the world," she pointed out.

He made a noise of disagreement. "And you don't?"

"No," she insisted. "I just want to make sure fewer terrible people live in it."

"You're not one of those terrible people. Just so we're clear."

"Oh, no. *I'm* exceptional," she assured him, closing her eyes. For just a few seconds. That was all she needed. A few seconds to regroup as her skin and sinew kept trying to heal and her blood kept pouring.

"Fuck it." She had no idea what Elijah meant with the curse. Not until he began to shift. Partial. Not all the way. Half man, half lion. But taller somehow. Bigger. Big enough to scoop her up with one arm and leave the other free to fight.

He was going to need to find pants again. That had to be a nuisance in his line of work. *Focus, Meghna.* So she did. Inhaling. Exhaling. Centering. Riding the agony as he carried her from their hiding spot in an undignified bundle.

Rapidly approaching darkness had made it harder to see the blood trail she'd left in her wake—a rookie mistake, one she could only blame on being so focused on evading her pursuers that nothing else mattered—and the night worked again to their advantage now. Blending with them as they kept to the shadows. The horses were still spooked, both by Elijah and the gunfire that had shattered the quiet grounds, but their hoofing and snorting wouldn't give away his position. Six of them. What looked like a few mares, a couple of great, hulking geldings. That about summed up everything Meghna knew about horses. She'd ridden several, but it was all part of her training, part of her cover as the high-society girl who did things like go to the Veuve Clicquot Polo Classic every year and show up at the Kentucky Derby in a gorgeous hat.

Commandeering a ride was out of the question. The horses wouldn't take Elijah. She was in no shape to keep them in line. And there was no guarantee that Mirko's gunmen wouldn't just shoot their mounts right out from under them. Aston's flunkies didn't respect human life. Why would a few animals be any different? Any way you looked at it, they'd be left completely exposed.

Elijah didn't seem too worried. He just gave a roar and sprang with her into the night.

19

SCATTERED, DISTANT GUNFIRE SOUNDED OVER the comm receiver in Grace's left ear. At odds with the various clinical hums of Third Shift's small medical bay. But none of the ambient and far-from-ambient noises distracted her from the unconscious vampire she'd been tasked with watching over. Finn had pumped Estrada with enough sedatives to keep him out for quite a while. Until he fed and fresh blood flushed his system. Since there were no live takers for the honor at 3S HQ, the blood was being trans-fused into the vampire's veins from the packs they kept for medical and vampirical emergencies alike. Estrada was no good to them unconscious. No good to *her* unconscious while the rest of her team was at Safe House 13. The last thing she wanted to be doing while they were endangering themselves was babysitting a living corpse. Even if Nate had been roped into helping her do so.

"He'll be ever so thrilled to see you both when he wakes up." Finn laughs, barely giving the insensate man on the bunk a glance. No, his eyes are on Nate. And her. Filled with the same surprise and delight as when he'd found Nate giving himself a tour of the floor after Jack pulled the operatives in for an emergency meeting in Command.

"I'm not insulted," Nate had assured Grace when the order came in

just as they got off the elevator. "I know I'm not in the club yet—that was my choice—and I think I can entertain myself while you do what secret agents do."

It turns out watching Tavi Estrada is what some secret agents do. While others go on a rescue mission in South Brooklyn. Finn doesn't look devastated to be leaving his old mentor and lover behind. No, he just grabs Nate, surprising him, and gives him a loud, smacking kiss on the cheek. It preps Grace for when he does the same to her. "Goodbye, my loves," Finn trills before rushing out of the medical bay.

My loves. Grace could still hear the echo of those two little words, even with all the comm chatter that suddenly burst in—both a relief and an annoyance.

"Is it just me, or does half the shit you guys come up with end up going sideways?" A low, belligerent huff. Already incredibly familiar though the new recruit hadn't been with Third Shift long.

"Shut up, JP!" multiple voices on the channel chimed in at once.

Across the small clinic area, Neha Ahluwalia let out a crack of laughter, nearly dropping her tablet. JP, formerly Joseph A. Peluso, was *her* love. He'd left her with the kind of kiss that men gave their partners before going off to war. The sweeping, emotional, almost-too-intimate kisses of big-budget Hollywood movies. And with the added assurance that he was "sure as hell" coming back. Grace didn't need those assurances from Finn anymore. He knew that if he didn't come back, she would find him and *drag* him back. Will him back from the dead if she had to. Like she had in that Brooklyn warehouse last month.

"Pendejo...what did you give me?"

The slurred words drew Grace away from her contemplation of Neha and Joe's nascent relationship versus her and Finn's long-standing one. Estrada was struggling to sit up, swatting at the tubes circulating the blood through him. Nate was trying to keep him still, but he was only human. No match for a vampire's strength. Grace was glad she'd thought to tie him down with restraints.

PRETTY LITTLE LION   173

"You were sedated," she said, gesturing Nate back from the narrow bed with a sharp tilt of her head. "You'll get over it."

In her ear, there was battle. The volley of gunshots. Curses. In front of her eyes was a different sort of war. Emotional warfare. Intellectual. Getting Octavio Estrada to crack. And if he wouldn't crack... Well, they'd have to break him down into manageable parts.

Estrada scowled, flexing one muscled arm and then the other. To no avail. And then he fell back, his brown eyes hot like the depths of a coal stove. "Was this the plan all along? Why not bring me in last night?" he demanded.

Grace prided herself on not being petty. At least not in her professional life. Over monthly margaritas with her girls from the neighborhood? Sure. She let a little bit of salt slip into her voice anyway. "You know why this had to happen. But I'm sure the board of the Queensboro Community Hospital would be happy to explain."

Nate's eyebrows went sky-high. Finn was rubbing off on him already. Grace didn't laugh, though. She simply acknowledged his reaction with a nod before turning back to their guest. "You made the mistake of thinking you were in control of this situation, Mr. Estrada. You're not. You shouldn't underestimate us."

He smiled then. The kind of smile that probably made other people drench their underwear. "Only a fool would underestimate a woman like you," he assured her, thinking charm would get to her when anger hadn't. "I trust your other job is secure?"

She hadn't spent years working with Finian Conlan without learning how to resist charm. And there was no point in answering the question. They didn't have time for trivialities. Not while her friends and colleagues were putting themselves at risk. Grace muted her comm. She shut out Nate and Neha and the fluorescent lights and the medical equipment. And she leaned forward. Then she yanked the transfusion needle out of Estrada's arm.

"Is whatever you're doing for Mirko Aston worth your life?" she asked softly. "Because I hold it in my hands. Not because I'm a supernatural but because I'm a doctor. I can hurt you or I can heal you. That's your choice." She was lying, of course. "First do no harm" was sacred to her. But her poker face, her carefully neutral tone, had been honed from decades in medicine…and decades living in brown skin. She'd learned, at too high a cost, how to hide how she really felt.

Maybe Estrada knew that, as a brown man if not a vampire. He nodded, like they'd achieved some kind of accord. "I hear you," he said softly. "I understand you. But, Grace, understand that there are bigger things at work here than just you or me. Or our connections to Finian."

"What bigger things?" Nate interjected, ever the lawyer. He perched on the edge of the hospital bed like it was his table in a courtroom, eyes narrowed with speculation.

Grace appreciated the assist. A competent closer for her operation. "Yes, what bigger things?" she echoed softly. "It's of no use to us if you talk in generalities, Estrada."

"Who says I want to be of use to you?" He looked down at the already closed hole in the bend of his arm, from where she'd pulled the needle. "I've lived nearly two hundred years, Dr. Leung. Your threats don't scare me, and neither does death."

"Then what *are* you afraid of?" Nate asked.

Tavi didn't look at him. Didn't look at Grace. He stared off somewhere past the clear glass walls of the tiny clinic. "Not finishing what I started," he said eventually. After what felt like eons. "Not making right what I did wrong."

They were vulnerable answers, but as much as they told her, they also withheld. He was like Finn that way. She could see how and why the two had come together…and what had torn them apart. Like seeing a bleed she needed to tie off. "We can help you with that. Why won't you let us?"

"Because I can't." Estrada was paling, his eyes growing heavy. He hadn't been given enough blood yet to flush out the sedative, enough to put him at full fighting strength. He'd used up his small burst of energy already. But before he slipped back into the eerie, inhuman coma of the underfed undead, a single sentence slipped from his cracked lips.

"Because I promised her."

Her? Grace met Nate's eyes across the vampire's still form. He nodded, seeing the opening they'd both need to explore at the next available opportunity. "It's always a 'her,'" Neha observed dryly from her spot on the other side of the room. "Even when it's a 'him.' There's a 'her' somewhere in there."

Grace wasn't about to parse what *that* meant. Maybe that everyone had mommy issues on top of their daddy issues. She just went for another blood bag and hooked Estrada up again. First do no harm. That was the oath she'd taken. The oath she believed in. But there was so much harm in this terrible world. Harm that Estrada was aiding and abetting by virtue of his associations with Mirko Aston. Were they supposed to just let him? In the interest of allowing him to play out whatever his personal agenda was?

The white noise of the comm turning into an urgent hail saved her from addressing those tricky questions. "Hey! HQ!" JP barked. "Incoming! Prep the med bay for one! Two GSWs!"

"Go!" Nate said, shooing her toward the sinks and scrubs in the adjacent room. "Neha and I will keep our eyes on Estrada."

It could be any member of the team. It could be Finn. That was the way of emergency hails. Of all these missions. Of being a part of Third Shift. Grace put away the thoughts of doing harm and let her mind flood with her next priority. Healing whoever came in. Taking out the bullets. Sewing up the incisions. So they could go back out and be a hero all over again.

Octavio Estrada wanted to be a villain.

Maybe the best thing they could do was leave him to that.

A severed limb went flying past her. Maybe it was an arm. Maybe it was a leg. Meghna was too disoriented to identify anatomical parts. It felt like Elijah had been fighting for hours. Like the trek to their exit point, to safety, was miles away. Gunfire and screams echoed in her ears. But nothing touched her. No more bullets. Elijah made sure of that. There was a Hindu legend of one of the avatars of Vishnu. Half man, half lion, Narsimha had vanquished a "demon" king unable to be killed by any human. Swimming in and out of consciousness, jostled like a passenger on an airplane experiencing turbulence, Meghna thought of that avatar now. Elijah was no supposed god in disguise. His foes weren't portrayed as demons. There was no violent and virulent casteist baggage framing his story—at least not of the Indian variety. But he felt like a warrior of old. Snarling. Lashing out. Shielding her as best as he could against what seemed like countless gunmen fanning out across the grounds. Had Elijah said there were only six? She couldn't remember. But this was more than six. This was a mini army. She was clearly out of her mind with pain. Useless to him in a fight. It was a problem. Inconvenient.

"Let me." She shoved ineffectually at Elijah's shoulder somewhere between the main clubhouse and the parking lot, eventually slipping from his grasp and onto her own unsteady feet. There were two shooters right on their heels, gaining. She pulled the blades from her hair, from her belt, and turned, nailing one pursuer in the throat and the other through the eye of their balaclava. They fell like dominoes. Black clothing splashed with red.

And Meghna could feel herself following suit. Her head swam. Her knees jellied. The brief burst of action had drained what little energy she still had. Before she passed out—before strong arms caught her up again—she had only one thought: *Where did they even come from?*

The question was still with her when she came back to

consciousness, however brief, in the back of an SUV. "We rescued your stuff from Jack's place. No bugs, no tags," she heard a vaguely familiar voice rasp from somewhere beyond her immediate vicinity. "No fucking clue how these bastards found you."

"Well, someone better get a fucking clue," Elijah growled. "I don't want a repeat." He was close. Near her ear. His thigh was warm beneath her head. And that was all she knew for a while.

When Meghna awoke again, it was indoors. Under bright fluorescent lights. *Safe.* There was no way of knowing that except she did. And the feeling of security was…uncomfortable. Worse than the throbs of agony in her upper arm and her thigh. She wasn't supposed to let her guard down. Couldn't drop her defenses. "Stop," she heard herself say, though she couldn't have said what precisely she was trying to stop.

"Shh." The rumble of Elijah's voice anchored her to a *now*, to a *here*. "We've got you, love. Gracie's got you. Just hang in there. You'll be right as rain soon enough."

No. No, she wouldn't. Meghna was never going to be right again.

The room is dim. For security as much as ambiance. She can't see her superior clearly. Just a sense of dark hair and dark eyes. Of supernatural light—what some might call an aura. "Are you up to this, Meghna?" the hypnotic voice asks. "This will take months, perhaps even years, of your life. And you will be entirely on your own."

"I can do it," she says without even pausing for breath, for debate. "I'm perfectly positioned. My quasi-celebrity status will be an irresistible lure for this mark. To waste this opportunity would be foolish."

"What's foolish is underestimating the toll this will take on you. We are supernatural, but we are still vulnerable, Meghna."

"We're Vidrohi," she counters. "That's all that matters."

Her superior laughs. For a long time. Uncomfortably long. Until Meghna, with all her media training and poise, is squirming in her seat. "That's not all that matters, betiya. Maybe you'll learn that before I did."

She recognizes her mother then. In the dimness. In this anonymous room in the middle of nowhere. And she wants to flip over the table between them. Almost as much as she wants to cry and scream. "You don't get to say that to me," she says softly, shoving down any other wild impulse. "Not when you walked away."

The first slice of the scalpel brought Meghna back to where she needed to be.

The second let her scream like she'd wanted to that day.

The third…she didn't feel the third. And she told herself she didn't feel Elijah's hand in hers either.

Then she felt nothing.

Nothing except the purpose she'd almost forgotten.

20

____

MEGHNA WAS OUT COLD FOR nearly a day after Gracie took out the bullets. Elijah barely left her side. He watched her body erase her once wounds with a vigilance like his mum's watchful eyes over him and his sisters. It was unsettling. Seeing the supernatural power enact upon her while she slept. Not so different from his own transformations but also completely different. Hers made her the beauty. His made him the beast.

There was a metaphor in that. He didn't want to unpack it. Meghna's pale-brown skin was her ticket to so many things that his darker skin didn't allow him access to. She counted on being fetishized for how she looked…and then struck, a weapon who was afraid to show remorse. Meanwhile, he was assumed violent at first glance. She'd been raised to be a killer. He'd been taught by Mum and Dad to present as anything but. And then the service had made one of him anyway.

By all rights, he and Meghna should've been enemies. Both the UK and the U.S. had been stirring that pot of hatred for decades. India too. Her lot despised his because it made them feel better, whiter. But the last thing he felt for her was hate. Or disgust for how she'd chosen to fight the injustices in the world. No. The emotions churning inside him, within the beast who lived at his core, were so much softer. As soft as the hair at her temple. As the curve of her mouth under his fingertips.

"Meg," he said because he couldn't stay silent at arse o'clock in the morning. "Meg, come back to me. We're not finished yet. Not with Aston. Not with each other."

She didn't stir. He hadn't expected her to. Not just because he'd said something passably romantic. That wasn't the sort of woman she was. No flowers. No movie dates. Not for this one. A beautiful badass who'd met him in a closet minutes after their first words were exchanged. Meghna needed explosions. Intrigue. A good blade. And a plan.

Elijah pulled his hand back from the fall of her hair on the pillow. His wrist comm vibrated with a message. Briefing and debriefing @ 0600.

"We'll get him," he said aloud. "Meghna, Estrada *will* cough up the auction details. Aston's not won yet."

Her eyes flashed open. Cold. Assessing. Clinical. He knew what that meant even before she spoke. Before she sat up stiffly, ripping the bandages from her arm and her bared upper thigh and tossing them aside. She was all in for the game...and nothing else. Walls up. Shields activated. Near death, or even just a hell of a lot of pain, had a way of doing that to a person. To a career operative. "How do you know that for sure? When do we move out?" she demanded as if she hadn't just slept the day away after multiple GSWs and major surgery.

"Easy does it, love." Elijah put his hands out, as if that alone could urge her back into the hospital bed. "Aston doesn't have to be your first priority. You just woke up."

"It's my *only* priority," she assured fiercely. "Anything else is a waste of precious time."

"Is it?" He arched an eyebrow. Then, when she didn't rise to the bait, he arched them both. Finn would be so proud. "Come on now, Meghna. Do you remember anything before you took those hits?" he prompted. "Because I do. I remember tasting every inch of you. And you doing the same to me. Putting that tongue of yours places no one's ever been."

She didn't even react to the gloriously lurid memory, her expression as flat as though he'd recited a laundry list. It would've hurt had he not anticipated it. "Do you know how many men I've fucked, Elijah?" she asked, her tone that of a bored socialite sneering down at someone not worth her time. "You're too old, too long in this business, to be this naive. That was nothing." She hurled these words with precision, like throwing stars. "*You* are nothing to me."

Their aim and trajectory were flawless. He still knew they were lies. He and Meghna had shared more than just some hard fucks these past several days. No matter how determined she was to pretend otherwise. He'd caught a glimpse of her soft underbelly. His beautiful, deadly assassin queen. A lioness in every way but blood.

"If I were nothing, baby girl, you wouldn't have to say it." The endearment with the pull of Patwah did exactly what he expected it to: infuriate her. Her cheeks flushed. Her eyes blazed. She was fucking stunning as she launched at him with a growl. Like she'd never been wounded, never faced death.

And he welcomed it, welcomed *her*. He half shifted, meeting her as what he truly was: a man and a king. As she landed a punch to his broadened shoulder, he lowered his fanged mouth to hers, taking infinite care to only nibble with his lips.

"Fuck you!" she cried, twisting in his grip and leaning into it at the same time, heedless of her newly healed arm, uncaring of her reknitted thigh.

It was everything, not nothing. This battle. This dance. This ritual. He was already a little bit in love with her. Maybe he had been from the very start. Meghna cursed and moaned in turns. Her legs went from kicking at him to winding around his hips. She wrapped his locs around one fist and tugged until the pleasure-pain coursed through him. He nipped at her throat just hard enough to bruise. It wasn't the calculated sex in a closet or her hotel suite or the frantic adrenaline rush in the car. Or even the idyllic interlude at the safe house, where they'd laid themselves bare. It was...a claiming. Flesh and spirit belying and overriding her defenses. His too.

Because this was what Meghna didn't understand. She wasn't the only one floundering in new territory. She wasn't the only one feeling flayed wide open by more than bullets. Lije was sodding terrified by wanting someone this much, needing someone this intensely. And the only way to quell the terror was to *have* her.

Clothing was hardly a barrier. A bed? Unnecessary. Did it even matter that the med bay was under surveillance? *No*. In just a few reckless moments, he was inside her. Clutching her with clawed hands as she took and took his cock. "That's it, baby girl," he panted as he stroked the shell of her ear with his tongue, rocked into her warmth, let her feel the truth of him. *Know* the truth of him.

And it only spurred her on. She fucked him violently, angrily, in a way that only proved how much more than fucking it was. They crashed into the wall. His pants around his knees, shirt torn to shreds. She punished him with her pelvis even as her sweet cunt rewarded him again and again.

"I'm. Not. Your. Baby. Girl." She punctuated each clash of their bodies with a harsh syllable.

"But you *are* mine, Meghna. Just like I'm yours."

Call it a mate bond. Call it fate. Call it seren-fucking-dipity. But Elijah was tied to this remarkable woman now. For better or worse. So he stole every last second of ecstasy he could. Until they were weary and worn and their limbs no longer supported their combined weight. When they'd gone to the floor and she'd wrung every last drop of come from him and she had no voice left to swear at him.

"You've got me, Meg," he gasped out, hoarse and sweat-slick. "I will always be here for you. Always." She turned her face into his neck and simply shuddered. But she didn't let him go. "Briefing's at oh-six-hundred," he told her softly. "We'll roll out after that."

———————

"This is bullshit!" Jackson exploded, his face even whiter than normal with rage. "The academy was secure. They shouldn't have been able to track us there, but they did. And I need to know *how*."

The hit squad hadn't breached his private suite. Or the secret room in the tack house. But Safe House 13 was still compromised. Their cofounder had managed to keep his temper under wraps for those tense hours when the reinforcements had gone in and after when Grace had been operating on Meghna and the cleaning crew had taken care of the bodies. But now? Now, there was no leash on his emotions. He pivoted on one foot, pinning each and every one of them in the conference room with his cold glare. Every inch the privileged, upper-class, society man he'd been raised to be. Staring condescendingly at those he deemed less worthy.

Grace hated this side of Jackson Tate. They all did. Even while knowing that it was this side of him that funded most of their operations. He'd been born into money, into prestige and power. An old New England family, an Ivy League legacy. While most of the men of his ilk and his age group had been radicalized to the right wing in Reddit forums and Facebook groups, he'd gone the opposite route…leaning more and more left the more actual war he saw. But he was still your basic angry white man at heart. And he still expected every single thing to go his way.

She was too exhausted for *his* bullshit. After pulling two slugs out of Meghna Saxena. After the verbal fencing with Tavi Estrada. All Grace wanted to do was clock out and take the R or the N train home to Queens. She wanted to put aside the dark distraction in Finn's eyes as he looked off in the direction of the med bay. She wanted to ignore how Elijah, their strength and their foundation, looked as though he'd been hit by a wrecking ball. She wanted to fight. She wanted to hurt someone. That, above all, was why she needed to get the hell out of here.

She pushed away from the conference table, startling Finn on her left and Joaquin on her right and causing Jack's gaze to snap to hers with alarm. "We've been working our asses off, and I understand your frustration, but you don't need to take it out on us," she said to him in her Dr. Freeze voice. "Security breaches on *your* property are a *you* problem. Third Shift has kept a safe house there banking on *your* word that it would stay secure."

"Fuck." He winced, rocking back on the heels of his overpriced loafers. "You're right, Grace. I'm sorry."

And there again was that benefit to being the Wendy among the Lost Boys. As much as she hated it, it defused tension and solved entirely too many intra-team squabbles. Neha's recent addition to the group was bound to shift the balance, taking some of the pressure off her shoulders, but for now Grace was still the one person who could regularly hold her bosses and her coworkers accountable for their shitty behavior. "Tell us how to fix this," she said, shoving all of the accountability and responsibility back where it belonged. "What do we do now?"

"You go to the auction." It wasn't Jackson who answered. Or Elijah. The voice belonged to the man in the doorway—a refreshed and revitalized Latinx vampire with a wary lawyer standing just behind him. "Meet Mirko on his turf," said Tavi Estrada, his copper eyes hot and intense. "Make him pay for what he did on yours."

"And what about *you*, Tav?" Finn spoke now. So uncharacteristically quiet when the team had returned from Brooklyn and during the debrief but not in this moment. Not as his eyes flicked from Estrada to Nate to her and back again. Oh, what a tangled web they'd woven. "What do you reckon we should do with you?" he demanded.

Grace wasn't the least bit surprised when Estrada crossed the threshold into Command and helped himself to an empty chair. "Let me go," he said, spreading his hands wide in a theatrical gesture. "I won't get in your way if you don't get in mine."

He was still dressed in the clothes Finn had brought him in wearing. Dark jeans. A maroon button-down shirt. A tan scarf and a tailored black wool coat, both more for fashion than for any concession toward the weather. She hadn't seen any point in undressing him while prepping him for transfusion. Maybe she should have. Perhaps it would dull the impact somewhat of this dynamic creature in a room full of dynamic creatures. But then again, Meghna was here. Recovered from her wounds. Sitting at the foot of the table in an oversized T-shirt and sweatpants. And she outshone them all. An apsara, Elijah had explained while Grace bent over the hole in her thigh. Some sort of unearthly Indian nymph. *"She'll heal as soon as you get the lead out, she says. Like nothing was ever even there."*

Estrada, too, looked as though he'd never been knocked out. A man in his prime. A *vampire* in his prime. But he had a weakness. Someone he'd kept a promise to. *Her*, he'd said. Grace slowly rolled her chair back toward the table. She reached for Finn's hand and interlaced their fingers. The cool sensation of his skin flush against hers was calming, centering, and suddenly she didn't want to go home nearly as much as she wanted to stay.

"You never got in my way before," Meghna said from her seat, pitching her voice across the room like a trained actress. "But you never interceded on my behalf either. Or on *anyone's* behalf. Is that what you're proposing now, Tavi? More of the same?"

"It better not be," Finn put in before his ex could reply. "Because we damn well expect more from one another than that, and you're among us now whether you want to be or not. That *counts* for something, Tav. Maybe you don't want to tell us what sort of game you're playing, but I'll be damned if you leave us to swing."

He was conveniently leaving out that he'd forcibly deposited Estrada among them. But Grace didn't disagree with Finn's point. Third Shift wasn't the best or the biggest black ops and security outfit in the country. They didn't get all of the big-money government contracts or the glory. They more often blundered into success than they strode deliberately. But what they had down, where they excelled, was in the trust they'd built with each other. She knew, without a doubt, that most of the people in this room—and Nate hanging back just on the other side of the doorway—would lay down their lives for her. The unknown quantities, Tavi Estrada and Meghna Saxena-Saunders, needed to sign on or shove off.

0600. That was when they were slated to break and roll out for their respective downtimes or departures. It was 5:56 a.m., according to Grace's phone. The remaining four minutes ticked down in tense silences and hushed whispers. In Elijah and Meghna trading smoldering, too-intimate looks and Finn squeezing her thigh beneath the table as he tried to maintain his composure. In Joaquin pulling out their tablet and Neha calling JP over to look at hers.

"Okay," Tavi said as 5:59 a.m. rolled to six. "You've got a deal." As if one had been put on the table. "I'll help in any way that I can."

"I know how you can start." Elijah rose from his chair, cracking his neck and rolling his shoulders. His locs seemed to grow several inches before their very eyes. "Tell us all about Mirko's little auction. And his big, bloody shape-shifter serum."

21

TAVI COULDN'T REMEMBER THE LAST time he'd been amid so many do-gooders—the virtue rolling off of them in waves, their eyes full of expectation as he made an untraceable call to Mirko. The would-be emperor of the western world barked a sharp "yes" into his mobile before launching into a barrage of insults at Tavi's parentage and his future spawn. Never mind that, as a vampire, the latter were implausible. The man didn't waste thought on such details. He did, however, waste a surplus of breath on things any supervillain worth his salt ought to keep to himself.

"These American mobsters are such fools. Aleksei's successor is of no use to me. His shipments have been seized twice in the last three weeks. Idiot!" Aston vented, as though he were talking to his therapist and not someone who'd sooner rip out his throat than listen to such prattle.

Half the room had cleared, clocking out, going off to separate operations, but Tavi was still very aware of his audience. Finian, the delicious and dangerous Ms. Grace, the silver-haired lawyer, the man who'd introduced himself simply as "Tate." Meghna and Elijah Richter—whose survival was giving Mirko fits.

He was on his third or fourth paragraph of a rant about how

they'd evaded capture after the clinic when Tavi decided to take pity on everyone listening in on the call and interrupt. "What do you mean they evaded capture? I was under the impression they'd been handled. Otherwise I would have offered my expertise."

Mirko spat a curse in Slovak. "They disappeared after crossing the border into New York. What am I paying my people for? Not this incompetence!"

Tavi saw the moment that the realization struck the Third Shift operatives. So many narrowed eyes and huffed exhalations. If Mirko's men hadn't been behind the assault on their safe house... *who had*? This was not a question he asked. No. "I trust those you are paying to arrange the auction are more trustworthy?" he prompted instead.

"I'm paying *you* to arrange the auction," Mirko snarled like the shape-shifter he wished he could be.

Technically, Tavi had been paid to facilitate the transfer of the serum. Which he'd done. But again, Aston was not a man interested in accuracy. Only the broad strokes. "Then you have nothing to worry about," he assured Mirko. "It will all play out as you require." And as *he* required. Every beat of this play was designed to move him closer to his goal.

He wrapped up the call soon after the dose of ass-kissing, handing the burner phone back to Tate. "Satisfied?"

"Far from," the man said, eyeing the device like it was a live snake. And then he gave voice to his most pressing concern. "If your boss didn't order the hit squad on the riding school, then who the hell did?"

"Particularly vengeful paparazzi?" Meghna suggested, arching one beautifully sculpted eyebrow. "I felt certain that I was the target. Chalk that one up to a celebrity ego."

One could almost believe she meant it. Except that Tavi recognized the detachment in her voice, the coldness in her dark eyes.

She was like him. She wore many masks. One for every day of the week, two on Saturdays. He'd seen that the first time she'd been allowed entry into Aston's inner circle. Upgraded from party-scene arm candy to someone who could circulate among the criminal element. A woman of her caliber would not choose such company without an agenda. He still didn't know what it was. And he had no desire to share his own. No matter how hard these operatives tried to break him.

You couldn't break someone who'd shattered into pieces more than a century ago. Finian had tried, in his way. And he was far from the only one. *She would hate what you've become...and she would understand it.* Tavi scowled at the errant thought. He'd spent a long time tucking such things away. Scrubbing any trace of her from his mind, as though a psychic might scrape his brain at any second. Why was it leaking out now? In this nest of heroes? What had been in that needle Finian jabbed him with in the FiDi? Liquid vulnerability? Superman's Kryptonite?

The operatives were still arguing potential new threats when he broke from his ruminations and came back to the present. Tavi did not envy them the task of ferreting out the threat. When you'd lived as long as he had, you made a lot of enemies. But their enemies weren't his problem. None of this was his problem. His only conundrum in this moment was getting the hell out of this office building and back to the bosom of Mirko Aston's organization.

So Tavi smiled. The kind of smile Meghna Saunders would appreciate. Full of sex and secrets. "Are we done here yet?" he asked lightly. "I've got things to do."

Things to do, people to betray. No matter how good these operatives were, no matter how much good they *wanted* to do, Tavi couldn't let them reel him in. They were Third Shift. He had a first priority. A vow to keep. A promise to see through.

Meghna hated mirrors. For all that she'd made her name through her beauty, she loathed being reminded of who she was and the image she presented. Sitting across from Octavio Estrada was like sitting across from a pane of reflective glass. Perhaps it was the same for him. And perhaps that was why he made his exit swiftly. So that he, too, wouldn't have to sit face-to-face with his own sins.

"We'll tail him, of course," Jackson assured her mere seconds after the vampire's departure. "He'll know it, but that's not the point."

What *was* the point? She was still trying to figure that out. Why was she here? Why had she come this far with Elijah Richter? All she'd done up to this moment was deviate from her path. She'd endangered her simple goal of finding Ayesha and ending Aston's plans, whatever they might be. And for what? *No. You mean "for who?"* All of this had been for *him*. There was no obscuring the facts. Meghna had blundered into the middle of a romance novel when her entire life thus far had been a spy thriller.

The echo of fucking Elijah just an hour ago was still on every inch of her skin. That beautiful violence. How he'd met her blows with kisses and caresses, shifted to match her anger and master it. He'd known he couldn't placate her with sweetness. So he'd given her the bitter. The dark. Her thighs still ached with it. Not the remnant of the bullet she'd taken. Just the remnant of the sex she'd had. That *they'd* had. She had no doubt that there were half-healed scratches under Elijah's T-shirt. Furrows from her nails. Marks of her weakness. She'd never left them on a man before. Never let herself go so wild. Even flying high on X in her midtwenties. Not with the man whose last name she'd kept…who was in the ICU, fighting for his life, *because of her*.

But Elijah? All he'd had to do was look at her to take down her walls. What kind of operative did that make her? Not a very good one. Probably a worse operative than she'd been a wife—which was saying something. She almost hated Elijah a little for how he'd burrowed to the core of her. Not just with his cock but with his steady, honest heart. Decades of constructing her barriers, of reinforcing her defenses, and he'd torn them down like tissue paper. Easily. And yet she couldn't regret the sex, even though it had been an epically bad decision. He was a fantastic lover. An even more fantastic person. Someone who, like Chase, deserved far better than to be entangled with her.

Meghna shuddered, rising from the cushy leather seat and following Joaquin and the other operatives out of the room. She didn't spare a glance for the big, beautiful man who occupied so many of her thoughts. He was under her skin already. In her blood. Looking at him wouldn't change any of that. But it might just make it a little worse.

Focus, Meghna. Her old mental mantra had proven useless, hadn't it? But there it was, whispering through her mind anyway as she stalked up the aisle of the open office floor. An exercise in futility. Because the chatter of Third Shift was rising around her, a reminder of what the Vidrohi lacked out of necessity. Camaraderie. Connection. *Joy.* She'd blocked so much out. Pushed so many people away. High-school friends. Dance mates in the Indian Students Association and FOGANA—where she'd been a non-Gujarati ringer helping win raas and garba competitions. Business-school classmates. Influencers, models, makeup artists she'd met through her professional endeavors. Even Em, her supposedly trusted personal assistant, only assisted her with a curated list of personal things. She was the woman everybody wanted to be and the woman nobody knew. Until now. Until Elijah. He'd learned more about her in just a few days than even her own father had discovered in three decades.

She wanted to wrap her arms around herself, to ward off the feeling of being stripped naked. But Meghna let her hands hang casually at her sides as Joaquin stopped her and apologized for the Instagram photos they'd mocked up not being a sufficient cover.

"It's fine," she said with a lightness she didn't feel. "Your work was impeccable. It's not your fault that Mirko didn't believe I'd flown off to Ibiza without him." No, the fault was solely hers. Pictures of an impulsive jaunt to a party hot spot meant nothing when she'd blown her own cover by getting caught on-camera at Dr. Schoenlein's facility. *Like an amateur.* One of the girls fresh from the training camp nestled in the mountains. The girl she'd once been and never would be again.

"Why me? Why now?" The questions tear from her throat like bandages ripped off wounds. "I didn't ask for this."

"Nobody asks for this." Her mother, her trainer, her cool-eyed jailer, tucks the contraband mobile phone into the pocket of her puffy down jacket. "It's what we are given by virtue of who we were born."

"I didn't ask to be born either!" she points out. "You planned that. You can't even call it an act of love, because you and Dad sure as hell didn't love each other." Being raised by divorced parents, by people who can barely tolerate each other and speak only through lawyers, is common in her friend group back home, but being the daughter of a celestial being who basically gave her up at birth definitely is not.

The dark eyes that look so much like her own—it's like looking at a mirror image—are equal parts pitying and oddly warm. The General, as they call her behind her back, reaches out and tucks a strand of hair back under Meghna's toque. "This is my act of love, Meghna. I'm preparing you for a world that has always hated us and always will."

Her mother had prepared her to face it *alone*. Something that Meghna had thought necessary. She'd bought the rhetoric. Leaned in to those old mythological stories of the apsara as a decoration and a tool of the mercurial gods. Signed on to the Vidrohi bylaws, as it were. And here she was now, thirty-five years old, wishing she were part of a team. *A family.* Was that irony? Stupidity? Or hope?

Maybe it was even more than that. Maybe it was her own act of love.

22

FUCK IT ALL TO HELL. Someone else was after them. Not a surprise, really. They'd made a lot of enemies in their time. What it *was*, though, was a needless complication. Something to split their focus and exploit their vulnerabilities. Elijah didn't like it. He didn't trust it. And from the look of Jack when the room cleared, neither did he.

"Dammit," he cried, tossing a chair across the room with a violent thrust of magic. "I really liked that property. And now I have to sell it off."

Right. So much for being on the same page. It was a cold-slap reminder of just how much Jack had in assets, in ready cash. Of just how different their worlds were no matter how united they were in running Third Shift. Jack was *old* money. Silver cuff links for every suit. Real estate in four major cities. "You can buy another," Elijah pointed out, tacking on a caustic "your lordship" for good measure.

"Sorry." His old friend flinched, the power still crackling from his fingertips. "I deserved that," he acknowledged.

That and more. But they'd have to put a pin in the ongoing discussion of Jack's white privilege. There were much bigger fish to fry. Probably sodding Jaws or one of those kaiju from *Pacific Rim*. Elijah tapped the tablet in front of him, pulling up the schematics for the riding school, already scrubbed of any evidence that the hit squad had been there. And already sanitized of 3S's presence, too. "What are we going to do about the breach, mate?"

"*You* are going to this auction." Jackson grimaced, dragging both hands through his absurdly well-groomed hair. "*I* will worry about the breach on Safe House 13. How the hell did it get compromised? Are you sure you weren't followed?"

There was no way to be one hundred percent sure of that. Between hackable surveillance drones and skyborne shape-shifters. But Elijah was reasonably certain he and Meghna had done the job of covering their tracks on the way from Connecticut to South Brooklyn. *Meghna.* "Speaking of compromised…" It was his turn to wince.

The tension drained from Jack's shoulders at that. He tipped back his head and laughed, all bright eyes and deep dimples. Showing off why they'd all nicknamed him "Pretty Boy" in the desert. "She's got you good, huh?"

"Up to my neck," Elijah confessed all too readily. He felt no shame in admitting it. There were worse things a man could say he'd done than fall too hard for a beautiful woman.

They didn't have time to dissect his love life any more than they had time to go over the advantages of Jack's whiteness. But Elijah appreciated the breath. The pause. Even the laugh at his expense. Outside the windows, conveniently unfrosted after the briefing, he could see Meghna on the floor. Speaking to Finn and Grace and Joaquin. Charming them, no doubt. Like she charmed everyone. The gorgeous girl at the party. He'd followed her into the closet at the Manhattan Grand thinking he'd hooked her, but she'd hooked him.

"This too much for you, Lije?" Jack grinned at him. Smug bastard. He had a lively public social life dating actresses and pop stars that landed him in the gossip columns every other week, but no one he'd ever felt seriously about. He could cast stones from his glass house.

"No, it's not too much for me. And she's no threat to us," he assured Jackson of the question he knew better than to even ask. As reckless as he'd been, as stupid as lust and other things he couldn't name had made him, Elijah was wise enough not to bring a powerful enemy right into the heart of Third Shift. He'd given Finn the same benefit of the doubt when it came to bringing in Tavi Estrada. Maybe they led with their hearts along with their heads, but their hearts seldom steered them wrong. "She's a good person. Even though she doesn't want to be."

Because that *was* Meg, wasn't it? His ruthless assassin, his single-minded seductress. She thought fighting for justice meant she didn't have to fight for herself, for her integrity. But it was there anyway. Shining so brightly. She was brilliant and strong and kind. Sharp edges and soft curves. He had only just begun to know her, and he wasn't done learning. What made her laugh? What made her sing? How did she look beneath a man when she trusted him completely? He might die during this mission—as he could during any mission—and if he didn't find out, he would be dying in vain.

"Christ." Jackson exhaled loudly, shaking his head. "You're a mess, Lije. I hope I'm never where you are." And wasn't *that* a surefire way to ensure that he'd be exactly where Elijah was soon enough?

He knew better than to point that out. Whenever Jack's number came up, he'd learn for himself. How swift and hard the descent was. How bloody beautiful the view was. How once you were in it, you never wanted to leave. It was paradise. Like the islands. And just as susceptible to natural disasters. To *super*natural disasters. He'd have to be prepared to lose Meghna and prepared to fight for her. And he was more than ready for it.

Elijah swiped through the mission files on his tablet until he reached the coordinates for their next destination. The building layout, already marked for entry and exit points thanks to Joaquin's speedy work. No hotels this time. No research facilities. This was one of Mirko's holdings through a shell corporation. A private hunting lodge and event center in the Finger Lakes region. One road in. Surrounded by woods. Wired for electric but not internet or Wi-Fi. Minimal cell towers in the area. It screamed "horror movie." Even came with its own vampire, if you factored in Estrada. Anyone willing to go out there with a bunch of other criminal types had to be off their rocker. Or just that desperate for what the serum could do.

Neither option worked in Third Shift's favor. Which fell in line with their run of rotten luck so far. Normally, their ops ran like a well-oiled machine. Both stateside and overseas. They'd sent JP on several short-burst missions abroad while his case dominated the news, and he and his teammates had reported no hiccups, no deviations from SOP. So why now? Why so many fuckups so close to home? Elijah couldn't help but think their unknown quantity—whoever had sent the gunmen to take out him and Meg—had something to do with it.

"Someone doesn't want us going after Mirko and his lot," he concluded aloud. Someone with even more power than an international arms dealer who had a small cache of missiles and chemical weapons at his disposal. Someone for whom the best possible outcome was that shape-shifter serum going to the highest bidder. "I think yesterday was their way of letting us know it."

A grunt of displeasure sounded from the other side of the conference table, where Jack had been busying himself righting the furniture his little sorcery fit had upturned. He popped around to Elijah's seat, frowning down at the blueprints still displayed on his screen. "So there's a bigger predator in this food chain. First the local bosses and vors like Vasiliev. Then Aston. Then…who? How far up does this go?" His brows winged together as he cursed under his breath. For all that he was high society, he had a mouth like he'd grown up in a gutter. "I can't even go to my DoD contacts with this. It's too sensitive."

"The call might be coming from inside the house," Lije agreed. "Or the Senate." It would've been a joke but for the fact that Congress was loaded with duplicitous arseholes who wanted nothing more than to finish the destruction they'd put into motion in 2016. And when you tossed in Homeland Security, the CIA, and the Supernatural Regulation Bureau? No matter the secret committee Jackson himself reported to, it was entirely too dangerous to let on to anyone that Third Shift was under attack. They had to proceed with extreme caution.

———

It felt almost anticlimactic to return to Finn's underground quarters when the meeting broke up. Or maybe it just felt natural—normal—for the three of them to go home. Grace couldn't explain why the inanity of it bothered her. Watching first Finn, then Nate cross the threshold, then take off their shoes in concert and set them in the rack in the entryway. Maybe because Finn had been gone with Estrada and then gone to Safe House 13. And Nate had been avoiding them for more than twice that amount of time. This was like picking up a conversation they'd started weeks ago after a long interruption. Only none of them spoke.

They hadn't said a word to each other after Meghna broke off from the group and went back to the conference room. As they took the elevator together, each processing their respective thoughts. A wonder, truly, considering how rarely Finn was silent. But he hadn't been himself for a few days now, had he? She was used to making diagnoses, to making assumptions, but that one felt a bit convenient. A bit selfish. Because there was another, equally reasonable explanation. This was just a side of him she'd never seen. A side he'd kept hidden for decades.

And he was sharing it with her and Nate now. As he stripped off his jacket and then his shirt. As he went for the tie Nate had loosened at some point in the past twenty-four hours—the buttons he'd undone while keeping Grace company in the med bay—and finished the job. Finn was as talented and efficient at undressing other people as he was at dressing himself. Though he did pause to press one kiss to the bared column of Nate's throat. And another to the inside of his wrist. When the men were both as naked as the days they'd been born, Finn finally broke the awkwardly comfortable silence. "Who's up for a shower? The hotter the better."

Grace didn't have to be told twice. She'd been on her feet for what felt like a week. Her fingers still felt stiff from wielding the scalpel and tweezers to take the bullets out of Meghna. Her shoulders ached. Maybe her heart ached, too. She whipped her clothes off, left her bra and underwear on the floor alongside Finn's silk boxers and Nate's more practical briefs. She didn't wait for them to precede her this time. She took the lead, heading down the hall to the bedroom and the en suite, putting up her hair as she walked. Finn kept silk wraps and shower caps for her visits, and she helped herself to the latter from the drawers beneath the dual sinks before continuing deeper into the master bath.

Once in the open-plan shower that could easily fit six people— should Finn ever feel so ambitious—she turned the taps, stepped under one of three rainfall showerheads, and let the steam rise up the tiles. *God, that feels good.* Her muscles nearly wept from the relief of the deliciously hot water and the perfectly pressured spray. And then they did cry…from the sweet, sharp, sensation of Finn's lips on the back of her neck. Her shoulder. The meaty flesh of her upper arm.

"Love bites." He chuckled as shivers of pleasure danced along her skin, at odds with the temperature of the water.

"Do you need to feed?" she murmured, tipped her head back, offering her neck.

"No. I just need you, Grace of my heart," he said, pulling her back against him. "You and this other one here."

"Can't scrub your back without help, huh?" Nate drawled, leaning against the dark-tiled wall, beneath the second showerhead. His prematurely gray hair darkened under the water, matching the dark whorls of hair on his chest and between his legs. And he looked to Grace like some sort of lean, long-limbed water spirit. He'd let Finn take off his clothes readily enough, but now he was holding him accountable. *See us. Hear us. Acknowledge us*, he seemed to be saying without actually using those words.

"Can't do anything without help," Finn bantered back as he stroked her hips and the tops of her thighs. As if he was reacquainting himself with her body. His touch was as exploratory as it was sensual. "Can't do anything without you. Without either of you," he added, mouth hot—hotter than the water—along the shell of her ear.

Grace wanted nothing more than to surrender to that mouth. To that seductive whisper. But she couldn't shake off the unease from earlier—the idea that they'd skipped things, fast-forwarded past the problem points in a movie. "Is that your guilty conscience talking?"

"I don't have a conscience," Finn lied cheerfully.

"Objection, Your Honor," Nate said, crossing the few feet between them. Coming close, so he stood just a breath away. "Witness is perjuring himself."

"I am not." She felt the outraged huff on her skin. More for effect than any actual release of air. "I'm not that flexible, for one."

Oh, *there* was the Finn they both recognized. Shaking with mirth at his own joke. Blue eyes bright when she twisted to meet them. Grace scowled at him. "Be serious first," she said. "Be honest. Then we'll let you play."

"Ah, Grace. I told you before. I'm always honest with you. Tav doesn't have a hold on me. Not like you think. Not like this." He squeezed her in a half hug, their wet, naked skin slicking together. "And spending time with him didn't bring anything back but regret that I chose to change but he didn't."

"What about me, Conlan? Where do I fit in?" Nate demanded, as was his right.

"Right here, I hope." Finn reached out with his other arm, obliterating that tiny but pivotal inch that held Nate apart, pulling him flush against them both. So she felt his erection hard along her side. "If that's where you want to be."

"Grace?" Nate tilted her chin toward him with two fingers. "What about you? Don't let him steamroll you into this just because he always does. Do you want this?"

He was so sweet. So gallant. Looking out for her even after their talk on the way back from Queensboro. Even after she'd assured him she knew what she had with Finn. Grace had half a mind to bite his fingertips. She licked them instead. "What is it that you said to me? I wouldn't be here if I didn't." Maybe not the exact words, but the same sentiment.

They were enough. For now at least. For Nate's mouth on hers and on Finn's. For too many soap suds and a few bumped noses. For hands and dicks and gasps and moans. If none of them managed to say "I love you"...well, that was all right. That was for a different day in front of the judge. A different day in what she was coming to see as their lives from here on out.

The conversation they'd begun all those weeks ago wasn't over. It was just beginning.

23

ELIJAH LIVED ON THE TOP floor of 3S HQ, in one of the two luxury apartments. "Perks of the job," Jackson liked to call it, especially seeing as how he lived in the other one. There were other, smaller units scattered throughout the building—including the underground lair that Finn called his own. Danny Yeo and his new bride had just taken over one. Joaquin ran their hacker empire from another. Lije had been tempted to become their neighbor when his teaching term at the Westchester Military School just outside of the city had ended two years ago. It burned him to even consider moving into a place that could fit the flat he'd grown up in into one room. Even his staff quarters at the school had been spare. But Jack put his Ferragamo-clad foot down. *"Absolutely not. You've earned your way to the top, my friend. You've paid for it and then some. Now let yourself enjoy it."*

He'd never seen Jack's point, never appreciated it, until he brought Meghna home after the morning briefing. Not that she spent much time admiring or exploring the space—which he'd furnished in dark woods and chromes from IKEA and Crate & Barrel, because you could give a man a posh pad, but you couldn't make him buy a $6,000 credenza. No, Meghna turned to *him* in the open living room, her gaze barely lingering on the high ceilings, the tall windows. She spent maybe moments more taking in the football posters on the walls and the record collection he'd been amassing since he was fourteen. *He* was all that mattered to her, not his fancy digs. But as he looked back at her, met those gorgeous eyes, all he could think was that she looked *good* here. She looked like she belonged in a place like this. And maybe that meant he belonged in it, too.

She arched an eyebrow. Her lips tilted in a rueful smile. The spokesmodel, the brand ambassador, saying everything with a single expression. "So this is you."

"Mm-hmm." He slipped his arms around her, pleased when she didn't resist. When she nestled in. Meghna Saunders, a cuddler. Who knew?

But her next words belied the physical softness. They were hard. Cynical. From social butterfly to black widow. "Aren't you afraid someone's going to burn it down now that I'm here?"

No. He was afraid of a lot of things, but not that. He dropped a kiss on the top of her head. That high hairdo with its deadly pins. And then he kissed the side of her equally sharp face. The bow of her scimitar mouth. "The only arsonists here are us, love," he told her. "You and me. Setting my bed on fire."

She didn't offer a counterargument. Maybe it was easier to speak with her body. With how she fiercely kissed him back and frenetically tore at his clothes. They stumbled through his fancy apartment, leaving bits of discarded clothing in their wake. Burning a trail to his bedroom. All the places they'd bruised and scratched just hours ago in the med bay, they now stroked and licked. Was that their cycle then? Violence and then tenderness? Frenzy and then the beautifully slow burn? He'd take it. Revel in it. He'd earned it, hadn't he? Now he was determined to enjoy it.

Later, much later, Elijah found himself puzzling over the same question he'd had when he discovered what and who she really was. "How do you do it?"

"Do what?" There was sleep in her voice, but suspicion too.

"This." Elijah glanced meaningfully at the strewn sheets and their entwined limbs. Somehow, they'd managed that tangle you only saw in movies and on TV. Her whole body covered, him bared to the waist.

"How did *you* do it?" Meghna turned the question back around on him, like she'd done so effortlessly the other day in the elevator—*fuck, had it really only been days and not months?* "You had no idea what you were walking into with me. Whether I'd respond to you. Whether I'd like you. Whether I'd be anti-Black. Conservative. My father voted red for most of his life," she said. "Obama was the first time he went the other way."

It shouldn't have surprised him. Her just putting it out there like that. She kept her secrets, sure, but she'd been free with her opinions. He rolled to his side, propping his head up on his hand. Studying her face. So open when it was usually closed. "We researched you," he said honestly. "Your voting records. Your friends. Even your Netflix queue. The paparazzi shots of you in Black Lives Matter shirts."

"Performative allyship," she pointed out. "Plenty of people wear the swag and don't believe it. As long as they hashtag it or retweet it, that's all that matters to them."

Elijah nodded, conceding the point with a short laugh. He and Joaquin had the same argument with Jack at least a few times a year over pints and darts. "So you're saying you're performative in all ways? Sex *and* politics?" he couldn't help but tease.

"Oh, fuck you." Meghna pulled one of the pillows out from beneath her head and hit him with it. Playful, but still hard enough that he could swear he tasted feathers.

"Ow!" he exclaimed with exaggerated outrage as he tossed the makeshift missile to the foot of the bed. It was strange to see this aspect of her personality. Strange and…encouraging. She was letting him in. Letting him see the side of her that pondered and the side that played.

"You researched. You moved forward with me. I have to do the same." She settled back against the headboard, chewing on her lower lip, measuring her thoughts and her words. "Even if it's someone I'd never associate with in my personal time."

"That's a helluva risk to take, Meg." He wasn't some hypocrite who was against sex work. His sister Amani had worked one of those XXX mobile hotlines for years to pay for uni and grad school. But what Meghna did... it was in person. And it wasn't just a transaction. It was espionage, if not more. She went to bed with killers and frequently woke up one herself. "You ever think there might be someone you can't charm? You can't overpower?"

"Like you weren't taking a risk with me?" Meghna fired back. "Even if you didn't know how much danger you were in at the time. That's the job we do, whatever shape it takes. It's not like 'dating across the aisle' or 'fucking across the aisle' or whatever cutesy thing all those lifestyle blogs want to call it. If it weren't for the work, I couldn't see myself even talking to a man like Mirko Aston. Much less touching him. He's against everything I stand for. Everything I *am*. Most of the men I've targeted over the years are fundamentally vile. Racist, homophobic, misogynistic abusers who want me to go back to where I came from—but only after they come their brains out."

It was a precarious dance she did. Public face, private body. Both with their own agendas. "You said your reputation was taking a hit for being seen with the likes of them. Aren't you worried your public persona will stop being effective cover?"

"Of course." Meghna made a face. "My badass publicist can only do so much. It'll work until it doesn't. But better my reputation than my life or someone else's."

Except that she *was* putting her life in danger. Willingly. Knowingly. While fucking men she loathed. He couldn't do it.

He couldn't fathom it. "You still haven't answered my question, Meg. How do you do this? Because I got one go at you and lost my whole head. No objectivity. No eyes on the mission. Nothing. But you? You've done this again and again. With people who'd probably want to see you debased, deported, or dead if you weren't in their bed. You let them close. And sure, sometimes you take them out, but sometimes they walk away with a piece of you."

Meghna was quiet for a long time. Touching his hip, the border of his rib cage, before pulling away. "It disgusts you, doesn't it?" she asked. "The sex work. The wet work. You can tell me, you know."

Elijah's chest constricted. Disgust? For this remarkable woman? *Never.* But was there worry? Yeah. Of course. "Killing people's not an easy thing, Meg. Even if you shrug it off. I know it lives inside you. And the other work you do to get there, the sex work"—he made himself say it so she had no lingering doubts about where he stood with the concept—"it scares the hell out of me. Because I couldn't manage it. Not even for one hot weekend. And you've done it for years without losing who you are and what you stand for. But disgust? No. You've got my feelings all wrong on that count. I'm in *awe* of you. Of your strength. Of your commitment to your cause. Of how you just don't give a damn."

Meghna scooted to the edge of the mattress. As far as she could go before falling off. He almost dreaded what she was going to say. Something cutting. Something that denied everything they'd been through so far. But she gave him none of that. "Now *you've* got *me* wrong," she said, tracing patterns on her kneecaps with her fingertip. "Because I do give a damn. With you." It was almost like she was talking to herself, not him. "All those marks? They've never taken anything valuable. Anything I didn't knowingly let them have. But you? Elijah, if I have anything good and real left in me to give anyone, it's yours."

Meghna. Fuck. The breath rushed out of him in a whoosh like he'd been punched in the gut. He reached across the divide she'd created. Put his palm over hers on her knee. What could he do but be as naked as she was being with him? "You have so much good in you. So much that's real. And *you* own it. Not me," he confessed. "I'm just falling for you because of it."

She didn't look at him. She bowed her head. He could hear her rapid breaths with his supernatural ears. "You're what?" she asked softly, like she hadn't heard exactly what he'd said.

He could walk it back. What he'd revealed. But Elijah had never been a coward. Mum and Dad hadn't raised a man who couldn't stand behind his words. He took a deep gulp of courage and air. He squeezed her knee. Just the feel of her squeezed at his chest. "You heard me. I have feelings for you, Meghna Saxena-Saunders."

She raised her head, face hidden by the curtain of her loosed hair. "Already?"

"Already." Because that was the truth, wasn't it? Maybe he'd fallen for her the first time he saw her, like some poor starstruck fan. Maybe he'd been off his head when she sank to her knees to seduce him and when she stared dispassionately down at Sasha Nichols's body. He couldn't pinpoint the exact second; he only knew that it had happened and he would never be the same.

Meghna covered his hand with hers. She stared down after doing it, as if memorizing or analyzing how it looked. Her smaller golden-brown hands sandwiching his dark-brown one. She was no less dangerous. They were both equally capable of meting out harsh justice, of dealing death. "Is it because you're a lion? A shifter thing?"

Oh. Oh, beautiful baby girl. She couldn't dare to trust. Not even now. He curled toward her. Closing the space she'd deliberately put between them. "No, it's an Elijah thing. A you-and-me thing." Because if she couldn't meet him…well, he was strong enough to go to where she was. To stay there for as long as it took to make her believe him.

Meghna held herself still. So painstakingly still. His pretty predator. Maybe she'd kill him now. Slice him with one of her blades. Or maybe she'd cut him with her words. Bound to be even sharper. "There's a 'you and me'?" She turned on her side. So they were face-to-face. Her eyes were like dark, drowning pools. Fuck, she was gorgeous like this. Sweated out of her makeup, her armor. "Are you sure about that? Because I'm not. I'm not sure of anything anymore."

This was a pivotal moment. He knew that without having to be given a clue. And Elijah had no problem rising to the occasion. With his prick, and with his heart. "Nothing performative here, love," he admitted. "Only the truth as I see it. As I feel it." And he felt *her*. The beat of her pulse under his mouth. The slightest trembling of her body beneath his as she digested his words and what they meant. *Oh, Meg. Sweetheart. Just let someone love you. Like you deserve.*

Yes, he was in love with her. He loved her. Perhaps he should've been embarrassed to put it all out there, but there simply wasn't *time*. They only had this small bit of respite before diving back into the game. And he wasn't going to waste it when he could die tomorrow. There was no sense in holding anything back. No shame in laying all of his cards on the table. He was mad for Meghna, and he wanted to be with her as much as he wanted his next breath. If they made it through Mirko's auction, if they survived the next week, the first thing he'd do was ask her for something real. Lasting.

"You're going to regret it," she murmured into his neck. "Anyone who cares about me usually does. Look what happened to Chase."

"I'm not Chase," Elijah said, pulling her more securely against him, stroking circles along the tense column of her spine. "I know who you are. More than that, I know who *I* am and how far I'll go for someone I care about." Third Shift. His family. Now Meghna. He'd protect them all with his life. No regrets whatsoever.

"I can't make any promises." Meghna was still speaking to his skin. To the hard line of his collarbone. Her hair spilling across his chest. "I won't give you any hope."

"I know," he said simply. Because he did and he understood why, too.

But then she gave him what she could. Her touch. Her affection. Her passion. And that spoke more eloquently than the words ever would.

———

Everything told her to go. Like that time in Reno. And the time in Montreal. Her molecules shoving her out of bed. Her blood screaming to escape. *Get out. Now.* Meghna was halfway to the front door, clothes bundled against her breast, exit strategies running through her head, when she made herself stop. When she remembered she didn't *have* to sneak off like a thief in the night. Old habits died so very hard. Because her instincts were telling her to run...and those things she'd only recently identified as softer emotions were begging for her to stay. *Elijah* was asking for her to stay, even though he was still asleep in the bed they'd nearly wrecked.

"You heard me. I have feelings for you, Meghna Saxena-Saunders."

Plenty of men had told her they loved her before. That they had feelings. That they wanted some sort of reciprocation. All but one had been lying...and it had landed him in the hospital years after the fact. Not exactly a rousing endorsement. Now here was this lion shifter, this gorgeous man, putting himself in the line of fire. Maybe *that* was why Meghna had such a strong desire to get the hell out of Dodge.

She let her hastily gathered up clothes spill to the floor as she made her way back to the bedroom. Where she just stood in the doorway for a moment. Two moments. Three. Studying the shape of the man tangled in the sheets. A week ago, she'd had no idea he existed. Now she knew the intimate curves of his body. How he smelled and tasted. How passionately he cared. It wasn't that she *didn't* care. Meghna wasn't...*cold*. But it had been so long since she'd let herself exist beyond the surface, beyond the roles she played. Emotional investment was just a step too far. If she started feeling, then she started thinking, and then she started second-guessing. And then she couldn't pretend she liked Mirko Aston's clammy hands on her skin.

But that jig was up, wasn't it? She'd never have to fake it for the arms dealer again. She'd just have to be real for the man across the threshold. *Can you handle that, Meghna?* That was the million-dollar question. She didn't have the answer. So she just slipped back into bed and fit herself against Elijah's back.

"Couldn't do it, hmm?" he murmured sleepily.

Of course. A shifter. An operative. He hadn't slept through her departure at all. "Don't be so smug," she said, dropping her arm around his hip.

He shook with barely suppressed laughter. "Not smug, Meg. Just happy."

Happy. That was another thing she was unfamiliar with these days. Unless you counted getting a swag box of lipstick from a prominent makeup brand or cashmere lounge wear from an athlete turned designer. What was happiness to someone like her except a fleeting feeling you got from two scoops of ginger ice cream and a good gin martini? *Fuck.* She didn't want to equate joy with the wild scent of Elijah's skin. With his solid bulk offering her something, *someone*, tangible to hold onto. She didn't want to equate joy with anything that was supposed to last.

Nothing lasted in her life. Not her parents' relationship. Not any mother-daughter bond. Not safety or security, citizenship or personhood. The only certainty she had was that things were shitty. And that it was her job to make things slightly less shitty. Meghna was a weapon. Just like the stilettos she favored. She wasn't a person. She didn't get to have real wants and needs. That was ridiculous. That was too much. That was…who she wanted to be. In a perfect world.

Goddammit. Meghna inhaled. Exhaled. Clung to Elijah like the life preserver he'd thrown her. And then his watch chimed with alerts that drove them both upright.

"Estrada's back on-site with Mirko," he rumbled, staring at the digital screen on his wrist. "Everything's going according to plan."

Was it, though? Was there even a plan? She shoved a handful of her hair out of her face and curled her legs beneath her. "When do we move out?" she demanded. "That's all I care about."

Elijah's brows rose. "Is it?"

No. No, it wasn't. And he knew that full well. She scowled. "In case you haven't noticed, we're in the middle of a clusterfuck that could have disastrous global implications," she pointed out. "Pardon me if I don't stop to be glad we have a break."

He wasn't the least bit contrite. His dark-brown eyes were soft. So were his fingertips along her cheek. "You can, though, love. You can breathe," he urged. "You can rest. The clusterfuck will still be there when you're done. It'll always be there."

"That makes us pretty bad at our jobs, doesn't it? If it'll always be there?" Meghna couldn't help but play the contrarian. Mostly because it was a legitimate question she had about the longevity of anyone in the game. The Vidrohi had existed in some form or another since the beginning of recorded time. Didn't that mean they'd *failed* in their core mission to set the world to rights? Or was it just that there would always be evil to balance out the good? You could only ever hope to be one step ahead before it caught up with you. "Or does it mean we can never retire?"

"Got plans for your 401(k), do you?" Elijah chuckled before settling back against the headboard and giving the question more consideration. "I don't know that I've got that much time left with 3S," he admitted quietly. "Either because I'm getting on in years, or because someone'll take me out. One way or another, my work will come to an end. But the threat…that'll keep going. That *doesn't* mean I was bad at my job. It means humans will always be humans. Supes will always be supes."

She nodded, because she understood that logic. "You're saying peace is not in our nature."

Elijah tugged her back toward him, so she was cradled between his massive thighs and sheltered against his chest. "Would you even be content with peace?" he asked, stroking her hair. So much comfort, even as he asked her uncomfortable questions.

"I don't know." She'd had no chance to find out. No opportunity to learn. Not just because of the charge her mother had laid upon her, but because of the direction of the country, of the world. A slow crawl to fascism that had turned into a free fall after the Darkest Day. And sure, plenty of the people she'd gone to high school and college with had clapped their metaphorical hands over their ears and eyes and ignored what was happening. Almost everyone from her MBA program was a corporate bigwig now, rolling in dough. They'd all continued on, luxury and denial allowing them to live just as they once had. While children were being thrown in cages and mass deportations were put into effect. Meghna wasn't plenty of people. She wasn't other people. She'd embraced the opportunity to make—to *force*—change. And if she'd wished, occasionally, to have a different life…well, the feeling hadn't lasted. It couldn't. Not as long as men like Mirko Aston walked the earth.

"Can I tell you a secret, Meg?" Elijah rested his chin atop her head…which would have annoyed her if it weren't an unconscious gesture. It wasn't patronizing. Just…natural. Like he felt he *could*.

"You're going to tell me either way," she pointed out dryly. This, too, was natural. To tease him like she knew this about him.

"Oh, I am, am I?" He huffed, tickling her side before letting his hand fall back to the mattress. "I want to believe we'll be okay," he said, picking up the thread like he'd never dropped it. "That by the time I'm old and gray, we'll have sorted it all out. Does that make me a fool?"

"No." It didn't. Not by a long shot. Meghna had known a great number of fools in her life. He wasn't even in the Top 100. "It makes you exactly who I thought you were. An idealist. A hero. A man with an overabundance of hope."

Maybe some of his hope and idealism would spill over to her. Maybe it already had. And that was why she was still here. Why she'd come back instead of running off to parts unknown. Meghna wasn't naive enough to call that love. Like she'd said to him earlier, *"I can't make any promises. I won't give you any hope."* But it was *something*. Something strong and real and binding that she wanted more of. That she *craved* more of. She'd been alone a very long time. Too long. Surrounded by people but forever by herself in a crowd. Her own doing, of course, but that didn't make it any easier. It just meant she knew precisely where to lay the blame.

Elijah was laughing when she snapped back from her self-reflection. A warm, rumbling sound, not unlike a purr. "I'm no one's hero," he said quietly. "I'm just trying to do what's right."

So was she. But their methods were completely different. Meghna saw most people as expendable. He saw every life as something worthy of being saved. She used men like tissues. Like Mrs. White in *Clue*. At best, they were "soft, strong, and disposable." Whereas Elijah had attempted his first seduction for this mission and failed spectacularly. Or succeeded and then some, depending on how you looked at it. After all, she was here, wasn't she? In his literal bed?

She was marveling at that, all of that, when simultaneous vibrations jerked her head toward the dark corners of the bedroom. Her devices. All of them. From wherever the Third Shift people had stashed her things. Meghna leapt from the bed like *she* was the lion shifter, finding her purse hanging off a hook attached to the wardrobe. Shit. *Shit.* She'd been out of touch for more than twenty-four hours. And if it was more than Em could handle…

Elijah was out of bed, too, like a shot. Beside her as she tossed
her silent burners aside with a clatter and pulled forth her three
"real" devices. Mirko had to be furious, she thought, as she
thumbed out her security code on the first phone and pulled up
the messages. He hadn't caught her yet. She'd gone to ground.
Slipped through his grasping fingers. Whatever this was, it was to
draw her out. To pay her back.

They were photos. Nothing but photos. Of Chase. First in what
was clearly his hospital bed at UCLA. And then…then in a chair.
Looking pale and wan, anything but the beloved action hero, in his
polka-dot gown. A saline drip on a stand the only concession to his
wounds. She stared down as if she was some odd sort of remote
watcher. Half-fascinated, half-horrified. Like rubbernecking at a car
crash. Surely this wasn't her ex-husband. Surely they hadn't *continued* to use him as a bargaining chip? How had they smuggled him
out of the hospital without raising a single alarm? *Oh hell.* Getting
him shot hadn't been enough. Now she'd gotten him kidnapped, too.

"I don't have to care," she said aloud. If her hands were shaking…well, that was just an unfortunate physical response. "This
doesn't have to mean anything." It was just a play. One she could
ignore. Chase could die in this anonymous warehouse, and it
didn't have to impact her goals in the slightest. Because Mirko had
miscalculated. Yes, she had a soft spot for Chase. For everybody
on her celebrity text chain, too. But would she risk her core objective for any of them? *No.* So why were her knees like jelly? Why did
she accept it when Elijah caught her and banded his arm across her
hips to keep her upright?

"It doesn't have to mean anything," he acknowledged with a
growl. "But that's not you, is it, Meghna? No matter how hard you
pretend. You care. They know you care. *I* know you care."

Chase was innocent. "Big, dumb, and tons of fun," so many
of the tabloids called him. As if a "himbo" couldn't have depth,
couldn't have feelings. He'd given her an escape when she'd

needed it. A chance to be the vapid little celebutante brat everyone thought she was. He didn't deserve this. To be a plot device in
a suspense novel. To be a cudgel they used to beat her. "We have
to get him out," she said. Slightly amazed that her voice was even
working. That she had the capacity for words. "They can't have
him, Elijah. I have to go."

"Not alone, you don't," he said fiercely into her ear. So warm.
Velvet heat brushing her lobe. "You've got me now, love. *Us.* The
whole of Third Shift. And we'll find him. It's all right."

When her phones all vibrated in unison again, it was he who
looked at the message. Who told her what it said. You can have
him or the serum. One location, one choice.

It was spelled too precisely to be from Mirko himself. Meghna
had to giggle hysterically as she registered that. Maybe it was Tavi
Estrada, so recently returned to the fold. Maybe another minion
in on the plans. But they'd made it easy. Efficient. Chase and the
serum all in one place. It was almost *too* easy.

Elijah didn't laugh so much as scoff. "Why is it always kid-
nappings with this lot?" he demanded. "They nabbed one of my
people last month. Now they've got one of yours. No imagination
whatsoever."

And why did supervillains always lay out these traps in such
obvious ways? Did they not think people could go to the police?
The FBI? The CIA? Meghna's father was a high-level defense
contractor, for fuck's sake. But such was their arrogance. Such
was white supremacy. They assumed they could take control, and
people like her, like Elijah, would just fall in line. No, she had no
intention of going to the police, the FBI, or the CIA, but she had
Third Shift. She had her own wits, her own skills. If things worked
in their favor, she wouldn't *have* to choose between her ex and the
shape-shifter serum. But maybe she'd have to choose between her
heart and what was right.

No. Maybe you already have. The nagging reminder sounded

more like the General than it did her own internal monologue. Like a smug "I told you so." She looked up at Elijah, at his beautiful bearded face. "I didn't want to compromise my mission objective for Chase…but I did it for you, didn't I? From the minute we saw each other across that room."

"Do you regret that?" he asked.

She gave him the only answer she could be certain of. "I hope I don't have to."

24

TAVI TOOK A CAR SERVICE back to the Financial District, lest he suffer another sneak attack while patronizing the MTA. But once he'd been back in Mirko's company for a few hours, he began to consider that being rendered unconscious was vastly preferable. The man was odious on the average day, but still on a tear about Sasha's untimely demise and Meghna's betrayal, he was insufferable. *The island*, Tavi reminded himself as Mirko stormed around his suite at the Cipriani throwing barware and expletives with equal fervor. *This is all to get to the island.*

He'd stuffed his true agenda so far down that he barely remembered it sometimes. It was easy, too, to play the villain. To be the kind of predator who didn't care who he hurt as long as he ended up on top. That was his reputation in the criminal community. Among the terrorists he'd made comrades of. Octavio Estrada, the vampire who could get you anything you needed whenever you wanted it. At the cost of anything he'd ever needed or wanted himself.

Tavi gripped the untouched tumbler of whiskey in his hand like a lifeline as Mirko flopped back down in his seat on the edge of his ugly brown suede couch. "This is a shit show!" Aston declared, brows knitting together with displeasure. "Three organizations have dropped out of the auction. My investors are displeased."

His investors. No, his *boss*, he meant. Because someone pulled Mirko's strings, even if he wanted to pretend he was a king. Someone who wanted the shape-shifter serum badly enough to orchestrate this entire game. Roman Hollister. This was the closest Tavi had ever been to confirming Hollister's involvement, his true aims. Finian and Third Shift had almost ruined his chances. So noble. So heroic. So utterly clueless.

Tavi wanted to hate them for his brief stint in their midst, but he couldn't. He actually admired Finian for his initiative. The young twentysomething he'd once known, so easily swayed from religion to sin, had a cause now. As single-minded and narrow as it was, it was nothing to be ashamed of. They wanted to save the world. It wasn't their fault that the world was beyond saving. That all you could really do was rescue a small number of people bobbing in the muck. Not that he was any kind of hero. He'd damned far more people than he'd saved.

Tavi leaned back in his chair, feigning ease he didn't remotely feel. "Are enough of your competitors confirmed? That's all that really matters."

Aston's petulant pout brightened. "Yes. Yes, the room is guaranteed to be packed."

Good. Not just for Mirko's aims but for his. "You should move it up," he suggested. Tate and Richter's idea, really, but he was loath to give them credit even in his own mind. "To keep everyone on their toes. Change it to tomorrow. If the venue is ready, then why wait? Those who are serious about the product will show. Those who aren't? They weren't worth your time anyway."

He'd been saying similar things for two hundred years. Most of them to arrogant men who thought their version of control was revolution. Aston and his ilk weren't new. They were just arrogant. Hungry. Greedy. Qualities people associated with Tavi as well.

Because of how he chose to spend his time. Where he chose to commit his loyalties. Maybe they weren't wrong. Maybe Finian was right to be disappointed in him because he reveled in this role.

"Do it," he urged Mirko. "Move up the auction. Show them your might."

The arms dealer seemed to like that idea. He scrambled for his phone, fingers flying across the screen. Tavi didn't dare count it a win. Not until a good ten minutes later when Mirko declared that he'd indeed moved the auction up to tomorrow and anyone "worth a damn" would be there. *Good.* But also *bad.* Tavi poured himself some more liquor from the bar set up beneath the hotel suite's windows. "What happens to the serum after the auction?" he prompted slyly. "We both know you won't let a single one of those people walk out of the room with it."

"It will go where it belongs," Mirko brayed like a jackass. "That is all anyone outside this room needs know."

So everything, everyone, had only one destination. Roman Hollister's island. The mysterious fucking island that Tavi had been trying to land an invite to for ages. He was trapped between elation and frustration. To be so close to one's goal yet so far away...it was more torment than even a vampire of his age could comprehend. But he'd promised. He'd *sworn*. It had given him a purpose that he couldn't abandon now.

Tavi was an excellent vampire. He'd killed and fed and triumphed in his immortality. He was not a good person. So be it. That was the price he paid. "I want to go," he said, taking that calculated risk. Because if not now, then when? "Take me with you, Mirko. I've seen you through this far. Let me see it through the rest of the way."

Aston sprawled back in his seat. Eyes bright with victory, with pride. He had no idea that a viper sat in his midst. Such was the arrogance of these kinds of men. "Yes," he said. "I will put you on the next flight manifest. You, as tainted as you are, should see what we have accomplished. What we *will* accomplish."

A backhanded compliment. Tavi had smiled through millions of such comments. And he did so again. Him and his tainted blood, his tainted skin. *Fuck you, you fucking pendejo*, he thought as he kept grinning. "That's all I want," he said. "I want to be witness to the future you've dreamed, Mirko."

He wanted to be witness. He wanted to tear it apart. But the latter was his secret, no one else's. Not his filthy, beautiful Finian's. Not that noble warrior Grace's. Let them continue to think what they would of him.

"Good!" Mirko crowed with laughter. His florid face, so flushed with liquor, showed his ease and his arrogance. "They can't stop the tide, Estrada. They can try, but they will fail."

Men like this had run the world for thousands of years. They thought themselves immortal. But they weren't. Not even the oldest, most powerful supernatural creature was immortal. Death came for everyone in the end. He'd seen empires rise and fall. Dictatorships wither. It didn't matter who was in the White House. Who maneuvered behind the scenes. Death was the one thing none of these megalomaniacs could escape.

"Why are you trying to stop me, Octavio? Our goals are fundamentally the same." She perches on the top of the crumbling wall, half over, half close.

He could reach her. One supernatural leap is all it would take. He can't say what keeps him from dragging her down by the ankle. "No, querida. You're a crusader for justice. I am a realist. So our goals will never be the same."

"Bullshit." She laughs. "And that's why you'll never catch up to me. No matter how hard you try."

Bullshit. If he had to kill a thousand people to get to her, he would. Tavi was so fucking tired of idealism. All he wanted was certainties. An auction tomorrow. A flight after that. Access. Answers. *Her.* Finian thought there was more to him than that. Some deep core of emotion that had made them fall in love more than fifty years ago. No. No, there was nothing deeper to be found than what Tavi displayed. He was undead. Not of the living. This was what they so conveniently forgot. He'd removed himself from the human equation. He was beyond their petty squabbles and pettier ideals.

"Liar." She laughs against his ear. "You're not stone, Octavio. Not impervious."

Carajo. No. He shoved her voice back into the far reaches of his gut. He'd been so good, such an expert, at pushing both her and Finian aside. At locking them away in boxes. That she was rearing her head now meant he was dangerously close to unraveling. Tavi sat forward, breathing deeply of stale apartment air that he didn't need to stay alive. Fuck, he hated this. When he let the mask drop. When he remembered. When he had those pricks of conscience, as small as they were. It was much easier to be cool and removed, to play at being the age-old creature with no mortal cares. He did that like he used to breathe. Without thinking. Without contemplating how exactly it moved him forward.

"And where are you moving forward to?" He could hear two voices asking him that simultaneously. One deploying a thick Irish brogue, the other a musical Bengali lilt that held just a dash of tartness. Like the sweet limes that grew in her homeland.

The ominous crinkle of tarp brought him forth from his dangerous ruminations. Two of Mirko's thugs, the ones he'd nicknamed Bobo and Tonto, had brought in a length of black plastic and spread it across the sitting room floor. Nothing good ever came of somebody laying down a tarp. The Cipriani's management was not going to be pleased with whatever came next.

"You want to bear witness, Estrada?" Mirko asked gleefully. "You can begin now."

A third henchman whom Tavi couldn't have identified if his undead life depended on it wrangled Dr. Gary Schoenlein into the room, tossing the unfortunate man onto the plastic like he was nothing more substantial than a sack of garbage. *Carajo*, he thought again, for far less pleasant reasons than before. The scientist had delivered the serum but failed in so many other ways when his clinic had been breached. He had to pay. Such was the way of things. That did not mean that Tavi wanted to see it.

He killed out of necessity. For sustenance. For his goals. He didn't *revel* in it. It didn't give him an erection. It didn't make him feel powerful. These little petty tyrants like Mirko Aston…this was how they made themselves important. By making underlings cower on a tarp, weeping for their lives.

"Please," Schoenlein begged. "Please, Mirko, I swear I'll do better. I'll be more vigilant."

For all the good it would do him. He'd handed over his research along with the product. He was expendable. The scientist who'd synthesized a variation of the miraculous serum that could transform mere humans into hybrid shape-shifters probably deserved a better death than this. Something that recognized the leaps he'd made, the risks he'd taken, in copying military secrets for private gain. He didn't receive it. He died like a traitor, like a prisoner of war. Shot in the back of the head, execution-style, as Tavi watched and didn't flinch. Tonto and Bobo, for all that he called them fools, were efficient. They left no blood spatter on the walls. And the tarp took care of everything else. Except for Aston's laughter. That splashed the walls and the ceiling, even more garish than streaks of gore.

Octavio Estrada *had* to be impervious. He had to be made of stone.

Because to be anything else was nothing short of self-destruction.

———————

Joaquin tried to get everyone on the stateside team together for a "Third Shift family dinner" every few months. They hadn't hosted one since losing Mack and welcoming JP to the fold. There just hadn't been a right moment, a time when almost everybody was on premises at HQ. So when the announcement popped up on his wrist comm, Elijah wasn't surprised. He was, however, slightly miffed at the timing. Now? Really?

Yes, really, Joaquin texted back within moments. Call it a team-building exercise. You and Jack love those, right, Bossman?

Jackson, much to his private dismay, had yet to earn the title of "Bossman" or anything else remotely respectful. And certainly nothing as personal as "Teacha." "You think I'm going to call a white man 'jefe'?" Joaquin had scoffed during one of their movie nights. "Dream on."

Jack still showed up to each and every dinner. Not necessarily because hope sprang eternal but because Joaquin's chivo guisado and mangú were beautiful enough to make angels weep. With a scant two hours until mealtime and entirely too much on his mind, Elijah had no hope of competing. He wasn't going to impress Meghna with his cooking skills today, though Mum had made sure he'd learned everything right alongside his sisters. "Up for dinner?" he murmured, gently elbowing her.

She'd been glued to her multiple phones and her tablet since the photos of her ex had arrived, growing grimmer and grimmer by the moment. He didn't know what to say to her to make it better. And maybe there was nothing he *could* say. Maybe being surrounded by 3S operatives was the best possible conversation.

"Food?" she said absently. "What's food?"

Blasphemy. Though it occurred to him that they'd barely eaten between now and Aston's party. Not unless you counted eating dick and eating pussy. And man could not live on that alone. So that was how they found themselves taking the lift two floors down to Joaquin's place, armed with two bottles of wine and some sort of appetizer out of Chrissy Teigen's *Cravings* that Meghna had whipped up in a pinch out of the paltry contents of his cabinets.

They were met with a *party*. Gracie and Finn and the lawyer whom Elijah suspected he was going to see much more often. Danny and Yulia, his wife, had surfaced from their honeymoon period. Jack was nursing a drink in the corner and pretending he wasn't enjoying himself. And of course Joaquin was handing out brimming glasses of pisco sour. It was a Peruvian cocktail, not Dominican, but Joaquin insisted they "didn't discriminate when it came to good booze."

That was far from the only debate of the gathering. Especially when Elijah dared show up empty-handed save for alcohol. "Excuse me. Active missions," he pointed out huffily. "Did Gracie bring something? Why am I the only one on the hook?"

"I brought the entertainment," Grace said dryly, tilting her head at Finn. "I don't cook if I can help it."

"Can't boil water?" Meghna asked sympathetically, only to be met with a firm shake of the other woman's head.

"I didn't say I *can't* cook. I said I *don't* cook," corrected Grace, gesturing with her beer. "Not for this bunch of cretins. You start cooking for a boys' club, next thing you know you're doing their laundry, and Elijah may think I'm Wendy Darling, but I'm certainly not Snow White. I don't need to see Sleepy, Happy, Dopey, and Groucho's dirty drawers."

"Just mine," Finn added helpfully. "Except I don't wear drawers."

"We *know*, you go commando," Elijah groaned at the same time that Nate said, "Objection, Your Honor, that's a lie."

Pandemonium broke out at that. Complete with Nate offering to introduce "Exhibit A: black silk boxers" into evidence and Joaquin protesting, "Not on my dinner table, you don't!" When Elijah looked over at Meghna, she was alight with laughter. Near to wheezing. Her glass of pisco was already empty. Her eyes…her eyes were full. Yeah. Dinner with Third Shift was telling her everything he wanted her to know. *You're welcome here. You're safe here. You belong.*

Everything Third Shift had whispered to him so many years ago.

"You're different, Teacha. Since you came back from the desert." Naomi swings his nephew up onto her hip, careful to shake her braids away from her son's curious grip.

He sets down a forkful of his mum's curry goat. He hopes this isn't a prelude to some lecture about PTSD, which the Apex doctors assured him he most certainly did not have. He's been doing all right, all things considered. Better than a lot of men who came back. "Different how?" he huffs.

"You visit more, for one!" Ciara shouts from the kitchen. The best ears in the family, the best hunter. "We actually remember your face now."

It's not much of a compliment. His visits while he was in the service were so rare as to be nonexistent. Now that he and Jack are busy getting Third Shift off the ground, he's got maybe five minutes more spare time than he used to.

Naomi ignores their youngest sister, dark eyes narrowed in contemplation. Of all of them, she's the most like Mum. A fierce protector of her kids. A taker of no bullshit. A person who sees straight through him. "I think you're almost ready," she says as little Winston grabs a braid with a crow of victory.

Knowing her, he already has a general idea. He shouldn't even ask. It's the same thing Mum's been after him about for years. A wife, little ones, a pride of his own. He waits while she rescues her hair from the baby's chubby fists before he can stuff it in his mouth and choke on the beads. Not that she can't multitask. "Ready for what?" he prompts once Win's been safely deposited in his playpen.

"To become who you were meant to be."

"A husband and father?" he suggests dryly, going back to his food before it gets cold.

Naomi gives him a look that makes him feel like a toddler being put in his place. Right next to Winston on the floor. "No," she says with a mix of amusement and patience. "A leader."

A leader. Elijah didn't feel like one most days. But right now?

With his team roaring with laughter and camaraderie around him? With Meghna barefoot on Joaquin's couch? He felt like he was a part of something bigger than just himself. This was why they did what they did. The fight was never going to be over, but this was what they were battling for. Friendship. Family. Love.

He reached out to Meghna, slipping his arm around her shoulders. And when she nestled into him, still giggling, he almost felt like happiness was possible. Like everything they wanted was in reach.

Did that make him a bloody fool? Probably. Did he care? Not one fucking bit.

25

GRACE'S PLATE WAS HEAPED WITH chivo guisado and mangú and rice and the patatas bravas Meghna had brought in while Elijah hemmed and hawed about not having time to cook. The fragrant stew and plantains were pure comfort. So were the spiced potatoes. Like her mama's greens and her ba's spicy Chinese dishes. When Joaquin made them gather like they were family, not coworkers, she almost felt like what they were pushing for was true. This was her family. These were her people.

She'd tried, the first few years at Queensboro Community, to join in the culture there. But they'd all been so suspicious, so resentful, of the Asian excellence and Black Girl Magic she'd cultivated in order to win her spot there. Ice Queen, Bitch Princess... all the nicknames that had plagued her in medical school came back with a vengeance. And then she'd realized that she could work somewhere else without having to dispel those myths. Third Shift. Sure, she still had hurdles. Like anyone who wasn't white and male. She was still a Black woman. Still Asian. Still struggling to teach the people around her that she wasn't their mother or their maid. Still hating that she had to teach at all.

Grace nudged Finian with her knee. She knocked Nathaniel

with her empty beer bottle. *I'm here.* She'd always had a good sense of self. You had to, when you grew up in America not looking like the people they'd etched on the charter. She was unapologetically Black. So proud to be Chinese. But she still felt like she was fighting to be seen. The snark about being Snow White was...unlike her. A thing she'd normally have kept to herself. But having Finn and Nate flanking her, with all of that warmth, had made her drop her usual defenses. So much about Finn and Nate made her drop her usual defenses.

Her security doors opened up so thoroughly that the words "I'm quitting" escaped her lips before she could stop them, surprising her as much as everybody else. Forks and spoons and plates clattered. At least a few glasses slipped from grips. Only Elijah's quick reflexes and Jack's magic kept red wine from spilling all over Joaquin's flat-woven rugs. Exclamations of "What?" and "Why?" flew fast and furious even as Grace struggled to clarify. "No! Calm down, everybody!" she said as she worked it out herself. "I'm not quitting *here*. I'm leaving Queensboro Community."

She was? *Yes.* She was. The impulsive words solidified into something tangible that grew in her chest. She'd been punching a clock at the hospital for years. Barely that in recent months, as more assignments for 3S took up her time. It was a chore to go in. She did her procedures on autopilot, relying on her rote skills instead of what had once been a passion, a challenge. Tavi's scheming to get her called in front of the board had only made clear how little she actually cared about being there. Having her contract terminated, getting suspended, would not have been the end of her world.

The end of her world and the beginning of it were in this room. So was her passion. So was her commitment. It was time to stop pretending Third Shift was her side gig. It never had been. Not in her heart and not in her head.

"I want to be a full-time operative," she said once the cacophony had settled and Finian stopped looking so much like he needed an emergency transfusion. "I want to be here, where I'm needed… and not just because I'm the only woman on the American side. Because that's not the case now, is it? We have Neha. And Yulia. And Meghna."

Yulia and Meghna both blinked at that but, to their credit, didn't vocally disagree. Whether they wanted to interrogate it or not, whether it was temporary or not, they were part of 3S now. Yulia by marriage and also by everything that happened with her brother, Aleksei Vasiliev, barely a month before. Meghna because she'd partnered with Elijah in more ways than one. They were witnesses to 3S's inner workings, emotionally invested in its members. And they meant she was no longer alone.

Grace swung her attention back to Elijah and Jackson. To her bosses and men she considered friends—but not at the expense of herself and her worth. "I want you all to value me for what I actually bring to the table. How I save your asses on a regular basis. And I'd like to go on more away missions, more extended ops. No more desk duty and waiting at home with the first aid kit."

"Sod it all, Grace. Why didn't you say something before?" Elijah's growl reverberated across the room. "You do save our arses on the regular, and if we haven't made you feel valued for it, that's on us. That's what that Snow White business was about, wasn't it?"

Score one for the lion shifter. Grace shrugged, leaning forward to place her empty drink on the coffee table. "Draw your own conclusions, Lije. I'm just saying how I feel. What I want. What I deserve."

And she wasn't done with that. She shifted her body just slightly, sinking back into the couch cushions so the men on either side of her were her focus. "I want this, too," she told them quietly. "I want to see where it goes. I want it to last. I want promises. And feelings—not just pants feelings," she added before Finn could make the obvious and expected joke.

He winced. "I haven't been making you feel valued either, have I, Gracie?" he murmured. It would have been for her ears only had they not been in a room full of shape-shifters and spies. Most of whom were now politely pretending to drink and chat and finish their food.

"I know who you are, Finn. I've never expected anything from you," she assured him. "I didn't need to. But then last month…in that damn warehouse…I felt you bleeding out under my hands. *Again*. It changed everything. I didn't want it to, but it did."

"It changed things for all of us," Nate said, the gentle weight of his body pressing along her side. "It woke me up."

"It had you running scared," Finn corrected. "If Grace hadn't called you, you wouldn't even be here right now."

"But I *am* here," Nate countered, ever the lawyer. "And I'm not going anywhere."

Good. That was all Grace wanted, really. Her job, her life, her men…some semblance of permanence. And to come first for once. To be the one cared for and cherished, instead of the one always doing the caring. She deserved that. She deserved *this*. And she wasn't ever letting it go.

———

Meghna knew what Elijah was trying to do with this dinner. It was about as subtle as a brick to the head. Making her feel welcome. Making her feel like a part of something. Showing her that she didn't have to fight alone. Third Shift and its people were as opposite to the Vidrohi as inhumanly possible. They counted on their bonds, on their mutual commitment to their goals, to help them. She'd been taught that self-reliance was the only way to keep everyone in the network safe. And yet…here she was. Being included, assumed a compatriot and colleague, all because she'd come in with Elijah a handful of days ago. Third Shift was either the biggest bunch of trusting fools to walk the planet or a crew of total geniuses.

They were definitely fantastic cooks. Her hastily compiled patatas bravas from the tinned potatoes and tomatoes made a decent
showing but couldn't possibly compare to the table that Joaquin
had laid. If only fighting fascism involved the best possible combination of spices, they'd have long since conquered it already. She'd
grown up in a house with servants who'd come with her father
from Uttar Pradesh. Ramu Chacha, their driver. Uma Auntie, the
housekeeper. Thakur, the cook, who'd snuck her sweets and treats
whenever she visited the kitchen. She'd taken them all for granted,
taken Thakur's skill for granted. And she herself had only learned
to navigate the culinary arts later in life. As an adult. For Instagram
more than anything else. Surely not personal enjoyment. Surely
not because she missed the heat of coriander and ginger and green
chilies on her tongue.

Good food made you feel things. Meghna hadn't really felt anything for years. Now she couldn't seem to stop. Anger. Fear. Lust.
Affection. Hunger. Joy. She couldn't remember the last time she'd
laughed so freely.

"You're having fun. Admit it." Elijah nudged her companion-
ably, his brown eyes sparkling. This was the man that women suc-
cumbed to in clubs and bars, if that was even a thing he did. The
beautifully charismatic flirt with the rich hot-chocolate laugh.

"I'll admit it. But it still feels...wrong somehow." To be smil-
ing, to be warm and well fed, when so many people in the world
were suffering. Had she convinced herself that being miserable,
cool, and aloof amid all her wealth and privilege somehow made it
okay? How was that any better? Meghna gripped her thrice-filled
pisco glass with both hands. "Do you always do this?" she wondered. "Party before you might die?"

"Not always. But it's a good reminder of what we might die *for*,
love. For our friends. For our families. For the freedom to be who
we are without fear." He huffed out a breath. Serious once more.
So passionate in his convictions that it took her own breath away.

He found the tendrils of hair falling along the right side of her face and wound them around his fingers, tugging gently. "We don't do it to be macabre, Meghna. We do it because it gives us hope. And it gives us fuel."

Fuel she understood. Cold vengeance for the wrongs perpetuated against the world's most vulnerable had been fueling her for decades. But hope? Hope was something she'd wiped out of her lexicon. Until Elijah Richter had given her that come-hither look across the VIP lounge at the Manhattan Grand and tripped all her internal alarms. "I should fuck him," she'd concluded, though that was the most ridiculous of conclusions if one was trying to be practical. *You wanted to fuck him*, the judgmental voices at the back of her mind corrected. *You wanted him from the first second you saw him.* How could anyone with a sex drive not feel the same? Elijah was perfect. Dark-brown skin and dark-brown eyes and muscles and smiles. Her palms itched even now to wrap around his locs and tug. To guide his face between her thighs. If she was going to die tomorrow, she wanted Elijah to lick her, to fuck her, one last time.

"Be my fuel," she told him softly, leaning forward to move her empty plate from her lap to the coffee table. "Show me what we're fighting for."

"Oh, Meg. I already have." He gestured with his bottle of beer before setting it aside. "But I'll do it again. And again. Until you see what the rest of us see."

"What's that?" she wondered, though she half suspected the answer.

"*This.*" And operatives and underlings be damned, he leaned forward and captured her mouth with his. Regardless of the food and alcohol they'd consumed. The fact that she tasted as much of garlic as she did of Peruvian liquor. Elijah Richter didn't care. This was a lion king claiming his partner before his pride. This was him speaking to her in the most basic, primal language on earth. With a kiss that overtook her, overcame her, consumed her. It poured honey and rosewater through her veins. Popped peppercorns and tamarind on her tongue. His palm on her neck was so warm and steady. Steadier than her pulse. If Meghna leaned into this man, if she breathed in his power, she would never lack for support.

Loving Elijah Richter back would be the easiest mission she'd ever undertaken. And the most challenging. Because love was the biggest risk in the world. The payoff was as big as the loss. She'd half-assed it with Chase. Not love so much as infatuation, helped along by copious amounts of designer drugs. Falling for Elijah was sober and clear. No substances in play. Just her. Just what *she* wanted.

Meghna couldn't recall the last time she'd gone after something she wanted for herself. Amassing *things*? Sure. She'd had the wealth and the connections for Birkin bags or Louboutins. All parts of her costume, her cover. But going after what filled her emotional well? Never. Because she'd internalized the lesson that wanting was selfish, destructive. Elijah was trying to show her that wanting was life. But all she could feel was to acknowledge that wanting was dangerous. It was heady and seductive beyond the apsara's duty and skills. This was why the old Hindu myths and legends warned against falling in love. Why they painted apsaras as selfish sluts who left their babies behind to be raised by mortals while they returned to the heavens. Why Draupadi's preference for Arjuna over her other four husbands was her secret sin and her lust for the warrior Karna even more forbidden. Because caring too much was a weakness. Attachment a vulnerability that targeted more than just mother and child. And yet these were the same stories that praised women like Savitri, who faced down Yama, the god of death himself, to bring her husband back to life. Vice versus virtue. Sinner versus saint. The virgin-whore dichotomy had been in play for thousands of years. Pitting women against one another. Pitting women against themselves.

Meghna wasn't even sure she was capable of love, but Elijah made her want to try. To dive from the plane without a parachute and just fall. For now, she would fall with him into his bed. Capture what could be their last hours together and hold them tightly. Joaquin and the others let them leave to do just that with obligatory commentary. A bit of good-natured ribbing. Warnings from Finn to "Beware of chafing!" The elevator seemed to reach Elijah's floor in a blink. Their shoes and clothing came off just as quickly.

"You're a good man," she whispered against his lips when they stopped just inside his bedroom doorway. A sentiment she'd put forth already but that bore repeating. "Too good be true."

"You haven't been listening to me at all, have you? Goodness isn't a lie, Meg." His fingertips skated down the curve of her cheek, leaving behind a trail of fire. His other hand had a good grip on her ass, and he gave it an emphatic squeeze. "It's a choice. You can make that choice for yourself. For your heart. And stop seeing yourself as the villain."

I don't see myself as the villain, she wanted to protest. But winding her legs around his waist and grinding against the rise in his jeans seemed like a more important task. Kissing him silent was far more vital. And living to the fullest until tomorrow was all that mattered.

26

LEAVING NEW YORK CITY'S LIMITS, whether by car or by air, was always a bit fiddly. So many passes to check and permissions to clear. Elijah hated it, but such was life in the wake of the Darkest Day. In the wake of the Sanctuary Cities becoming true sanctuaries—or open-air prisons, depending on how you looked at it. There was a lot of shite that Third Shift could skip, given their various connections, but one wrong move could change all of that. Red tape was something you never escaped.

"Get on with it," he growled at his tablet, which didn't answer back. Meghna was still asleep beside him—not for long, knowing her. She slept uneasily. With the proverbial one eye open. He wondered how long it had been since she'd truly let herself rest.

They were heading up to the Finger Lakes soon. Surprise guests at Mirko Aston's big to-do. Finishing what they'd started. It didn't make much sense when you looked at it from the outside. Why Elijah and Meghna? Why Finn and Grace on B team to retrieve Chase Saunders instead of a whole squad? But since when did black ops make sense? This was efficient. A simple, two-pronged assault didn't waste extra resources, extra manpower. They knew the target. They knew the product. They knew the hostage. Elijah dispatching Sasha Nichols had sped up the whole sodding thing's timetable. *"Clean up your own mess, Teacha,"* he could hear his mum say. He'd never forgotten that lesson. Any of her lessons, really.

Past girlfriends said that having a strong mum and sisters had made him a better man, a better boyfriend. He couldn't speak to that. Because Meghna was an only child and she was pretty damn amazing, even if she didn't want to see it beyond what she projected to the world. She'd worked so hard to isolate herself. To be exactly what people saw in the tabloid news, all those papers he'd gorged on before meeting her. But the woman curled into the sheets beside him, her hand on his hip as if she didn't want to let him go, was so much more. Layered and rich like a chocolate cake. Just as decadent and dangerous.

He was loath to wake her, but he climbed out of bed and went about doing his pre-mission morning routine. Quick shower. Shave of the head. All those beautiful locs that she'd gripped in passion falling away. He'd grow them back after. Right now, he needed the illusion of camouflage. The fiction that the shifter at Safe House 13 was someone else. Like a spy donning a wig. Sometimes it was just about maintaining plausible deniability.

By the time he emerged in the bedroom, Meghna was gone. Not far, fortunately. Just sitting on a stool at the kitchen counter, sipping coffee. One of the few things he remembered to keep stocked in his cabinets. She'd cleaned up in the guest bath. She wore the same trousers from the day before and one of his black T-shirts. Her hair was pulled back from her face in a severe bun— needles jabbed through it crosswise in a decorative but deadly X. Just as beautiful as she'd been that night at the hotel. As she'd been two hours ago in his arms. He'd never stop finding her beautiful. No matter what she wore or what she did.

Elijah poured himself a cup of coffee—a good, strong Jamaican blend that one of his aunties sent him every few months without fail—and perched on the stool next to Meghna. "Ready to go?"

"We have to go whether we're ready or not. That's the mission, isn't it?" A cynical smile tugged at her gorgeous lips. "That's always the mission."

No. It wasn't always the mission. But it was *her* mission. He understood that. He didn't judge her for it. He admired her. The strength and skill she'd cultivated to do everything she needed to do. Always moving forward, always moving on. He just needed to convince her that she could stand still. That she could *stay*.

———————————

Meghna's coffee had long since grown cold, though she'd mimed drinking it for Elijah's sake as he dropped down next to her at the counter. She was too busy staring down at her business phone to remember she needed caffeine. God, she was sick of her cache of devices. The Apple products. The burners. The tablet. In the past two days, the oh-so-necessary tech had brought her nothing but bad news. Those photos of Chase. The demands from Mirko. She was glad to be leaving them behind at Third Shift HQ. But she wouldn't be leaving *everything* behind. *Fuck.*

To the untrained eye, the newest email at the top of her inbox looked like garden-variety spam. Something the filter on her official influencer account hadn't caught. It was a string of Devanagari characters for the subject line and another string in the body. And a suspicious link. The latter went nowhere, she knew without even clicking, but the strings? Oh, they were tied to something, *someone*, very real.

We need to meet, the letters said when she mentally unscrambled the anagrams and translated them into English. Urgent. I will find you in the lakes. The message was short. Cryptic. Unsigned. And yet she knew exactly who'd sent it. The General. Her mother. Purva Saxena—the surname was a formality leftover from a marriage that had meant nothing to her. A convenient formality. It kept people from digging deeper. From discovering that her entire legal identity had been manufactured by the Vidrohi. Such was the case for many of their supernatural operatives. And then there were those like Meghna, born in human hospitals, raised in "regular" society, told of their birthright, their powers, whenever a parent or guardian felt it was time. Like fifteen years after divorcing Daddy and fucking off to Sikkim.

And now Purva wanted to meet. In the middle of an op. How the fuck was she going to make *that* happen? How did she even know they were headed up toward the Finger Lakes? Meghna's arm tingled, more with a sense memory than actual pain. The men at the safe house. That black-clad hit squad who'd put a slug in her. They hadn't been Mirko Aston's crew. Was her mother involved somehow? Was this "urgent" meeting related? The tingles moved from her arm to her spine. And across her skin. She looked up at Elijah, found his gaze patient but questioning.

"What is it, Meg?" he asked gently. "Another message from Mirko?"

To tell him or not to tell him. He'd drawn so much honesty from her in such a short time. More than any other man. She trusted him and his team as much as she was capable of trusting anyone. But to speak of the General was to speak of the Vidrohi. And that would betray everything she'd worked for over the past two decades. The network counted on secrecy, on shadows, and it wasn't just *her* truth to share. There were hundreds, if not thousands, of active Vidrohi agents around the world. All embedded in deep cover. In big business. In government. In science. Committed to rooting out evil in every realm. There was no reason for Elijah to know that…was there?

"No messages," she told him before she could second-guess it. "Unless you count Waheed Ali and Honey Morgan arguing about duvet covers versus top sheets." Bless the text chain. It could, and would, go on without her.

"The *Washington Post* bloke and the lady who won the Best

Actress Emmy last year?" Elijah whistled, the sound a blatant tease. "That's some company you keep."

"Kept," she corrected, taking a sip of her tepid coffee. "I don't imagine I'll be in those circles much longer. It's too dangerous for them. And that's if I live through the next day."

"You'll live," he assured her almost immediately, eyes blazing yellow-gold as they frequently did with the change of his moods. "We're going to finish this, Meghna. We're going to stop whatever that son of a bitch has planned. And we're going to win."

It was the kind of rousing dialogue Chase spouted in his action movies. All Elijah needed was the swell of orchestral music in the background. She couldn't give him that. But she could give him a big-screen-worthy kiss. She leaned forward, placing one palm against his newly smooth cheek, and brushed her lips over his. Softly at first. Delighting in his warmth. And then parting his mouth, increasing the pressure and mating their tongues. He tasted like minty toothpaste and the same coffee she'd just been drinking, but it was richer on him. A true jolt to her system. She'd lied to him about the General, but she wouldn't lie about *this*. About how good it felt to kiss him. About how easy it was to slip from her barstool and move between his knees.

Just like last night, she clung to him, to this one bit of joy before they faced uncertainty once more. And he drew her in, against the broad bulk of his chest and into the shelter of his arms. "You'll live," he said again, making it a promise before he dragged his mouth along her jawline and they kissed again. And again.

Her frustration with tech reared its head anew when his wrist comm vibrated, pulling them apart. He checked the screen and cursed quietly in Patwah. "We've got to head out. The helo's waiting for us at Teterboro. Jack wants to check in again before we go."

27

THE MCCAMMON LODGE AND EVENT Center was just what one would imagine such a place to look like. Half luxury cabin, half corporate retreat. Owned by one of Mirko's many shell corporations. Tavi had been here before, during his years affiliated with this circle, but never under such particular conditions. Never with such grim intentions. And he didn't even have the serum in his possession. No, Mirko had tasked two more of his henchmen with guarding the prize, cuffing the reinforced briefcase to one of his pet bear shifters' wrists. How Vladimir felt about such a responsibility was of no consequence...but he had no problem mauling anyone who tried to take it. Tavi had filed that away just as he filed away everything else he learned from these people.

Now, he paced the halls of the lodge, watching the guests arrive throughout the day. Some by car, others by helicopter, landing on the private helipad just behind the building. Many of the same people who'd been at the party, their confidence in Mirko bolstered by the amount of coke that had gone up their noses. But then, that was all part of the plan, wasn't it? To gain their confidence before he gained control. Tavi knew all the pages of this playbook. He'd seen far more ambitious and capricious men use it…and fail miserably.

"Are you ever going to do more than watch?" she'd taunted him once. More than once. Dropping into a spindly seat across from him at a café in the Marais. Sliding into a seat beside him at a bar in Havana. And New York. Always New York. Funny how it was the place that captured so much of his past and all of his mistakes. Her. Finian. His conscience made sentient.

Tavi had been an operative and an operator longer than most. A double agent. A triple agent. A traitor to so many causes, barely true even to himself. But one thing he knew for certain: Every living creature in this building was going to die before the night was out. According to Mirko, it was the only way to move forward. The only way to be sure. Not Tavi's personal choice, not his favorite method of dispatching competition, but you couldn't make lemonade without squeezing the lemons. That they were racist lemons went a long way toward easing any of Tavi's discomfort on the matter.

He'd been making such rationalizations for a very, very long time. Very few people had called him on it. Because he let so very few people get close. His family was long dead. He'd kept deliberate distance from their descendants. His lovers remembered him fondly, if they remembered him at all. Finian had been an exception on that count—and a costly one. But none had cost him more than the person he was doing all of this for. The person he'd never once taken to bed.

"Are we going to do this dance forever?" he asks her when she slides into the seat across from him.

"Yes. Until we can't anymore." She has a drink in her hand, untouched and just for show. Something fruity with loads of rum. There's no shortage of such cocktails on Hector's menu. *"And that might be sooner rather than later."*

He doesn't like the sound of that. It's jarring. At odds with the music *from the stage. At odds with everything he's come to know of her. "Are you in some kind of danger? More than usual?"*

"More than usual," she affirms. "And so I need a fail-safe. Backup. In the form of someone no one will suspect."

Him. She means him. "Whatever it is, I'll do it," he says instantly, though he'll likely regret that later.

"Find me," she says with an odd intensity. With flames in her eyes. "I'm always the one finding you. I need you to return the favor."

So yes. He was finally doing more than just watching. All because she'd asked. If his methods were crude, crass, less than desirable…so be it. He'd let dozens of men die if it meant she lived.

28

THEY'D DRIVEN TO THE AUCTION site. Five and a half hours. A few checkpoints. Finn chattering most of the way, all of the typical flirtations and innuendos—even with the guards who'd demanded their IDs. Like she hadn't clutched his and Nate's hands the night before, clung to their naked bodies in the dark. Or maybe like she had. Maybe this was Finn assured of his place in the world. Grace was still getting used to the new normal. Even when they finally pulled up just outside the lodge and conference center.

"You up for this, Grace of my heart?" Finn wondered as she steered the car behind a thick copse of bushes.

"I wouldn't be here if I wasn't," she assured him coolly. This was what she'd wanted since signing up with Third Shift. To be a part of the active teams. Not relegated to first aid and triage. To be beside someone she loved. She was ready.

They made sure the car was appropriately camouflaged before they headed toward the lodge. It wasn't far. Less than five klicks. She ran more miles on the treadmill four times a week. Getting inside the actual compound was the tricky part. There were few open access points—which probably worked in its favor as a getaway for criminals. The front entrance. A loading dock. The patio with the outdoor pool, covered now for the season, that sat adjacent to the indoor pool. Olympic-sized with two Jacuzzi tubs. That was their best bet, since no one was likely to be swimming during a supervillain serum auction. They had thieves' tools to get in the glass patio doors, one of Joaquin's prized Honeybees to disrupt the security feed, and maybe five minutes to get in and grab Chase Saunders before being discovered.

"No pressure," Jackson had joked while briefing them. But Grace *thrived* on pressure. On knowing that mere seconds could spell the difference between a clean operation and one that would require a follow-up. So her blood was pumping when Finn broke into the natatorium. When they crept along the side of the long pool, their footsteps barely making noise on the white tile. Finn could probably smell it on her. The thrill, the focus, the adrenaline. He grinned at her, a distinct gleam in his eye, as they hurried through the narrow room and into a hallway. He didn't have to speak. His eyebrows said everything she expected and more. He loved this part of the operation, too.

According to the heat signatures Joaquin had transmitted during their drive, Chase was being held in a second-floor room on the resort's east side. With the Honeybee engaged, they took the east fire stairs up to the room in question. A measly two guards stood in front of the door. Honestly, Grace was a little disappointed. One would think that a celebrity would require more security than that. An entire retinue of henchmen. With giant guns that screamed overcompensation, not perfectly reasonable shoulder holsters. Maybe Aston's people were cocky. Maybe they just didn't care.

She tranqued one while Finn bit the other. Their bodies barely made a thump on the threadbare hall carpet. Once they were taken care of, the dim, dark room where Mirko's men had stashed their hostage was easy to access. Especially if you had a vampire who could just break down the door with one well-placed shove. No additional guards inside. Nothing except an incredibly famous, and incredibly sedated, man on the dusty comforter of the room's king-size bed. The maid service in this place was clearly lacking, but they'd kept him hooked up to his IV, so that was worth a tip.

"Oh, this one's a beauty. Even half-dead with his arse hanging out of his hospital gown. I see why Miss Meghna had to go and marry him." Finn's words were typical, but the look in his eyes and the downturn of his mouth didn't quite match them. As if he was still practicing being himself again.

"She shouldn't have married him," Grace murmured as she unhooked the saline drip from the stand and wrapped it, dropping it into Chase's lap. She then stepped back, gesturing for Finn to lift the unconscious man in his arms. "It wasn't fair to Chase. He didn't know what he was getting into."

"When is it *ever* fair, Grace of my heart?" Finian countered. "We do what we have to do. And *who* we have to do. Sometimes, if we're lucky, we find someone who understands that."

She knew he was thinking about Nate, whom they'd left in his bed with stern admonitions to go nowhere in their absence unless it was absolutely necessary. Another human who could so easily become collateral damage in this ongoing war—who had already seen more than his fair share of violence. Were they cruel for loving the Chases and Nates of the world? For willingly and knowingly bringing them into dangerous lives? Grace was human, too, but she'd made the conscious choice to join Third Shift. To use her superhuman skill as a doctor, hard-won through years of education, to aid in their fight. Growing closer to Finn had been as accidental as it had been a foregone conclusion. He'd *insisted* on it, bulldozing through the professional walls she'd tried to erect. But Nate? A civilian? What right did they have to do this to him? To risk his life and also make him worry constantly for theirs? It was a heavy burden for any one person to carry. Far heavier than the armful of wounded actor who Finn transported like nothing at all. Nate claimed he was ready. He claimed he could handle it. But Grace wasn't even sure *she* could handle it and she'd been living this life, a double life, for years.

They emerged in the hallway with its ugly, dated carpeting. The entirely too quiet hallway. "Trap?" Finn suggested with the quirk of one brow.

"Trap," she agreed.

Finn shifted his grip on Saunders so he had a defensive shoulder forward and one hand free for his gun. She drew both of her own weapons, one with bullets and one with tranqs. And moments later, bears filled the hallway. Fully shifted werebears.

"At least it's not birds," Finn offered optimistically. "I still have PTCS from the last time."

Grace frowned. "Don't you mean PTSD?"

"No." He grinned. "Posttraumatic cock-sucking."

She should've known better than to ask. She didn't have time for more than a cursory eye roll before a huge brown bear shifter charged her. She shot him neatly through the forehead and then gave Finn momentary cover as he dropped back and returned Chase Saunders to the room they'd found him in. He was dead-weight, safer out of the fray. And it freed Finian to use his teeth—which he did, to great effect. They worked in bloody concert, the surgeon and her closer. She took down two more supes with head shots. Finn snapped three necks after taking a chunk out of each. It was exhausting and invigorating. Like an eight-hour procedure compressed into less than eight minutes.

Had Aston thought Meghna would be overwhelmed by bear shifters? Had he wanted her torn limb from limb? This was overkill for who they assumed was a human woman. A man who would order such an attack deserved no mercy. His minions deserved no quarter. And Grace and Finn didn't give them any. Before long, bodies littered the narrow hallway. And they stood ankle-deep in them, bloodstained, sweating, but *victorious*.

Finn and Grace were in. Their comms were muted, and Elijah didn't wear his during ops where he was likely to shift, but he trusted the timetable that had been set before Go Time. And, of course, he trusted his people. The two operatives had taken the more circuitous route into the McCammon Lodge. He and Meghna, since she'd technically been invited, were using the front door. Brazening it out as guests of the esteemed Mirko Aston. They were patted down in the foyer of the event center by a big blond bear shifter whose nostrils flared when he caught Elijah's scent. Apex predators didn't particularly get on. Shocker. His handling was rough, and he pulled the gun from Elijah's ankle holster with something like glee…not realizing it was there for that very purpose. It made him focus on that as the threat and not Elijah reeking of lion. After all, there were probably dozens of shifters already here for the auction. What was one more?

But Elijah *was* a weapon. Just as Meghna was—and the hulking, humorless shifter, who lingered on the curves outlined by her formfitting black sweater, missed the stilettos in her hair entirely. If they needed extra firepower, they could always take a weapon off some unlucky bastard who wasn't going to be using it anymore.

They'd dressed for black ops work more than whatever party Aston was throwing. Dark clothes. Nothing loose that anyone could grab hold of. But Meghna still looked like a million dollars. The conversion rate to pounds would be even higher. Stretchy black pants, glittery and out of the club wear section of the Locker, clung to her long legs. Her boots were practical for combat, with stacked heels that hid wicked blades. His own were more utilitarian. Same with his trousers and shirt. He'd be losing it all at some point in the proceedings, so he hadn't picked his Sunday best.

The chopper had left them a few klicks from the event center. The middle of a clearing. It would circle back a few times before the agreed-upon return at 2300 hours. And Joaquin was monitoring all comms in case immediate action was necessary. So far, though, Elijah reckoned they were all right.

They were led through a reception area that must've been grand once. Now it just looked faded, sad, like its glory days were sometime in the 1970s. Frayed wall hangings, dusty columns. An empty marble check-in desk on a slightly raised bit of floor.

"Lovely," Meghna said dryly. "Maybe we should have our wedding reception here. The aunties would have *so* much to talk shit about."

"Are Indian aunties anything like Jamaican aunties?" Elijah asked, laughing lightly. "Because I'd never hear the end of it."

"We should get married just so we find out," she bantered back.

Their escort was not amused…but he was also not threatened, which was far more important. He made a grumpy noise as he herded them toward a set of double doors to the left, continuing to underestimate the people he was bringing into Mirko Aston's midst. Maybe he hadn't been briefed about the things the two of them had got up to. Elijah wasn't about to enlighten him. Because he was too busy enjoying the moment of light before the storm, the bit of respite. It made something catch in his throat. In his chest. *Wedding receptions. Marriage.* She wasn't serious. It was all part of the persona she slipped on and off like a favorite gown. But he was gobsmacked by how much he liked the idea. Marrying Meghna Saxena-Saunders. Flirting, fucking, and fighting side by side for the rest of their lives. However long that might be.

He held to that idea as they were prodded into a small anteroom…and tried not to find it too ominous when the bear shifter locked the doors behind them and left. This was expected, after all. They'd been formally invited for a purpose. And that purpose soon became clear. A large flat-screen monitor was the focus of the makeshift green room, which boasted a few upholstered dining chairs and a paisley-print sofa that had seen better days. As well as two more doors. One set into each flanking wall. The monitor was on. Showing an intimate party room filled with people.

"Well, this feels familiar," Meghna said, grimly observing the gathering that looked very much like the one where they'd met.

Vodka fountains. A few tables with cold appetizers. Still other tables with clear glass tops, for cutting lines. And the room was full of entitled white men. Many he recognized, a few he didn't, and some he associated with pictures from the FBI's Most Wanted list. Elijah had been in many rooms like it before, not just the one at the Manhattan Grand Hotel last week. Even from the outside, he was painstakingly aware of his Blackness, his Otherness. Just as Meghna was likely conscious of her Brownness. The temperature in the antechamber had dropped to an icy chill the moment they'd been pushed over the threshold. Nobody in this building wanted them here. Everyone here intended them harm and would waste no time in enacting it. He felt that; he knew that. He was poised to shift, his lion rising inch by inch and pushing against his skin. This was not a safe space. But they'd come here explicitly knowing that. The serum was far more important than his discomfort, than his every instinct screaming at him to get the fuck out. They had to get it away from these assholes.

He and Meghna were left alone for several interminable minutes. After assessing their own confines, checking the perimeter of the room, and testing the doorknobs, they returned to the monitor. Watching the movements on-screen. Listening to the chatter. *Waiting.* The California movie producer was there. Rick Keegan. Maybe that was how Mirko had gotten to Chase. And Tony Rossi, the head of a Chicago crime family. They both looked well recovered from their binges at the VIP party, eager to bid on Mirko's secret product. These people were all enemies as much as they were Mirko's allies. Competition. Once the show got started, it was liable to turn into the Hunger Games.

"Twenty-eight guests, in all kinds of criminal flavors," Meghna murmured, her side pressed to his in the most beautiful benefit of forced proximity. "No waitstaff. Locked doors. This doesn't look good." He could smell her skin like this. Her hair. Her essence. It didn't matter that she'd used the basic soap they kept at Third Shift HQ; he recognized *her*. His inner lion knew her just as well as it knew him and his mum and his sisters. She was part of his pride, whether she accepted that or not.

And she was right. This didn't look good. At all.

Still, they couldn't afford to wade in too early. Not before sussing out the situation. Not before finding out why they were in *this* room and not *that* one. "We need to wait this out. Whatever this is," he cautioned.

"Why?" she challenged. Because that was who she was, a person who would always challenge him. "What are they going to do if we don't wait, Elijah? If we leave and get in there? Kill us? They're going to try that no matter what."

Meghna wasn't wrong. That was the hell of it. All of the strict operational maneuvers he'd learned in the military, at the Apex Initiative, they went by the wayside when you were actually in the field. This was when you went by instinct, by whatever the situation called for. But before Elijah could barrel through a door, locks be damned, and discover whether there was a lady or a tiger shifter behind it, a commotion in the party room drew his and Meghna's attention. A door had burst open *there*. Revealing Mirko Aston and a handful of guards. Suited up. Heavily armed. Estrada was behind them. Dressed more for thieves' work. Without visible weapons. And his dark eyes seemed to tilt upward, as if signaling to a hidden camera. Signaling to Elijah and Meg or someone else? Whoever it was meant for, Lije got the message loud and clear. *Danger. Be ready.* And then Estrada slipped away in the direction from whence he'd come.

Mirko Aston didn't seem to care that he'd lost one minion. No, his gaze flashed over the crowd like a searchlight. Gleaming with something so cold that it sent a shiver down Elijah's spine. Meghna squeezed his hand. He could feel her vibrating beside him as Mirko began to speak.

"Thank you so kindly for your attendance!" the arms dealer boomed with movie villain menace, his Eastern European accent thickening for show. Like he was one of James Bond's enemies. "Your sacrifice will not be in vain, I assure you."

Oh. Bloody. Hell. The implication clicked just a few seconds too late. While Mirko and his men were already putting on gas masks. It wasn't an auction. It was a *slaughter*. Gas seeped in from the air vents, and men began to clutch at their throats. People broke out in ugly red hives, writhing as they sank to the floor. Whatever agent Mirko had pumped into the room, it was not bringing death instantly or kindly. It was meant to make his rivals suffer. To let them know precisely who was behind their untimely demises. And he no doubt reveled in the fact that Elijah and Meghna were being forced to watch.

Mirko stood across the ballroom, masked and…and ecstatic. The line of thugs behind him like pawns in a macabre chess match. That Estrada had skived off from his disgusting show of strength wasn't a concern. That the floor was strewn with corpses of those he'd done vodka shots and coke with… It was a source of pride.

The people who hadn't died immediately scrambled in vain for their firearms. Tried to get across the carpet to the gloating son of a bitch who'd double-crossed them. Whatever chemical agent they'd been exposed to made the efforts futile. Some of them were done for within minutes. Starved to death before the Hunger Games could even begin. Still others…they tried to shift, tried to take on a defensive form. That was when the bigger guns came out. Literally. Aston's guards pulled out AR-15s, spraying what was left of the crowd. The sound was amplified. From the monitor and from their surroundings. Wherever this party room was, it was well within earshot.

"The poison is targeted," Meghna concluded aloud almost clinically. "Whatever they used, it didn't work on the shifters. So they had to switch to semiautomatics."

As if on cue, a hissing sound drew their gazes up toward the ceiling. Where vents sat at high points along the walls. Gas wended its way out of the slats and floated down toward them. "Fuck!" Elijah instinctively moved in front of Meg, like that would somehow shield her from its path.

"It's okay," she said, still with that remote and robotic tone. "Mirko thinks we're human. It's not affecting us at all."

"*Yet*," he corrected. "It's not affecting us *yet*, and I don't think we should wait around to find out." If Mirko Aston assumed they'd been taken care of—disposed of as ruthlessly as his auction attendees—then that gave them an advantage. However slight. They had the element of surprise on their side.

Meghna nodded, the set of her jaw grim as the chemical cloud wafted closer. And Elijah took that as his sign to take action. He pivoted back to the entrance they'd used and plowed through the locked wooden doors. Putting his back and shoulder into it, thankful for shite 1970s style and equally shite upkeep. They splintered under his assault and let him and Meghna loose in the reception area. Gas dispersed in their wake, but they kept moving. No telling what they'd encounter if they stood still.

The thunderous *rat-a-tat* of automatic gunfire had petered off into eerie silence. And Elijah spotted another set of thrown-open doors just a little bit farther along. Odds were, Mirko and the guards had only just made their getaway. They were likely still on premises somewhere. He'd memorized the site schematics. There weren't that many entry or exit points. The pool. The front door. The back, which led out to a parking lot and a private helipad. The compound was secluded, very upstate New York meets *The Shining*. And he had no desire to go stark, raving mad trying to get the fuck out of this bloody hotel.

Meghna was oddly silent, unresponsive, almost doll-like as he tugged her along down the center hallway. It was unnerving, but he didn't have time to be unnerved. To be off his head with worry. He just had to hope she'd come out of whatever fog she was in. Shock. PTSD. He'd seen men in combat freeze the same way after an IED took out a supply lorry or a Humvee, or a scout party ahead set off land mines and didn't live to tell the tale. You could tolerate death and violence up until you couldn't. Until it finally sank beneath the skin. And then you cast up your guts or woke up sweating every night or started fights in the canteen.

He'd been lucky. He had his regiment. Then he'd had the Apex Initiative and Jackson, his best mate. As strange as it was to hit it off with a rich, white Yank. And, of course, he'd had Mum and Dad and his sisters. When he'd come home on leave, all that support and all that joy brought him back to what mattered. Life and love and laughing. If Meghna couldn't come back on her own, he'd remind her. *They* weren't dead. They were still here. And as long as they were here, they could still change the world.

29

DEAD. MIRKO'S CRONIES WERE ALL *dead*. Men she'd done shots with. Whose pinches and gropes she'd batted away. But not just that. They hadn't *all* been evil. Rick Keegan and her uncle went back decades in the film industry. She'd helped Dima Popov's teenage daughter find a modeling agent. Questionable men, amoral certainly, but they hadn't deserved to end like this. Choking, falling, burning from the inside out, being torn to pieces by machine-gun fire, bodies scattered across a ballroom in upstate New York. She'd long considered herself an arbiter of who lived and who died. This...this was completely out of her control.

Stop it. Pull yourself together. Meghna had to shake free of the death trap. She had to lock away the images, the thoughts, the sickness in her stomach. Just like the doors that had locked behind her and Elijah. She had to remember who she'd been before this week. Meghna Saxena-Saunders, ruthless assassin, cold-as-ice deep-cover operative. The woman who didn't care and didn't second-guess herself. It was that woman she needed now. So she could pursue Mirko Aston and end him. But her brain was slow to get the message. Her limbs too. She was still an automaton, pulled along by Elijah's firm grip.

They were heading down a center hallway at a clip, as if that would actually help if the chemical gas could hurt them. Had Mirko assumed it would? Had he gotten off thinking of her writhing on that floor in agony? She'd known when she took the assignment that Mirko was the lowest of the low. That he sold weapons of war to fascists and trafficked women and supplied drugs to children. That he was involved with something even worse, even bigger. She'd never once guessed it would be *this*. The creation of a shape-shifter army. The mass murder of his enemies and then... then anyone and everyone else he deemed a threat. And even people who weren't a threat. *Like Chase*...who'd hopefully been extracted by Grace and Finn by now.

Did it make her naive to think there was any difference between brokering evil and committing it? The entire United States of America had learned years ago that there was really no such thing as a slippery slope. That people always began as they meant to go on, but onlookers just chose to wave away the signs. *Oh, he's sexist? Surely, he can't be racist. Oh, he's racist too? Well, he can't possibly be genocidal.* Mirko had always been this person. He'd always had this agenda. So Meghna couldn't forget hers. Kill him. Find Ayesha. Stop the project.

The center hallway split off into narrow corridors. Not as suffocating as the clinic duct they'd crawled through just days ago, but certainly no comfort either. If she remembered correctly from the blueprints, one corridor terminated at the building's south side. A loading dock. The perfect place for a supervillain to park their getaway vehicle. There was also sufficient space on the flat roof for a helicopter to land, as well as a formal helipad about a half mile out. There was a fifty-fifty chance of Mirko picking *that* as his mode of escape.

Except... "He hates flying," she murmured just as they hit the T intersection at the end of the hallway. Mirko had always popped some benzos and demanded blow jobs on their private plane trips.

Hand jobs in first class on the two commercial flights they'd taken together. She shook out of Elijah's protective grasp, her senses and her blood flooding back.

"Meg?" Elijah didn't take the brush-off personally. He just keyed to her mumbled words with his supernatural hearing. "What're you on about?"

"Right and then straight back," she explained as she pivoted in that direction without even breaking stride. "Loading dock."

Just like *that*, Elijah was off again. Without her this time. Running gracefully and quickly like the big cat he was. She appreciated that he didn't patronize her by slowing down and waiting. That he trusted she'd keep up. In the brief time she'd known him, he'd *always* trusted that she'd keep up. And she'd trusted him in general—any mental protests to the contrary be damned. He'd reeled her in with one look from across the room. She'd plotted seduction, but he'd already succeeded in it. He'd made her one of his people. Even the true apsaras of old would be in awe of such a dance.

Meghna could've spent hours, days, months analyzing this revelation, but she didn't have any of that time. Not with the hallway narrowing and the gray metal fire door visible ahead. Elijah hit it at full speed, throwing it open with such force that it didn't matter if it had been locked. It fairly flew off the hinges. She burst out just minutes after him, onto one of three loading docks that jutted out to the building's back parking lot. In time to see Aston and his crew emerge on one of the others. *Fuck.* A large brown van was parked equidistant between them. Because of course.

Noticing the same thing, Elijah cursed a blue streak, adding some words in Jamaican Patwah that she'd never before heard in her life. "They can't get away," she cried out hoarsely. "They have to pay. They have to die."

"All of 'em?" He looked at her askance, as if to confirm her edict.

"All right," she acknowledged. "Just Mirko." Though she

wouldn't complain if Tavi Estrada took a few bruises with him as a parting gift.

"Then let me clear a path for you, love." Elijah flashed her a dazzling smile. A devious smile. One morphed into lion's teeth within seconds. Partially shifted, he leapt easily from one loading dock to the other. Like Superman taking a tall building in a single bound…and then taking down three of the burly henchmen on Mirko's left side. He knocked them over like bowling pins, scattering them across the concrete. Leaving the pickup for her.

Meghna vaulted off the dock and landed on the lot below. The impact on her knees was no picnic, but not so bad that she couldn't keep going. She pulled her blades from her hair as she rounded the front of the brown van. It had been parked facing outward—ever so helpful when quickly transporting murderous global terrorists to their next lair. But no one was going to be making a quick getaway. Not if she could help it.

She took out two guards in two minutes. One with a pin to the throat, the other with a jab through the heart. Mirko had only fled with a small cadre of men. Estrada not among them. At least not right now. Between her and Elijah, they made short work of their opposition. A series of bland-faced, forgettable brutes right out of one of Chase's movies. Human men charged them, bear shifters sprang at them…and then fell. Bodies hit the concrete like meat for the butcher. It was a whirlwind of everything she'd learned in training and everything she'd learned in the field. And watching Elijah fight, out of the corner of her eye, was like watching art in progress. She'd been too disoriented to appreciate his fighting style during their last fracas. Now, she had the full picture. The way he leapt, graceful and deadly all at once. How he easily batted at bears with his claws. The sheer power of his roar. It was chilling and energizing at the same time, and it served as a soundtrack as she delivered a roundhouse kick to a gunman's neck, slicing his carotid with the blades embedded in her shoes.

And then Mirko Aston was the only one left standing. On the opposing loading dock still. Alone. He scrambled down to the ground, so he was on equal footing with her and Elijah. A strange choice. An arrogant one.

It hadn't even been a week since she'd last spoken to Mirko. Since she'd last endured his clammy hands on her body. Since she'd seen him up close. It felt like years. Lifetimes. As far as her odd sense of detachment was concerned, the man standing in front of them was a veritable stranger. A little red in the face. Wild-eyed. His suit, usually impeccably fit, was rumpled. Anger rolled off him in waves. Anger and...something else. Some noxious combination of triumph and desperation. Elijah could probably smell it. Meghna could only absorb the vague essence. But they didn't have to rely on only their supernatural senses for long. Mirko made his intentions more than clear with a snarled curse and a swiftly raised weapon.

"You bitch!" he spat out, centering his gun for a kill shot, aiming just to the left of her sternum. "You thought to cheat me? To steal from me?"

No. Those had actually been unintended consequences. But "actually, I thought to kill you" probably wasn't the wisest correction to make to a man who looked as on edge as this one. A silver briefcase sat by his right foot, discarded and momentarily forgotten after coming face-to-face with them. Elijah's gaze flicked to the big-ticket item just as hers did. Their eyes then met in silent communication. *The shape-shifter serum.* It couldn't be anything else. It was the most valuable commodity Mirko had, and he wouldn't trust it to anyone else at this stage in the game. How convenient. Almost everything they'd come for in one tidy package.

Meghna didn't even blink at the weapon trained on her. She affected her most bored expression in the face of his ranting, the kind that would make a great GIF for a viral meme. "I upgraded, Mirko. That's all," she said. "I got tired of you."

She felt more than saw Elijah bristle beside her. The incredulous *"What are you doing?"* might as well have been asked aloud. But she knew her former lover. The wound to his ego didn't make him pull the trigger; it pushed him to more bluster. Buying them time.

"Tired? Of *me*?" He scoffed, patting his thin blond hair with his free hand. Vain to the end. "*I* was the upgrade, you ignorant tramp. A way out of your petty celebrity pool to *true* power. But people like you…you don't understand that, do you? You're content to leech from your betters. To whore."

People like you. Ah, there was the racist dog whistle. Right on cue. During their months together, he'd made no secret of how he was *doing her a favor* by being with her, by having her on his arm in public spaces. Never mind that, in reality, it was actually damaging to her professional and personal image. Or that Mirko's lust for her went hand in hand with his desire to dominate people he considered less worthy. "I'll admit to the whoring. Hell, I'll even take pride in it," she shot back, slowly moving to one side, bringing Mirko's focus with her. "But who's the leech? You're not even pulling the strings here, are you? You're taking your precious serum to somebody else. Somebody with 'true power.'"

He sputtered with outrage. So busy cursing her out in Slovak that he didn't notice Elijah edging to the left. "You're a middleman," she continued, sneering back at him. "A lackey. Whatever the big agenda is, do you think you'll be a part of it? Do you think you'll get a dose of that magic elixir?"

"I'm first in line for it!" Mirko insisted, but she saw the doubt flicker in his watery gray eyes. And in the next instant, he was loosening his grip on his gun, reaching down for the briefcase. Probably to inject himself right then and there. Prove her wrong. Grab for the power he so craved.

He would never get the chance. Elijah sprang, his shift swift and seamless. A huge tawny lion, soaring through the air, leaving tatters of clothing behind. He tackled Mirko to the concrete as easily as a house cat batting at a toy. Elijah's massive paw fell just below Mirko's throat. But he didn't rip it out. No. Her beautiful lion just rocked back on his haunches and looked up at her with amber-gold eyes. Offering her the kill. She'd read somewhere once that male lions hoarded their kills, didn't like sharing with the pride. Probably Wikipedia, which couldn't even be trusted. But male lion shifters...they were clearly of a different sort. Elijah *yielded* to her. Because this was *her* right.

She didn't have to be asked twice. Meghna whipped one blade from her hair and fell into a crouch. And then she leaned in close. Until she could count the streaks in Mirko's blown-wide pupils and feel his frantic, fetid breath fanning her cheek. Had Ayesha felt it, too? Was this despicable face the last thing she'd seen? "Where is she, you bastard?" She hissed the question, a deadly whisper, though Elijah could no doubt hear it. "Where do you send the women you're done with?"

Mirko's bloodied lips cracked open. A smile. A smirk. He forced out just one winded word. "Hell."

Of course. And he would take the truth to the same fiery place. Meghna zeroed in on the organ that had allowed him to underestimate her. That had caused her so much grief. That defied her now. No, not his dick. That was too simple, too puerile. She jabbed the stiletto straight through Mirko's eardrum and right into his brain. The blood was minimal, the death almost instantaneous. His body took a few seconds to catch up, jerking on the concrete before it finally went still. A dark stain spread across his tailored trousers as his bladder let go. Not the first time she'd seen that happen. She'd experienced enough blood and piss and shit, enough death rattles, for two lifetimes. And this probably wouldn't be the last.

"Meg?" Elijah's voice was a gentle prompt near her ear. He'd shifted just enough to use his human vocal cords. He was mostly near-black mane and golden fur. Still a massive cat, his weight comforting against her side. Just as well, because they'd forgotten to bring pants this time.

"American pants or British pants?"

"I think you know where I stand on British pants."

She clapped one hand over her mouth to stifle the ill-timed laugh, used the other to retrieve her blade before she scrambled back from Mirko Aston's corpse. "I'm all right," she insisted, even though it wasn't entirely true. "I'm okay. We should get out of here." Back to the clearing where the chopper had dropped them off. And then back to New York City, to Third Shift HQ. Back to the drawing board as far as Ayesha's whereabouts were concerned. She wiped her stiletto off on Mirko's trousers and then stood, dusting off her clothes and her hands.

The sun was no longer high in the sky, but a shadow still fell across them. A shadow...and a pair of gray sweatpants. They landed on Elijah's flanks as Tavi Estrada strolled up like he was arriving late to a garden party and not a scene of carnage. "The compound is clear," he said, brown eyes cool and unconcerned, voice as chilled as a glass of good champagne. "Finian and the good doctor got the hostage out. He'll live to make a dozen more mindless blockbusters."

Chase was safe. *Oh, thank god.* Meghna allowed herself one small sigh of relief. If she hadn't seen Mirko in days...she hadn't seen her ex-husband in months. And she couldn't afford to see him now, here, lest he connect her to his kidnapping. But he was *okay*. That was the most important thing.

Elijah shifted back in the moments it took her to process Chase's fate. He tugged on the sweats with no self-consciousness whatsoever—not that he had anything to be self-conscious about, hewn like a work of art as he was. His expression was thunderous. "And just where were *you*, Estrada?" he demanded. "Keeping those hands clean? Doing your taxes? Watching a little telly? We didn't let you go so you could do absolute fuck-all."

"You have your missions, I have mine," the vampire said with a shrug. He grinned, snatching up the silver briefcase from where it still lay by Mirko's side. "I'm sorry. I have a prior engagement." And with a blur of movement, a burst of vampiric super speed, he was across the parking lot. Gone. With the shape-shifter serum.

They needed to go after him. Even if he posed no immediate threat, he couldn't just run off with something so valuable. "Well, shit." Meghna sighed wearily, rolling her head and cracking her neck. "We should've seen that coming." Understatement of the year, but it still felt necessary to say. To own their glaring mistake.

"Once a backstabbing arsehole, always a backstabbing arsehole." Elijah snorted, shaking out his arms as he prepared to give chase. "Finn had his number all right."

And then the McCammon Lodge exploded behind them. Around them. On top of them. They should've seen *that* coming, too. It was Meghna's last thought before she felt the sharp prick of a needle in her neck—*Dart? Hypodermic?*—and she passed out cold.

———————————————

They were three klicks from the lodge, nearly to where they'd left the car, when the cacophonous boom shattered the mid-evening quiet and red-orange flames and smoke rose up in the distance behind them. Finn stumbled in surprise, nearly dropping Chase Saunders, heartthrob extraordinaire, in an inelegant heap on the ground. Grace reached out to steady them, even as dread crawled up her spine and out her throat in a sharp scream. It all happened in seconds, and then they were swiftly pivoting to stare back at the inferno. The actor's head lolled against Finn's shoulder, but he was still out like a light. If they were lucky, Chase would write this entire kidnapping escapade off as some kind of post-gunshot fever dream.

Grace couldn't do the same. Because this was the job she'd

signed up for. The one she'd long ago chosen over full-time medicine. Sometimes it bled, and sometimes it burned. Like the old,
dusty resort that might still have people in it. Her skin prickled.
First do no harm, right? "Should we go back?"

"No, love." Finn didn't hesitate. "You know the protocol. We
keep moving forward. Straight on."

Because that was the life *he'd* signed up for. A vampire who
watched the decades fly by and kept going. How many fires had
he walked away from? How many partners had he buried? She
had some inkling, but she would never know all of it. Of course,
they also had to get Chase to safety and back under round-the-
clock medical care. That was the priority, regardless of Finn's past
choices or her present ones.

Grace set her fingers to the pale, clammy skin of Chase's throat.
His pulse was weak but there. His chest moved with regularity
under the loose drape of Finn's arm, indicating that his lungs were
in working order. And his wound hadn't reopened. He was hanging
in there despite his ordeal. But there was no guarantee that he'd be
stable for long. She tapped her earpiece and reactivated her wrist
comm. "We'll need a pickup. Just north of our drop-off." The car had
never been an option for their return trip and had probably already
been removed by someone from the 3S motor pool. "The lodge is a
literal hot zone," she added, though HQ had likely already registered
the blast. "Possible casualties. I assume you're already en route."

"Affirmative." Joaquin's voice crackled in her ear. "Jack's got
the helo headed your way. Sit tight. Stand tight. Whatever you're
doing, make it tight."

"I'm not even touching that one. It's too easy." Finn laughed,
hefting Chase more securely in his arms.

"Your restraint is noted," Jackson interjected on the same channel. "ETA five minutes. Keep your eyes on the sky. I've got a cranky
lawyer at HQ swearing to sue me if I don't get you two back in one
piece."

Nate. Sweet, steady, gentlemanly Nate. Grace met Finn's gaze, and the personal feelings they'd banked for the op blazed up in that space between them. "Well, we don't want any lawsuits now, do we?" she murmured before muting her comm once more.

"Wouldn't be the first time someone went to court over me," Finn said in that outrageous way of his, eyebrows doing double time.

Chase shifted then, a small moan escaping his lips. But he stayed mercifully, conveniently unconscious. Finn frowned down at his charge. "Hush," he chided. "No one asked you." If he was tired of hauling the actor around, he gave no indication of it.

The two men were as different as the proverbial night and day—and not just because only one was conscious and the other was the only one technically human. Or because Chase was blond and Finn a brunet. Chase was adored by millions. He craved the spotlight. Finn, for all his flirtation, lived in the shadows. They were both objectively beautiful, but it was only Finn's face that moved her and irritated her in turns. She'd put up a decent resistance to his charms…until she didn't. *Her* restraint could also be noted.

Nate's arrival in the picture had changed everything for them. Pushed them together when, by all logic, he should've moved them further apart. Grace had watched enough TV shows to know how this went. The Black woman sidekick never got her happily-ever-after. The two white men got all the fans. But Nate was Jewish and Finian was a vampire, and reality was stranger than fiction.

The chopper landing, though eerily quiet as far as helos went, jerked her from her thoughts. She hadn't kept her eye on the sky, and it had come to ground without her vigilance. Grace watched as JP ran a gurney out to scoop up Chase and secure him. His movements were quick, efficient. And his wolf-shifter strength meant that he could practically carry the entire contraption, Chase and all, back onto the Black Hawk with little effort. The newest Third

Shift operative was acclimating well, for all that he'd been on the run from mobsters and law enforcement alike just last month. He'd had some training as a medic while in Afghanistan, and that meant Grace wasn't the only one on staff who could hand out bandages and insert IVs.

"Well, that's a relief." Finn sighed, making a show of shaking out his limbs. "I do love holding a handsome man, but I prefer them awake."

"Nate's probably staying up for us," she said with a smile. She could picture him sitting up in a tangle of black silk sheets, his reading glasses perched on his nose and a tablet full of casework propped on his knee. Funny how that felt familiar already. Comfortable. Even though it was new.

She followed Finn to the helicopter and accepted his hand for the step up into the hold. And then she held onto it for a few extra seconds. Grace had always thought medicine was her calling. Medicine. Surgery. Performing miracles in the OR. But no. She understood the truth now. She'd made the right choice in deciding to quit that work and embrace Third Shift full-time. Her calling was saving lives in general. And saving loves.

30

CONSCIOUSNESS DIDN'T RETURN TO MEGHNA slowly. No, it slammed into her in a burst of sight and sound and physical sensation. Everything was too bright and too loud and too painful... and then it suddenly snapped into focus. The sun was dropping low in the sky. The evening was quiet. The ground beneath her was cool with frosted-over grass. She wasn't hurt. And she wasn't alone. But it wasn't Elijah who stood over her as she scrambled to sit up and instinctively patted herself down for her blades. It was a woman dressed in all black, save for the pale fur lining on the hood of her slim-cut ski jacket. Her oval-shaped face was a careful mask of indifference, her dark eyes remote. She was beautiful the way a statue was beautiful...and Purva Saxena would take that as a compliment. Meghna hadn't seen the General in almost a year and, like every time she did, it was like looking at a familiar stranger.

"Where am I?" she demanded, scanning their surroundings. A wooded area. It could've been miles or just yards from the lodge. "Where's Elijah?" The last thing she remembered was the building blowing up, debris starting to fall. What if he'd been injured? Had Purva helped that along? Ice clinked around in the bowl of Meghna's stomach. "What did you do to him?"

"I gave him a stronger dose of the same sedative I gave you." The General shrugged, as if injecting someone with drugs was a normal thing people did. "It was the most efficient way of separating you. By the time your lover wakes up, you'll be back at the loading dock. This shouldn't take long."

"How do you know he's my lover?" It wasn't the first question Meghna had meant to ask, but it slipped out anyway. And try as she might, she couldn't keep the annoyance out of her tone. It was like being fifteen again. Off-balance and out of her depth. Unsure of how to handle this person who'd never been a part of her life but whose shadow had never quite left it.

The slight but somehow enormously smug smile that curved Purva's lips telegraphed that she knew exactly what impact she was having. She tucked a strand of her straight black hair behind her ear, watching Meghna stand without offering a hand to help. "I know *you*," she said crisply, her posh British-Indian accent sharp enough to cut glass. "Better than you know yourself."

"Bullshit," Meghna spat, checking her weapons again. *All present and accounted for.* The stiletto she'd killed Mirko with was a comforting weight against her palm, and she curled her fingers around it. "You have no idea who I am." *No idea what I'm capable of.*

"Don't I?" Purva's coal-black eyes glittered like diamonds. "You think I don't know how you hate me for leaving you and divorcing your father? How you've called me 'the General' all these years because you don't want to call me 'Ma'? Do you think I haven't watched you push people away because it's easier than letting them close? You may think I'm heartless, but one thing I'm definitely not is stupid."

Meghna had never thought the General was stupid. Cold, calculating. Ruthless and practical. But never stupid. And hearing her private thoughts dissected like this stung like wasps. "Is that why you wanted to meet? So we could have a warm and fuzzy heart-to-heart about our dysfunctional relationship?" A thermos of chai would've been more appropriate for that than a syringe full of sedatives. "Did you think I needed some very belated motherly advice about boys? No, thank you."

"No, I think you need a warning about who you're working with," Purva said. "Any advice I have is just a bonus."

"I know who I'm working with," she assured. She'd learned every inch of Elijah over the past few days. Memorized all of his tics and tells. Wrapped herself in how he tasted and smelled. And, strangest of all, she knew his heart. His big, brave, generous heart that even had room for a soulless cynic like her.

The General—*my mother*, she mentally corrected as if that would somehow prove the woman wrong—arched an imperious eyebrow. Her full lips curled. It was an expression that telegraphed *I know something you don't know*. And it raised Meghna's hackles.

"Did you bring down the lodge?" she wondered, though she already suspected the answer was in the affirmative. Tavi Estrada was too self-motivated, too cagey, to do something so showy. No, blowing up a building was more her mother's style. She loved setting worlds on fire and then going back to her mountain and letting everyone else deal with the fallout.

"It had to be done," her mother replied, without even the barest nod toward regret or concern. "The Committee burned this location as well as the clinic near Farmington where you had that unfortunate encounter with Dr. Gary Schoenlein. The situation needed to be contained."

"What?" The ice clinking in her stomach had spread to her veins. Her throat. And it froze her feet to the ground. "What committee? How do you know about Schoenlein?" The puzzle pieces weren't fitting together. Not in any way that made sense. And then one incongruent, ugly piece hovered in the forefront of Meghna's mind. "D-did you send that hit squad to the safe house? Did you try to *kill* me, Ma?"

"No! Never!" For the first time in twenty years, Purva Saxena's mirror-smooth facade cracked, the fractures spider-webbing out until even her eyes held damp emotion. "Everything I have done, I have done to *save* you, Meghna. To build you up and make you strong and prepare you to fight. And when I learned that Hollister was using the Committee to work at cross-purposes...to further his own agenda...I knew you had to be told."

Hollister. The Committee. Meghna spoke eight languages and she had no idea what those words meant. "What the hell are you talking about?" Surely Elijah had awakened by now. He'd realize she was gone. She didn't have time to play guessing games.

"Third Shift," Purva said. "They're one of many black-ops mercenary groups who take their cues from a committee inside the American government. But it's not just a national committee. It's a global group cooperating on a shared purpose. I represent the Vidrohi's interests. Roman Hollister represents..." Her mother broke off, mouth twisting in a grimace. "He represents himself. That much has become clear."

It clicked then. Roman Hollister was a billionaire industrialist and financier. Like Jeff Bezos and Elon Musk's older, wealthier template. His social tier was much higher than hers. He had a private island where he reportedly threw lavish parties and private orgies. He hobnobbed with presidents, kings, and dictators alike. Meghna suddenly remembered Mirko bragging at last week's party about a Moscow brothel and the prime minister...*oh*. There was where the puzzle piece fit in. "And you think Third Shift is doing Hollister's bidding? No. It's not possible. They wanted to take Mirko down."

"Maybe he did, too. Have you considered that?" Purva challenged, crossing her arms over her chest. "Do you know where that scientist's coveted serum is going, Meghna? Who it was marked for all along? Roman Hollister has been using his influence for *decades* to make this happen. Right under all of our noses. On that fantasy island of his. Only the rich and famous come back. None of the working women and party girls ever do."

Meghna hated every bit of this. The eleventh-hour exposition was like something out of a bad spy movie. One of Chase's early box-office bombs. And she'd never expected the woman who gave birth to her to be the one delivering the cheesy dialogue. "So what? If Hollister's some sort of evil billionaire supervillain who wants to breed his own shape-shifters…what does have to do with Elijah and 3S?"

"Ask them. Find out." The General was back. The vulnerability she'd displayed earlier was all but gone. Her gaze hardened. "Do what you've been taught to do. What you've taught yourself to do."

A frustrated scream tore from Meghna's throat and her fingers clenched around her stiletto hard enough for the blade to cut into her skin. It began healing almost immediately, but that was little comfort. "Why don't you take down Hollister yourself?" she demanded. "If you're in this Committee together. Why don't you blow it up from the inside just like you blew up that resort over there?"

"Because the balance at the top is too delicate," Purva said with another careless shrug. Maybe she had a whole collection of shrugs. One for every fuck she didn't give. "It's far better to let you destroy the foundation so it crumbles. I just thought you would like to know what you were truly up against."

"So that's it? That's what you had to say to me that was so important?" she asked. This was the epitome of a meeting that could have easily been an email. "Are you going to walk away now that you've delivered your little message?" *Like you always do?*

"No, Meghna." Purva shook her head as she pulled a pair of black gloves from her pockets and slipped them on one by one. "You're going to walk away. You're going to walk back to Elijah Richter. And I truly hope he's as trustworthy as you think he is. There's one lesson I did not bother to teach you, and I should have. Apsaras don't *have* to leave," she said in a gentle tone reserved for lullabies, for lories. For songs Meghna had never heard her sing. "You can choose to stay."

What bubbled up in Meghna's throat then wasn't a scream so much as a sob. For the little girl who'd never been told such a simple thing. For the young woman who'd never believed it. For the adult who'd insisted she didn't need it. "Then why didn't you?"

The General, Purva, *Ma* just shook her head, something almost like sadness playing across her face before it went impassive once more. And then she gestured for Meghna to go. "You're running out of time."

No. Meghna dashed hot tears away with the backs of her blood-stained hands before she clenched them into fists and pivoted toward the opening in the trees. She had all the time in the world. And she was going to use it to do what mattered. To change what she could. The future. Not the past.

The force of the blast must've knocked him out for a good fifteen to twenty minutes. Maybe even longer, Elijah reckoned, when he came 'round to Meghna crouched over him with concern written all over her gorgeous face. And a Black Hawk helicopter hovering in the sky about half a klick away, a ladder hanging out of its open belly. He sat up with a groan, cataloging the bumps and bruises from tangling with Mirko's guards. Funny thing was, his head didn't hurt like he'd cracked it. But shifter biology was strange that way. Every day a new surprise.

"About time you woke up, Sleeping Beauty," Meghna said, offering him a hand.

"Don't let the team hear that nickname," he warned as he accepted her help and levered up from his ungainly sprawl on the ground. "I'll never hear the end of it." He made quick work of brushing concrete chips from his arms and shoulders. Great slabs of stone and brick had rained down all around them, and the building was still coming down.

Meghna watched him get sorted with such intensity that it was almost unnerving. And when he caught her at it, met those big dark-brown eyes, she looked away. "We should go," she said, all business and no nonsense. The teasing tone she'd adopted when he woke was safely tucked away. "The helicopter's only been here for a few minutes, but I can't imagine they want to linger much longer."

She was right. Estrada was long gone with the briefcase and its sought-after contents by now. There was no use in standing here and faffing about. So they scarpered, closing the distance to the Black Hawk and clambering up the ladder. Meghna swung inside like she'd been born to it and he followed with much less grace. Which was all right, because the actual Grace was waiting for them in the hold. Along with Finn and Chase Saunders, who was settled in on a gurney with a saline drip. *Thank Christ.* Elijah had never doubted they'd complete their mission and get out safely, but visual confirmation sent palpable relief coursing through his veins.

"Cheers, mate," he said to Finn with an appreciative nod while Grace helped JP check over Meghna, every inch the doctor even if she wasn't planning to do it professionally anymore.

"I'm fine, I promise," Meghna was protesting as he turned toward the open door to pull in the ladder and close everything up.

"You're definitely 'fine,' ma'am, but let's make sure you're okay" was apparently JP's version of bedside manner...or maybe that was for Elijah's benefit, because the wolf shifter laughed when he growled his displeasure.

Elijah focused his attention below so he wouldn't toss JP out on his arse on principle. The hunting lodge looked like it had been nuked from space. Fire and ruin. A mushroom cloud billowing up and out across the surrounding land. He waited until they'd cleared the smoke, pulled up into the clouds beyond it, before he got up and walked to the front of the helo, where Jack was on the controls. He was a fair pilot, but he didn't take the seat often.

He must've been beyond worried to fly the rescue himself. The modified Black Hawk was a stealth, quieter than a baby's nursery, but Elijah still raised his volume when he spoke, like he had to be heard over the engines. Some habits never died. "What's the early assessment?" he asked. "Was that a total fuckup or what?"

"You tell *me*," Jackson said, keeping his gaze trained out on the clouds. "It sounded like a shit show, and I'm beginning to think they're all going to be shit shows from here on out."

"Shit shows and clusterfucks all the way down," Elijah agreed, taking the empty copilot's seat—which JP must've filled on the way in. The uptight boss and the mouthy new recruit flying the friendly skies together…that would've been one awkward ride. Elijah didn't envy that. "Estrada nicked the serum. So that's bad news and it's good news. We didn't secure the package, but we do know where it's going, yeah?"

"Yeah. He took the getaway plane meant for Mirko. It took off just before the lodge lit up, and Joaquin's already tracking the flight," Jack confirmed. "We'll be able to plot our follow-up without too much difficulty. And you'll get to sit it out. You've had entirely too much face time lately, my friend, and discretion is the better part of valor."

So that was one bit of a bright spot amid the literal fire and brimstone. Elijah glanced back at the helo's belly, where JP was patching up Meghna's scrapes despite her protests that she would heal. He was more hands-on than Gracie, that one. As if every patient he helped could make up for a life he'd taken. Would Meg follow in his footsteps? Doing penance for what she thought were her sins? Elijah didn't know and couldn't say. But he knew she wouldn't rest until they closed the book on this entire operation. It wasn't done just because Elijah was being benched. It wasn't done just because Mirko Aston was dead. It was just getting started.

"We did learn one other valuable thing before all hell broke loose," he told Jack. "We were right about how high up this goes.

It's got tentacles all over. Hollywood. High society. Government. But Mirko answered to someone even higher. Someone who wanted him to take out his competition. Means we can't trust anyone but ourselves."

"Maybe we can't even trust ourselves," Meghna's voice came from behind them. She'd shaken off JP and his pervy mother-hen impression. Her face was smudged with soot but already devoid of bruises. Her gorgeous eyes were hard. Focused not on Elijah but on Jack. "Maybe there's a perfectly logical explanation for why all your missions seem to go wrong, and maybe it's currently piloting this helicopter."

The hell? Elijah's fur bristled and he growled, immediately defensive. "What? What in the bloody blazes are you talking about, Meg? How is *Jack* the problem here?"

She shook her head. Still staring at his friend, his partner. "Ask him about Roman Hollister," she demanded. "About Hollister's private island. Paradise for his rich friends but hell for all the women he's trafficked there. There's no way Jackson doesn't have *some* idea that he's been involved all along."

"Roman Hollister?" Jackson wiped the back of his hand across his mouth, as if the name tasted foul. Sparks shot from his fingertips like the world's most inappropriately timed Fourth of July sparklers. His face bleached of what little color it had. "You're sure? *That's* who's orchestrating all of this?"

Dread crawled up Elijah's spine as he forced down his shift. "You know him?"

"Yeah." Jack's gaze was bleak. His smile macabre and mirthless. "He's my biological father—and one of our bosses."

Lije didn't know which bizarre piece of information to process first. "What?" was all he could manage, and fortunately, it covered all the bases. "What the fuck does that mean?"

"The committee I report to," Jackson explained. "It started as purely U.S. government, but in the last few years, it's been a cooperative effort between global powers. Made up of military and civilians. Roman Hollister is one of the members. He brought me, and by extension Third Shift, in."

"He's been playing you, using you for his own purposes. And it's highly likely he sent the phantom hit squad," Meghna added darkly. "Probably to clear the chessboard for him and whatever his endgame is. Congratulations." She made a sound that was a cross between a groan and a curse, dropping her head into her hands and scrubbing at her hair. If Elijah hadn't shaved off his locs, he'd have done the same. This was worse than a shit show and a clusterfuck. Infinitely worse.

"And he's your dad?" he prompted Jack incredulously. "You never breathed one word of that to me and I've been your best mate for near a decade." He'd never, *ever* considered that the person at 3S keeping the most secrets had been by his side from the jump.

"Sperm donor," Jack corrected, a muscle twitching in his jaw. "Jonathan Tate is and always will be my dad. We come from an old family of sorcerers, but Dad had prostate cancer in his thirties. It rendered him infertile. No magic exists that can beat what cancer does to you. When he realized he and Mom couldn't have their own children…he turned to Hollister. His old friend. His old *sorcerer* friend. To ensure that I would still be born with powers. Hollister's job began and ended there as far as my parents were concerned. But he's always…taken an interest in me."

He said those last words with a fair amount of distaste, but Elijah couldn't offer any comfort. Not when Meghna was looking at them both like they were the enemy. "That interest of his has us compromised and we didn't even know it. *Fuck.*" Hollister had been one step ahead of them—maybe three steps ahead—this entire time…just to lead Third Shift in circles.

Jack's fists clenched around the Black Hawk's controls. "But why would he try to kill you? It doesn't make any sense," he huffed.

"He had to know Safe House 13 was *mine*. The riding academy is attached to an LLC under my name."

Meghna made that harsh noise again and sharply shook her head. But when she spoke, it was oddly soft. Pitying. *Disappointed.* "Why do men do anything?" she asked rhetorically, walling herself up behind her crossed arms. "Power."

It was too much all at once. The fighting. The explosion. Getting knocked out. Jackson's revelations. And now this. Her pulling inward and pulling away. Elijah couldn't have it. He wouldn't. "That's not the only reason men do things, Meg," he said, rising from the copilot's chair. Going to her in just two long strides. Stopping just a hairsbreadth away. "Sometimes they do them for love."

She tilted her head, looking up at him. He'd never before thought of her as small, as fragile. She was just as fearsome in flats as she was in heels. But there was something breakable about her now. Something JP and Gracie hadn't been able to patch. And he was suddenly aware of just how much taller, bigger than her he was.

Until she cut him down with one quiet sentence and walked back into the hold. "Sometimes love just isn't enough."

He went after her. Of course he went after her. There was hardly any other place to go on the helo besides that. "How would you know, Meg?" he said to her back—as stiff as a board and impenetrable as a brick wall. "You ever been loved like that? Ever let anyone that close? I don't think so."

Not until him. And it wasn't ego to think that. He'd seen it first-hand. How she'd opened up to him, opened up *for* him. Not just physically, in bed, but emotionally and intellectually. She'd shown him corners of herself he damn well knew Chase Saunders had never seen.

"I failed my mission," she said, turning slowly to face him. Her voice was heavy with anger and self-judgment. With JP and

Finn and their supernatural ears onboard, there was no point in whispering. In trying not to be heard. And she pitched her words accordingly. Like an accomplished public speaker. "I let myself believe we had a common purpose, that we could both succeed. But I gave up our objective in pursuit of yours. And then we both failed, didn't we? Estrada took off with the serum. I didn't find who I was looking for. That's what matters more than love in our line of work."

There were so many things to tackle, both personal and professional, and Elijah didn't know which to pluck out first. "*Our* objective?" he repeated. "The apsaras?" He mangled the vowels, but Meghna didn't flinch or correct his pronunciation. She just shook her head.

"No," she said. "Though apsaras are a part of the Vidrohi, they're not the sum total."

He saw Finn shift in his periphery. Like he recognized the word. Elijah couldn't say the same. *Vidrohi*. It didn't ring any black-ops bells. Not military either. Meghna saw the questions in his expression. He didn't even have to prod her to go on.

"Vidrohi means 'rebel' or 'revolutionary.' There's a famous Bengali poem with that title. And thousands of years ago, we took it as ours. Third Shift...you still operate inside the lines," she said, moving across the Black Hawk to the unoccupied section by the door they'd climbed through. "Keyed into the government. The military. The Vidrohi know no lines, have no official rosters, no creed except justice. We were antifa before antifa," she murmured, twisting to look at him again. "My mother brought the organization—if you can even call it that—into the new century. And then the Darkest Day happened. And it all got worse. Here. Europe. Asia. My mother actually reached out to other factions to form an oversight committee. United in purpose to combat evil around the world. That's Jackson's Committee."

He didn't care about that. Sod that connection. It was the least important part of what she'd said. "Your mum got you into this?" Elijah felt the growl rumble through him and vibrate within the words. "She…she put you out to work on your back for the greater good?" *Christ.* What kind of parent did that to their child?

"*No.* That was *my* choice," Meghna assured instantly and vehemently. "I saw it as a natural progression of what my powers can do. It was efficient. A tactical advantage. Just like the military utilizing shifters in war…except on *my* orders only."

He flinched as her barb about his time in the service struck sharp like one of her blades. JP's grunt from where he was monitoring Chase's saline drip told him he'd felt the hit, too. They were both veterans of their respective countries' military as well as of the Apex Initiative. They'd lost friends in Afghanistan, in Iraq. Sacrificed relationships. Put their lives on the line.

"Here now, that's not fair…" Elijah began, only to stop and shake his head. "You're right," he said after a moment. Because she was. They'd lost friends…but they'd taken friends, too, hadn't they? Someone's brother, someone's father, someone's son or daughter. People, both human and supernatural, who were fighting for *their* leaders' ideas of what was right. "I've done things I'm not proud of," he admitted. "We all did. Out there in the desert. In the name of queen and country. For progress and patriotism and all that shite. And it was all 'on orders.' Just doing what we were told. Like automatons. As if we couldn't choose different."

He could've listened to Mum and refused to fight in a white man's war. But he'd gone ahead and done it. Again and again. And maybe Meghna saw some of that recognition in his eyes, because she sighed wearily and gestured him close. He crossed to her in two long strides, taking the hand she reached out to him.

"What would you have done if you did choose differently, Elijah?" she asked softly. Just for him now. No matter who was pretending not to listen.

"3S," he said without hesitation. "I'm doing it now." Putting together this team with Jackson was the best thing he'd ever done.

Meghna nodded, her eyes bright with understanding. "That's what embracing my heritage, what joining the Vidrohi, was for me," she said. "Choosing something besides mindless conformity and swallowing the party lines we've been spoon-fed our whole lives. Peace doesn't have to come at the expense of brown lives across the ocean, Elijah. It can come because we fight white supremacy right here at home. You know that and 3S proves that. That's all I've been trying to do."

"Alone," he pointed out, bringing their joined hands to his chest. "And you don't have to do that anymore. You can try doing it with me, with *us*. We can fight all of this, untangle all of it, together."

"Even if you don't like what we find out?" she wondered, one eyebrow arching with challenge.

"Even then. Having people is what makes all the difference, Meg." *Stay*, he wanted to tell her. *Stay with me. Join me. Join us.* But he half suspected she'd grab a parachute and jump out over the Hudson River if he pushed it any more right now. She was still skittish. With good reason. Too much had happened too quickly. And if what she and Jack were saying about Roman Hollister was true, Third Shift only had more difficult work ahead. "Just think about it," he urged instead.

"I will," Meghna assured before releasing his hand and stepping back. "I promise I will."

And he knew her well enough by now to believe her.

31

THE PRIVATE AIRFIELD WAS JUST that. Private. Damn near deserted except for the car and driver waiting to take Tavi and his briefcase full of presents to Hollister's luxury lair. That he'd arrived alone garnered not even a blink from the white human who guided the Audi along the five-mile journey. Maybe the henchman was paid not to blink. He'd no doubt seen a great number of disturbing things. A sleek, white supersonic jet without Mirko Aston and his entourage barely rated on the list. And someone had likely notified Hollister of the bulk loss of several useful toadies. No matter, surely. There were always more criminals to recruit. An endless supply. That was going to be Tavi's party line when questioned at least. He needed to make himself just as indispensable to Roman Hollister as he had to Mirko. And if he was lucky, the men would meet the same untimely end.

What he saw of the island between the airfield and Hollister's estate was boring to the point of being suspicious, even under the cover of night. Beautiful foliage. A smooth road. Nothing and everything that screamed of hidden ugliness. It was enough to sharpen his canines, and he felt the prick of them on his own tongue. The wounds healed before he could even taste the blood.

This is where it ends, one way or another, Tavi thought as he stepped out of the car and onto a long, winding driveway that led up to a columned portico. He'd made it here…but he was far from out of the woods. That was patently clear when he took in his welcoming committee just a few yards away on the perfectly paved basalt drive.

A woman with a few guards behind her. Lit by the lampposts situated at intervals along the border of the lawn. She appeared pale-skinned, blond-haired, like the Aryan ideal. Clad in a sharply cut gray business suit and wearing ridiculously impractical high heels. None of that masked who and what she really was. Not to his eyes. Because he *knew* her. The brown-skinned beauty who'd bedeviled him for more than a century. Her riotous black curls rippling across her shoulders. Her ripe curves, barely contained by the confines of her suit. A jinn's glamour could only do so much. It couldn't cover up his memories. Or the essence of her that had long ago seeped into his bones.

She realized immediately that he saw through her facade. She had never been a person slow on the uptake. And she *knew* him too, didn't she? Uncomfortably well. A wry grin quirked the lines of her full lips. "Octavio. You came. You found me," she said in perfectly bland and unaccented English that jarred his ears. She'd always been a fair mimic, but combined with her business-school Barbie exterior, it was unnerving.

He curled his fingers tightly around the handle of the hermetically sealed briefcase that had guaranteed his safe entry to this island. Yes, he knew her. It didn't mean he *trusted* her. But he did… he did *miss* her. "I promised I always would, didn't I?"

"As if you keep promises?" she snorted, sounding a bit more like the person he remembered.

"As if you've ever made one?" he countered. "Just how many men have you lured to this place besides me? Am I merely your latest mark?"

Her glamour slipped then. Just a fraction. Revealing the woman he'd been playing cat-and-mouse games with for more than a century. Her gorgeous hair. Her eyes, as deep brown as the wrapping of a good cigar and just as smoky. His greatest enemy. *His greatest love.* "You bastard!" she cried as she pulled her mask back up, hand flashing out in a slap that rocked his head back. "How dare you?"

Tavi could almost feel the borrowed blood blooming under his skin in the shape of her fingers and thumb. And he smiled. *Here* she was. The wildly unpredictable jinn with the fiery temper who'd tossed a drink in his face in 1922. "A thank-you would've sufficed, Ayesha."

"Thank you," she said tartly before leading him up toward the grand building ahead.

If the guards were at all concerned about their odd exchanges, they were as well paid as his driver to feign indifference. They were all white, fair-skinned and light-haired. Tavi wondered, not quite so idly, if they were prime candidates for the serum. Test batches had been used on "less-than-ideal specimens"—Mirko's words, not his. Women no one would miss. Somehow, Ayesha had avoided being one of them. And he suspected that had a lot to do with her extreme blond makeover. Was it voluntary, or had Hollister wished for it? Either way, it was a complete anathema. Repulsive. To cage someone so vibrant, so thoroughly herself, in what amounted to a white-woman skin suit. It was like something out of a horror novel. Being such a thing himself, he recognized true abomination.

Oh, Ayesha. What the hell is going on here? As he followed her under the portico—where the car could have pulled up but didn't, a clear intimidation tactic—he let his gaze fall to her hands. Pale, slender, unfamiliar fingers. She'd had a ring. A jeweled ring that never left the middle finger of her right hand. It was gauche to ask a jinn about lamps, about talismans, but he'd always assumed it held meaning or magic. It was gone.

Fuck. He'd come to rescue her. To rescue all of them. If this went sideways, who the hell was going to rescue *him*?

━━━━━━━━━━

Third Shift HQ was buzzing with activity for hours after they all swiped in, bone-weary after the drive from Teterboro. Jack had almost said "fuck it" and landed on the roof in Hell's Kitchen before remembering he didn't have a strictly legal helo pad up there. Grace appreciated the concession to practicality. And she even—grudgingly—appreciated having to go through the checkpoint to get back into the city. The last thing they needed was the NYPD and the Sanctuary Alliance cracking down on them for fudging the rules. Especially when they had to sneak a major Hollywood star back to his California hospital before any of the tabloids realized he'd gone missing. The checkpoint guards hadn't looked too closely at the mound of blankets in the back of their van. Not after Jack flashed his pearly whites and his government clearance.

And now they were back on their home turf. Splitting up for med bay and showers and debriefings. When Grace finished the first two out of the three, she came back to Command to find Finn sprawled in Jackson's favorite chair at the head of the table. He'd changed out of his gear and cleaned up, too. He looked pale and tragic in a dark-red silk shirt and leather pants. Like he was headed to an anniversary showing of *Interview with the Vampire* after they wrapped things here instead of straight down to bed with her and Nate—who he'd no doubt seen when he put on his goth-inspired outfit.

Grace could imagine what that reunion had looked like. The soft touches. The fierce kisses. Finn saying something absolutely awful and Nate countering it with something smart and sharp but kind. She'd been caught up with getting Chase stabilized for transport and had cleaned up in the Locker for the sake of efficiency

and speed. Because if they'd all been at Finn's place together…
well, the only debriefing would've involved their underwear. Even
with how exhausted she was, how very *done*, her pulse jumped at
the idea.

Down, girl! She reined in her urge for post-mission sex and
closeness, leaning one hip against the conference table. "You
heard about Estrada?"

Finn scoffed, tapping out a restless rhythm just inches from her
perch. "That he did a fuckin' runner with the shape-shifter serum
and left us all looking like fools? Yeah. Jack and Lije made that
quite clear."

"How do you feel about that?" she asked, fully aware that she
sounded like a high-priced therapist who should charge $200 an
hour for the answer. But despite her fascination with the brain,
psychiatry had never been her field of interest. The only mind she
wanted to unlock was Finn's.

"How d'you think I feel about that, Gracie?" He made a dis-
gusted noise. "I'm considering hiring a plane to fly a banner over
HQ that says 'I told you so.'" But then his defensive shoulders
dropped. He dragged one hand through his dark hair, scrubbing
his scalp with frustration. "And I'm…disappointed. I've been on
this earth forever and a day, and I still thought that maybe, just
maybe, he'd see what we're doing here and want in. Maybe I'm the
biggest fool of all."

He was a lot of things—a pain in the ass, a gorgeous hunk of
undead man—but he wasn't that. Grace removed his fingers from
the rat's nest they were making of his hair, squeezing them. "No.
You're not. I think part of the reason we're *all* here is because we
want to believe it's the right road. The best way for us to fight
everything that makes us mad or hurts us. It's why I chose this
over my job at Queensboro. But *I chose*, Finn. You can't make that
decision *for* anyone."

Finn interlaced their fingers, studying the pattern they made for a few seconds like he was sorting out a puzzle. "That's why you resisted me for so long, isn't it?" he murmured, glancing back up at her. "Didn't let me railroad you into an affair with your coworker. It had to be on your terms."

It was on the tip of her tongue to make a crass joke about him railing her plenty in the end. He'd appreciate it. Probably follow it up with a lewd quip about him rubbing off on her. But Grace knew he appreciated her sincerity and her no-bullshit approach more. "If we'd slept together at the beginning, would we be here now? Best friends? Partners? With Nate? I like how we got here," she said. "And for all you pretending that you're a sexual harassment lawsuit waiting to happen, that was a choice we made *together*. You respected me, Finian. And I grew to respect you as a result. Maybe Tavi Estrada needs someone to do that for him."

"And maybe he needs to go fuck himself," Finn suggested in return, his tone thankfully more amused than angry.

"That is also a distinct possibility, yes," she agreed. "Honestly, that would be my suggestion for him before any personal growth he might attempt."

Finn laughed, reaching for her and pulling her close. Until she was verging on falling right into his lap. They kissed in full view of the surveillance cameras, office rules and surly bosses be damned. "I love you," he whispered as he traced a sensual trail from her jawline to her ear and back. "I hope you know that, Grace of my heart."

"I do," she said simply. "And I know I love you." It was both the easiest and most challenging thing in the world…loving this outrageous and beautiful vampire.

Maybe they both could love the man waiting for them downstairs. Nate Feinberg was everything Tavi wasn't. Trustworthy. Kind. *All in.* They could, the three of them, choose each other over and over again. As many times as it took to stick. Grace was actually looking forward to it. She was all in, too.

32

COMMAND WAS IN CHAOS. LUCKY for all of them, it was a familiar chaos. Post-mission meetings, reports being filed, Joaquin being Joaquin. "Gimme!" they insisted, wiggling their fingers for the Honeybee that Finn and Grace had taken on the op. Danny swiped the device off the conference table and chucked the device across the conference room like a grenade, narrowly missing hitting Elijah in the head. "Oi!" he shouted irritably. Danny didn't even bother looking sorry, the little shite.

Fuck, he was utterly knackered. But it was hours yet till the team could wrap up and head to their quarters. He rubbed at his temples, slouching down in his chair and returning his attention to Jackson—who'd been ranting about the shape-shifter serum for the past seven and a half minutes.

"How do we know Estrada won't try to sell it to the highest bidder in a *real* auction?" Jack demanded of everybody and nobody. "Aston took out his direct competition, but there are still takers out there."

"Like the U.S. military?" Meghna suggested, with no small amount of accusation. She'd taken the seat furthest from Elijah. On the other side of the table. Looking as exhausted as he felt.

He was trying not to take her cooling off too personally, trying to be a mature adult and give her space to breathe. But all he'd wanted to do for hours was hold her. In the transport on the way back to HQ. When she haltingly told everyone about the Vidrohi and Ayesha. Even while she was having a go at the armed forces. "The scientist, Schoenlein, he'd mentioned something about the military doing their own experimentation. Who knows what kind of shifters they've created? Maybe they want more?"

The flurry of sound and motion in the room ground to a sudden halt. *Oh. Right.* With back-to-back crises taking up their full attention, he'd neglected to tell her a very important detail about himself. Or expand on the salient points. Half the eyes in Command went to him and Jack. The other half swiveled to JP, who barked out a laugh. The former Marine straightened just slightly from his usual sprawl and raised his hand. "Me," he volunteered. "I'm the experimentation. Or one of many, anyway. Pretty sure the Apex Initiative has hit on its perfect recipe, though," he shrugged. "They ain't in the market for more juice."

"And we would know," Elijah added. "We've a pipeline from them to 3S. They feed us recruits, occasional intel."

"How's that operation any different from Aston and Hollister building their own army?" Meghna's contemplative frown furrowed her brow. The disapproval was heavy in her voice.

Jack, their golden boy with a dress uniform in his closet, protested immediately. "It's entirely different and you know it."

But she wasn't so easily dismissed. "Why?" she demanded as she leaned forward. "Because the military does it for their country? For their ideals? I'm sure Hollister has ideals, too. I don't know exactly what you've done in the name of patriotism, what your Apex Initiative claims to be, but I do know that it results in the same thing we left back at the lodge: senseless death. Collateral damage in the form of innocent civilians. Drone strikes killing brown women and children."

Elijah winced. He could hardly dispute that. "I reckon that's a row we're never going to stop having, Meg," he admitted, accepting the discomfort. The responsibility. The questions he, Jack, and JP were still working out among themselves. "It's not something we're gonna solve in our lifetimes. Not while whoever has the biggest guns or the sharpest claws runs the world."

"Can we move from the philosophical to the practical?" Jack was the irritated and tired one now. The sad state of his suit—rumpled, tie discarded—should have been Lije's first clue that his friend was nearing the end of his tether. "Our next move is the island. Joaquin found the falsified flight plan for Mirko's private jet and hacked it. We have two options: assume Estrada took the plane to its intended destination and kill two birds with one stone. Or split our focus to look for him *and* pursue Hollister."

Pursue Hollister. Jack's biological father. Elijah was still wrapping his mind around that tidy bit of what-the-fuck. But they had other pressing priorities besides Jack's personal episode of *Coronation Street.* "Finn said to assume Estrada went to the island," he recalled from the vampire's debrief. "He said, and I quote, 'The two-faced fucker had his own reasons for being up Mirko's arse.' Something about where the bodies are buried. And accessing the cemetery. Tavi wouldn't have come so far not to see that through."

"I know how that feels," Meghna interjected wearily. "I can count my mission failures on one hand. I didn't want this to be one of them." She scrubbed at her hair, loosening several strands from her messy ponytail. Neha reached over and squeezed her hand. Some silent message passed between the two women. A moment of solidarity. They barely knew one another…and yet understood some things instantly.

"Maybe the woman you're looking for is there, too, with the rest of the trafficking victims," Neha said. "Maybe she got to Hollister first."

Coupled with Tavi Estrada's whereabouts, that was a lot of

maybes. But Elijah wasn't going to let the uncertainties hamper whatever Third Shift did next. They'd worked with thinner intel before. Pulled off last-minute miracles. Faked a man's death and changed his identity in a matter of weeks. They'd flip that bloody island upside down if they had to, in order to see who or what fell out.

"We've got this," he told his team. "What happened upstate was a setback, yeah, but I've seen us do some brilliant things when we thought all was lost. We're fighters. And we're family. We'll figure this one out as well," he promised.

Something flickered in Meghna's gaze. Warmth. It went from a flicker to a blaze. And her lips tilted up in a faint smile that gradually widened. *"It makes you exactly who I thought you were. An idealist. A hero. A man with an overabundance of hope,"* she'd said to him not too long ago, in the comfort of his bed and his arms. Was she thinking of that now, as he was? In the end, it didn't matter if he was any of those things—idealistic, heroic, hopeful. As long as he was here with Third Shift. As long as he was hers.

Meghna had never been so thankful for paperwork. For all the things that came *after* an op. The debriefings. The additional medical examinations. Logging the gear used and returning borrowed items to the Locker. Making sure Chase had been put on a private flight back to California. All of it meant that she had most of the night and the early morning filled with mundane tasks that kept her from thinking too hard about what had happened during that last hour in the Finger Lakes. Mostly her mother. Worse, her mother being *right*. When she at last found herself alone in Elijah's suite of rooms, washing up in his en suite bathroom, she gripped the edges of the sink with slippery hands and tried not to crumble.

"I think you need a warning about who you're working with."

"*Apsaras don't have to leave.*"

Those were statements that did not, on their face, intersect. And Meghna was too exhausted to try and figure out how they made any kind of sense at all coming from the same woman who'd kept her at arm's length for nearly thirty-five years. She was too tired for puzzles, for games. Maybe she'd been tired of them this entire time. And that was why, when Elijah appeared in the mirror, looming behind her and haloed by the track lighting, all she could think was *good. Good, now I can rest.*

They hadn't spoken much after the helicopter ride back to HQ. He'd given her space. She'd taken it and then some. Now she fell back against him, obliterating the inches between their bodies. And he caught her. Banding his arms across her. Turning her and settling her head beneath his chin. It was silent. Simple. Not an end to what they'd said to each other on the helo or a continuation of it. A *hug*. Meghna couldn't remember the last time she'd been hugged or given one. Maybe some red-carpet cheek press for the cameras. This was different. It was for no one's eyes but their own, reflected in the glass. And it enveloped her. Sent warmth melting through her skin and her bones. There was nothing transactional about Elijah's arms around her, nothing asked for and nothing taken. It was pure and shared and safe.

They stayed like that for the longest time. Minutes. An hour. With his heartbeat steady beneath her ear and his fingers drawing gentle circles between her shoulder blades. "What *is* enough, Meghna? What do you need?" he asked after a while, like they *were* continuing the conversation from earlier. "Tell me, and I'll give it all to you."

"I don't know," she admitted. "I might never know." She'd lived so much of her life alone. And the rest of it superficially. As she'd told herself dozens of times before, all she really knew of happiness came in gift boxes or wineglasses or from a perfect murder. Seeing Purva hadn't magically fixed that. Maybe only therapy would. Years and years of therapy. Not to mention that she was going to have to tell Elijah that he hadn't been taken out by debris but by her *mother*. When he was already highly suspicious of the General's motives. That wasn't exactly an auspicious start to a relationship.

Plus, Ayesha was still missing. Meghna was no closer to finding out what happened to her than when she'd started seeing Mirko so many months ago. And they still didn't know enough about the Committee and Roman Hollister's plans, though Jackson had sworn to get to the bottom of it all. What if the General was more involved than she'd claimed? Meghna still didn't fully understand the ins and outs of her mysterious oversight Committee. Why the insistence upon anonymity among the Vidrohi ranks if Purva was going to spill their secrets to some global cabal? Her mother had promised her "later" as she pushed her back toward the event center. *"I'll tell you everything later. For now…do what you must."* And wasn't that always what Meghna did? What they both did? What they must? What if it put her and Elijah on opposite sides? What then?

"You don't need all the answers right now, love," Elijah murmured, his deep and rumbling voice vibrating through the top of her skull and down to her toes. "All you need is to believe me. To believe in *us*. You and me. Right here. And I know you already do. We've crossed that hurdle."

He was right. They had. She'd trusted him quickly, too quickly. Probably from the minute he'd slashed Sasha Nichols's throat. Maybe even before. When she'd felt his eyes on her from across the VIP room. She never would've gone with him to Connecticut, to the safe house and beyond, if she didn't believe in him on some basic, implicit level. If she didn't care about the same things he cared about. Truth and justice and friends and family. She could have, should have, left at any time and continued on her solo path. But she hadn't. She'd chosen to stay.

Apsaras didn't have to leave. *She* didn't have to leave.

Meghna raised a hand to Elijah's face. His stubborn, beautiful, strong-featured face. His beard had grown in even thicker over the last day, the hair soft on her palm. She'd kissed him a week ago to seduce him, to distract him. Now she did it to claim him. To promise him. *I'm here*, she said with the first teasing whisper of her lips against his. *I believe you*, she said as she traced the bow of his mouth with the tip of her tongue. *I trust you.* She peppered wicked little pecks at the corners of his lips.

"I love you," he groaned as he opened to her, hot and hungry, and met her equally ravenous kiss. "I know it's too soon, it's mad, but it's the truth."

I love you, he repeated as he hitched her up in his arms, wrapping her legs around his hips. *I love you*, he said again as he walked her to the bed and came down with her to the mattress. *Love you, love you, love you*, he echoed as he stripped her of her clothes and her every defense. Because she didn't need defenses with this man. He saw her for who she was and loved her—wanted her—just the same.

Meghna couldn't say the words out loud yet. She could barely string them together in her head. But she hoped he felt them in the stroke of her hand. In the welcome of her thighs. In how she rose to meet him when he shucked his clothes and bared his cock. *I think I could love you, too*, she told him as he sank deep inside her and she anchored her blunt nails in the tight cheeks of his ass. She showed him with every cry of pleasure he drew from her throat. With a hundred openmouthed kisses. With her foot tracing restless circles on the back of his thigh. With how she didn't let go. Not during. Not after. And never again. Elijah Richter was hers. Her man. Her lion. Her heart.

Later, while she drowsed in the warmth of his massive arms and broad chest and he absently threaded his fingers through her hair, a little bit of reality returned. Hollister. His island. Third

Shift. There were so many things left undone, so many loose ends to tie up. "What are we going to do now?"

Elijah pressed a kiss to her temple. "Remember that world tour of closets I promised you?"

She groaned. Hadn't they killed that joke days ago? Now he was resurrecting the corpse. Was Finn the bad influence on him, or was it the other way around? She had a feeling she was going to find out in the weeks ahead. "I'm breathless with anticipation," she said with a heavy dose of sarcasm.

"Oi. There's no call for that." He tugged at a lock of her hair. "I've got some downtime coming up, and I think we should start with Jamaica. Maybe head on to London."

Downtime. Jackson had made a similar suggestion to her. To lie low, stay out of sight, as Chase recovered from his wounds and Third Shift moved into their next phase of operations. It didn't sound entirely bad. She would have legitimate vacation photos to post on Instagram. Nothing Joaquin would have to doctor. She propped her chin on Elijah's chest and arched her brows with speculation. "Let me guess: You want me to meet your aunties?"

"And my mum and sisters." His eyes were like two gold coins flashing in the early morning light. They practically twinkled. "They've got a wedding to plan."

She didn't even bother stifling the laughter, letting it ring out as her shoulders shook and tears gathered in the corners of her eyes. "Our venue blew up," she pointed out when she had a measure of control over the giggles.

Elijah reached out and stroked the lines bracketing her smile. Like they were precious. Like *she* was precious. "Yeah, but *we* won't."

Maybe it was foolish to be with him. Maybe it was the biggest risk she was ever going to take—falling in love, trusting his people, joining his team so they could finish together what she'd started alone. Maybe it *would* all go up in flames. But she'd be ready.

She'd been training for this her entire life. She was ruthless. She was fierce. She was committed. And she never, ever let a target get away. Meghna moved in increments, until she was kissing his fingertips. And she whispered one soft word against Elijah's skin.

"*Boom.*"

They call him a monster. More wolf than man—
more dangerous than any predator.
They have no idea.

Please enjoy this glimpse of
Big Bad Wolf, **available now.**

THE MAN WHO SAT ACROSS from her looked like he wanted to eat her, and Neha Ahluwalia had no doubt that he could. In great big bites. Laying her to waste with swipes of his claws.

Would it be kinder than what he'd done to land himself behind bars? *That* she had no inkling of. But she did know he was guilty. Guilty and a killer. One was a legal distinction, the other largely genetic, but they were both equally true. It wasn't just the look in his eyes. Not just speculation or suspicion or her overactive imagination. It was the facts. Spelled out in fine print, looped in strands of altered DNA. Joe Peluso was the monster in the closet, the creature you were warned about in fairy tales…and still, somehow, not the scariest white man Neha had encountered while doing her job. What passed for humanity these days terrified her far more than the things that went bump in the night.

His first trial had dominated the headlines for months. "Unknown Sniper Spurs Gangland Chaos." "Brutal Killer Caught!" "I Did It: QueensBorn Shooter Confesses." You couldn't walk by a newsstand or flip past the local news without seeing Peluso's face. His police mug shot. Broad features spattered with cuts and bruises. Ears that stuck out in almost comical contrast. He looked dangerous. He *still* looked dangerous. Like someone who would absolutely cut down four members of a Russian drug ring while they were eating dinner—leaving them facedown in their borscht—and then stab another two guys in close combat in the parking lot.

"*Yeah, I fuckin' did it! Is that what you want me to say?*" he'd shouted in court, according to the transcripts. "*Let's just get this bullshit over with!*"

What the transcripts hadn't said was that he'd almost *transformed* while raging on the witness stand. It wasn't that much of a surprise to people in law enforcement, like her—all kinds of new species had inched their way into the light since the Darkest Day in 2016, and she had more than a few in her own family—but the ripple of fur across his body, the *fangs*, had been enough to throw the court into a tailspin. Pun fully intended. That he'd shot people, stabbed people, but hadn't turned berserker—hadn't *devoured* his victims—had put a whole different spin on his case. Instant mistrial. Instant cover-up...at least as far as the press and the public were concerned.

Neha should've been terrified at the prospect of this new client *and* of the reality of him sitting across from her right now. And, sure, maybe she'd freaked out a little that morning at the firm. She'd spilled coffee on her second-best blazer and asked her favorite senior partner to repeat himself. "*I want you to sit in, Neha,*" Nate had obliged. "*I think you could learn a lot on this one...and I think we could learn a lot from your take. I want your profiling skills on full display.*"

As a junior associate, she was practically begging to log some more billable hours and hack away at her law-school debt. But the Peluso case? *Not* one she'd been expecting to have land on her plate. *Not* high on her list, since it wasn't exactly going to help pay the bills. But she'd said yes anyway. Because how did you turn something like this down? A vigilante shape-shifter in a Sanctuary City? It was the kind of opportunity that could make or break her career...even if it didn't break the bank in the process.

Now here they were at the table. Her, Nate Feinberg—the first chair on the case—and his second chair and partner in defending crime, Dustin Taylor. With Joe Peluso himself staring back at them. His bruises were fresh. Probably from a recent tussle in jail as he waited for the new trial date. But everything else was the same as in his picture. His dark-brown hair chopped short in a blunt cut. A harsh-featured face only a mother could love. Those ears. And his dark, cold eyes. Meeting them, acknowledging his blatant perusal, Neha knew without a doubt that he was capable of taking lives. Professional. Efficient. Ruthless. But there was something else there, too. Not vulnerability. Not softness. Nothing like that. Just…depth? A hint of something below that chilly surface, something charismatic or compelling. A mystery waiting to be solved. Was it the monster? Or was it the man? Either way, Neha couldn't—*wouldn't*—take her eyes off him.

There were too many things about him, about this case, that didn't add up quite right. Like Peluso's heavily redacted military files. Like how he had only gotten caught because, of all things, he'd called in a tip after his hit. A twominute, forty-second phone call telling the cops about a shipping container full of "goods" scheduled to arrive later in the week. While one set of law-enforcement officials had tried to trace the burnerphone call and crossreferenced the security cameras and drone footage from nearby, another had intercepted the drop. The shipping container in question hadn't been full of drugs or bootlegs or weapons. It had been full of people—mostly human women—slated for sex trafficking.

Joe Peluso had cut down six criminals without blinking…but spared one thought to save dozens of lives. A man who'd clearly done his homework about the security drones that circled the city, he'd figured out their patterns. Even though they were supposedly on a randomizer and changed circuits every day, he had chucked all of that—risked being recorded—to make a call. What she didn't know, and didn't remotely understand, was *why*. And she hoped that the why would help them win their day in court, despite all the odds that were stacked against them. Not the least of which was the fact that this guy had taken out a bunch of Russian nationals, and all of the current president's New York-based cronies were calling for Peluso's head. So that the Russian government didn't retaliate. So they didn't lose all their cushy connections. Add in the supernatural factor—which called into question rights and personhood and whether he was even *entitled* to a new trial—and it was a mess.

There was buzz around the firm that the rest of the senior partners had balked at Nate taking this case, fearing public backlash. *"Sanctuary fucking City,"* he'd reportedly said in response. *"Last I checked, mobsters, pimps, and white supremacists were still the bad guys, and all Americans are still entitled to due process. No matter what's going on in Washington with birthright citizenship and humanity verification legislation, Joseph Peluso is* still *a citizen."* And that was that. As long as the mayor and the governor kept fighting the dark curtain that had dropped across the United States over the past few years, the legal firm of Dickenson, Gould, and Smythe would keep holding the line.

How Nate managed the other partners so efficiently was a secret well above Neha's pay grade. And, frankly, she didn't want to know. The enigma sitting across from them was more than enough to deal with. She just had to trust that both Nate and Dustin knew their shit. As for herself…? She'd come into law after doing a doctorate in behavioral psych. It was her job to know Joe Peluso's shit.

"Get him talking, Neha. Find out what his public defender missed. We don't want to repeat those mistakes."

Too bad the man across the table didn't seem particularly inclined to talk at the moment. His posture was closed-off, sullen. He answered questions in monosyllables. It was no wonder that first trial had been an epic disaster. Peluso screaming he did it. Gavels banging. Everybody and their mother shitting their legal briefs. The presidential cronies and rightof-center government officials calling for oversight on sanctuarycity legal procedure.

That made the governors and mayors who were part of the nationwide Sanctuary Alliance push back and cite the Sanctuary Autonomy Act of 2019. All of it had kept Peluso on ice in prison for months without even a question of retrial. Nobody at DGS wanted a repeat of that threering circus.

And on a more local level, nobody really wanted to mess with Aleksei Vasiliev, the Russian mafia *vor* whose underlings Peluso had eliminated so ruthlessly. Vasiliev owned a string of clubs and bars in the old-school Russian enclaves across Brooklyn and Queens, but it was fairly common knowledge that (a) they were a cover for drugs and sex trafficking and (b) he was just one cog in a larger operation run by a criminal network that both local authorities and Interpol had been watching for years. Plus (c) his potential supernatural affiliation—there was no confirmation in the legal community, but rumors had him as everything from werewolf to sorcerer. Oh, and there were also (d) his ties to several Aryan militia groups. The overlap between white supremacy and organized crime was such that the Venn diagram was practically one circle.

Aleksei Vasiliev was a nightmare. It was just Neha's luck that Joe Peluso had messed with him—and then some—by taking out a bunch of his pals. Peluso had basically kicked over six hornets' nests. And, looking at him now, it certainly seemed like he did not give a single fuck about it. He was slouched, almost bored. Staring at the table or the wall more than paying attention to his lawyers. There was a slight tension to his shoulders, to the lines of his mouth, but that could be attributed to any number of things. A problem with authority. General surliness. Constipation.

Dustin's smooth baritone betrayed not one bit of annoyance that their new client wasn't playing ball. "Would you say you were under duress when you left Queens on the night of September 14?"

"'Under duress?' What kind of bullshit phrasing is that?" Peluso rolled his eyes. "No one forced me anywhere. Loneass gunman, remember?"

Nate offered his most charming smile in response. "Was it a full moon?" He knew the answer to that already. The date of the hit was well documented. But he wasn't fishing for calendar confirmation. "Were you perhaps driven by…impulses?"

This, too, met with disdain. And zero acknowledgment of what Nate was referring to. "Do I look like the Weather Channel?" Peluso sneered. "The fuck do I know if it was a full moon?"

Neha struggled not to laugh, to not give him the satisfaction of a reaction, and applied herself to taking notes while Nate and Dustin went over the prelims again. But mostly she just watched their client. Studied him. Recorded what questions made the veins on his neck stand out. When he clenched his fists. He didn't like talking about his past. Bristled when asked about motive. On the surface, he seemed like the classic alpha male with authority issues. Push the wrong button and he would blow.

But then you added in the shifter factor…and she was stumped. From all reports, Peluso hadn't changed forms, or attempted to change, since his outburst in court. The medical staff at Brooklyn Detention had done as much blood work as their limited capability allowed, monitored him for weeks afterward, and only logged a few minor signs of supernatural ability. Bursts of increased aggression at certain times of the month—something she could actually relate to. But he hadn't gone full wolf or bear or whatever he was. He'd done nothing that required putting him in solitary. Aside from being a surly asshole who clearly got in a few dustups here and there, he was a model prisoner. Not so much the model client.

It was the world's most personal *Law & Order* rerun—movie-star handsome Nate and suave and serene Dustin trying to get a bead on the chillingly charismatic killer they'd agreed to defend. The contrast was almost comical. Their suits probably cost more money than Joe Peluso would ever see. Hell, Neha knew without a doubt that their suits cost more than her entire wardrobe. They were almost incongruous in the spare, utilitarian, private visitors' room. Two shining beacons of Armani hotness surrounded by cinder block and reinforced steel—an ad for a fashion house versus the Brooklyn House of Detention.

Halfway through the meeting, she realized Peluso was looking right at her. Leaning back in the chair bolted to the floor, chained fists on the table before him like he'd been ordered to pray. There was something like a smile on his face. A glitter in the black ice-chips of his pupils. *Oh. Of course.* She knew what was coming. She'd worked as a grunt in the DA's office for two years before DGS fished her out of the shallow end. This was when the client said something like "Who's the bitch?" or "She a perk?" or "Can I see your tits?" The veritable sexual harassment buffet.

She braced for it. It never came. Peluso just flicked his gaze back to Nate. "Why's *she* here?" he demanded. "You trying to soften me up or something? It ain't gonna work. I know what you think I am, but you can't bribe me into good behavior like a dog."

He was angry. And she wasn't sure what to unpack first—that he thought she was a bribe, or that he'd compared himself to a dog. There was definitely a chunk of the public who thought he was a rabid monster off the chain, even without knowing his true nature. There were certainly people at the firm who thought she was just a diversity hire with great legs and a pretty face—a showpiece. But he was wrong. Nate hadn't brought her here to soften him. Just to get to him. And the fact that he'd noticed her meant she was *in*.

She leaned forward, folding her hands on the metal table in a parody of his. "I'm here to learn, Joe," she told him. "Nothing more, nothing less." The skin around his left eye was black and blue. His right cheek looked like someone had taken a cheese grater to it a week ago. But it was his gaze she focused on, his intensity that held her fixed.

Nate's hand settled on her knee. A warning squeeze, not a stolen grope. He was in no way interested in any of her body parts besides her brain—not just because he was gay, but because he

didn't subscribe to the toxic male posturing that seemed to perme-
ate most law firms. He'd likely brought her on board because she'd
profiled his boyfriend a few months back over Friday night drinks.
His now *ex*-boyfriend.

"Tread carefully," he was saying with the squeeze. "Tread carefully but work it." She was thirtyfive. Older than a lot of her fellow
junior associates. She didn't need the warning. She knew how to
be careful.

"Bullshit," Peluso pronounced, that almost-smile returning to
his face. Bizarrely, she kind of wanted to see the real thing. "It's
never 'nothing less.' You want something from me. And good luck
with that, 'cause I got nothing to give."

He was guilty, but he didn't seem to have any guilt. Not about
what he'd done. That much was clear. And he wouldn't stand for
more bullshit. So, she told him the truth as she knew it. "Okay. Here's
the bottom line, Joe. They're here to defend you. I'm here to break
you down. Get inside your head. Find out what makes you tick."

It amused him. He tilted his head, sizing her up with his good
eye. "I'd like to see you try."

The way he said it—a cocky, casual threat—should have sent
a chill down her spine. It didn't. It just got her back up. "That's the
beauty of it, Joe," she told him. "You won't see it. You'll be halfway there, looking around and wondering why you told me every
secret you've never told another soul."

She'd tried that line on a few clients here and there. Most of
them laughed, because they didn't believe her. They didn't realize that she'd been cracking people like safes since long before
the psych degree. When one of her older brothers had held her
Malibu Barbie for ransom, she'd gotten the doll's location out of
him in four minutes. She'd been eight.

People told her things. Whether they wanted to or not. People
connected to her. Whether she wanted them to or not. It was a
blessing and a curse. Maybe it was *her* supernatural gift.

"You'll give me everything," she assured.

Joe Peluso didn't laugh off the challenge. Instead, he seemed to mull it over. His brows winged together. His eyes went distant. He interlaced his fingers, cuffs clinking against the tabletop. He watched her watch him. Nate shifted beside her, obviously unsettled by the standoff, but he wouldn't have asked her along if he hadn't thought she could handle it.

She could handle this. She could handle *him*.

She knew Joe was guilty...and she knew she was just that good.

ACKNOWLEDGMENTS

___

Writing a book in a normal year is a challenge. Writing a book during the COVID-19 pandemic and the 2020 election cycle was probably the most painful thing I've ever done. And that includes the time I cracked a rib tripping on the sidewalk. (Moral of that story: drop the pizza box and save yourself!) That ache eventually went away. This was months upon months of creative struggle chased with despair and depression. I honestly wasn't sure I'd ever finish *Pretty Little Lion*. I thought my writing career was coming to an end. Sometimes I *still* think that. Particularly as the world around us continues to grapple with COVID and political strife and racist violence and natural disasters. (Yes, I'm a proud SJW—a social justice warrior—and if you've made it all the way to this page, I assume you figured that out already.)

But I'm very lucky in that I have people around me who remind me again and again why we keep fighting and why romance authors write the books we do. Because *hope* is always an option. And so is love. That's the message I want readers to take away from the Third Shift series. Sure, I'm penning lusty over-the-top plots, but there's a lot of reality in these stories as well. Too much for some people—and that's okay. I get it. There's nothing wrong with wanting pure escapism in romance novels. I'm often in the mood for those myself! But with Third Shift, I'm writing my way *through* the darkness, not around it. Because I have to believe that hope and love will win out in the end, not just for my characters but for all of us.

And that's enough maudlin navel-gazing out of me! Let's get to the fun stuff! As you might guess, I took some liberties with a few things in *Pretty Little Lion*—from super serums to government and military doings to how tech doohickeys work. There's no spy hideout at an equestrian center or secret training camp in Sikkim, and if shady dudes are having coke parties in Midtown hotels, I've never personally witnessed them. I've definitely made the walk from 8th Avenue to 11th Avenue in Manhattan late at night, but I've never been to the Finger Lakes.

The beautiful poem excerpted at the beginning, by Bangladeshi poet laureate Kazi Nazrul Islam, is one I had to memorize as a kid and *perform in front of people.* In the original Bengali, not English! (Please don't ask me to do that now. I would fail miserably!) Apsaras are a real part of South Asian and Southeast Asian mythology—albeit not quite so murder-y. That is purely my own invention. While Meghna and *Big Bad Wolf*'s Neha are from different parts of South Asia than I am and as different from each other as night from day, they both reflect some of my own experiences growing up in the United States. South Asian American people aren't a monolith, but there are ties that bind us, rooted in both worlds. And I firmly believe that those of us with privilege need to reckon with it and use it for good.

Maybe that's also a little bit of why I write these books. And the result, *Pretty Little Lion*, wouldn't be here without help and input from *so* many people. It took a village that spanned a decent chunk of North America. Audra North read the earliest version of Meghna and Elijah's story, back in 2015 when the characters were human. So did Elizabeth Kerri Mahon, who later did a read

on t
Jacki
PLL
stars (
me through
saved me with last
my eternal gratitude for b
through 2020. Michelle Bell an
needed it, as did Dave. My South Asian
and also gave me a safe place to fall—fro
chats to TikTok lessons and fielding my f
Sonali, Alisha, Namrata, Mona, Tahmir
Farah, and Falguni…I'm so blessed to k

Of course I must thank my agent
for always fighting for me and lendi
needed. And thank you to my editors
Mary K. Altman and Christa Dési
Diane Dannenfeldt, Stefani Sloma,
and everyone else at Casa who help
you have in your hands right now.
Stephanie Gafron and illustrator
cover art that graces both *Big Ba*
Tessera Editorial's sensitivity reade
resource for this series, and I can't

Finally, I want to shout-out my
my back—but is still not allowed
Yoda! Because shouldn't we *all*
through 2019 and 2020? (I'm st

Sulei

LITTLE LION

thank you both! Charlott
lso put eyes on this it
than I can possib
shara Deen pat
moments. Or
ints. On
achin

e Stein,
eration of
y say. Rock
ently Skyped
nd Zoe Archer
el Young Jr. has
me and this book
de me smile when I
sisters lifted me up
up texts and video
rantic phone calls. Nisha,
ha, Kishan, Sophia, Sona,
now you all!

Courtney Miller-Callihan
g a supportive ear when
t Sourcebooks Casablanca,
, as well as Jessica Smith,
Katie Stutz, Sabrina Baskey,
ed shape PLL into the book
A special thanks to designer
Kris Keller for the gorgeous
d Wolf and Pretty Little Lion.
rs have also been an invaluable
recommend them enough!
big brother, who has always had
to read my books. Oh, and Baby
thank Baby Yoda for getting us
ill not calling him Grogu.)

Xoxo,

kha Snyder, Chicago, IL, April 2021